UNUSUAL SUSPECTS

UNUSUAL SUSPECTS

■

AN ANTHOLOGY OF CRIME STORIES
FROM BLACK LIZARD

Edited by *James Grady*

VINTAGE CRIME / BLACK LIZARD

Vintage Books   A Division of Random House, Inc.   New York

A VINTAGE ORIGINAL, MAY 1996
FIRST EDITION

Library of Congress Cataloging-in-Publication Data
Unusual suspects: a new anthology of crime stories from Black Lizard /
edited by James Grady.—1st ed.
p.   cm. —(Vintage crime/Black Lizard)
ISBN 0-679-76788-6 (pbk.)
1. Crime—Fiction.   2. Short stories, American.
I. Grady, James, 1949–   . II. Series.
PS648.C7U58   1996
813'.087208—dc20   95-52041
CIP

Book design by Mia Risberg

Random House Web address: http://www.randomhouse.com/

Printed in the United States of America
10 9 8 7 6 5 4 3 2 1

CONTENTS

Contents

INTRODUCTION:

ALL THE UNUSUAL SUSPECTS

James Grady

Crime wears a million masks—murder, rape, robbery, casual mayhem, and calculated cruelty. Our current plague of crime is probably no more virulent than the evils that stalked London's human warrens in the time of Charles Dickens or lay in ambush in the pungent alleys of Yen Shu's Forbidden City, but today's tally of terror cascades over us in an endless waterfall of instantaneous electronic information.

Ironically, the crime that terrorizes us has always been a major source of our entertainment. Perhaps by fictionalizing our fears we can better face their facts.

No matter what the reason, from the court intrigues of *The Tale of Genji* to the vicariate poisonings of Agatha Christie, from

the lethal espionage of *Hamlet* to the back-alley courage of
Dashiell Hammett, crime sates our yearning for diversion, and so
victims fall like crimson rain from the pages of novels and the
flickering rainbows of cinematic screens.

Crime provides a workable milieu for writers and artists, a con-
flux of humanity in which all the forces of drama swirl: good vs.
evil, courage, ingenuity, greed, madness, deceit, despair, love, tri-
umph, tragedy—conditions and episodes capable of being shaped
into a coherent, depictable event with a beginning, a middle, and
an end, with as much action and character and theme as the artist
is capable of portraying. And because crime touches everyone, the
art it generates bears the potential for a universality that is difficult
to match.

Those of us who labor as writers work crime for the love of the
drama we find there, not for the love of the horrors we portray.

Those of us who read and watch crime fiction do so for the
solid drama that the genre requires be given us. In crime fiction,
we may confront horrors that sear our imagination, but we will
not be frustrated by a theme- or style-saturated stream of prose
that begins somewhere and goes nowhere around characters who
do nothing.

Crime fiction fans are an exacting audience. They may forgive simplistic style, formulaic plots, and predictable endings, but
they will not forgive a writer who fails to do the fundamental
work necessary to create a complete story. Nor will they accept a
writer's work if that writer fails to perform one simple miracle: in
every crime story, no matter where or when or how the story is
set, somewhere and somehow the writer must brush the reader
with the inescapable truth that we can all be victims, villains, and
even heroes—we could all *be there*.

But *where we are* is not a book or a short story or a movie, it's
real life, and in our real life we live with crime. To raise our lives
above the crime around us, we must do more than merely walk on
by and hope we're lucky. To do nothing is to surrender to whatever crime fate sends our way. Such an abdication of our power is

itself a damning sin, and perhaps our only certain redemption can be found in our willingness to struggle against the forces of evil. So we must work, we must fight back. What is true here for the individual is true, too, for society: crime threatens all of us; therefore its solution must be an effort involving all of us.

Literal crime requires law makers, law enforcers, law breakers—and victims. Those are tangible issues worthy of all the sweat, blood, and tears our culture devotes to them.

But crime is more than literal. When humanity defined itself as more than a herd of beasts, when cognitive laws replaced the instinctive rules of the pack, we created a concept that goes beyond behavior enforced by laws or pack power: we created justice.

And so in the best part of our hearts, we realize that crime is more than a function of what is legal and what is not, crime also encompasses acts of unjust suffering.

Suffering and justice defy yardsticks, but consider that in 1996's ultramodern America the number of personal computers in use by our citizenry is almost equaled by the 20 to 30 million Americans our Congress had documented as suffering from hunger. Slice the hunger data another way, and you discover that one out of every twelve American *children* suffers from hunger. Fourteen percent of Americans live below the mystical poverty line, a dollar figure based on an annual earned income that is less than many people spend for a new, nonluxury family car. As horrific as is the sum of these sorrows inside America's borders, the calculations for pain in the rest of the world are far higher and more intense.

There are few laws against such dramas, yet they, too, can be called crimes, for they violate our sense of justice. We cannot ignore these crimes any more than we can ignore a serial murderer cruising America's highways, if for no other reason than the simple, selfish universality of all crime; what can happen to *someone else* in this world can happen to *us*.

Perhaps to death we must add a second certainty for humanity: crime will probably be with us always. But that still doesn't mean we can't or shouldn't fight back; that means we *must* fight back.

Fighting back—or rather, fighting for—is the central purpose of Share Our Strength, an organization dedicated to battling homelessness and hunger by drawing on the talents of those of us lucky enough to escape such fates, and then turning those talents into vehicles to help others help themselves.

Since its founding in 1984, SOS has distributed more than $26 million in grants to over eight hundred antihunger organizations in the United States, Canada, and developing countries—and 94 percent of the money SOS raises goes directly to organizations that distribute food, treat the consequences of hunger and malnutrition, and build self-sufficiency programs designed to meet immediate needs for food while investing in long-term solutions to the crises of hunger.

One of SOS's projects has been to combine the talents of writers and the desires of readers, publishing anthologies of fiction and essays in which writers donate their work, readers buy an excellent product, and royalties go to help SOS fight the good fight for all of us. Everybody wins.

Now, with the help of the readers of this volume, SOS attacks the crime of hunger and homelessness by marshaling the talents of writers known for their skills at creating literatures of crime.

SOS's roundup netted a wonderful crew of "unusual suspects" for this battle. As a group, the contributors to this volume have sold millions of books. Our authors include such literary stars as Joyce Carol Oates and Andrew Vachss, such multiple–national award winners as Ben Schutz and John Lutz, and such rising-star new writers as Jessica Auerbach and George Pelecanos. Bestselling author James Lee Burke donated our collection's classic, a story that critics agree transcends any genre. This collection even contains one once-believed "lost" treasure: a short story by the legendary Jim Thompson.

As writers of fiction we are no less grounded in the facts of life than anyone else. We know full well how the cycle of hunger and poverty rolls like a big wheel through time. We harbor no illusion that giving one short story to this anthology will end the hunger and homelessness that have been with us since the dawn of history. But as writers and as human beings we know more than the bitter truths about *what has been*. As historians Will and Ariel Durant noted, the wheel of history is attached to a cart, and that cart is going somewhere. Already, the cart has rolled mankind out of the swamps of smallpox and universally accepted slavery. How much effort will be required to roll the cart beyond the muck of hunger and poverty is unknown, but to do nothing is to surrender to its wheels.

We're all worth more than that. We may not see the end of crime and injustice in our lifetime, but we need not surrender. Shoulder to the wheel, we fight and push to rise above the mire.

UNUSUAL SUSPECTS

Jessica Auerbach

POLICE REPORT

The coroner's report listed the cause of my wife's death as a gun-shot wound to the heart. A six-foot-tall man stood in my back-yard (two acres, wooded, small stream and very private) and fired one warning shot and one shot which killed her. He was a police-man. It was an accident. He meant to pull the trigger, but he misidentified her. He thought she was a burglar. His partner wit-nessed it from the window above.

The partner is somewhat overweight, not quite as tall. He told me: "Anybody might have done the same, seeing her come out the window like that." Both officers have pins and badges all over their uniforms. Dunbarton, the one who shot her, has a red bar pin with gold lettering on the left side of his chest. It reads, "Marksman."

The coroner's report is quite thorough. It enumerates every abrasion and scratch. Contusions on her hands and knees from where she hit the ground when she jumped from the window onto the patio, for instance. It mentions scratches on her left leg as being old. Those were from the pricker bushes over by the stream. I have told them they shouldn't worry: I don't hold them responsible for those scratches. The report doesn't mention that her jeans were ripped at one knee, nor that her sweatshirt was torn when she jumped. I do hold them responsible for those damages.

There were no hidden ironies discovered in the autopsy. She was not, for instance, found to have every internal organ filled with cancerous cells. Her body organs and tissues were compatible with her age, the report said. If the Metropolitan Life statistics can be believed, she could have anticipated another forty-three years. Under other circumstances.

This is condensed and from memory: 2:24 P.M.: Report of suspicious male on property of 14 Dunleavy Road. Officers observe old model Chevrolet parked at 27 Dunleavy and proceed to back door. Door is open and officers draw guns and proceed into residence. Upon trying upstairs bathroom door, it is found to be barricaded. Officers identify themselves and warn suspect to open door. Sounds indicate an escape is being attempted, so Officer Dunbarton proceeds to the exterior. Dunbarton observes suspect running, fires a warning shot, and when the suspect continues to run, fires at the suspect.

There was nothing in the police report about what she was thinking when she went out the window, nor what she thought when they identified themselves. What she thought while she soaked that piece of wallpaper for the spot next to the door and she heard their footsteps approaching.

This was the first murder in the town except for a man who shot his wife and killed himself seventeen years ago. They correct me when I say *murder* and say, "Mr. Burns, *killing*, please."

4

"Murder is a legal term," Eldon reminds me. "But," he reassures me, "the manslaughter charge will hurt them quite enough." Eldon is my lawyer, but he isn't from this town. He was our lawyer in the old town. We hadn't been here long enough, nor had enough trouble, to meet the lawyers and doctors.

Did she hear the first shot? The second? Are they telling the truth about the first shot? Yes, I know, I tell Eldon, they found the spent shell, but couldn't it have been fired later? The bullet entered her back when she was on the run. I told Eldon I wanted to see the gun. He said it would be difficult and he rattled off a list of hypothetical arguments they were likely to propose. "Why do you want to see the gun?" he asked me. "You're not a ballistics expert."

But I thought this: maybe she saw the gun when she came out the window, or maybe she looked over her shoulder when she was running and saw it.

"What is it you want?" Eldon asked me. "Do you want to sue for damages?"

I said, "I want to see the gun," and he arranged it. It is smaller and squatter than I had thought and not as shiny. The opening of the barrel is very large. Not at all like Danny's cowboy guns.

She was in the bathroom, putting up the wallpaper right behind the door. The door seemed to be barricaded, they told me. Her step stool was there, blocking it. Or maybe she did try to barricade it deliberately when she heard them coming. She was wearing jeans and a sweatshirt. A gray sweatshirt. "From the back," the younger officer said, "she could have been a man." I threw out the piece of paper she had soaking in the water tray. It had begun to disintegrate. Then I cut another and soaked it and put it up. There's still another wall yet to paper, but I won't do that. I just wanted to work on that one piece. The one she was in the middle of when she heard footsteps.

Was the door to the house wide open? I have asked them, repeatedly. Unlocked, they say. I want it changed in the police record to unlocked, not open, but they say it means the same thing in

5

police terms. "Words are different to police?" I once asked one of them. "Sometimes, yes, sir," he said to me.

The suspicious car out front was her car. Twelve years old and rusted through. "Not the kind of car we see too often in this neighborhood," they said.

"She liked it," I told them. "She didn't want to worry about scratching or cracking up a new one."

"Yeah," the younger officer said, "my wife's like that too."

"My wife's dead," I said to him. That was in the hospital corridor when they were telling me how sorry they were for their tragic mistake.

I don't let the kids use that bathroom. And I only use it when I'm going over things again. I didn't take the step stool out or clean up the tools because they're all right behind the door and when I open it, I'm always just a little startled at how it's blocked. It's a good way to start going over things. Feeling startled, I mean.

I call the police station when I have questions. The officers speak slowly. They are careful not to contradict themselves. They think I call only to catch them in such a contradiction, but trapping them is not my interest. I just want to hear it again. I often ask them if it is standard procedure to enter a house without knocking or ringing and they always say something like, "Yes, sir. We had a suspicious call. It was Mrs. Bradley, the woman across the road who put in the call." Perhaps they think I should take my case to Mrs. Bradley. The suspicious character in the complaint turned out to be the town surveyor checking a boundary.

When my children stepped off the school bus that afternoon, my wife was not there to meet them. They probably waited a few minutes, but then, growing impatient, crossed the street by themselves and walked down the long twisty dirt road to the house, alone. They might have been excited when they first saw all the emergency vehicles parked out front near their mother's car. They rang the front bell. Nobody answered so they walked around to the back.

At night I hear footsteps in the hallway. If the children cry out, I am afraid to cross the hall and go into their rooms. They would be better off somewhere else.

When she heard the footsteps, what did she think? Did she think that must be Jack, home early, and call out? They said she didn't call out. Did she open her mouth, soundlessly, mimicking an Edvard Munch painting? Perhaps she couldn't even breathe, hearing the footsteps. Was that why she went out the window? Was she gasping for oxygen? In all the years we were married, I came home early from work only once: about two years ago she called me and said she was sick. So she knew, listening to those footsteps, that they weren't mine; that I was not arriving home early with surprises. I never brought gifts except on occasions like birthdays or Christmas. And even then I was often remiss.

Were they loud footsteps, indiscriminately placed here and there, dashed this way across the room to check behind the living room curtains, then back again to open the guest closet door? Or were they quiet, steady, surreptitious creepings that sent her out that window?

They thought no one was home. Then they heard the scurrying in the bathroom, they identified themselves and told her to open up. That's when she went out the window.

"We assumed she had something to hide," they have said to me. Yes I told them, she had begun to think of two acres as private. She wanted boundaries on her home, her bathroom, her self, her brain.

Some of the women in the neighborhood have told me they, too, would have gone out the window. "Couldn't any robber or rapist claim he was the police?" they've said, explaining it to me, though I already understand that much.

I have started to sit at that window. Right on the sill. The window is actually over the bathtub, so it's difficult to get myself through it. With practice, though, I am getting better at it. The window is high. She would have had to pull herself up fast and hard to make it up there. It is not a particularly wide window, either, so it's a squeeze going through and I have to put one hand on the exterior wall of the house to get the proper leverage. The frame of the aluminum storm window sticks into me from below as I sit there. But she didn't pause and hover on the sill as I do. She might not have noticed it sticking into her at all. I have measured the drop to the ground below. It is more than eight feet. Eldon said to me, "You never know how you're going to react under stress. You can't know what she was thinking."

I want to know, although I've never actually gone through the window. It's a long drop, for one thing.

I sit on the sill and I know I must jump one time. I wait till the children have gone to bed, but sometimes they knock on the door, wanting to use the bathroom. "Use the downstairs one," I say, "I'm busy." They only forget because they are three-quarters asleep. In the daytime they would never try to use this bathroom. Everyone tells me to send them to Elsa's mother, but they don't know her mother went home after the funeral and got into bed. She gets up to go to the bathroom. She lifts the bedside phone, dials my number, and weeps, but that's all she does anymore.

The children would be better off elsewhere, although there are no lurid bloodstains or bullet holes to point to. After the police finished pacing around the patio, someone scrubbed away the blood. He got down on his hands and knees with a scrub brush and a bucket of detergent and washed it all away.

The children lock the doors when they come in now. They like the windows shut, too. With the weather getting warmer, the rooms feel as though they're swelling up around us. I know it would be better for the kids—healthier—if the doors and windows were open wide, but I can't help them with that. The only one I can open is the bathroom window.

I go to work. I get them off to school in the morning. I only sit on the windowsill in the evenings. My magazine is a biweekly, so the pace is fast, the deadlines frequent. I do the cover and feature art layout and I think I do it well enough. I am working with larger blocks of color than before. But this probably has nothing to do with her. I work shorter days now so that I can meet the children after school. We go to the supermarket together and we buy things for dinner.

"We deeply regret our part in this, and the resultant suffering from this tragic, but well-intentioned act," the police chief wrote in his letter to the local paper. Eldon says they're worried that I'll sue. I say, "Tell them I am thinking about it," although I'm really not. Eldon said money for the children might be something to consider. And a new house, he says. "Do you think you want to move?" I tell him I haven't thought about it. I'm still thinking about how she felt when she crossed that windowsill. I'm still wondering if she saw the guns. And whether her head hit the concrete patio when she was still alive. I write that one down so I can call the coroner and ask.

I asked Eldon about purchasing a gun. I could see that this made him very nervous, but he didn't talk of psychiatrists or vacations in the mountains. I asked him to tell me the law, and he did so, very matter-of-factly. I know Eldon, and I think he's hoping that such offhanded responses will help me to move on and to begin to forget.

So I follow the rules he has laid out to me. I apply with proper ID and go home during the forty-eight-hour waiting period. I bring my money back to the store and collect my gun. And I do not burden Eldon with knowledge of any of that.

Sometimes I stand where Dunbarton stood and hold the gun, although I don't know what angle or stance would be correct. I'm getting more of a natural feel for it, though, the more I do it. Once when I was watching she came through and did pause, like a small bird—a nuthatch—slender and quick-seeming, and she moved her head from side to side, surveying the options, not troubled by me standing with the gun, and then she flew off.

I have chalked in Dunbarton's footprints on the patio surface so I can sit there on the window and glance toward them. I have put the gun down on the ground there. But it would be better if someone else stood down there, while I went through the window. So the gun would be at the right height, so I would know if she could see it as she came through the window. Who could I ask to do such a thing? Certainly not the children. Eldon's patience would be tried by such a request were I to approach him. He's been good through all this, and I know I've pushed him to his limits. He says, "At least you and the children have each other to get you through this."

I don't say what I am thinking, which is, Eldon, face facts. These children would be better off with just about anybody else. Pick someone at random on the street, Eldon, and my children will be better off. For a moment, just thinking about that, I can imagine them whole again, laughing, even. Find someone, I say under my breath, and I cross my fingers, as my children do, one digit pressed down hard against the other; hope against hope. When Eldon turns his back, my fingers uncross, my fists clench—I cannot help it—and I bow my head at what I have done to them. Find someone for them, Eldon, do that much for me.

What Eldon cannot know, and what I cannot tell him, is how nearly I have crept into her skin. I say nearly, for the transition isn't whole just yet. But there is one thing in which I still believe: in time, I will know every detail—the angle of the sun, the temperature of the air, the quality of the breeze. "Eldon," I will write, perhaps as early as next week, "find someone for them."

Jim Thompson

THE CAR
IN THE MEXICAN QUARTER

I

It was about three in the morning at Mexican Joe's. A dingy lantern hanging from the unused electric chandelier cast an eerie light against the cobwebbed walls. Everything was quiet except for the gentle snores of Joe who lay beneath the counter. I was eating hot tamales while I waited for my relief on the Mexican quarter beat.

There was little sound on the brick street outside. Occasionally a giant beetle whirling around the street light would crash to the pavement. At least it sounded like a crash. Then you could hear, furtively, the smothered wail of an infant or the half-muttered speech of someone turning in his sleep. That was about all.

The buildings were two and three stories high and all wood. In some there were windows; in fact, practically all had windows on the street floor, but the other apertures were largely boarded up or stuffed with pillows and sacks. Only the distant swift transit of light through a crack told you that people lived, loved and died behind those dirty gray boards.

I wrapped the husks from my tamales up in a newspaper, laid it on the table and placed a quarter on top of it. Then hearing footsteps outside I lit a cigarette and sauntered to the door, thinking of something sharp to say to Flannagan for being late.

I was about to raise the match to my cigarette when something about the footsteps made me hesitate. I dropped the match and listened, holding my breath. The heavy-footed Flannagan had never walked like that. I felt for the butt of my gun. Except for the police there are only two kinds of people who walk the Mexican quarter at night, crooks and strangers.

A man in a pure white suit passed the doorway. He was wearing white canvas shoes, too, so that a look at the back of his coat convinced me that he was in a uniform, a hotel uniform. The kind that bellhops at the Lansing wore during the summer.

This did look pretty rotten. The Lansing is one of the biggest hotels in town, but I knew that it stood for a lot of dirty work from its employees. One suicide a year is plenty for a big hotel and the Lansing had one almost every month.

I craned out of the door as far as I could and followed the nattily dressed figure with my eyes. His hair was black and slicked down with some sort of smelly grease and his head was too small and sharp for an honest man. There was something treacherous, too, about his easy skipping walk. He looked like the fellow you're always afraid of finding behind you on a dark street.

Then, at the corner beneath the streetlight he turned and I recognized him. Skippy Kahn.

If you'd been around town as long as I had I wouldn't need to tell you that Skippy was about the worst rat living. He was a sneak thief, a dapper for crooked games and about everything else that a decent man shouldn't be. But, because he was a stool pigeon he managed to keep out of jail. At that, I didn't see how he had managed to land at the Lansing. He was too tough an egg to work even in a place of that kind.

Naturally, I didn't have to guess but once to figure that something dirty was about to happen with Skippy Kahn in the Mexican quarter. What I didn't think about was that it would happen to him. We all get fooled though.

He stood behind the lamp post evidently waiting for someone while I tried to keep out of sight and at the same time watch him. As I waited he lit a cigarette and flipped the match into the air. And almost as he had done it I heard the faint hum of tires on the rough brick.

Slowly the car came on. It was without lights, I could tell, because there was no reflection against the sallow walls of the buildings about me. The motor was practically silent. It was, perhaps, a minute and a half after I first heard it until it had passed the doorway in which I stood. I opened the screen and I stepped out to the walk.

A little chill ran down my back. There was something so ghostly about that car. The curtains were drawn on front and side and with its slow easy movement it resembled nothing quite so much as a hearse. At the last minute I noticed that it bore no license plates. Somehow, with premonition of what was about to happen I almost opened my mouth to shout.

Then, without warning the lights went on and Skippy who was almost in the center of the street was directly in their focus. He was at least a hundred feet away from me but in that brilliant glare I could see the expression on his face clearly. It may sound queer but he looked like a rabbit being hunted by searchlight. And like a rabbit he stood there, paralyzed, and waited for death. For it was death.

The quiet motor suddenly hummed like a giant wasp. There was a sudden quick clash of gears. In a moment, that easily gliding car assumed a breathtaking speed—the tires fairly hummed with the sudden acceleration. Then it was all over.

Skippy never moved out of his tracks. He didn't have time. The speeding black car caught him full-center with its bumper, downed him, spun him against the bricks, then with one last roaring effort sent him crashing against the shoddy frame of the building with a shock that shook the whole street.

Then the car was gone and for that matter so was Skippy Kahn.

Flannagan came panting up at that moment, derby hat in hand.

"Been watchin' 'im . . . why I was late . . . shall I call headquarters?" he gasped.

"Afterwards," I said. "Call the coroner now."

That morning I dropped in at the Lansing. Byers was the name of the superintendent of service. His clothes and his manners were a little too good for his job and he had a smile that he could turn on and off. I didn't like him.

"Got a boy working here by the name of Skippy Kahn?" I asked.

He raised his eyebrows.

"Charles Kahn, you mean, I'm sure," he said. "He was one of our best bellmen. He was killed last night. Didn't you read about it?"

"I saw it," I said. "And it wasn't an accident. He was murdered. I'm trying to find out why. Where was Skippy going last night when he was killed?"

Byers smiled helplessly. "If we only knew," he said. "But you see, there's really no way of telling. It's all a mystery here to us."

I got down to business.

"Listen," I said. "I know something about hotels. Don't you keep a record of the rooms that your bellboys go to? Don't they have to write down what they went to that room for? If they don't and you don't the Lansing has been breaking a state law for a long time."

I didn't have to mention the law but once to make Byers see the light. He folded up like a camp chair, took me across the lobby and presented me to the bell captain, and in a minute I was looking through the record of the room calls for the night. Then, assuring me that he would do anything within his power to solve the mystery, Byers faded out of the picture. I didn't bother to thank him.

It had been a fairly quiet night so my job was easy. Skippy Kahn had only two calls between two and three o'clock. One of these had been to the room of an established guest of the hotel who wanted some aspirin. The other room looked as if it might be a clue.

I got the occupant's name from the clerk and caught the elevator up. A small nervous man with quick, jumping eyes opened the door. I showed him my badge and went in.

"What was Skippy Kahn doing up here last night?" I shot at him.

"I don't know who you mean," he answered.

"Well, the bellboy that got killed."

Only his eyes betrayed the speed at which his mind was working, for his words rolled from his tongue as smoothly as if the answer had already been there.

"Why, I called for a blanket about two-fifteen," he replied. "The boy, Skippy, whom you mention, answered the call. He told me that the linen room was closed and that it would be impossible to get one. I asked him to try to procure one from a vacant room and I guess he did make some effort to fulfill this request. But he was unsuccessful and came back and told me so and I gave him a quarter and dismissed him. That was all I saw of him and all I know of him."

I didn't say anything. I stepped across the room and turned off an electric fan that was placed to blow across the foot of the bed.

Then at the head I turned off another. The sweat began to roll from his brow and from mine too.

"It was only about ninety last night," I said. "Why didn't you turn off these fans if you felt chilly?"

He turned as white as a sheet. "Say, what do you want anyway?" he blurted.

"What have you got?" I asked. And before he had time to answer, I continued. "Now, listen here, Jack. You're likely to get into a whole lot of trouble about this mess. In fact, I'm going to see that you do get into plenty if you don't break square with me. Personally, I think you're on the level. If you want me to keep that opinion you'd better tell the truth. Now, I don't care about your personal habits or anything else. All I want to know is what Skippy Kahn was doing up here this morning."

When I mentioned "personal habits," his eyes fell and I almost felt sorry for him. I knew his trouble.

"You won't have me locked up?" he asked, finally.

I said I wouldn't.

"All right then." He came over to where I was sitting and looked me squarely in the eye. "I'm a dopehead," he said, quietly. "I don't suppose that's any secret to you. I've been out of the stuff for two days. Last night I took a chance and called this bellboy. He said that he could fix me up. I gave him $50. That's the last I've heard of him until you came in just now."

I got up and looked him over carefully.

"Your story sounds pretty good," I said, "especially since we found a fifty on Skippy. And you don't talk like a crook. As far as I'm concerned you can check out anytime you want to. But one more thing: Did Skippy give you any idea as to where he was going to get this stuff?"

He shook his head slowly. "I'm afraid he didn't," he replied. "He did say that he could get it in less than five minutes, although I don't suppose that will help you much."

"You never can tell," I said, and left him.

Five minutes did mean something to me.

II

The Lansing is practically in the center of town, which means that there are no suspicious dives within a radius of several blocks. Five minutes would not allow a man time to descend and ascend on the elevator and to run to the drugstore on the corner. The drugstore was closed at night anyway. That meant that Skippy Kahn was depending on delivery service and I believed that I knew just the place most likely to peddle dope.

I got off at the mezzanine and found my way around to the telephone room. The chief operator showed the night's records of outside calls willingly. I found the number I wanted in a short time.

"Where did this call come from?" I asked.

She laughed. "We're still trying to find out," she said. "The room it was supposed to come from was vacated at ten o'clock last night so there really shouldn't have been any call. Probably the girl who took it just made a mistake in the room number."

"But isn't it possible," I asked, "for there to have been a call from this room after ten o'clock last night? Couldn't the man who checked out of it have gone back later and called?"

She nodded. "He could have, but it isn't logical. A man who leaves his room at ten wouldn't be likely to go back at two in the morning to 'phone. He'd probably be picked up in the hall by the house detective if he tried it."

I thought a minute. These telephone operators are pretty reliable girls, regardless of what you say about wrong numbers. Besides, I wasn't quite ready to give up my pet idea.

"How does this sound," I asked. "This fellow that checks out of his room leaves his door open when he leaves. Someone passing by takes advantage of the opportunity to use the 'phone without spending anything. Possible or not?"

"Now," she said, "that sounds like what actually happened; in fact, I'll bet it did happen that way."

I thanked her and hurried out. In just two minutes (I timed myself) a taxi had taken me to the Owl Rent Car stand.

Dago Red Ivers was inside at his desk. I have known Dago Red for several years, but he did not offer to get up or to shake hands. He merely stared at me out of his cold brown eyes.

"Well," he said, finally, "what do you want?"

"The man who killed Skippy Kahn," I replied, without hesitation.

He sniffed. "So do the police."

I grabbed him by the shoulder and whirled him around facing me.

"None of your wisecracks," I snarled. "I've got you dead-to-the-pin at last. I've known for years that you were peddling here but I couldn't prove it. I can now.

"Listen. This morning between two and three Skippy Kahn called this place and gave you an order. You've had it in for Skippy for a long time, he knew too much. But you didn't want to take a chance on bumping him where you might get caught. So you got him to go down into the Mexican quarter on some pretext and had him wait for the order. Then you ran him down.

"You didn't have any license on your car and your lights were off but I recognized you and I saw the car sitting in the back when I came in. Flannagan was with me and he can testify about the car and you too. Now, do you want anything more or are you willing to own up?"

Red looked at me coldly. Then he broke out into a nasty laugh.

"So you and Flannagan recognized me?" he said.

"Yes."

"And the car too?"

"I'm telling you," I repeated.

Still laughing, Ivers picked up the telephone and called a number. He motioned for me to listen.

"Give me the chief of federal revenue," he said to the voice at the other end of the wire. Then, "Hello, Chief. This is Red Ivers. One of our local detectives is here accusing me of a murder last night. Tell him something for me, will you?"

He handed the 'phone across the desk and I took it. "Marshall speaking," I said.

"Oh hello, Marshall," came the chief's voice. "Sorry but I'm afraid Red's got the laugh on you this time. We've had him padlocked for the last week pending investigation. Just unlocked his joint about an hour ago."

Dago Red's laugh trailed me through the door as I went out. I felt my ears burning. What a fool I had been not to realize the fact Skippy Kahn's calling that number by no means meant that he had got it. But I didn't mind the personal humiliation so much as I did seeing the case go to smash. My detective work had been fine. It just hadn't worked. Fault enough.

Disappointed, I headed for the station. And for want of anything better to do I went over to the morgue from there and had a look at what was left of Skippy Kahn. He was pretty badly jammed up, but there were a number of scars that had never been made by a car.

That gave me an idea too, but I couldn't do much with it. The fact that he had used dope himself only puzzled me. For if he had had a supply why had he not sold it instead of sending for more? Probably out I decided.

I sat down on a bench and thought back through every angle of the affair. Studying, I could see that I had been wrong in trying to pin the crime onto Dago Red. In the first place, it was an amateur's job at murder and Red could hardly qualify as an amateur. He might shoot, poison or knife a man; running over him would be too crude. Then, there was the matter of those missing license plates. A professional would have exchanged plates, realizing that their absence would be likely to bring down undesirable attention.

Then, I thought of the way the car had approached Skippy. It had traveled very slowly until it was almost on top of him. What had been the idea? Had his death been the act of a mind that worked upon the spur of the moment? Had it been unpremeditated? It looked that way.

I had this much then. Skippy had called some friend. The friend had been afraid to make a downtown delivery so Skippy had met him in the Mexican quarter. There, the friend had suddenly decided to run him down. With this much, I called headquarters.

"What friends did Skippy Kahn have?" I asked. "Who did he run around with most?"

The answer came like a flash.

"Skippy Kahn didn't have a friend in this town and no one would have run around with him for fear of being taken for a stool pigeon."

I was desperate. "How about relatives?"

"Only one. Wife. Here; I'll give you her address."

I caught a car to the address given and knocked on the door. In the driveway was a neat, black car. It shone like glass from bumper to taillight. There were thousands of others in the city just like it.

I was pretty curious about the kind of woman that would marry a man like Skippy Kahn. Naturally, I didn't expect much. I was in for a surprise.

The woman who answered the door was practically everything in a woman that Skippy was not in a man. Oh, of course you can't go through the mud without getting splashed but she had come as near to it as anyone might. Her brown hair was neatly combed and her eyes were large and matched her hair. I liked her hands, too, firm and well kept.

She knew what I had come for, of course, and invited me in

without delay. When we were both seated in the front room she spoke: "You don't need to tell me about Skippy. I heard about it and frankly I'm not very sorry. But I'll be glad to give you any clue in the matter that I can."

I twisted my hat in my hand. I had not expected her to take things so calmly and it rather upset me.

"Well, it's this way, Mrs. Kahn," I said, at last; "I really don't expect you to shed much light on the matter. It's more for the idea of leaving no stone unturned than anything else. You might tell me though whether anyone used your car last night. To your knowledge, of course."

She shook her head, looking me in the eye.

"No one used that car last night. You can see for yourself that it's as clean and new as the day it was driven out of the shop."

I nodded. "Yes, I noticed that." I studied her for a moment while she met my gaze. Then I looked at the carpet. It was a trifle muddy.

"Well, Mrs. Kahn," I said, "there really isn't much use in questioning you further. You may get a call from the station, but that's just a matter of form. I wish you luck." I arose and extended my hand.

She took it hesitantly, as if fearing some trick. Casually I stepped to the window and looked out at the car.

"By the way," I said, "did you know that your front license plate was upside down?"

I heard her gasp. Then she crowded past me and looked out at the car. The plate was in its proper position. She turned on me, fear mixed with courage on her face.

"A trick? Well, you can't trick me. You haven't got a thing on me and you know it. You may as well leave."

"Afterwhile," I agreed. "In the meantime you might tell me what Skippy called you about between two and three in the morning. Also, why you washed and polished your car this morning."

"He didn't—I didn't!" Her voice was almost a whisper.

"Oh yes he did," I insisted. "The call is on record at the hotel. And it's pretty plain that you just got through dolling up the car. Now, spill it."

"I won't!"

It was hard of me but I had to do it. I walked over to the 'phone and removed the receiver. "Police headquarters," I said, holding down the hook.

She was across the room in a flurry, grabbing my arm. "I'll talk. Oh, give me a chance!"

I put the receiver back on the hook. "All right. Go ahead."

She cried as she talked, but they were the tears of nervousness more than remorse. So her story was fairly coherent.

"Skippy kept a supply of the stuff here in the house. He was too much of a coward to keep it with him. I know that if it had ever been found here he intended to shove the blame onto me. He didn't have much. Only enough for his own use; so I was very surprised last night when he called me and told me to bring it down.

"My first idea was to refuse. Then I knew that I would have to pay in more ways than one if I turned against his wishes. But I was afraid of being caught and like a fool thought that taking off those plates would make me safer. I didn't realize that they would be almost sure to lead to my arrest.

"I have never driven a car a great deal so that I was deathly afraid as I went along the dark streets of Mexican town. I had laid the package on the floor where I could crush it and scatter the contents in case anyone tried to stop me. But without lights I lost track of its position.

"You saw the result. I did not know that I was so near to my destination, but I knew that I would have to have that package ready when I arrived. Skippy would not stand while I hunted and fumbled. So for just a minute I risked turning on the dash light. But I was unfamiliar with the switch and I turned on the headlights. That frightened me more than ever, especially when I saw that I was almost to Skippy. I tried to turn them off again, but was unsuccessful and being short on time I let them go and leaned over to look for the package. It was under my heel.

"I had my elbow against the rear lever and my foot was over the accelerator. As I slid down in the seat my toe naturally came down on the gas. The jerk threw my arm against the gear lever and clashed the gears. Thoroughly frightened now, I jerked at the gear desperately bringing my foot down on the gas harder than ever. Then, I shut my eyes. I don't know how I got around the corner nor how I got home. But here I am, wanted for the murder of Skippy Kahn."

"Will you tell me one thing more?" I asked. "Why you ever happened to marry Kahn?"

She shrugged her shoulder and grimaced. "I don't know. People do foolish things. Then he wasn't always as bad as he got to be. After we were married I had to stick with it. He wouldn't listen to a divorce. I know he would have killed me if I'd ever tried to get one. He usually had a pull with the police, too, so it wasn't any use to go to them."

"Well, he won't bother you anymore," I said. "I've got to be going now."

I started toward the door.

Frightened, she stopped me.

"Where are you going?"

I grinned. "To look for the party who killed Skippy Kahn."

"But I just told you—"

"You didn't tell me anything," I interrupted. "Not a thing. That's the only thing you'll have to remember. Can you do it?"

For the first time she really smiled. "You're square," she said.

I went out the door.

. *David Corn* .

MY MURDER

Ever have a notion that you couldn't get out of your head? No matter how hard you tried, it was still there. Always creeping around, whispering to you: here I am, here I am. Becoming part of you. The notion does not wither. You might forget it for a while. But turn a corner, and there it is, and the game you play with yourself of not thinking about it—for how can you think about not thinking about it?—is lost again. Sure, you recognize this feeling. Pulled into such a state, the answer many of us reach is this: yield. No choice is there. To be free, you must do it. And then figure out how to deal with the consequences. Start that affair with your officemate. Tell your boss how bad he smells. Cook the books. Steal from the collection plate. Hurl a brick through your neighbor's window. Answer that adult services ad placed by that person who specializes in you-know-what. I, too, took the yielding path. I killed a person—just to kill, for no other reason—and I have gone unpunished.

"There it is, the opening page of *My Murder*." I watched Hal Hemmings shut the book and stare into the camera. "This week, this book is on best-seller lists across the country. A fanciful exercise in imagination? Or, as the author claims, a true confession of a senseless murder he committed and got away with? Today we have with us the author of that book, Webb Seiden."

The red applause light ticked on. The studio audience began clapping.

"Stay with us. We'll be right back with the man who says he is a cold-blooded killer."

Gail Renda ran her fingers through my hair and complained about the makeup artist. I watched the monitor and worried about the strands her long fingers were collecting. Her broad, moon-shaped face was flush.

"There's not enough under your eyes. They probably want you to look evil. Remember what I told you: If I were them, I would load the audience with relatives of victims of unsolved homicides. They'll spring them on you in the second segment. We negotiated with them an exclusive—no other guests on the show—but we cannot control how they might fix the crowd. Be ready. Be natural. Talk to him, not the camera. And say the title whenever you can—especially when you come back from a break."

I listened to my agent, as she again straightened the tie we had purchased this morning. Ready, I was ready. The first time out is the hardest, everyone said. Get past this, it all will be easier. In my pocket I fingered the small stone I had picked up years ago at the grave site of Faulkner. Margaret had been with me then. We thought we soon would be married. Now she was gone. Now I was about to step before television cameras. With no complaints: this was what I had asked for. Now I was a published author.

"Say the title," Renda said, as I left the room.

A producer guided me to the chair. The audience stared. The host stood on the other side of the stage. He did not say hello. Someone shouted, "Fifteen seconds." The lights were hot. On cue, Hemmings did his lead-in. He then ran toward me, yelling his first question: "Mr. Seiden, did you actually kill someone just to kill them?"

"Yes."

"And then you capitalized on this heinous crime by writing this book?"

"Well, I did write . . ."

"So you're making money—I'm told the book is flying out of stores—off this act of murder?"

"I do have a book out. Its title is—"

"Mr. Seiden, you do understand why many people—myself included—are outraged that . . ."

He carried on. I waited. I knew I would be waiting for weeks to come. Just one moment after another, I told myself. I answered the questions when he allowed me the chance. Yes, I had tried to be a screenwriter. Yes, I had not succeeded. Yes, the only script I had been able to sell was the one for a B movie called *Lust Island*. Yes, I had committed a murder merely to see what it would be like. But, no, I didn't do it to write this book. In fact, several years passed between the event and the publication of *My Murder*.

"The event? What a sterile term. And who was she? The other person in this 'event.' You do say in the book your victim was a woman."

"Actually, Mr. Hemmings, I made it clear in the book that I would not disclose details that might assist any investigator. I explained that I would refer to the victim as 'she'—I never knew the person's name—but that did not mean that the victim had been a woman. It's all in the book."

"Excuse me, I haven't read it. Nor do I plan to. And I would urge anyone watching not to buy your . . . your deplorable book."

Before I could respond, he jumped into the audience and placed his microphone in front of the face of a white-haired mountain of a woman wearing thick glasses.

"Pretty sick, isn't it?" he said.

"Hal, he's a real sick fuck," she said. Later I would learn that someone in the control room had dubbed a tone over the last word of her sentence.

"We'll be right back," Hemmings said.

In three minutes, we were. We covered some details of the event. I had been driving, picked up a hitchhiker. Talked a bit. Stopped an hour or so down the road. Used a knife. Ditched the body in the woods. Went on my way.

"Why? I don't get it. Why?"

"Read the first page. That's the best explanation."

"Here's another page," he said.

The power. The surge. It can only sound like a cliché. But, then, this must be one of the oldest acts known to our species. I felt I had joined a club. Yet, strangely, not one that meant a great deal—or as great a deal as I had anticipated. I half-expected another club member to find me out, to come to my home one night, present his credentials, and tell me the secret. "You see, it's not as special as you thought. But welcome anyway." As with so much in life, it was the joining that was notable, not the ever-after state of having joined.

"Mr. Seiden, I respectfully submit you are full of you-know what and should be locked up with all the other murderous creeps. Why should we believe you won't do this again, if your sorry little heart so desires?"

Time for another break—no answer.

Renda had been wrong. It was not until the third segment that

Hemmings introduced audience members related to the victims of unsolved murders. "Maybe you killed my Janey," an older man shouted. "My Manuel," a woman said. "My Daddy," a girl shouted. "No details," I said, "none."

"Can't you even have the decency to look at these people and tell them that you are *not* responsible for the death of their loved one?"

"Was it on Route 38, near Yucaipa?" yelled a man in the front row.

I front of me were the images: the road, the sky, the face, the woods, the body, the leaves, the stillness.

No details, I repeated, no details.

"Some people think this is a hoax, that you didn't kill anyone, that you're in this only for the big bucks and some perverse ego thrill. I don't know which would be sicker."

"Mr. Hemmings, I stand behind my work."

"The book or the murder?"

"*My Murder,* my book."

58:10 into the hour. Done. An assistant escorted me off the set and to the green room. The makeup artist wiped my face clean. Hemmings came in. "Great show," he said and departed. Renda and I left the building through the rear entrance. We stepped into a waiting limousine. "Terrific," she breathed into my ear.

More shows. More confrontations. Newspaper columnists condemned me. Members of the clergy sermonized against me. Politicians promised legislation. The President pronounced me despicable. I was all that was wrong with society. A national newsmagazine put my face on its cover, above the line, "The Most Hated Man in America?" I was grateful for the question mark. A tabloid television show reported I was having an affair with an older actress. I had never met the woman. A supermarket gossip sheet claimed that Renda secretly had offered to provide to that magazine proof my book was false, if it would pay her

$150,000. She released a statement denying the story. I bought a black convertible. There were symposia across the nation on the responsibilities of publishing houses. Doesn't promoting books such as this one, ponderous moderators asked, only encourage people? I declined invitations to all such affairs. A former professor of mine called Renda. I lost the message. My parents were snubbed at their tennis club. The obsessed pored over each page, searching for clues, some to crack the case, some to prove I was a fraud. Development execs at the studios rang. They promised I could write the screenplay. The book sold. My roommate moved out of the Melrose bungalow we shared. I retained a realtor to look for a place in the hills. I changed my phone number three times.

Renda kept pressing me on the next "project." She never called it a book.

"Move fast, capitalize on all this," she said one afternoon, while we ate salads at a sidewalk restaurant in Santa Monica. "No turning back, honey."

She suggested the next project chronicle this whole episode. Another bestseller, she said. The advance would be high six figures, initial shipping of two hundred thousand at least. She even had the title: *The Murder Wars.*

"A little too violent?" I asked.

She looked crossed at me when I informed her that I had begun a novel based on a series of hunting trips taken by my great-grandfather when he was a young man in Montana. She said nothing while the waiter poured sparkling water into our glasses.

"Webb, dear, people have stood by you. Taken flack, a great deal of it. Been talked about in none too pleasant fashion. Don't abandon them to follow a fancy."

"I am always with you," I told her. She leaned over and tussled my hair, again taking several strands with her.

"I am almost always here," I told the police detective who came to my front door later that day. It was my way of apologiz-

ing for having missed her earlier. Look over there, I directed her.
I had placed by my phone the note—written on LAPD station-
ery—she had dropped in the mailbox. This was proof of my intention to phone the number she had left. I had been intrigued
by the name on the note: Anna Rixt. How could one pass up the
opportunity to meet an LAPD cop with this name? But I had
been distracted by a host of e-mail messages I had received that
day from members of a Gothic literary electronic conference I had
joined under a false name.

Now Anna Rixt stood a foot or two into the living room. She
began by noting that I did not have to let her in or speak with her.
I waved aside her obligatory remarks.

"German?" I asked. "Flemish?"

"Dutch," she said, as I invited her to sit.

Her father had been a Dutch jazz drummer; her mother,
a black American movie extra. At her prime, the light-skinned
mother had a lovely, smooth and oval face. That was before the
heroin. I learned all this later. Anna Rixt had kinky, sandy hair,
wide lips, sharp lines at the side of her hazel eyes, broad shoulders,
long, slender arms. Thirty-seven, I guessed silently. She wore no
wedding ring.

"Lemonade?" I asked. "Fresh from my own tree."

"As long as there's not too much sugar."

I went to the kitchen and fetched the lemonade.

She informed me she had not come to question me directly
about the murder in my book. But she wondered if she could dis-
cuss with me in general terms the subject of killing.

"It might help me in my work."

I did not believe her, but felt like helping her. My contact with
the police had been on the cool side during these past weeks. A
sergeant at the local station had called twice to notify me that the
department had received a death threat concerning me. Each
time he noted brusquely that a patrol car would swing by period-
ically. I, too, had received threats in letters and calls, despite having changed my number. But it would have been bad form to

request assistance from the authorities. On a couple of evenings in a row, I noticed the same car slowing when it passed my house. Another victim's relative or a detective from Nevada assigned an unbreakable case, I guessed. I waited for a confrontation, but the car never stopped. My book, my choice, my problems. No need to burden the police.

I felt sympathy for homicide detectives who believed my book mocked their arduous existences. So whatever I could do for Rixt—within reason—I would do. And I was curious. She told me she had wondered about the internal justifications that occur within the psyche of a murderer ever since her first case—a woman found with her mouth and nostrils glued shut by epoxy. That case, Rixt noted, was never solved.

But I suspected that another imperative had brought her to me. I pictured a scene: Detective Rixt at her desk. The phone rings. Some Higher Up had just been ripped a new anus by another Higher Up for not doing anything about that jerk on television who is making a million for having bumped off a party unknown with complete impunity. Down the chain of command, the order came: do something. And Rixt, at her cluttered desk in an office in dire need of a fresh coat of paint, was the order's final recipient. She had to visit the most hated man in America.

"There's a portion of the book that intrigued me." She sipped the lemonade and took a copy of my book out of her bag.

"I hope the office paid for it."

"No, I did." She did not get the joke. She began to read:

Guilt had been my greatest fear. I realized before I acted that I could not be sure what emotions, what compulsions would be borne of this event. Would they be as powerful— or more so—as the original impulse, the original sin? Would the commission of this murder create another force within me that was beyond control? I thought of the old cinematic depictions of the murderer so racked by remorse he confesses. I had no desire to be found out. Yet who could predict with rock-fast certainty that he—and he would have to be speaking for his entire conscious—would stick to this path? Who could be truly sure that some Sunday-school part of him would not rebel, without any declaration of intent, and purposefully drop a clue? There was now a killer inside me, and I could not be certain that I saw all of him in broad daylight.

I waited for him to cause trouble. For him to leverage the guilt. Nothing came. Yes, there were pangs. This had been a shitty thing to do. I realized that. But no heavy weight descended. And, as far as I could tell, there was no inchoate urge for penance. Someone might argue that the writing of this book is driven by guilt. It is not. If I were not fully convinced that I could write this book and escape legal punishment, these words would never have appeared. All of us have read a news report of a grisly action—a thug raping a nun, a colonel torturing a child, an army destroying an entire town of civilians, bayoneting babies, dropping napalm—and wondered, "How could they do it?" I would hazard a guess that many of us harbor the innate knowledge that no matter what horrible deeds we may do, eventually we will be all right. That the guilt, if present at the start, will fade. One of the few universal lessons of human existence is that everything fades. The guilt I never knew is gone. There might be others who are consumed by guilt, but I happen to be one of the lucky ones.

Anna Rixt put down my book. "No guilt at all?"

"As I said."

"When dealing with murderers, many of us count on, if not guilt, then the nervousness that we assume is the product of guilt."

"Nervousness might be of assistance," I said, as I placed my hands behind my head and gazed at the ceiling. "But I can only advise that you do not unduly associate it with guilt. A person in your custody would have reason to be nervous with or without guilt."

Good line, I thought.

We chatted for almost an hour. I did my best to answer her, until she checked her watch and said, "Thank you for your time, Mr. Seiden." She stood up and knocked over the pitcher of lemonade—it shattered on the floor.

"Don't move," I said and got the broom and dustpan. She stood by awkwardly in the puddle as I cleared the broken glass from around her. When I was done, she headed toward the front door. I asked if she intended to call on me again. She turned to look at me but did not reply. When I returned to the living room I saw that she had left her copy of my book. I opened it. She had underlined passages and written notes in the margins, in some spots rather extensively. I shut the book. It would be an intrusion upon her privacy, I thought, to read her jottings.

Several days later, I sat at the kitchen table, thinking about Anna Rixt, wondering if she would return. It was late afternoon, that portion of the day that cinematographers call "magic hour," when the long rays of a declining sun cast a glow. I was sifting through brittle letters my great-grandfather had written as a young man to an uncle in Philadelphia. One described when he was trapping near Flathead Lake in Montana and met an Indian man and a white woman who lived together in a cabin. The pair were startled to have a visitor, but with a storm front moving in, they invited him to supper and offered him a spot on the floor for the night. Neither the man nor the woman said much. They never mentioned their names nor asked his. In the morning, as he packed up to head out into the rain, the woman said, "We'd prefer you not say anything to other folks about us." My great-grandfather vowed not to and in his letter allowed himself but one observation on this episode: "Only far away from the rest of us could they find civility."

The phone rang. "Turn on the television."

"Who is—"

"Turn it on, you damn idiot," Renda said and hung up.

I went to the living room and picked up the remote. I only had to flip through several channels before I found where I was supposed to be. A woman surrounded by a group of reporters stood in front of LAPD headquarters: ". . . he's making all this money off of"—she was crying, stammering—"off of . . . of me." She paused while the cameramen jostled in front of her. The woman was thirtyish. She wore oversized sunglasses. A red scarf covered her hair. Not much of her face was exposed. An older woman in a business suit touched her hand, and she continued. "He tried to kill me. It was awful, I never wanted to ever see, to think about— but then I was watching television and there he was. He was right up there, talking about this as if it were nothing, as if I were not even a . . . a dog."

The older woman introduced herself as the speaker's attorney and declared that her client had been my victim, that I had not killed her as I had written, but that I had severely wounded her and left her for dead. Six years ago, the lawyer said, the woman in the red scarf was the hitchhiker I had picked up. After being stabbed repeatedly and then dumped in a ravine, this woman had managed to crawl a few hundred feet and had been discovered by two hunters. The attorney noted that her client barely survived the assault and emerged traumatized, with a murky recollection of her assailant and no memory of his car. She had been able to provide only sketchy information to the local police. The attorney read from the police report: "Victim identified assailant as male Caucasian in mid-thirties, of slim build, about six feet tall and 170 pounds, with dark or light brown hair." Close, I thought, but heftier than me.

"I never could remember the face," said the woman in the red scarf. "I never wanted to. Such a horrible, horrible. . . . But I saw his face on television. It was like I was there again. Everything came back. Even how, when he thought I was dead, he came over to me and said, 'Thanks for the company.' Then walked away. And I remember hearing the engine of the car turn over."

The attorney took charge. She explained that she had turned over relevant information to the LAPD and that the police in Yermo—where her client had been assaulted—had requested assistance from the Los Angeles department. "Would there be a lawsuit?" one reporter yelled. "Anything is possible," the lawyer replied. "A book deal for her, too?" "If anyone deserves money it's this poor woman."

"How do we know this is for real?" another journalist asked.

"Real? Real?" the woman shouted. "How's this for real?" She lifted her blouse. Her abdomen was covered with ugly scars. She pulled down her collar. A thick, crooked scar on the neck. She took off her glasses. Another one below her eye. "Real enough?"

I picked up the phone. "Is it—" Renda began to ask. "You know, I've never once asked you."

"I know. Are you asking, now, Gail?"

"No, not really. But are you prepared for all the shit that's about to rain down?"

"No."

"Well, I hate to say this, but this will sell more books. I'll be right over."

The reporters arrived before Renda. When a pack had gathered, I stood outside the front door and said that I could not corroborate the woman's account.

"She's not the one who you cold-bloodedly executed for the hell of it?" I could not see who had asked that.

"I've said before that I would not address any specifics."

"You deny her story 100 percent?"

"No denials, no confirmations."

"When you kill someone, they stay dead, don't they?"

I waited for the next question.

"What is your response to the statement from LAPD that it will examine these allegations?"

"It's what I would expect the LAPD to say."

"If the police ask you to supply an alibi, will you?"

"I will try to be helpful, in accordance with the guidelines I've already established."

"Do you think this is a publicity stunt to cash in?"

"By who?"

Renda's aquamarine BMW pulled up. She jumped out of the car, pushed through the crowd and grabbed me.

"Thank you all for your time," she said to the reporters and pulled me into the house.

Renda left several hours later—aggravated. No, I would not reappear on the Hemmings show with my accuser. No, I would not grant any magazine an exclusive interview. No, I would not hire a high-priced Beverly Hills defense attorney. No, I would not reconsider my refusal to write a follow-up book. Yes, the appearance of this woman would provide an entirely new dimension to such a book.

"You're going to have to fight back," Renda said as she walked toward the street.

Why?

"Because that's the way it works." She climbed into her BMW.

"By the way," she said as the window glided shut, "this fellow named Shea keeps calling me. Says he taught you at USC. He's a pain in the ass. Will you call him or something?"

The waitress brought me my second beer, as I waited for the ceviche and read an article in a science magazine about a type of DNA that passes only from mothers to their children. So, I thought, no men in these near-infinite chains of evolutionary evidence. And then Rixt appeared. She explained she had been directed to this tacky Mexican restaurant by a neighbor. I knew which one: the retired claims adjustor, who tracked all the details of my life that could be discerned from his windows. I suspected him of falsely informing a tabloid that I had received nocturnal visits from the leading actress of a popular situation comedy.

"I hope I am not disturbing you."

She sat at the table and with no further conversation asked me if I could account for my whereabouts on a specific date six years ago. I told her I would check my records, but I doubted they were organized enough to be of use. She said that she had DMVed me and discovered that I did not own a car at that time. "Living in L.A. without a car?" she asked. I told her that I had been sharing a car with a friend. "And that was?" I gave her Margaret's name and asked if she would like a drink. She ordered a rum with ice and lime.

"This is going to be a waste of time for you," I said.

"Her story is a persuasive one."

"Entirely convincing?"

"Well, her cousin is the assistant sheriff in Yermo and the one who signed the police report she's handed over to LAPD."

"Are you suggesting this might be a—"

"No. Just one more item to check."

"If the point was to murder someone, don't you think whoever did that would make sure the subject was murdered?"

"If people didn't screw up, I'd have no job."

My food came, and I pushed it aside. "What's her name?"

"Haven't you watched the news?"

"I did but I blanked on her name."

"Connie Dicomini."

"You think there is a case to be made here?" I asked.

"There is a point to be made."

"A point?"

"That you cannot smartass the law. Let more people think that and the world will be even nastier for cops and people like me."

"So better any resolution than the accurate one?"

"Everything depends. Every time is different." She finished her drink.

"What if the wrong person is used to make the point?"

"That would be a terrible thing. And it happens. Most people in jail deserved to be there long before they were caught. But I know a few who don't. They're living their own private hells. No system can process all the intake we get these days and not screw up. But I will say one thing. When the wrong person is blamed and punished, a small good is still committed."

She waited for me to ask, but I did not.

"And that is, all the rest of us are shown it's not getting any easier to rob, beat, shoot, slice, rape, kill and avoid the consequences."

"Yes, but in those cases the person who performed the deed falsely credited to another learns that this lesson is a lie."

"That's why I called it a 'small good.'"

She stood up to leave. I offered to walk her to her car. She declined and said she would stop by in the morning, after I had had a chance to check on the date in question. I listened to her boot heels click against the floor tiles.

"You left your copy of my book at my house," I called after her.

"That's okay," she said. "I don't think I need it right now."

Rixt did not come by the next day. I screened all my calls, refusing to talk to an assortment of journalists, a bevy of lawyers, and Renda. "We must develop a plan," an agitated Renda said to my machine. "And do something about that professor of yours. He keeps bothering me." I tried to work on the Montana novel, but every half an hour another television producer rang the doorbell. I sent them away.

Shortly after noon, the bell sounded again. At the door was a woman who looked familiar. I impatiently asked what she wanted. She stared for a moment. I asked again.

"You don't know, do you?"

The red scarf. Connie Dicomini. And behind her was a mob of reporters, photographers and camera operators.

"I wanted to see you," she said.

"Now that you see me, are you still so sure?"

"Yes, yes I am. It was buried in my mind. Now it's not. Answer me one question. I have to know: how could you?"

Lines of water ran from her face; her expression remained steely. The end of a scar peeked out from behind the sunglasses. The scene was being broadcast live.

"I can't say anything," I told her.

"Yes, you can. You choose not to say anything. So you can continue to torment me and collect millions. But I won't stand for it. Maybe they'll put you away, maybe they won't. But I want an answer. I don't care how long it takes. I'll be waiting. I'll be everywhere until you can tell me why what happened to me happened to me."

She spat in my face and walked away.

"Got it good," one cameraman said to his producer.

For the next week, she was constantly nearby. Wearing her sunglasses and red scarf, she sat in a car outside my house. She followed me when I walked to the corner each morning to get a coffee and a paper. Her car was in my rearview mirror whenever I checked. She never said another word to me. At night, I stayed up late, sitting at the window, with the lights out, and watched her alone in her car. For the first couple of days, the news people followed her as she followed me. I stayed away from the television to avoid the alleged-victim-keeps-lonely-vigil stories. Renda, who paid daily visits, never mentioned her.

I considered crafting a response for Connie Dicomini. But nothing came. I would not be able to satisfy her. I waited too for Rixt. There was no word from her. But early one morning, I heard from Margaret. She had not returned any of the calls I had placed to her when my book was about to be released. Now, she informed me, she was calling as a "courtesy to the past."

"I'll accept any courtesy I can get."

"This detective came by last night, she had an odd name. She asked me questions about you. But mostly she wanted to know where you were on a certain weekend six years ago."

An obliging Margaret had checked an old personal calendar for Rixt and discovered that she had been traveling that weekend. In the calendar, she had written "Webb—Joshua Tree," which she interpreted as a reference to one of my many solo overnight trips to the national park. Margaret had gone through phone records and found that no long-distance calls had been made from our phone on the relevant days.

"Webb, I couldn't say I knew where you were."

"I probably can't either."

"I did ask her, what if we assumed you had gone to Joshua Tree, would it still have been possible for you to, to . . ."

She was crying.

"And she said, 'Maybe.'" The old silence. "And I can't cover for you. I can't."

"If you want to know Margaret, I'll tell you. No one knows. But I'll tell you."

"I've got to go. Goodbye."

I stayed in my house as much as I could. I kept up with the e-mail correspondence I maintained under various screen names. I listened to all the one-way conversations people held with my answering machine.

There were several calls from Maury Shea, a washed-out screenwriter whose course I had taken at Southern Cal. Decades earlier a script of his had been nominated for an Oscar. And every screenplay he wrote after that had gone unproduced. By the time I had come to sit in his classroom, he was dishing out stale recitals of his eight principles of successful screenplay writing and recounting for the millionth time the stories of his lunches, dinners and drinks with Welles, Huston, and Brando, during which they beseeched him for the opportunity to direct or appear in his next film—the one that never came. His eight principles were conventional but useful. I recalled being quite pleased that I had incorporated seven of them into the script for *Lust Island*.

I had no particular feelings toward Shea and ignored his calls as I did all others. Then when I was picking up the phone to order a linen jacket from a catalog, I found Shea on the line, trying to call me. He was mad that I had not returned his messages and told me that we had to talk right away.

"Let's talk," I said.

"No. No. Not like this. Come see me. I have to show you something."

"I'm pretty busy."

"If you don't, I'll, I'll go and . . . I already told . . . I can prove you a fraud."

"How so?"

"Just come, if you want to know. Believe me, you want to know."

He was right. I wrote down his address. We agreed I would drop by the next morning.

When I woke up I engaged in my new daily ritual. I went to the living room and, shielding myself behind a curtain, peered outside. She was still there. I realized I was waiting for two women to act. I wanted Connie Dicomini to vanish; I wanted Anna Rixt to reappear. For the first time since my book had come out, I wanted an end to all this.

Another ring of the doorbell. Two detectives from the homicide division of LAPD introduced themselves and asked if they could come in and talk to me.

"About what?"

"About certain allegations that have been made," one said.

I told them that I did not think I should talk to them without a lawyer present. The tall one—only he talked—informed me that they would appreciate it, then, if I came down to their office later in the day with my attorney. He handed me his card.

"If that is not convenient for you," he said, "we will be happy to call upon you again."

"What about Detective Rixt?"

"We're handling the case," the talking detective replied with a frown. "We'll be seeing you."

I found the note Rixt had left me and called the handwritten number on it.

41

"You have reached Anna Rixt, please—"

Voice mail. I phoned the station house and asked for her. Someone there suggested I contact headquarters. "Rixt, Rixt— sounds familiar," a downtown desk sergeant said. "Hold on." He checked and then asked if I wanted to speak to someone else in homicide. "Detective Rixt left the force two years ago."

I picked up the copy of my book that Rixt had left behind. I found a passage next to which she had scribbled a few words I could not decipher. I had not read the book since it had been in galleys and now could not recall having written these lines.

I was keenly aware that this was a dividing point. Whatever change occurred in me between the "before" side of the event and the "after," there would be no returning. So much in life can actually be undone. You can divorce a spouse you come to hate. You can quit a job. You can de-clare bankruptcy and start anew. You cannot undo a death. Once I had a conversation with a friend before he had a tat-too of a cup of coffee drawn above his right shoulder-blade. What if you change your mind someday? I asked him. What if you grow to dislike your tattoo? That's the whole point, he said. It is forever. How often do you do something that is forever?

Renda pounded on the door until I let her in. She held a fax. "See this. See this. They want a deal."

I told her I was not interested.

"Even with all the shit with that woman—or because of it— and they still want a deal. Some people have been scared off. You better take it now. They could easily turn around and offer it to her."

"Not interested."

Renda tried to convince me. I knew that she saw this as a step toward obtaining a studio job—her dream for many of her forty years. "What's the point," she shouted, "in representing someone who doesn't want to be represented?"

"Gail, what would happen if I declared that the whole book was a ruse?"

"That would be it for you. Nothing, no more. Not too good for me, either."

She sat down on the couch and was silent for a moment. "Would that be the truth?"

"I was only thinking aloud."

I made her a cup of tea, and she settled down. I didn't mention the detectives. I told her I was going to visit Shea.

"What for?" she asked.

"Old times, I suppose. Get him off your unduly burdened back."

Before she left, she tousled my hair. I thought about complaining this time. I was becoming possessive about the hair I had, and I never cared for this overdone display of tenderness. But there already was enough tension between us. Let the small stuff rest, I decided. "Honey," she said, "please think about the deal. But I can see I am going to have to start searching for other opportunities."

Connie Dicomini followed me onto the freeway. I did not know what Shea wanted, but I figured it would be best if I arrived without my usual escort. I brought my black convertible up to 90. I assumed that Dicomini would be caught off guard; I had never tried to escape her watchful gaze. She dropped behind, but soon was back, matching my speed. I slowed to 40; she slowed. I returned to 90. She was there. I repeatedly switched lanes, and she stuck with me. I moved into the right lane and cruised along. She remained close. As I was coming upon an exit, I checked the mirror. The lane to the left was open, and there was little traffic behind us. I jerked the wheel to the left and slammed my foot on the brake pedal. Connie Dicomini went flying past. I then pulled the wheel to the right—in time to jump across the right lane and make the exit. Too many hours of television, I told myself and rode along surface streets in Universal City.

Shea lived in a seedy portion of Van Nuys. I drove past his house, parked down the block at a 7-Eleven, picked up a package of cigarettes—I had not smoked in years—and walked back to Shea's house. I rapped on the frame of the screen door, and he opened it for me. Shea was tall, gaunt, pale, covered with liver spots. Dull gray stubble ran across his face. Long strands of limp white hair hung from the back of his head. He wore a fraying bathrobe over pale blue pajamas. He led me in, relying on a cane and shaking as he walked slowly. "Aneurysm operation," he said by way of explanation. All the blinds were drawn inside the house. Old newspapers and magazines were piled in various corners. Movie posters from the 1960s were crooked on the walls. He shuffled to a couch and fell into it. As I made contact with the Barcalounger, a cloud of dust emerged, and I coughed.

"You sick too?" Shea asked.

"No."

"Never let them operate. Three years ago they said they had to fix this aneurysm. It didn't bother me any, but they said she could blow any moment. So I let them. Now I can hardly walk. Can't drive. Tired all the time. All these damn headaches. And I haven't had a boner since. Insurance covered most of it, but it's cost me thousands. Rehabilitation, physical therapy. Can't afford the cable now. Look a lot different than when you last saw me?"

"A little."

"You don't look different to me, 'cause I can't remember what you looked like. My memory's almost as useless as my pecker."

From lunch with Brando to a San Fernando Valley hermit, I thought. On the mantel were framed photographs covered with dust.

"So if I had seen you on any of all those television shows or read about you in the paper—but I don't read the paper anymore—I wouldn't have remembered you at all. Nothing. Nada. Like thousands of people I once knew—a zero to me now. All gone."

He looked up from his hands. "Name them."

"What?"

"The fuckin' eight principles."

"Professor Shea, what did you want to tell me?"

"Okay, okay, screw the fuckin' eight principles. Maybe there were nine and I missed one."

He pulled on his hair. A woman came to see him several weeks ago. He can't remember her name. She said she's a reporter. She found out that I had been a student of his. She asked if he remembered anything about me. He explained to her all about the aneurysm operation, the bad memory, the bad pecker.

But, he told her, he has boxes. In the other room, boxes and boxes. Everything is in the boxes. Together they went through dozens of boxes—until they found the one from USC. Took awhile because it was labeled "insurance forms and warranties." And in the box are all the records from all his classes. Had this exercise he made all the little shitheads do, he explained to her. Sprung it on them like a trap. Came into the classroom, said, no lecture today. You have thirty minutes to write ten fuckin' fantastic film ideas—each no more than two sentences. Let's see what happens if you run into Mr. Studio Big-Dick this afternoon at a car wash. I graded them and gave them back, he told her.

But not before copying them. Not that he was going to swipe their ideas, most of which sucked. Not that. But they were good kicks to his own brainstorming. Sometimes he'd pull out the ten-idea sheets, rummage through them, get the juices flowing. And he still had every damn paper. Including mine.

I had forgotten all about Shea's ten-ideas exercise.

"Right here," he said and knocked a stack of *TV Guide*s off the table in front of him. He held it up for me. I reached out my hand.

"No, no, no. . . . Let me read it to you."

Number one: the Devil, disguised as a high-power lawyer, takes over a large New York corporate law firm. A young associate in the firm discovers this and attempts to thwart him.

"Not bad. I can see that," Shea said.

Number five: Instead of being blackmailed by a political opponent, the President of the United States, at the start of an election campaign, announces he is a transvestite. He then tries to convince the country—and his wife—that he deserves another term.

"Ahead of your time, Mr. Seiden."

Number ten: A washed-up minor-league pitcher, who is a former Special Forces veteran, stumbles upon a terrorist plot to blow up the Astrodome during the World Series. He and his teenage punk-rock nephew derail the scheme.

"Clearly, you were running out of steam. Oh, I skipped this interesting one."

Number four: Someone claims responsibility for a murder he did not commit and then proceeds to cash in on it.

"A little on the vague side, but we can easily fill in the details."
Shea wanted money. He said he would let me start the bidding. What did I think was fair? "Never done this before," he said.
"What about the reporter?" I asked.
She had wanted to take it. He had demanded she pay for it. She said that if she needed it she would come back—and then she never did.
"Drink?" He pointed to a bottle of bourbon and two crusty glasses on the table.

"No, thank you."

"Need some ice." He stood up and grabbed my list. "Think I'll keep this close." He hobbled off to the kitchen.

I tried to think quickly and thoroughly. The list was not solid proof my book was a ruse, but it was strong evidence for that proposition. He thought I would want it buried. In a perfect world, yes. But perhaps it now was more important for the paper to be disclosed. If so, how the paper became public would be crucial. If I refused to pay him and stormed out, would he find another reporter to sell it to? Or would he consider Connie Dicomini's accusations and come to realize that the paper, if revealed, might help me? Then would he sit on this list until I paid him? But if I bought it from him, could I release it myself? Probably not. I would be accused of having faked it. Shea would not be a reliable source for confirming the origins of the paper. A reporter had seen it. She could attest to its validity. But her name was lost.

The door to the kitchen squeaked, and Shea entered the room. One hand held the paper. The other grasped a bowl of ice and the cane. A finger slipped, and the bowl fell.

"Shit," he said—and slipped on a piece of ice and fell backward. He landed hard and did not move. I rushed to Shea. My paper lay next to him. I kicked an ice cube away from it. He was still, but breathing. I heard a car drive past and saw that the front door was open. What if someone came in now? Shea on the ground, my paper beside him, me in the house. All easily twisted. Taking the paper would do me no good—unless I was certain I never wanted it to become public in a credible way. The postman could be next door and heading this way. But I had to proceed through all the calculations. When Shea came to, no doubt he would call me and we could start negotiations again. Let's say he didn't revive. Would it be better for my list to be there by his side or not? I could not figure that out. Should I stay with the path chosen, do what had to be done, round out rough spots, tidy everything up, be in control? Or leave him this way? I considered dragging Shea

<figure>47</figure>

to the couch. Go, said a voice. Do it, said a voice. I realized I had not touched anything in the house, only the armrest of the Barcalounger. If—just if—he was not going to be fine, it probably would be best for my fingerprints not to be on the chair. The voices in my head were hard to separate. They created a fog. I stood over Shea. I felt lost in the fog. Then it lifted. I wiped the chair and walked out the door without looking back at him.

The trial lasted less than three weeks. The jury needed seven hours to declare me guilty and another five to decide upon a sentence: death. It had been easy for the prosecutor to convince the jurors that I had been the person who had bashed a bourbon bottle into the front of Shea's head and had killed him. Connie Dicomini testified that I had lost her on the freeway, heading in the direction of Shea's home. Gloria Renda testified that I had informed her I was off to see Shea. After her testimony, on the courthouse steps, Renda announced that she would be representing Dicomini in negotiations with several publishing houses. A clerk at the 7-Eleven told the jury that she remembered recognizing me that day as "that awful man from the TV shows." A criminologist appeared with charts and showed that hairs found at the crime scene were consistent with my hair. The deputy county coroner noted that Shea had experienced blows to the back and front of his skull. He could not be positive which had been the lethal one, but he assumed it had been the one to the frontal lobe. Throughout the trial, there was no mention of any paper that had fallen next to Shea. It apparently had not been there when Shauna Fowbray—yes, of the U.S. Postal Service—had discovered the body.

I never took the stand. My lawyer advised me not to do so. During preliminary hearings he had fought successfully to prevent the prosecutors from referring explicitly to my book. The judge ruled that the prosecution could only mention my book if I testified. My lawyer also argued that due to my notoriety I could not receive a fair trial. The judge angrily replied that there was no

way on God's green earth that he would allow the fact that I had
bragged about committing one murder to prevent me from being
tried for another. Throughout jury selection, he asked potential
jurors if they had heard of my book. Most said yes. He asked
those whether they could judge this case purely on its merits and
the evidence presented in court. All said yes.

The district attorney's office only had one problem: my motive.

"We will admit we are puzzled by the 'why' of this murder,"
the lead prosecutor said during his summation. "We can only
guess at what goes on in the mind of such a heartless, soulless person." The media reported that the prosecutors, having learned
that I had been in Shea's class at the time of the assault on Connie Dicomini, believed that Shea had known something about my
supposed attack upon her. The tabloids reported that Shea and I
had been lovers.

My lawyer complained that he had no case. I had told him why
I had gone to Shea's home and about the paper. "But it was not
on the police list of recovered items," he said. Had I kept the original? he asked. I could not recall. I was being held without bond,
so he rummaged through the filing cabinet in my garage and
found nothing there. There was a possibility that my graduate
school papers might have ended up in one of the boxes that Margaret had taken, but whenever my lawyer phoned, she hung up.

During a pre-arrest interrogation—to which I had submitted
voluntarily, against my lawyer's advice—I had told the detectives
on the case, the two men who had come to my home, about the
paper and where I had last seen it. "There was no paper to save
your pink-ass butt," said the talking member of the pair. "You did
it. You know you did it. Read your million-ass-dollar book: *No,
it didn't feel like a dream. But time was odd, soft. Not until I pulled
over for a coffee, did I reenter my own life again.*' The expert
speaks. Tell yourself you know, and you'll remember. You say it all
got foggy when you were standing there. People tell us that all

the time. You wouldn't believe how many people. 'It went dark,' 'It went hazy.' 'It went fuckin' mauve.'"

During the preparation for the trial, I had told my lawyer about Rixt. He promised he would have an associate check on her. A week later he handed me a file. Rixt had been a cop, with a solid performance rating. One night she shot her partner. The newspaper articles told how they had been caught in a shoot-out in an alley behind a warehouse. Her story was that they had been responding to a tip and were fired on by unknown assailants. She returned fire; her partner went down. The review board concluded that he had been killed by a bullet from her gun. Prior to his death, the newspaper clippings noted, her partner had come under internal investigation for trafficking drugs. Rixt was cleared of any wrongdoing in the shooting—and refused to talk about it publicly. She left the force and became a private detective. The file contained an old publicity still of her mother in her heyday and a few jazz magazine references to her father.

My lawyer went to see her. She had a small office above a copying store in Silver Lake. She had been hired by a client to look into my case, she explained. She would not say who the client had been. Nor would she say whether she had discovered anything of use to my defense. Rixt did disclose she had been visited by the detectives working my case. I told them the same thing I am telling you, she said. My lawyer concluded she could not be of any help to us. But I never stopped wondering who had retained Rixt.

Throughout my incarceration, I considered the alternative scenarios. Assume Connie Dicomini managed to follow me. After I left Shea's house, she knocks on the door. Not hearing anything, she enters and spots the old man on the ground. She picks up the paper, reads it, and realizes it might be proof that the man she is accusing might be innocent of the charge. Does she kill Shea to protect her version of the truth?

But she could not have trailed me. I had lost her on the highway.

Had Renda seen Shea's address at my house? Say she did. She then drives there and it's the same setup as with the first scenario. Renda does not want to be the partner of a proven fraud. There's no deal in that. Maybe Renda's association with Dicomini began before the trial, before my trip to Shea's house. Could she that day, on the way out of my home, have stopped by Dicomini's car and slipped her Shea's address?

How about this: both arrive and enter the house after my departure. Renda had this habit of tousling my thinning hair and grabbing a few strands. So she plants the hair in Shea's house and collects the paper. Who grabbed the bourbon bottle—and then walked away with the broken-off neck of the shattered bottle, the other piece of evidence that the police never found?

You have no proof, my lawyer reminded me repeatedly.

Renda never visited. I read in the paper that she had brokered a book deal for Dicomini. My lawyer, with no great enthusiasm, worked on an appeal. Months after the trial, I was able to start working again on the Montana novel.

I was in the prison library fruitlessly searching for information on the silverite movement in the West in the 1890s, when I realized that I had overlooked something. The first chance I had I called Rixt collect. She hung up on the operator. I wrote her. There was no reply. Over the next six months, I called whenever possible and wrote her a letter every day. Finally, one Sunday morning, I was informed a visitor was waiting for me. I was brought from the wing reserved for those sentenced to death to the high-security visiting room. Behind a thick pane of plastic, there was Rixt.

"Hello," she said through the small holes in the plastic.

"You saw Shea, didn't you?"

Rixt shifted in her seat. "I came because I want you to stop writing and calling."

"So, then tell me. Did you go to Shea's house?"

"It doesn't matter."

"You told him you were a reporter—like you told me you worked for LAPD."

"I never actually told you that. You'll have to forgive me if I don't apologize for that. You should always ask to see a badge."

"And you were working for Renda, right? Trying to find out if the book was true or not?"

"I can't tell you who I was working for."

"Did you ever look into Dicomini's cousin in Yermo, the one who signed the police report on her case?"

"The client took me off the job before I got to that."

"But you saw that stupid test of Shea's. You read it. Did you tell Renda about it?"

"I can't—"

"And the cops came to see you and you didn't say anything."

"I don't work for LAPD anymore."

"But you have to say."

"Listen, it wouldn't help you now. If I did say that the test existed, what would that mean? It could mean that it was there and you killed the guy so he wouldn't blackmail you with it, and then you destroyed it. Maybe you did want it to come out because you were worried about Connie Dicomini. But how can you prove that? And if that's the case, maybe the old jerk wouldn't part with the test, so you knocked him."

She was right. I shut up for a moment.

"If you had said something at the time," I said, "it might have made a difference. You can't say it wouldn't have."

"You did too good a job in your book. I couldn't find any clear evidence one way or the other—that you did it or that you made it up. But I was willing to believe you. I've always found that when somebody declares himself an asshole, you're better off taking him at his word. So I never had much desire to help."

"None of the Shea business would have happened had it not been for you. He'd still be alive today. That doesn't bother you?"

"You should talk. I don't live in a make-it-up world. Where I come from, something goes wrong and some fool you don't care about is dead. I can't change that. You get used to it. It'd be great to keep an old man alive or maybe even help prove a fucker was framed, if he was. But you don't always get to write your own story. At least, I don't. And I can live with that—or I try to. So, yeah, you and me are in a way tied together by Shea. But it's not a bond that means anything. It's just there. And I've got plenty of it's-just-there in my life. I don't like what happened. But I don't like a lot of things."

"You came because you feel guilty."

"I suppose I'm not one of the lucky ones."

"Then will you tell me?"

"It won't help you any."

"Yes, it will. I want to be sure that I didn't kill him."

I often think about Rixt's reply. She shook her head and said, "You know, it's odd what you can convince yourself of."

Then she left. I never contacted her again.

Dicomini's book was published. An emotional highlight, one critic said, is the scene in which the victim meets my agent, and Renda breaks down. I found that the book was ambiguous as to when this encounter occurred.

During the publicity wave that accompanied Dicomini's book, a reporter wrote me and asked for an interview. I had spurned all such requests so far, but accepted this one. He came with a photographer. We were allowed to use a conference room for an hour. For his first question, he asked if I had any regrets. I'd be a damn fool not to, I replied.

"Did you really kill someone for your book?"

"I have nothing new to say about that. A death sentence doesn't change everything."

"No jailhouse confession, then?"

I had nothing to confess.

We talked about the appeal. I was not hopeful, I explained, but I did view it as a way to postpone my execution for a year or two.

In that time, I could finish the Montana book. I am really pleased with it, I told him. I sent the first three hundred pages to a small press in Vermont, and the editor there expressed an interest in publishing it.

But please don't print that, I asked. I had submitted the manuscript under a pseudonym.

▪ *Benjamin M. Schutz* ▪

CHRISTMAS
IN DODGE CITY

Sharnella Watkins had never walked into a police station in her life. She'd been tossed in delirious or drunk, carried in kicking and screaming, and marched in on a manacled chorus line. But walk in on her own, never. That would have been like sex. Another thing that if it was up to her, she'd never do.

She checked both ways before she crossed the street, searching for witnesses not traffic, and clattered over on her nosebleed heels.

She knocked on the bulletproof plastic at the information center.

The desk sergeant looked up from his racing form. "Help you, ma'am?"

"I'd like to talk to that detective, the big one. He's bald and he gots a beard down in front, ah, you know, ah Van Dyke they calls it, oh yeah, he wears glasses, too."

"That's detective Bitterman, ma'am, and why would you like to talk to him?"

"It's personal."

"Well, he's working now. Why don't you come back when his shift ends?"

"When's that?"

"Six o'clock."

"I can't wait that long. Can you give me his phone number? I'll call him."

"Sorry, ma'am, I can't do that. Unless you're family. You aren't family, are you?" The desk man sniggered. Big Bad Bitterman and this itty-bitty black junkie whore.

"No, I guess you're not. Sorry 'bout that." The desk man looked down, trying to root out a winner in all those optimistic names.

Sharnella knew the truth would be pointless, but along with a nonexistent gag reflex, the other gift that had kept her alive on the streets all these years was the unerring ability to pick the right lie when she had to.

She leaned forward so that her bright red lips were only inches from the divider and sneered. Then, shaking her head, she said, "You think you're so smart. Well, lets me tell you something. It ain't me what needs him. He's been looking for me. He wants to talk to me. And now, I'm telling you both, to go fuck yo'selves. I ain't coming back, and I ain't gonna talk to him and . . ." She got close enough for the desk man to count her missing molars: "I'm gonna tell him it was your sorry bullshit what pissed me off and he should see you 'bout why he can't solve no cases no more."

The desk man had been following her little breadcrumbs of innuendo and found himself ending up face to face with Mount Bitterman. The explosion wouldn't be that bad. Bitterman had made enough enemies that if he declared you one, you'd as likely be toasted as shunned. Bitterman never forgot and never forgave.

The desk man had endured too much inexplicable disappointment and loss to risk an angry Bitterman.

As Sharnella turned to walk away, the deskman said: "Hold your horses, bitch. This is his number at headquarters." He wouldn't write it down for her, hoping her memory would fail. She'd be fucked and Bitterman would have no cause. As she backed away, mouthing the numbers to fix them in her disloyal mind, the deskman said, "You know Bitterman only listens to the dead. I hope you find him soon."

Across town, Detective Avery Bitterman reached down and pulled on his dick. One of the advantages of a closed front desk. He'd notice himself doing this more since his divorce. A dispassionate review told him that it wasn't for pleasure but rather to reassure himself that he was still all there, a feeling he had less and less often these days.

The receptionist at headquarters told him that he had a call from a Sharnella Watkins and that she said it was an emergency. "Put it through," he said.

"Is this Detective Bitterman?"

"Yes, it is. How may I help you?"

"You probably don't remember me, but I remembers you. You arrested my boy Rondell. You was the only one who didn't beat up on him. You wouldn't let nobody hurt him."

Bitterman shook his head, remembering. That's right, ma'am. I wouldn't let them lynch him. I thought it would be more fitting if your son got sent to Lorton, where he could meet the two sons of the woman he raped, sodomized, and tortured to death. Those mother's sons and some friends tied him down, inserted a hedge shears up Rondell's ass, opened him up and strung his intestines around him like he was a Christmas tree. When, to their delight, this didn't kill him, they poured gasoline over him like he was a sundae and set him on fire.

"No, I do remember you, Sharmella."

"SharNella." She knew she was right to call this man. He remembered her. He would help her.

"It's my baby, Dantreya. He's gone, Mr. Bitterman. I know he's in some kind of trouble . . ."

What a fuckin' surprise. "Ma'am, I'm a homicide detective. You want to go to your local district house and file a missing persons report. I can't help you with this."

"Please, Mr. Bitterman. They won't do anything. They'll just say, 'That's what kids do,' and with me as a mother why not stay out all night. But he's not like that. He's different than my others. He's a good boy. He goes to school. He's fifteen and he never been in no trouble. Never, not even little things. He likes to draw. He wants to be an artist. You should come and see what he draws. Please, Mr. Bitterman, he's all I got left. It's Christmas tomorrow. I just want my baby home." Wails gave way to staccato sobbing.

Sharnella's tears annoyed Bitterman. I'm a homicide detective, that's what I do, he said to no one. I can't deal with this shit. It ain't my job. Come back when he's dead. Then I'll listen.

"Ma'am, I'm sorry. I understand how you feel. But the beat cops can keep an eye out for him. You tell them where he's likely to go. That's your best bet, not me. I'm sorry. I gotta go now."

Bitterman hung up over her wailing "No's." Where was he going to go? He was head of the cold case squad. These days, everything was a cold case. Arrest and conviction rates were lower for homicide than for jaywalking. The killers were younger, bolder and completely without restraint. The law of the jungle, "an eye for an eye," would have been a welcome relief. The law of the streets was "an eye for a hangnail." Everything was a killing offense. Motive was nothing, opportunity and means were ubiquitous. Children packed lunchbox, thermos, and sidearm in their knapsacks for school. The police were the biggest provider of handguns. Three thousand had disappeared from the city's property rooms to create more dead bodies that the medical examiner's office couldn't autopsy, release or bury. That for Bitterman was the guiding symbol of his work these days. Handguns on a conveyor belt back to the streets, and the frozen dead serving longer and longer sentences in eternity's drunk tank.

The phone jerked Bitterman back from his reverie.

"Mr. Bitterman, this is Sharnella Watkins. Don't hang up on me. I can help you. My boy's gone, 'cause they want to kill him."

"Who's they, Sharnella?"

"The 6th and O Crew."

"Sharnella, you said your son had never been in trouble. The 6th and O Crew is nothing but. Why am I listening to this?"

"He didn't do nothing. He was coming home from school with a trophy he got at a art show, and Lufer tried to take it from him, but my baby wouldn't give it to him and when Lufer tried again he hit him with it and knocked him down and my baby ran off. He said Lufer went to get his gun and was yellin' that he'd kill him for sure. And he would, that boy's purely mean. He kill you for no reason."

"Sharnella, this still doesn't help me. Get to the help-me part or I'm hangin' up."

Sharnella had never given a policeman a straight answer in her life. But her baby was in danger. Sharnella never stopped to think why she felt so differently about this child, her fourth, than any of the others, only that she did and that his death, after all the others, would kill her too.

"This boy, Lufer Timmons. He's killed a bunch of people. That's what everybody says. Everybody afraid of him. They say he's the Crew's main shooter. But he does it when it ain't business, just 'cause he likes it. And he said he'll kill my boy. Doesn't that help you, Mr. Bitterman?"

The Crew favored death as a solution to all its problems. Giving the delivery man a name was a help. "Tell you what, Sharnella. You go over to the station house like I said and give 'em all the information about your son. Bring a picture, a list of all of his friends and where they live, and where he's been known to hang out. Tell them to fax me a copy of all that. I'll look into it."

Her story was probably 90 percent bullshit and 10 percent horseshit for flavor, but Bitterman knew he'd check it out. You turned over every rock and picked up every squiggling thing. That was his motto: No Corner Too Deep, No Corner Too Dark.

Bitterman tried to remember Sharnella from her second son's trial. She'd started dropping babies at fourteen and was done before twenty. That'd make her around thirty-five now. She looked fifty. Flatbacking and mainlining aged women with interest. Beginning as a second-generation whore, Sharnella's childhood had been null and void; her prime had passed unnoticed, one sweaty afternoon in a New York Avenue motel.

Bitterman was more aware of time than ever before. He'd lifted and run and dragged his ugly white man's game to basketball courts all over the city. Elbow and ass, he rebounded with the best even though he couldn't jump over a dime. No one ever forgot a pick he set or an outlet pass that went end to end, but he remembered not to shoot too often or try to dribble and run at the same time. His twenties and thirties didn't seem all that different, but now at forty-five he knew he wasn't the same man. Bald by choice, rather than balding. Thicker but not yet fat, slower both in reflexes and foot speed. Maybe mellowing was nothing more than realizing that he couldn't tear the doors off the world anymore. The long afternoon of invincibility had passed.

Sharnella's second son, Jabari, had killed a rival drug dealer in a rip-off attempt that also killed a nursing student driving by. Her only daughter, Female, with a short "a" and a long "e," so named by the hospital and then taken by Sharnella, who liked the sound of it, had died of an overdose of extremely good cocaine at the age of sixteen. Everything she delivered died or killed someone else.

Bitterman called down to Identification and Records.

"Get me the file on Lufer Timmons. If there's a picture make a copy for me and send it up with the file. And see if there's a file on Dantreya Watkins."

Bitterman sat at his desk awaiting the files, massaging his eyes.

Bitterman had tried to catch a case of racism for years, a really virulent one, but to no avail. He had mumps when he needed anthrax. It would have made his job so much easier. No sadness for the wasted lives, no respect for the courage of the many, no grief for the victims, no compassion for the survivors.

He'd been a homicide cop in a black city for almost his entire adult life. He'd seen every form of violence one person could do to another. He'd seen black women who'd drowned their own babies, and ones who'd ripped their own flesh at the chalk outlines of a fallen son. Men who'd shot and stabbed an entire family then eaten the dinner off their plates and men who'd worked three jobs for a lifetime, so their children wouldn't have to. Bitterman just didn't get it, how anyone could conclude that they were all of a kind, that they were different and less. He wished he could, it saved on the wear and tear.

When he opened his eyes again, he saw the Lufer Timmons file on the desk and a note saying no file on that Watkins. Maybe he was his mother's pride and joy.

Lufer Timmons had been raised by strangers, starting with his parents and moving on to a series of foster homes, residential treatment centers, detention centers and jails. Now at seventeen, he was well on his way to evening the score with a number of crimes to his credit starting with the attempted rape of his therapist at the age of eleven.

Bitterman studied the picture of Timmons. Six one and a hundred sixty-eight pounds. He had a long face with deep crevices in his cheeks, thin lips, a thin nose, prominent cheekbones, and bulging froggy eyes. Bitterman pocketed one photo, Xeroxed the page of known associates and family and put the file in his desk drawer. A call to operations yielded the very pleasant news that one of his known associates was currently in custody at the downtown detention center.

Bitterman drove slowly along "The Stroll" looking for Sunshine, as in "put a little Sunshine in your day," her marketing pitch to the curbside crawlers. Sunshine was a six-foot redhead, natural, with alabaster skin, emerald green eyes and surgically perfected tits. Bitterman had decided that Sunshine was going to be his Christmas present to himself. He wasn't even sure he wanted to have sex with her. He just wanted to look at her, all of her, without having to hurry, like when she was on display, so he could memorize her beauty. Lately he'd been thinking about what he had to show for forty-five years and all the fucks of a lifetime hadn't stayed with him as sharply as his memory of her on a warm summer's eve, leaning against a lamppost, trying to stay one lick ahead of a fast-melting vanilla cone. Her tongue moving rapidly up the sides of the cone until anticipating defeat, she engulfed the whole mound and sucked it out of the cone. Beauty baffled Bitterman. It seemed fundamental and indivisible. He could not break down his response into pieces or explain it away by recourse to another force or power. Sunshine was perfect and her beauty touched him in a way he couldn't avoid. He hoped that she wouldn't be easy to find. He knew that she would turn out to have bad teeth and bray like a donkey.

Lafonzo Nellis was waiting for Bitterman in interrogation room six. Bitterman sat down and the guard left.

"So, Lafonzo. Tell me about Lufer Timmons."

"Fuck you."

"Glad we got that cleared up. Let me give you some context, here, Lafonzo, before you get into more trouble than you can get out of. Because it's Christmas, God gave me three wishes. The first is a known acquaintance of Lufer Timmons, in custody, that's you. The second is to have you locked up but not papered. The third is up to you. See, if you don't talk to me, that's okay. I hear that Lufer is a reasonable man, fair with his friends, not likely to do anything rash. I'm gonna leave here, head over to 6th and O and start asking about Lufer, and talking loud about how much help you were to me. The street bull who brought you in hasn't papered you yet. He can let you go and he doesn't have to explain a thing. You're just DWOP: Dropped Without Prosecution.

Now, I hear that a lot of your buddies saw you get busted and righteously, too. How you gonna explain being out of here right after we talk? Huh?"

"You ain't got the juice to make that happen."

"Oh, yeah. You been around, Lafonzo. Let's get a reality check here. You know that a street bull's got two jobs. His shift and court time. Court time is time and a half. You sit on your butt, you drink coffee, you tell lies, you hit on the chippies, nobody's shooting at you, and it's time and a half. Now, I just promised that guy I'd list him as a witness on my next two homicide trials. They're usually three or four days each. Easy time, easy money. What do you got to offer him?"

Lafonzo had a friend who was a cop and he'd pocketed $100,000 in court time and he'd only made three arrests all year. Lafonzo had a vision of trying to 'splain everything to Lufer. Lafonzo made his mind up immediately and forever. "Okay, okay. What do you want to know?"

"We'll start with the easy stuff. I got a picture of Lufer from his last arrest. Look at it, tell me if he's changed any."

He slid the picture across the table. Lafonzo didn't pick it up. "Yeah, that's him. He ain't changed none."

"Okay, so tell me about him. What's he like?"

"He's a crazy man. I mean, what you want to know? He's in the Crew, 6th and O. You know what that means. I don't got to tell you. Let's just leave it at this, if there's trouble, Lufer fixes it. Period. Understand?"

"We're getting there. If I was to go lookin' for him, where would I find him?"

"Dude moves around a lot. See, there's plenty of other people, like to find him, too, you see what I'm saying. If he has a pad, it's a secret to me."

"What kind of car does he drive?"

"A 'Vette, a black one."

"You know the year, the tags?"

"No, man. Why should I care?"

Bitterman knew he'd find no such car legally registered to Timmons.

"Okay, where does he hang out? I'm gonna put a man at 6th and O with his picture every day from now on. So where else will he show up?"

Lafonzo was running out of room for evasions; a full-blown lie was called for here. But present danger prevailed over the future.

"They's a few bars he fancies. Nairobi Jones, Langtry's, the Southeaster."

"What else can you tell me? Any trademarks, things that he favors?"

"I don't know. He always wears that long coat. You know, the ones that go down to your boots."

"A duster?" Bitterman was finally interested.

"Yeah."

"What color?"

"Dark. Dark red."

"Like burgundy?"

"Yeah."

"What's it made of?"

"Leather. Musta cost plenty."

"What about a bandanna?"

"Yeah, that too. He wears it around his neck, not on his head."

Glory to God. The red leather duster and the bandanna could make him "Johnny-Jump-Out" wanted in six daylight shootings. Bitterman put what he knew from the files together with Nellis's information and began to understand his quarry a little better.

"He fancies himself quite a shootist, doesn't he?" Bitterman began. "No back of the ear, hands tied, in a dark room for him. I admire that. Straight up in your face, shoot and shoot back. He must have quite a reputation in the 'hood. You don't fuck with Lufer Timmons, do you?"

"What do you need me for? You seem to know everything."

"That I do, Lafonzo. I know that Lufer steals a car when he's gonna whack someone. He's got a driver he trusts. He cruises the

64

streets till he finds his target, then he jumps out, which is why we call him 'Johnny-Jump-Out,' no pussy bullshit drive-bys for our Johnny, no, he jumps out, calls the target by name, pulls his piece and does it right there, trading gunfire on the street, broad daylight, then back in the car and he's gone. Cool customer, our Lufer, drawing down on a man telling him you're gonna kill him and then doing it. Nice gun he uses, too, .44 magnum. Holds on to it. Does he wear a holster, Lafonzo?"

"Yeah."

"Tell me about it."

"What for?"

"Because I want to know, Lafonzo."

"It's on his left hip, facing the other way."

"A cross-draw, how elegant. And so cocky. Most guys just shoot and throw down. He doesn't think he's gonna get caught. I know he wears armor because one guy hit him right in the chest before Lufer put one between his eyes."

"So how come you know so much, you ain't got him yet?"

"All we had was an M.O. No pattern to his killings. Now, I know that there isn't one. Lufer gets hot, you get shot. Now I've got a name, a description, and some places to look for him. He got a name for himself? All the great ones had nicknames. What about Lufer?"

"Fuck man, he don't need no nickname. You hear Lufer Timmons looking for you, that's like hearing the Terminator wants you."

Bitterman pocketed his photograph and smiled at Lafonzo. "I guess you'll be wanting to spend some time indoors, right?"

Lafonzo sat up straight. "Don't you be putting me out there, now. That motherfucker'll kill me."

"Relax. I'm not gonna screw around with you. I'll make sure you're papered and held, maybe get you a nice high bond you can't post. How's that sound?"

"Great. Fuckin' great. Thanks."

No other city in the world had as much of its population behind bars. Even the bad guys prefer to be in jail rather than on the streets. Bitterman was optimistic about nailing Timmons. A guy so caught up in building a reputation wouldn't be able to wait for it to be bestowed upon him. He'd help it along with plenty of boasting. All they had to do was find the right pair of ears. Secondly, he liked his gun too much. Holding on to that was a mistake. If they found that, they'd match it to bullets in his six victims. Once he was off the streets, they'd go back and talk to the deaf, dumb, and blind who'd seen and heard everything and convince just one of them to talk. Once gone he would not be coming back.

Bitterman left the detention center to get an arrest warrant from a judge. If he got it soon, it'd make the 3 P.M. roll call for the next shift. By tomorrow morning, every active duty officer on the streets would be looking for Lufer Timmons. A Christmas present to the city.

Dantreya Watkins had been going about this all wrong. He'd approached the "gangstas" on the street looking for a piece and received the short course on urban economics: Desperation drives the price up, not down. Once his ignorance of makes and models was established, his "brothers" tried to sell him .25-caliber purse guns for four hundred bucks. Poverty only served to delay his fleecing. After three unsuccessful tries, he knew enough to ask for a .380 Walther. That seemed to be a respectable gun. He found a kindly gentleman who sold him such a gun and a full clip of ammo for three hundred bucks, which was all the money he could steal from his mother.

It wasn't until later, in an abandoned warehouse when Dantreya squeezed off a practice round and saw the cartridge roll out of the end of the barrel that he learned that the clip was full of .32-caliber ammo and completely useless. Dantreya was now armed with a three-hundred-dollar hammer.

Dantreya's descent into the all-too-real world, far from the comics he read, rewrote, and illustrated in his room was now complete. He was waiting nervously at the side of his friend TerrAnce's house for TerrAnce to get his father's gun for him. In exchange, Dantreya had offered TerrAnce his entire collection of *X-Men* comics, which they would go get as soon as TerrAnce lifted the gun from his father's holster in the closet.

TerrAnce pushed open the ripped screen door with his shoulder and, holding the gun carefully in both hands, took the steps, one at a time. He walked around the side of the house and approached Dantreya, both hands grasping the trigger and pointing the gun at him. Dantreya stepped aside as gracefully as any matador and took the gun out of his friend's hands.

"Thanks man," he said, as he spun the chambers of the revolver. The bullets looked like the right size. Now, all he had to do was find Lufer Timmons. His older friends could help with that.

TerrAnce looked at him expectantly. Dantreya slipped the gun into his jacket and shrugged, "Hey man, I gotta go. I'll get you your stuff and bring it right back."

That said, he took off across the street and ran up the alley away from his friend TerrAnce, now crying with all the disappointment an eight-year-old has.

Bitterman pulled up to the corner of 6th and O. He got out and put the cherry on the roof to simplify things for the locals. Up here, a white man with an attitude had to be crazy or a cop. Bitterman wanted to make sure they made the right choices.

Fats Taylor was poured over a folding chair.

"The fuck you doin' up here, Bitterman," Fats asked, his chest heaved with the effort of speech.

"Just came up to hear myself talk, Fats. You bein' such a good listener and all."

"I hear everything, sees everything, and knows everything." Fats chuckled and smiled.

And eats everything, Bitterman thought.

"I'm looking for a faggoty little nigger, name of Lufer Timmons, you know him?"

Fats's face sealed over, as smooth and black as asphalt in August.

"Well, you listen, Fats, and I'll talk to myself. This little queer thinks he's a real pistolero, a gunslinger. Well, I think he's a coward. I know who he's shot, where, when, and why. Pretty tough with kids, and cripples, spaced-out druggies, welshing gamblers that don't carry. You tell him I'm looking for him, Fats. And you know who I've put in the ground."

Bitterman closed his show, went back to his car and drove away. Fats could be counted on to spread the word, emphasizing every insult. A punk like Timmons, to whom respect was fear and fear was all, wouldn't let this pass. Bitterman was already wearing armor and would until Lufer was taken in. Although facing a .44 magnum he might just as well be wearing a sunblock.

Bitterman repeated his performance in Nairobi Jones and the Southeaster.

For fun, in Nairobi Jones, he told them he was Charlie Siringo, the Pinkerton who single-handedly tracked the Wild Bunch until they fled to South America. In the Southeaster he was Heck Thomas, one of the legendary "Oklahoma Guardsmen."

Bitterman wanter Lufer to stay put, and challenging him would do that. He wanted him angry and impulsive, so he insulted him. He wanted him confused, so he multiplied his pursuers.

Bitterman drove over to Langtry's via all the "cupcake corners" in the first district. His latest ex-partner had suggested that the politically correct term for these young ladies was "vertically challenged" and they should be so described in all police reports. Bitterman got himself a new partner. He'd seen only a few working girls out on the sidewalks. Cold weather and the new law that allowed the city to confiscate the cars of the johns caught soliciting had forced one more evolution in the pursuit of reckless abandon. Now the girls drove endlessly around the block until they pulled up alongside a likely customer. The negotiations had more feeling than the foreplay to follow. Then a quick sprint to lose a police pursuit and the happy couple was free to lay down together take aim and miss each other at point-blank range.

Sunshine's Mercedes was off line. Bitterman figured she was probably curled up with some rich young defense attorney in one of the city's better hotels. Next to a Sugar Daddy John, a Galahad Defense Attorney was a girl's best chance to get off the streets and get some instant respectability. Just another reason to hate those scumbags. Bitterman gave up after talking to Betty Boop. She'd shown up around the same time as Sunshine, and Bitterman had fancied her, too. Now her looks had gone like last week's snow.

Bitterman pulled up across the street from Langtry's and started over when he saw Sunshine's Mercedes. He turned back and got into his car to consider his options. If she was in Langtry's alone, he'd pick her up and put her somewhere until he was done looking for Lufer and then celebrate Christmas Eve with her. If she was somewhere else nearby and he went in looking for Lufer, he'd miss her when she came out. He didn't like that plan much. Of course, she could be with someone else already. As long as it wasn't some fuckin' defense attorney he'd flash some badge, heft a little gun and requisition her on police business. Bitterman decided that this year the city could wait to get his gift.

He hadn't been this excited since he was four years old and came down in the middle of the night to see if Santa had brought the baseball glove that would make him Willie Mays. Just give me this one thing, Lord, just because it's something I can ask for. Everything else I lack is so huge, so vague, so damned close that I don't even know what I'm looking for.

Dantreya Watkins hurried halfway down the alley, then slowed and moved cautiously along the wall to the intersection with the street. He was trying to think of what his heros would do. Batman would swoop from the dark and knock Lufer down, then disarm him, tie him up, and leave him for the police. The Punisher would kick down a door and come in guns blazing. Dantreya tried to conjure courage but all he got was a tremor in his legs and a wave of nausea. He turned back to the alley and threw up all over his shoes. Courage had not delivered him to this place. He had nowhere near enough money to pay for Lufer's death, and he could not imagine running away to live elsewhere. He could leave his world as a superhero, but not as himself. Like his mother he had an allergy to the police and would not take a step toward one. He knew Lufer was a guarantee of death, only the date on the death certificate was missing. His fears and beliefs, what was impossible and what was certain, had brought him to this alley. His mind had painted him into a corner and it didn't bother with a small brush.

The tremor in his legs increased and Dantreya gripped the pistol in his pocket even tighter, hoping that would slow down the shaking that surged through him. He thanked God for the gun. Without it he knew he was a dead man looking to lie down.

Forty minutes later Lufer Timmons in his long red duster pushed open the door to Langtry's and stepped out onto the sidewalk. Avery Bitterman sat up, cursing his luck that Timmons would be the one to show first. Timmons held the door and his companion stepped out into the night. She really was lovely, a thick mane of brick red hair, pale skin and deep dimples when she smiled. Sunshine, in her knee-high boots, towered over Lufer, who traveled up her length slowly, appreciating every inch of her. He was gonna love climbing up this one. Lufer wasn't particularly fond of white meat, but that crazy honky who'd been jivin' with him put him in the mood to fuck this bitch cross-eyed, then maybe mess her up some. Called him a faggot, a punk. He'd show him who the real man was. First he'd teach this white bitch about black lovin'. That'd ruin her for white dick. Then he'd go find that motherfucka, kneecap him, make him beg for the bullet, then shove his gun all the way up his ass before he did him. Lufer smiled, goddamn that felt good. Life was good to Lufer, offering him so many avenues to pleasure.

Sunshine slipped her arm through his and they walked down

the street, Lufer showin' off his prize and she whispering in his ear about what she had in mind for him. Bitterman let them pass his car, then got out and walked up the opposite sidewalk. Oh my, he said to himself as he felt something leak out of him. Sunshine was still as beautiful as ever, but her smile as she lay her head on Lufer's shoulder was not one he wanted anymore. He couldn't kid himself about what they would mean to each other, not any longer anyway.

Lufer pushed open the door to a three-story walk-up between a Brazilian restaurant and an erotic lingerie store. Bitterman pulled out his radio, gave his location, who he was watching, and called for backup. If he'd been able to see down the alley across the way, he'd have seen a slim figure back away, turn and run to the fire escape and quickly begin to climb.

Bitterman crossed the street and stood by the door to Timmons's crib. He opened his jacket and thumbed back the strap on his holster. A level-three vest was supposed to be able to stop a .44 provided it wasn't too close, but they said the shock would flatten you and you got broken up inside even if there wasn't penetration. Where the hell was backup, Bitterman thought.

He scanned the street in both directions and saw nothing. Right now he was the thin blue line.

A shot rang out, then another, then a scream and a third one.

Bitterman yelled into his radio, "Shots fired, I'm going up." He pulled the door open and heard things falling, scuffling and screaming from above. Both hands on his pistol, he followed it up the stairs. He hit the second floor and pointed his gun at all the doors and then up the stairs.

The noise was coming from the door at the far end. Bitterman closed rapidly and pressed himself against the wall. He reached out with his right hand and touched the doorknob. It was unlocked.

"Wonderful, I get an open door but no backup," he said to himself.

Bitterman slowly turned the knob. The noises had stopped.

No banging, no screams. When it was fully turned, he flung it open and stepped through into what he hoped was not the line of fire.

Lufer was on the floor. His pants were down around his knees. Sunshine was under him, twitching. Lufer's cannon was in his hand and there was a bullet hole in the sofa. There was also one in his neck, and the blood was pooling under his chin.

Bitterman saw a young boy to his left, holding on to a snub-nosed .38. The gun was jumping around like it was electrified. His left leg tried to keep time but it couldn't. There was a large stain on the front of the boy's pants.

"Put down the gun," Bitterman barked, but the boy didn't respond.

Bitterman searched his face. His eyes were wide open and unfocused.

"Put down the gun," Bitterman asked, more gently but to no avail.

The boy was clearly freaked out by what he'd done. Maybe he could get close enough to disarm him.

"Son, please put down the gun. You're making me nervous the way it's shaking there. I don't know what happened here, but I know he's a bad man. Why don't you tell me what happened here."

Bitterman edged closer to the boy, who was facing away from him. Maybe he could get his hand on the gun, then hit him in the temple with his pistol. At this range he couldn't afford to let the boy turn. Even shooting to wound him wouldn't work. An accidental off-line discharge could be fatal this close. Should he tell him he was going to reach for his gun, or just do it? And where the fuck was backup anyway?

Bitterman moved slowly toward the boy until he was about two feet away. If he turned on him he'd have to shoot him. He had no choice. Why wouldn't he just put the gun down and make this easier on both of them?

Bitterman slowly reached out for the gun. The boy's eyes

snapped into focus and he tried to pull away. Bitterman grabbed for the gun. It swung up towards his face, he pulled it down towards his chest and slammed the kid in the head with his pistol. The .38 went off and Bitterman fell back gasping. Dantreya Watkins hit the floor and lay still.

Bitterman, on his back, reached up and touched his chest. He could feel the .38 imbedded in the Kevlar. God, did he hurt and was he glad he could say it.

He lay there on his back, like a Kevlar turtle, his hands clenching with the pain of each breath. He saw Sunshine push Lufer Timmons up off of her, until she was clear of his now and forever limp penis, roll out from under it, stand up and stagger to the door without a backward glance. Bitterman tried to call out to her for help but could only groan instead, as she banged her way down the stairs. The front door slammed and Bitterman lay there in the enveloping silence waiting for the sounds of backup: screeching tires, sirens, pounding footsteps. Above all else he wanted there to be someone in a hurry to find him. Bitterman closed his eyes and whispered, "Merry fucking Christmas."

■ *Joyce Carol Oates* ■

THE STALKER

After it happens. She will quit her job, and perhaps her profession. She will move away from Detroit and she will break off relations with her colleagues and even her friends who will speak of her for years afterward pityingly, wonderingly *Does anyone ever hear from Matilde?* and *What has happened to Matilde, do you know?* and *We warned her, didn't we? We did!* As soon as she recovers from the episode she will put her aunt's house on the market (after eight years of occupancy she still thinks of the brownstone at 289 Springwood, Mittelburg Park, as her deceased aunt's and not her own) and accept the first offer any buyer makes no matter how low. Because she isn't a woman to care much about money. Nor is she a sentimental woman. *After it happens* she will never be inclined to sentimentality again, she will have earned that distinction.

The handgun. She'd already had the permit, issued by the county, when she went to the Liberty Gun Shop on North Woodward. A cream-colored stucco building in a mini-mall between Adult X-Rated Videos & Supplies and House of Wong Restaurant & Carry-Out. Liberty Gun Shop advertised handguns and long-guns, new and used, sales and purchases. The manager's name was Ted, call me Ted O.K.? but Matilde did not call him anything except a cool murmured schoolgirl *sir* once or twice. His eyes lighting on her, the tall poised height of her. Her forward-tilt-ing head, slender neck, eyes that pebbly-gray gaze her first lover, twenty years ago, had called the hue of infinite regret, though possibly he'd said infinite regress, it had been something of a joke (between Matilde and her lovers there had always been odd, awkward, ongoing jokes she'd never quite got, though like a good sport she'd laughed on cue). The gun shop owner pressed Matilde to consider high-capacity semiautomatic pistols but Ma-tilde insisted on considering only the most conventional and eco-nomic handguns, a used .38-caliber Smith & Wesson was what she wanted, ex-police issue and good enough for her purposes. Ted was disappointed, she could see. And when she took up the gun in her hand, and found it heavier than she'd anticipated, and her hand shook until she steadied it with the other, Ted expressed doubt he should sell the gun to her at all—it went against his "code of ethics" to sell any weapon to anyone who might not be capable of using it. Because a gun can be taken from you and used against you. Because to freeze with a gun in your hand can be a worse predicament than to be caught unarmed. Because you have to be prepared not just to shoot but *to kill*—and she didn't look like she'd be tough enough. But this, too, was a joke—of course. Matilde had her checkbook in hand. There was never any doubt that she, who believed in a total ban of firearms to private citizens, would be sold the revolver of her choice in the Liberty Gun Shop

on North Woodward: a medium-barreled six-shot secondhand
.38-caliber Smith & Wesson. And a small box of ammunition, two
dozen bullets. Though Matilde knows, if she uses the gun at all,
she will only use it once.

The heartbeat is her own, of course. Yet so frequently now she
seems to be hearing it, feeling it, at a distance. Like the myriad
unnamed noises of the city, ceaseless grinding-thumping, ceaseless drilling you hear without listening, planes passing high overhead in the night, invisible contrails of sound, ceaseless. *I can feel
your heartbeat!—Jesus.* And then he'd laughed, she didn't know
why, doesn't know why. Was he laughing at her, or in sympathy
with her. She has thought of it, of him, obsessively. But she
doesn't know.

The heartbeat is her own, of course. Yet it's his, too. *Look, my
name is*—what sounded to her ear like *Bowe, Bowie—I'd like to see
you, soon. Tomorrow? Tonight?* Lying in this bed with its bone-
hard mattress (Matilde has had a tricky back for the past several
years) her eyes shut tight and sticky sweat-pearls glistening on
her face *I see him:* the rain-splattered blue Volvo with a frayed
Clinton/Gore sticker on the rear bumper, he's behind the wheel
parked at the entrance to the high-rise garage where Matilde
parks her car while she's at work and she sees him then quickly
not-seeing hurrying to the elevator to take her to C-level, to her
car. And his telephone messages *Matilde, Please call*—his home
number, office number (he's a lawyer, a litigator, does volunteer
work for Legal Aid)—which Matilde replays and erases. *Not ever
again, please God. I can't.* She sees the Volvo slowly passing the
brownstone at 289 Springwood with its wine-dark, slightly corroded facade, its single splendid bay window, she isn't watching,
still less is she waiting, but she sees. What does he want of her,
what is the connection between them, their blood commingled,
she guesses *Bowe, Bowie?*—first name *Jay,* or was it the initial *J.?*—
he's married, she'd caught a glimpse of a ring on his left hand.

He'd been breathing quickly, she felt the heat rise from him. *No. Not ever again. I can't.*

Fate. Why, Matilde Searle has often wondered, do we so crave romantic love as if it were our destiny?—our private, secret, individual fate? As if romantic love, yes let's be candid and call it sexual love, the real thing, might define us in a way nothing else (our families, our hard-won careers) can define us. *I've never known who I am except when I've been in love* Matilde has said *and I haven't recognized that self and I haven't admired that self and I can't bear being that self again.*

Vital statistics. Born November 11, 1953. Ypsilanti, Michigan. First daughter, second child of a Roman Catholic family that would burgeon—the word "burgeon" is Matilde's, she'd used it perhaps one thousand times while growing up to speak with fond contempt of her parents and their restricted, to her restrictive, world—to six siblings. Six! people say, smiling. Your parents must have liked babies! and Matilde used to roll her eyes and say, dryly, I think it just took my mother that long to figure out what was causing it. (Now she's an adult, and her mother has been dead for three years, Matilde never jokes like that. She rarely jokes about *family* at all.) But the unexamined and wholly unquestioned Roman Catholicism of her parents and grandparents was a heavy, tacky wool overcoat that never fitted *her:* she's proud of having given up even the pretense of belief at the age of twelve. Went to Ypsilanti public schools, graduated summa cum laude from Michigan State University, 1976 (B.A., American history, politics), received a master's degree from the University of Michigan, 1978 (social work). Positions in East Lansing with the Michigan State Bureau of Youth and Family Service (1978–1982) and in Detroit with the Wayne County Clinic of Counseling of the State of Michigan (1982–present). At the Wayne County Clinic, one of the state's most massive and bureaucratized agencies, Matilde Searle is an assistant supervisor for Family Services but she is also "on the floor"—she has a caseload of never less than twenty families, involving never less than one hundred individuals, and frequently twice that number. Her annual salary, determined by the Michigan legislature's budget allotment, is $41,000, and she has not had a raise in two years. There is no medically recorded "nervous breakdown" in the file on Matilde Searle, nor do rumors circulate among her colleagues that she has tried to commit suicide, as certain of her colleagues, over the years, have: the Clinic is notorious for burning out its social services staff, female and male, but mostly female, on the sixth floor of the ancient buff-brick Wayne County Agencies building at Gratiot and Stockton where Matilde Searle has a corner-window office shared with another social worker with a master's degree from Ann Arbor, also female, five years older than Matilde, but black-Hispanic. *She* is Caucasian, a distinct minority in the city of Detroit.

The stalker. Matilde is awake yet the fevered pulse of her body suggests sleep, the paralysis of sleep. A soft, urgent, quickening heartbeat. She'd felt it—*his*. She has kicked off the quilted-satin bedspread sometime during the night and is covered now only partly by a sheet damply clinging to her lower body leaving exposed her sweat-slick chest, her small girlish-hard breasts, painfully prominent collar bone, shoulders . . . Is she naked? Where's her nightgown? She is not a woman who waits yet night is a time of waiting, sleep and bed and nakedness a time of waiting, inescapable. The .38-caliber revolver is inches away in the drawer of the bedside table and the drawer is ajar perhaps an inch. *Because you have to be prepared not just to shoot but to kill.* She's naked sweating in her bed listening to the myriad sounds of the nighttime city and to the closer, mysterious sounds of her aunt's house and to the soft urgent quickening heartbeat she understands is her own and not another's *and yet she sees him, hears him.* She knew he'd been stalking her for weeks, she even knew his name, Ramos, Hector Ramos, he's the estranged husband of one of her battered women clients, a woman she'd arranged to be admitted to the Wayne County Women's and Children's Shelter and for this he is furious with her, he hates her, wishes her grief, death—oh, Matilde knows. Briefly Hector Ramos had been her client too, the previous year, but whatever was thrumming along his veins—alcohol, coke, manic juices—had been too much, too intense, he hadn't been able to sit in the chair facing Matilde for more than three minutes without squirming and jumping up, and he hadn't been able to speak coherently, his eyes glistening, his lips sparked with spittle, still less had he been in a mood to fill out forms for the county, produce identification, sign his name *Hector Ramos* except in a grandiose unintelligible scrawl. He's a short, lean-muscled man of thirty-one, unemployed carpenter, a single conviction aged nineteen ("assault"—for which he'd served a brief eighteen months in Michigan State Prison), with stark-staring black eyes, black oily-kinky hair. His forehead is deeply, tragically creased. That baffled ravaged look, that look of ancient desperation Matilde sees in so many of her (male) clients, in so many men on the streets, Detroit's citizens. *Think I can't read, eh?—think I don't know words, eh?*—throwing the forms down on Matilde's desk. She sees him now, fierce betrayed Hector Ramos, approaching her, something metallic and glinting in his right hand which is pressed low against his thigh. He's wearing a simulated leather jacket like vinyl, trousers with a tear in one knee, high-top sneakers like the black street kids. Swift and silent as a snake, no yelled curse to warn her, a gleam of damp teeth, then he's on her. They are in a crowded place, the outer foyer of the Wayne County Building and Ramos hasn't passed through the metal detector which is farther into the interior nor has he been sighted by the pair of sheriff's deputies who are on guard, Matilde Searle will not have seen him until he's on her.

Terror of death. In the abstract, it's absurd. Has not Matilde argued so, many times. Where there's no consciousness there can be no pain, no sorrow, no humiliation, no loss, no regret, no terror. Where no consciousness, no memory. Where no memory, no humanity. You, no longer living, are not *you*. Yet, warding off the slashing jabbing knife blade wielded by the madman, pain so swift, intense, unexpected it seems to be a phenomenon of the very place, the air, like deafening noise. And the woman's cry, childlike, terrified—*No! Don't! Help me! I don't want to die!*

Vital Statistics. Nineteen years old, a sophomore at Michigan State, when she'd lost her virginity. Odd, archaic language: *lost*. Lost what, precisely? Later, her first intense, serious love affair, yes then she'd lost something more tangible, if undefinable: her heart? her independence? her control of, definition of, *self*? That first true loss, the furious bafflement of it. And never again quite so assured, confident. Never again quite so certain *Yes I know what I am doing, for God's sake leave me alone*.

What if: she has taken, not one of the elevators that open out onto the front foyer, but the stairs at the rear of the building. Which she has done, occasionally: five flights down. Exiting then by the rear doors, guarded also by Wayne County Sheriff's men, out onto Stockton. And so she'll avoid him. For that day. How many days she's been *not seeing* him. The lone figure in the periphery of her vision. Footsteps echoing hers to her car in the high-rise parking garage, slow angry smile as she drives past him she's *not seeing* because she's calm, resolute. Determined not to be intimidated, still less terrorized. Long before Hector Ramos there had been threats against Matilde Searle's life, and there had been stalkers in her life, before even the term "stalker" came into general usage. *Look, I'm a professional woman. I can take care of myself.*

What if: she has taken, not one of the elevators that open out onto the front foyer, but the stairs at the rear of the building. And so she would not be assaulted that day by a madman wielding a ten-inch carving knife newly purchased at K-mart. And so *he* would not step forward to intervene, even before he hears her screaming, and the screams and shouts of others around her. *He,* having legal business that day with the Child Protection Department, but otherwise infrequently in the county building, would not seize hold of Hector Ramos taking a knife-slash in the face, a stab in the forearm, wrestling the knife from Ramos before the sheriff's deputies have even drawn their guns. . . .

So human! so absurd!—to make of a purely random incident, an event of no greater significance than the encounter of microbes, or molecules, or subatomic particles an event charged with *meaning.*

So human! so absurd!—to make of a man's desire for her anything more significant and more profound than a man's desire for a woman, any woman. Because he'd intervened, and her blood was on him, in streaks on the front of his coat, and on his hands; her blood, and his own. Afterward insisting *Look, we've got to see each other, Matilde—you know that, don't you? That's your name, Matilde?*

The heartbeat is her own, of course. Even when making love, grasping a lover's shoulders, the small of the back, the buttocks, moving her body with his, her loins against his, the smooth heated skin, mouths sucking mouths, even then she had known which heartbeat is her own, which his. But it has been so long.

Fear of death?—not fear of death but fear of sudden helplessness, violence. A shattering of glass downstairs and the breaking-in of a door (it will be the rear, kitchen door: this, the door forced open two years ago by an unknown burglar or burglars who trashed Matilde's kitchen, living room, study before taking away what could be carried of Matilde's valuable possessions which in fact added up to very little) and the sound of rapid footsteps. How many times in the night before even the assault by Hector Ramos has she wakened dry-mouthed to hear sounds belowstairs like a rough-rocking dark tide rising to drown her. How many times waking her body quivering taut as a bow from which an arrow will fly. Then, she'd had no handgun in her bedside table. She had wanted no gun, no weapon. She would rise swiftly and lock the door of her room and she would dial the emergency number 911 if the sounds persisted and if she was truly awake and not dreaming which in fact so often even before the assault by Hector Ramos she was. And so there was no need, for there was no danger. For when the house had indeed been broken into, she hadn't been home. (Though she'd left lights on, a radio turned up high.) And when Hector Ramos had so carelessly stalked her those several weeks, late September through October, into November, it was always in the vicinity of the Wayne County Clinic or in the high-rise garage in which she parked and she'd never been really alone, not really alone, as now, in her bed, upstairs in the elegant old crumbling brownstone at 289 Springwood she'd inherited from her aunt, she is.

Naked woman. She throws off the damp sheet that smells of her body though she'd showered and washed her hair before going to bed. Rises from bed, unsteady on her legs, she's a thin-legged bird like a flamingo, or an ostrich. Corrective lenses required for driving, especially night driving. When depths flatten to the thickness of playing cards and even bright, primary colors are drained of their brilliance. She's in excellent physical condition except for occasional migraine headaches, bouts of insomnia, irregular and painful menstrual periods. She drives forty miles to be examined by a (woman) gynecologist in Oakland County, north of the city. She has no internist in the city since the doctor she'd been seeing was shot to death in his office near Wayne State University by black youths demanding drugs and cash, a year ago last Christmas. No prescription drugs now, not even birth control pills. There are other methods of contraception if contraception is required. . . . She's staring at something on the floor. She knows what it is, only the sweat-soaked nightgown she'd yanked off over her head and tossed away. She knows what it is, a puddle of cloth, still she stares.

Infinite regret. Infinite regress. There's something about a naked woman, one of Matilde's lovers whom she has not seen, nor spoken with, since 1981, once said. A naked woman in a man's close proximity always appears so . . . unexpected somehow. Fleshy, overpowering. Too big. *Even,* he'd said thoughtfully, *when you're not.*

How many years ago in another city before Matilde's life was her own. In the grip of an obsession, sexual love making of her body a vessel of yearning, of hunger *This is not me! Not Matilde Searle* she'd driven slowly and methodically past the home of her (married, law professor) lover, at dusk, and at midnight, one mad desperate lonely time at dawn, not truly wishing to see the man (with whom, shortly, she would break) and still less wishing to be seen (for what shame to be seen! so exposed! where her lover fantasized twenty-seven-year-old Matilde mysterious, elusive, too young and too idealistic for him, to be so exposed!) but simply to be in physical proximity to him who at that time in her life had seemed to Matilde Searle the very center of her life, her life's radiant core. Which is why we say *I can't live without you* meaning *your life gives life to me, who am otherwise an empty vessel, nameless.*

Is she a feminist, yet thinks such thoughts?—but Matilde Searle does not think such thoughts, nor express such thoughts, no one of her acquaintance has ever heard such thoughts, certainly no one of her female clients whose lives, ensnarled with men who mistreat them, has ever heard such thoughts articulated by Matilde Searle. In her aloneness is her strength. As in ours.

White bitch, scumbag cunt! Only after the bloody carving knife has been wrenched from him, when he's been pounded to his knees by the man named Bowe, Bowie, does Hector Ramos begin to scream at Matilde Searle. *Bitch! Cunt! I kill you!*—she's too surprised, too stunned to register what has happened, why she's bleeding from cuts on her hands, a three-inch slash on her left forearm, why she's staggering on the verge of fainting and strangers' hands, arms are holding her up—suddenly such a commotion, an outcry, the sheriff's deputies rushing with their guns drawn—why, what has happened, why has someone wanted to injure *her?* The man in the camel's-hair coat splattered with blood—his own, hers—is holding Matilde up, supporting her head, strong fingers gripping the back of her head. Her handbag stuffed with wallet, wadded Kleenex, notebook, papers, comb, plastic drugstore compact has fallen to the dirty foyer floor, someone takes it up and passes it quickly to the man comforting Matilde, here, here's the lady's purse, watch out it don't get stolen and afterward Matilde will hear this murmured solicitude, a gray-haired black man's voice, she'll hear and be touched to the heart *Here's the lady's purse, watch out it don't get stolen.* Her assailant who had? hadn't? intended to actually kill her is being handcuffed by the deputies, on his knees struggling with them shouting obscenities and lunging to escape and his face is more youthful than Matilde recalls, it would be a handsome face except it's distorted with rage and pain as the deputies clamp on the cuffs and, police style, yank the man's arms up behind his back so he's screaming in agony, begging *No! no! no*—To all this Matilde Searle is a witness but she isn't capable of comprehending. She is calm enough, her pride won't let her give in to hysteria nor even tears in this public place and in any case it's impossible for certain individuals—liberal, educated, idealists by temperament and training—their lives dedicated to "helping humanity"—to believe that anyone knowing them might wish them harm. Impossible!

The handgun. She has not practiced. Not once firing the gun though it's fully loaded: six sleek bullets in the oiled revolving chamber. She has not cashed in her coupon from the Liberty Gun Shop redeemable at the Crossroads Indoor Firing Range on North Dexter, in the suburb of Ferndale, which would give her a free hour's session with a "licensed" firearms instructor. From time to time during the past several days and nights she has removed the gun from the bedside table drawer, she has weighed it in her hand *ugly thing! ugly!* with the air of one weighing a profound and inexpressible yearning. The .38-caliber Smith & Wesson is a dull metallic blue, cool to the touch. Its surface, presumably once smooth, is covered with minute scratches, tiny near-invisible figures like hieroglyphics. The gun has its secrets— how many times has it been fired, how many bullets flying into flesh, how many deaths. There's a wholly objective statistical "life" of Matilde Searle's handgun inaccessible to her. *Because you must be prepared not just to shoot but to kill.* She won't be able to do it, when he comes for her. If he comes for her. He, or his brothers, cousins . . . there are so many of them, and time is on their side: any night, so many nights, she's alone, she's waiting. Better not to think of such possibilities. A gun heavy in your hands, you don't think. Except it's always heavier than you expect, which *is* a thought.

She has told no one about the gun, her shameful purchase, her purchase of shameful expediency. Not any brother or sister, not any of her friends who have so frequently expressed concern for her, worry that she continues to live in Mittelburg Park surrounded by encroaching "urban decay." Not her colleague Mariana with whom she shares an office and who has a handgun of her own—a compact, snub-nosed .45-caliber automatic with a pretty mother-of-pearl handle. Not the man who intervened to save her life, the man whose name she doesn't quite know, Bowe, Bowie . . . the man whose telephone calls she doesn't return, the man of whom she is not going to think. She lifts the gun glancing up shy and bemused seeing her reflection in her aunt's mahogany-framed

mirror a few feet away. Amid the faint, cloying fragrance of tal-
cum. And a faint whiff of cedar and mothballs from the aunt's ca-
pacious step-in cedar closet. Matilde Searle, a deadly weapon in
her hands, barrel upright and slanted across her breasts. *Is this me?
Is this the person I've become?* She has told no one, and will not.

Sucking. Lifting the gun, Matilde feels a sharp sensation of faint-
ness rising from the pit of her belly. Frightening, and delicious.
Upward flowing like water, a dark undertow. It's a familiar sensation but Matilde can't recall it then suddenly she remembers: this
is the way she used to feel, many years ago, when a boy or a young
man first touched her, when they first kissed, the remarkable sensation of another's mouth on hers, another's tongue prodding
hers. So suddenly, the gesture of intimacy irrevocable. And Matilde, young, dazed in delight and revulsion, excitement, dread,
relief—sucking on the kiss, a stranger's tongue, as if there were no
other nourishment she craved.

I can feel your heartbeat!—Jesus. In the front seat of the Volvo,
awkward, the man's arms around her, gripping her tight. They'd
been treated for their wounds, stitched, bandaged in the emergency room of the Detroit Medical Center. And he was driving
her, not home as he thought wisest, but back to her car in the
parking garage—as Matilde said, she'd need her car, she was going back to work the next day. The man who'd intervened to save
her life, the man whose name was Bowe, or Bowie, said,
concerned, Maybe you'd better not, you're obviously upset, for
Christ's sake *I'm* upset and that maniac wasn't trying to kill *me*.
He was a lawyer, a litigator. And he was articulate, though shaken
as Matilde was, and excited; a man she understood was accustomed to attentiveness, respect. You didn't contradict this man if
you wanted to live in peace with him but Matilde was firm,
Matilde insisted no, thank you very much, you've been very kind
but no, I'm all right. Trying not to look at his face more than she

needed to, the square patch of gauze beneath his left eye; trying not to meet his eyes. That locking of the eyes—no. There was already a palpable tension between them and Matilde put her hand on the passenger's door to open it and she winced with pain, slashes in the palm of her hand that had seemed to be numb but now she winced with pain, and in the Volvo parked on Stockton Street at the rear of the county building she lost her composure at last, suddenly choking, crying, her stiff face crumpling like tissue paper. *Don't touch me!* she might have cried but the man touched her. Put his arms around her. Matilde, it's going to be O.K., it's over now—his breath coming quickly, he was sexually aroused Matilde could tell, adrenaline pumping his veins. Then, I can feel your heartbeat!—Jesus. And he held her, and Matilde clutched at him, she could not control her choked breathless crying which was a wild laughter too but when the man tried to kiss her Matilde wrenched away. *No.*

Not a victim! She has been strongly advised to take at least two weeks' leave from the Clinic and to see one of the staff trauma counselors but she has declined. Apart from the wounds, which are only flesh wounds, and not infected, Matilde is certain she hasn't been traumatized. And Hector Ramos is still in custody and no one, so far, has posted bail bond for him ($2,500 bond on $25,000 bail)—Matilde calls the Detroit House of Detention daily, she knows how quickly even murder suspects are released back to the streets in Detroit. Back to their victims but *I am not a victim: I can protect myself.*

A fever. She's awake for hours, then sleeping fitfully, kicking at the bedclothes. Sees again the flying flashing knife which she tries again to deflect with her bare hands, forearms. If that man, that stranger, had not intervened perhaps she would be dead. And if then dead—where? Through the window beside the bed a tattered luminescent night sky, moonlit clouds like rock fissures. A harsh whining November wind. It's only 3:20 A.M. If she can make it through the night. *And the next night?—and the next.* She isn't going to quit the job for which she's been trained, the profession to which she's given her youth, her passion, her unmediated heart. She isn't going to move from her aunt's house. . . . But hearing, with a stab of panic, a car at the curb, or is it in her driveway: *his* car: the Volvo. *Matilde?—I want to see you.* Matilde stands cautiously beside the window looking down, sees no car in the driveway, nor at the curb; goes to the other windows, looks out and sees nothing; hears nothing. (Except the wind flinging leaves against the windows. And the myriad ceaseless noises of the city.) Thinking, But he wouldn't come here. Uninvited. At this time of night. That's absurd. That's madness. Of course. I know. Yet unable to return to bed for some time staring at the street, the windswept trees, the sky marbled with light—a scene weirdly dilated as if, violently shaken, it hasn't yet settled back into place, into its normal proportions.

A case of nerves. That morning at eight-fifteen leaving her car parked on C-level of the high-rise garage Matilde experienced a sudden jolt of panic—ridiculous!—as a coffee cup, Styrofoam, glaring-white, blown by the wind, rolled clattering in her direction. And every time the phone rings, and it's a man's voice. And a late-afternoon call from one of the women counselors at the shelter, a call having nothing to do with Mrs. Ramos, and Matilde steeled herself expecting to hear that Ramos had been released, and had murdered his wife. Steeling herself waiting to hear what was not told her even as, gripping the telephone receiver tight, oblivious of the pain of her scabby-stitched flesh wounds, she believed she was actually hearing what was not told her amid the pounding in her head, the *beat! beat! beat!* of her brain. *The madman. Ramos. Now coming for you, Matilde.* And tonight as previous nights the telephone rang several times—at nine, at eleven, again at eleven-thirty. Matilde has shut off her answering machine, she knows who it is. *Let's just see each other, let's talk.*

Matilde?—I'm not going to give up. Methodically Matilde has shredded his notes left for her at the Clinic as, that first evening, her wounds still smarting with pain, she'd thrown away the printed card he'd given her. *No. I can't. I won't.*

Wounds. A dozen cuts of varying degrees of depth, severity on her palms, knuckles, wrists, forearms. All but two were not deep enough to require stitches. Where the angry man had slashed her on the left side of her neck there's a burnlike scab of about three inches—it looks like a birthmark, or a pursed mouth. Matilde contemplates it frequently, noting the progress of its healing. How lucky you were they told her at the hospital, your scarf (she was wearing a thin cotton-knit scarf tied casually about her neck) blunted the knife blade, an artery might have been cut. Matilde caresses the crusted scab with her fingertips, prods it into pain, scratches it gently when it itches. A fact: there's a quickened, feverish heartbeat inside the wound.

Infinite regret, regress. It's only 4:10 A.M.! Flattened on her bed on the rock-hard mattress a hand on her burning, slightly sunken stomach, another hand, the back of her hand, on her burning forehead. She had felt his heartbeat, too. His mouth, the heat of his breath, the adrenaline charge. Yes I want you, but what does that mean: *want*. A woman wants a man, it's a mouth wanting to be filled. No but I don't want you, I don't want *it*. Her eyeballs glaring up out of the dark mute ignominity, anonymity of desire. *I want I want I want.* Turning her head, her stiff neck, to see the time: only 4:11 A.M.!

Pissing. Her bladder's full to bursting, and this pleases her: how *real*. And how *easily remedied*. Groping her way through the darkened room to the adjoining bathroom, switching on the light and she whimpers with pain, momentarily blinded—sees in the cabinet mirror a woman she hardly recognizes, matted hair, sweat-slick tendrils on her forehead, swollen eyes, lips; the angry little scab on her neck. Yet of all the skin that envelops her, there is little that is, in fact, marked, scarred. Matilde smiles at this revelation. Sitting then on the toilet seat with its numerous hairline cracks, emptying her bladder of hot splashing urine with a relief so profound it brings tears to her eyes. Relief of pissing profound as the relief of sexual hunger. Yet—no romance! Yet in fact more profound, since you can die of your body's toxins, but no one has ever died of sexual hunger. Matilde laughs aloud at this revelation and the thin girlish breathless laughter turns into the groaning-wheezing of the toilet's protracted flushing.

The stalker. Headlights trail across the ceiling, thin and fleeting as another's thoughts. She hears footsteps below her window, on the narrow asphalt drive between her house and her neighbor's. She has been asleep—a jagged, serrated sleep like wind buffeting sails—on the bedside table a bottle of red wine, an empty glass—the house is locked and the door to the bedroom locked and the .38-caliber Smith & Wesson revolver is in the drawer of the bedside table only a few inches from her hand. Now in fact—as in a film suddenly speeded up, to indicate not just the swiftness of time's passing but the insubstantial nature of time—the revolver is *in* her hand. She winces with pain but it's a wakeful, tonic pain. *Not just to shoot but to kill.*

The heartbeat. Unbearable. Pulsing everywhere like the air charged to bursting before an electrical storm. Matilde, in a state beyond fear, in a sleepwalker's calm beyond panic, has thrown on her white terrycloth bathrobe and she's barefoot, advancing to the top of the darkened stairs, the revolver in her hand: her right hand, shaky but steadied by her left. Scabbed cuts on both hands now throbbing but Matilde doesn't notice. The *beat! beat!* in her eyes so pronounced that her vision is blotched, wavy as if she's undersea. As if the air's choppy vibrations have become visible, tactile. Beneath the sound of the wind she has heard a sound of

footsteps at the rear of her house, a sound of breaking glass. It is
5:15 A.M. and the moon is gone, layered over in cloud. After the
Detroit riot of 1967 Matilde's aunt had installed a burglar alarm
but the system gradually broke down, the fierce frantic din was
triggered by wind, or the slamming of a door, or squirrels in the
attic, it rang in the night and it rang in the day and it rang when
no one was in the house, nor even near it, and the police rarely responded to any homeowners' alarms in Mittelburg Park because
they were always going off and so when Matilde moved into the
house she never replaced the burglar alarm system which would
now be ringing as the kitchen door is being forced. Matilde at the
top of the stairs descends slowly, the .38-caliber Smith & Wesson
in her hand, aimed at an invisible target in midair. She calls out,
Who's there? Who are you? I've got a gun—She believes that she is
utterly in control, composed as one who has rehearsed a scene
many times, yet her voice is oddly faint and shrill, shrunken like
a child's piping voice, a doll's voice, a dream-voice. She speaks
louder, *Is someone there? Go away! Get out! I've got a gun*—These
words echoing as if they are not Matilde's but another's, mock-
ing—*gun, gun, gun*. Someone has broken into Matilde's house,
and he's heard her. An intruder, or intruders. As if Matilde can see
through the door at the rear of the hall that runs the length of the
house, from the front vestibule back to the rear door, the door
that's been forced, she knows that the intruder, or intruders,
are deliberating what to do: to escape, or continue. They are
strangers to her, or they know her—*Matilde Searle*—very well.
Her body is covered in a rank animal sweat and prickly beads of
moisture have formed on her forehead but Matilde is utterly
calm, as a sleepwalker is calm, never in her life so keenly awake! so
alert! her slender bones bright-brittle as glass! She has positioned
herself on the stairs in such a way that, crouching, aiming the gun
through the banister's rails, if the swinging door that separates the
front hall from the rear is pushed open, nudged even an inch, she
will fire.

The wind. The November wind, flinging leaves, bits of grit, scraps of paper, blowing the clouds in tatters across the sky that, over the industrial stretches along I-75 downriver and west of the city is a faint flamy-red through the night, has confused her: so Matilde tells herself. Barefoot and shivering at the rear of the house finally daring to investigate, switching on lights, making of herself a bold, white-glaring target should anyone be outside watching, she sees to her embarrassed relief that the door has not been forced, after all: but a pane of glass measuring about five inches square has been shattered. Maybe a would-be intruder had smashed it, maybe it had been cracked and the wind broke it, Matilde shines a flashlight out into the backyard where tree limbs, debris have fallen, the tunnel-like swath of light quivers, she darts it quickly about the leaf-strewn browned grass but sees nothing, no one.

Dawn. At 7:05 the telephone beings to ring. Matilde has not gone back to bed but has showered, shampooed her hair, she emerges from the fragrant steamy warmth of the bathroom as the phone rings, rings. A harsh glaring-gray light porous as moisture is pressing against the bedroom windows. The wind has subsided to fitful gusts, another day of Detroit no-weather, dull blank vacuity as if the sky has sunk beneath its polluted weight and it's a joyless world of cloud, fog. As if the catastrophe has already happened, it's over and now another day rolling from the horizon. Matilde winces at the light, there's a tall narrow window beside her bed where the blind is broken, months ago the damned thing snapped up to the very top of the windowframe and Matilde hasn't replaced it, countless items in the old house she should replace or repair but the thought of making an inventory leaves her dazed, exhausted. It's 7:05 A.M. and the telephone is ringing and whoever is calling Matilde at this hour must have something crucial to tell her unless of course it's a wrong number. Always the possibility, having steeled herself to hear his voice, the voice she doesn't want to hear, she will not in fact hear it. *Matilde?—I'm not going to give up*. At 7:05 A.M. taking pride she's made it through the night—another night. The gun returned to the drawer of the bedside table and the drawer shut tight. Matilde wonders, Would it be easier, believing in God? At 7:05 A.M. of this November morning which in fact is the morning of her fortieth birthday this is a thought that strikes her as urgent. She lifts the receiver of the ringing phone believing that whoever it is on the line, wanting to speak to her, or to someone, will have the answer.

▪ *James Grady* ▪

KISS THE SKY

Flat on his back at night when the TV and radio whispers and the coughs and sobs faded away, Lucus felt like he could kiss the sky.

Then Lucus would let his arm float up. Press his fingers against the concrete above him that told him where he was.

Grounded, man: Got to maintain. All day. All night.

Night only meant the Admin killed the cells' overheads and dudes with desk lamps had to snap them off. Unblinking walkway bulbs still ate shadows on the tiers and cast their shimmer into the cells. And unless a lockdown was on, anybody who'd saved enough to buy a TV could leave its screen flickering in his cell.

Same as ever, cell lights snapped on at 7 A.M.

From the bunk under his, Lucus heard H.L.S. whisper: "Think they's gonna go for it today?"

Lucus said nothing.

Jackster lay on the cot an arm's length from H.L.S.'s bunk, waiting to take his cue from the two gray men the Admin had sardined him with, waiting before putting his feet on the floor and figurin' on whether to take his meal card, make for breakfast.

"Maybe it's all cool," said Jackster, careful about carving his words in stone but still, like, reminding the older guys he was there. That he counted. "Maybe it's chilled."

"They been rocking the cradle," said H.L.S. "Put a dude to sleep with *it's-forgot's*, put steel in him when he's dreaming."

"They thinks they got a beef," added H.L.S., "they got a beef, and it don't blow away in the wind. Hard luck."

"I know what you're saying," said Jackster, not backing down like a punk but not pushing like a fool: "What you gonna do, Lucus?"

Silence answered those whispers in cell 47, tier 3, Administrative Building 3, Central facility.

Then from down the tier came the buzz of a cell door as Officers called a D-Dude out, the tinkle of chains as they strapped him in full restraints—hands linked to a chain belt in front, ankle hobbles, a lead line and row of tail links chained to the next guy in line.

D-Designate Residents were linked up to be marched to and from the mess hall, the first cons for breakfast and last for dinner; lunch got carted to them in their cells, a universally unpopular feeding system negotiated between Eighth Amendment court rulings and the Administration.

When they moved the D-Dudes to the mess hall, other cons were supposed to stay in their cells. Their gates might be locked, but often it was easier for the guards to yell the corridors clear and march the D-Dudes past open cells as fast as the shackled men could shuffle. The D-Dudes shuffled fast: in full restraints, you were a soft mark to get tore up. The guards weren't much protection: they kept their distance from D-Dudes to avoid a blade or whack from one of those angry boys.

Two years into his stretch, Lucus became a D Designate after he and Marcus jumped the hospital bus guards, stole the bus and damn near made it to the freeway before the troopers threw up a roadblock. Lucus shot a trooper in the leg with a bus guard's pistol. When SWAT sharpshooters cracked Marcus's head open from three hundred yards, Lucus was able to press the guard's revolver in Marcus's dead hand, then surrender unharmed. The trooper who got shot couldn't make a positive I.D. on which blue-jumpsuited convict had pulled his trigger, so dead Marcus ate that beef. Lucus only got tabbed for an escape.

That adventure added five onto his forty, kept him in chains for the next seven years.

Chains tinkled past the cell. Lucus drilled his eyes into the chipped white concrete ceiling.

H.L.S. swung out from under Lucus's upper bunk, went to the seatless toilet, urinated.

"Man," he said, shivering in the cold dank air, "hard luck, my plumbin's so creaky, can't go but half the night without hitting porcelain and I still got's to go first thing in the A.M.!"

"I hear that," said Lucus.

A rhythm worked its way down the tier, squeaky shoes followed by a loud clunk, then the rhythm replayed, coming closer: the Guard Rawlins, musclebound and faceless, unlocking the manuals on each cell door. Rawlins threw their bolt, squeaked down the line.

Jackster whispered: "What *are* you going to do, Lucus?"

Respectful. Wary. But pushing. Maybe checking if his ass was on the line, too.

The warning Klaxon echoed through the five tiers of Building 3, then came the sledgehammer clang of all the cells unlocking electronically.

Lucus sat up.

Cell doors across the way were slid open by their residents. Lucus wore prison blue sweats, a white T-shirt, a denim prison shirt. The seven-inch shank slid along his right forearm inside the shirt. The knife pricked his wrist, but the blade stayed up his sleeve, hidden by how Lucus held his arm and by a fuzzy red wristband like the iron-pumpers sported. Two winters before, a fish with a machine-shop job thought he could wolf out Lucus with the shiv he'd made right under the Jerks' eyes. Lucus broke both the fish's arms and one of his knees, kept the blade and left the fish to gimp around the walls like a billboard.

At their cell sink, H.L.S. splashed water on his face.

"I'm hungry," said Lucus. He slid to the floor, slipped into his sneakers. Glanced to the man at the sink whose hair was white: "You hungry, Sam?"

H.L.S.—Hard Luck Sam.

"Hell, yes," he answered. "If it's gonna keep running out, got to put more in."

"Want to stroll, Darnell?" said Lucus. *Darnell,* not *Jackster:* deliberately not using the dude's street name. Not dissin' the younger man, but underlining who was who.

"Think I'll hang here for a while," answered Darnell.

The Jackster, thought Lucus: you keepin' safe distance?

"I ain't that hungry," added the young man.

Justifying, thought Lucus: which means he's wanting to be sure I bought what he sold.

"What's hunger got to do with it?" Sam put on his shoes.

Could have been just H.L.S. running off at the mouth again. But Lucus knew better.

And the flicker in Darnell's eyes said that he *wondered.*

Central Facility's dining hall could hold all 2,953 of its residents, but by the time Lucus and Hard Luck Sam made their way through the checkpoints out of their cellblock, then through the chain-link fence tunnel to the Dining Hall, half of the bolted-down, picnic-style tables were empty.

Lucus recognized several crews of younger inmates clustered at their usual tables, a politicization of geography that mirrored neighborhoods from which those men drew their identity. Here and there sat old timers like Sam and him, neither apart from nor a part of any group. Tattoos from a biker gang filled a corner table; they were laughing. Spanish babbled from three tables. Two Aryan Brotherhood bloods sat close to the main doors—close to the Control Station where two guards sat. Two more guards punched out inmates' meal passes as they moved into the food line. Three guards strolled the aisles, their faces as flat as the steel tables.

The dining hall smelled of burned coffee and grease. Breakfast was yellow and brown and sticky, though the cornbread from the prison bakery was fresh.

Sam carried his tray behind Lucus, sat with him at the table that emptied of other convicts as soon as Lucus arrived. The exodus might have been coincidental, Lucus couldn't be sure. He was grateful for Sam's company, for the man staying where he didn't have to be.

"You lookin' good this morning," Lucas said.

"Hard luck is, I look like myself."

"Looking good," said Lucus. "Looking good to me."

Five tables away, Lucus spotted the Twitch, 6' 3" of too-tight piano wire, a guy with kinky hair like the man who kinda thought up the atomic bomb—Lucus couldn't be sure, he'd seen the picture in the prison library encyclopedia before he'd started The Program and learned to read real good. The Twitch bunked four cells down from Lucus. Twitch lifted a spoonful of yellow toward his grim mouth—the spoon jerked, and yellow glopped down to the tray. Nobody laughed or dissed Twitch: he was a straight-arrow postal worker who'd bought his ticket here when he beat a man to death who'd complained about slow mail service.

Twitch met Lucus's eyes.

Hope you taking your medication, thought Lucus. Twitch's lawyers lost the insanity plea, so their client bussed it to the prison population instead of a loony bin, but the courts let Admin make sure Twitch took pills to keep him rational.

Crazy, thought Lucus. What's that?

In the chessboard of tables, two men occupied steel slabs to themselves. One was thin and coughed; the other looked fine. The Word was they had Ultimate Virus, and once that was the word, those men were stuck where they were.

Someone snickered to the right.

Easy, casual, Lucus drifted his eyes to the laughter.

Two tables over, sitting by himself, bald bullet head on top of three hundred pounds of barbell muscle and sweet-tooth fat: Cooley, pig blue eyes and thick lips. In the world, Cooley cruised for hitchhikers and lone walkers, made Page One when the police tied him to three corpses.

Why ain't you a D Designate? Lucus asked himself, knowing the answer, knowing that Cooley played model prisoner, 'cept for maybe once or twice a year when that hunger burned in his eyes and he found some unconnected sheep where the Admin wasn't watching. Cooley left 'em alive, which kept the heat off, and always washed his hands.

The Twitch heard Cooley snicker, jerked his head toward that mountain of flesh.

Don't do it, Twitch, thought Lucus. He made his mind a magnet for Twitch's eyes. Don't be a fool today. Crazy as you are, Cooley'll eat you alive and love the memories in his lockdown. Ride your pills. Keep it cool.

Magic worked: Twitch's eyes found Lucus; blinked. The piano wire man bused his tray and left.

Cooley snickered, but nobody rose to his bait.

"Hard luck," muttered Sam. "The Twitch losing a cushy government job like that."

Lucus smiled.

Sam lowered his voice and talked with tight lips: "Ears?"

Lucus shook his head. Sam told him his back was empty, too, then said: "So what are you going to do?"

"I'm in the flow of events," said Lucus.

"Just you?"

"Gotta be who it's gotta be, and it's gotta be just me."

Sam said: "Believe I can—"

"You can't help me enough," said Lucus. "That'd just be one more body in the beef. That'd force it up to big time, but it's not enough to back it down. I won't let you stand on that line and get slaughtered if we both know it ain't gonna do no good no how.

"But Bro," finished Lucus, "I hear you. And thanks."

"Hard luck." The older man sighed. Lucus wasn't sure if it was with sorrow or relief. Sam said: "So you're in the flow."

"There it is."

"I be on the river banks." Sam shrugged. "Never know."

Then, for all the room to see, he held out his hand, and slapped five with Lucus.

Sam said: "What about the Jackster?"

"Yeah," said Lucus. "What about our Darnell?"

Darnell had folded the cot, leaned it next to the toilet. His footlocker was jammed up against the wall facing the bunkbeds. With the small desk, the sink, the rust-stained toilet and built-in footlockers for the two planned-for prisoners in this Resident Containment Unit, enough space remained for him to pace eight steps along the front of the cell bars.

"You getting your exercise, Jackster?" asked Lucus as he and Hard Luck Sam came back home.

"No, man, I'm working on my tan," answered Darnell.

H.L.S. stretched out on his bunk—feet facing the front of the cell. "Why didn't you take it to the Rec? They got three new Ping-Pong balls and you loves to watch that talk show lady strut her stuff."

"Figured I'd just hang here," said Darnell. "Wait for you."

"Wait for us to what?" Lucus kept his voice flat, easy. He perched on top of the desk, the open front of the cell and the pacing Darnell filling his eyes.

"Shit, man, I don't know!" said Darnell, pacing, staring out across the walkway, across the yawning fifty-foot canyon between their wall of tiered cells and the identical scene facing it. "We're partnered here, I figured—"

"Partnered?" said Lucus. "Don't recall signing on with anybody when they signed me in here. You remember anything like that, Sam?"

"I disremember nothing and I don't remember that," came the words from the lower bunk.

"Shit, man," said Darnell. Not turning around.

"Course, we do have to live together," said Lucus.

"Yeah," said Darnell: "That's what I'm talking about."

"I mean," said Lucus, "we all gots the same cell number." Darnell humphed.

"Numbers, man," chimed in Sam from the lower bunk, "they can be hard luck for a dude."

"What you mean?" snapped Darnell.

"Why, nothing, Jackster," said Sam, flat on his back, hard to see. "Just talking about numbers. Luck.

"Like when I went to that sporting house outside of Vegas," continued Sam. "Man, they trot the women out in a line, I'm gassed, blow and booze and riding a hell of a score, squinting at them long legs, them firm—"

"Stop it, man!" hissed Darnell. "Don't kill me like that!"

"How do you want us to kill you?" said Lucus, sweet and low. Jackster didn't reply.

"Just a story!" came the words from the lower bunk. "It ain't about women, it's about numbers. Them ladies all had these number tags on 'em, kind of like our designations, only you couldn't tell as much from reading theirs, just their number. Some of 'em were dog meat, but I spot Number 9 and she's so fine—"

"I heard this shit already," said Jackster. Leaning against the wall now, watching nothing real deliberately.

"And I choose her, tells the Man the hit parade bullet I want, pays him, go to the room and skin down—and who strolls in all what-the-Hell-for-you look on her face but the skaggiest bowser in the line! I find out my girl, she's so untogether, she's Number 6 but she ain't tumbled to her number's on upside down!"

"Hard luck," said Lucus, rolling out Sam's punch line.

"Yeah," spit out the Jackster, "kind of like when old H.L.S. here, him already a two-time fall man, cases his apartment rip so bad that the lady done showed up coming home—"

"She got sick at work," said Sam. "She wasn't supposed to."

If the Jackster knew what he was hearing, he didn't show it.

"Yeah," he said, "and it was hard luck when that lamp you whomped her upside the head with—"

"She wasn't supposed to be there screaming—getting in the way of me getting clear to—"

"And hard luck when you dropped out her window and the alley Dumpster lid caved in on you, and hard luck it was empty so's you hit steel bottom and busted your foot instead of bouncing off a pile of dirty Pampers, and—"

"You talking about *my* crime."

Even Darnell heard solid cement in the man on the bottom bunk.

Can't let this shit roll down today, thought Lucus. He said: "Enough hard luck out there to fill our happy home."

Zero the score so H.L.S. won't need to, thought Lucus. He said: "Kind of like when somebody sells three bags of rock to a roller wearing a beard over his badge, deal going down just in time to catch the Man's new mandatory sentencing guidelines."

Darnell's eyes risked flicking from the lower bunk to Lucus.

Lucus smiled: "Some guys just ain't cut out for the spy game."

"I don't play no games," said Darnell. But his edge was jagged, backing away.

"Hard luck. There it is."

"Should have been thinking about that *then*," muttered Darnell, not ready to give it up, not certain who he was talking about.

"I wasn't thinking about now *then*," answered Sam, softer,

sadder. "*Then* I was thinking about doing what was in my face. Scratching itches. Cool schemes that had to work for sure."

The air inside the room eased out the open cell door, whirled into the cacophony of shouts and radios and sweat in the cellblock.

"The point of the story," said Sam, his words round and smooth again, "is numbers. Some people get their number wrong, and look what hard luck that brings."

"I got my number," mumbled Darnell, "don't worry about it."

"I won't," said H.L.S. "I be glad for you."

"What about you, Lucus?" said Darnell.

"What about me what?" answered the man sitting on the desk.

"You gotta be working on your number," said Darnell. He met Lucus eye for eye. "Like you said, we live together, choose or no. That means your number's chained to mine, we on the line together."

"I know about chains," said Lucus.

"Me, too," said the Jackster. "And ain't nobody here don't know your number's up. Us being linked, it's righteous I should get to know what's what and figure my score around your play."

Jackster shrugged: "Ain't saying I'll throw with you, but I gots to do the stand-up thing by the guys I'm bunking with—"

"The right thing," interrupted H.L.S.

"Time for me to hit the shower." Lucus snagged his towel, stepped past Darnell saying: "You boys play nice while I'm gone."

Then Lucus was on the walkway, strolling down the tier, his towel looped in his left hand. Inside his right sleeve waited steel.

Split the walkway toward the right, stay closer to the rail than the cells. Not so close it's an easy bull-charge to push you over, but better close to the rail with its long drop-off than walking next to the bars where you were an easy push into a cell for a pile-on of badasses and blades. Ripping it up on the walkway meant that the tussle might get seen by the Tier Monitor in the bulletproof tower. The Tier Monitor could punch the horn, maybe get Nightsticks there while you still had some pieces left. In the cells, you'd fall into a setup so savage it'd be history before the Man got there, even if the Monitor saw you snatched.

Usually when Lucus walked the tiers, dudes sang out to him, gave him a nod or even strolled up to jazz. That morning, the guys hanging outside the open cells and doin' their busies inside sent him no words. Guys in his path rolled away.

"Hey, Sir," Lucus told the fat guard behind the desk at the cage entrance to the shower rooms, "OK if I catch a shower so's I won't stink up the Boss's office today?"

Architectural plans for the Central Facility called for two Corrections Officers to be on front desk duty at the Cleansing Units' facility entrance, and for one Officer to be stationed "in visual range" of the actual showers in each of the five locker rooms. The architectural plans took the "custody and care" charge of the incarceration laws seriously. Under the latest budget plan, enough Cleansing Units manpower existed for one front desk officer.

The fat guard had seven years left to his pension-out of the prison. When this guard found a dollar bill on a walkway, he'd been known not to smell homebrew being cooked anywhere in a three-state area.

Not a bad Jerk, thought Lucus as the guard skimmed the clipboard of demerit denials and didn't find this inmate's name or designation.

"Everybody likes clean residents," said the fat guard.

"I hear that."

"Number 2 and 4 are busted out."

"Believe I'll try 3," said Lucus, signing his name and number on the second line of the logbook.

The fat guard frowned, spun the logbook around and double-checked the scrawl on the line above Lucus's name.

"I thought you could read, boy."

Keep it level—Hell, slam joke it straight back at the fat son of a bitch: "Do my numbers, too."

"You know who's in there?"

"I don't care."

Flat out, the power mantra.

The guard shook his head, scrawled his initials in the OK column. Said: "Never figured you for that scene, Lucus."

Like all its counterparts, Unit 3's locker room had no lockers. Wooden benches were bolted to the floor. A set of prison clothes and a Day-Glo undershirt were neatly stacked against the deserted dressing room when Lucus walked in. From inside the tiled shower area came the sound of rushing water and billowing steam.

Lucus stripped to his skin, stacked his clothes on the wall opposite the other pile. A scar snaked around his left ribs where he'd been too slow seven years before.

The shiv he held pressed against his forearm, his other hand swung open and free, fanning a path through the warm fog.

There, against the far wall, under the last of the twenty spraying shower spigots, shoulder-length permed tresses protected by a flowered shower cap, watching Lucus emerge from the steam, saying: "And lo, it is the man himself."

"Who you expecting, Barry?" Lucus walked down the line of lead-heavy rain.

Barry was six feet three inches of rippling muscles. Long, sinewy legs that let him fly across the stage of the city ballet or lightspeed kick the teeth out of dudes inside who were dumb enough to think Barry's style equaled weakness. The showers' steam made mascara over Barry's right eye trickle down his cheek like a midnight tear.

"Expecting?" Barry turned his bare shoulder toward Lucus, flashed his floodlight smile and swung his arms out from his sides, up above his head, hands meeting in a point as Barry stretched to his tiptoes, eyes closed in ecstasy. He held position for a full count, then fluttered his arms down, cupped his hands shyly above his groin and lowered his chin, eyes closed: a sleeping angel scarred by a midnight tear.

One heartbeat.

Barry's eyes popped open and he beat his lashes toward the man with a shiv.

"Why I've been waiting for only you." Barry cocked poses with each beat as he sang: "Just *you*, indeed it's *you*, only *you*, yes it's *true* . . ."

Whirling around, dancing, singing: ". . . no-body bu-ah-ut—"

Cobra coiled, shrinking back on one cocked leg, both pointing fingers aimed right at Lucus's heart: "*Yooou*."

"Good thing you came," said Lucus.

"What else is a girl supposed to do?" Barry leered: "My pleasure."

"No, man," said Lucus: "My payoff."

"Oh my yes," said Barry, washing. "Lucus to Mouser to Dancer—why, you'd think we were playing *baseball!*"

"We ain't playing shit."

"Certainly not, manchild." Barry smiled. "And right you were. The play's been called, the sign is on for a hit."

"When?"

"Well, that nervous nellie was all *denial,* you see, as if he hadn't been cruising around the yard, too scared to make a move, afraid his bros would put him down. Those savages! As if *they've* never grabbed a punk in these very tiled walls and made the poor boy weep! So since this was his first time, and since *my man* wasn't really doing it, you understand, just accepting this evening of sin I'd thrown at his feet as evidence of what a *stud* he is—"

"When?"

"Let a girl tell her story or you'll never get anywhere with her!"

"We're where we are and where we're going. You been paid, you come across."

"Always." Barry savored the moment. "What did Mouser owe you that he swapped my debt to him for?"

"Enough," said Lucus. "Now give me what I bought: when?"

"Why, *today,* Dear Man."

Lucus showed nothing.

"Probably in afternoon exercise."

Yard time, thought Lucus. Starts at 3:30. About five hours away.

Barry washed his armpits.

"My simple little use-to-be-a-virgin's crew has traded around and rigged flooding the stage and done the diplomacy and even *rehearsed* wolf-packing. They have a huge enough chorus to smother any friends of their featured star who try to crimp the show and make it more than a solo death song."

Water beat down on the two men.

"What else?" said Lucus.

"Nothing you'd want. He cried. I think he actually feels guilty. That's the only charming thing about him—though he does have nice thighs. Not as nice as yours."

"Does he got any notions that he was set up with you or that he ran his mouth too much?"

"He's mere ego and asshole," said Barry. "He can't conceive that's he's been bought and sold and suckered clean."

"How about his bros? By now, they might know about you two."

"Not from him. He's too scared of getting stigmatized to confess, and he's cagey enough to not let it slip out—for a while. If they do know, no worry: Like you said, I used to middleman powder for upscale customers from a boy tied to their crew. That makes *moi* acceptable."

"We're square." Lucus stepped back, his eyes staying on Barry as he made toward the shower room door.

"How about a little something for the road?" Barry smiled. "It'll calm your nerves. For free. For you, from me."

"I got what I need for the road."

"Oh, if only that were true for all of us!" Barry shook his head. "If only we could all *believe* that!"

Fifteen steps away, Lucus turned, disappeared in the steam.

"Good luck!" cried Barry.

Lucus dressed. Don't run. Don't show one bead of sweat.

"You'll get what you was after?" asked the fat guard as he signed Lucus out.

"Guess I did."

"Guess I did—*Sir.*"

"Yeah." Lucus saw his reflection in the fat guard's eyes, saw how it shrank because of what that guard thought happened in the shower.

That's his problem, thought Lucus. He went back to the cell.

Spent the morning on his cot, like he had nothing to do.

Jackster and H.L.S. puttered about, neither one leaving Lucus.

"Lunchtime," announced Lucus, swinging off his bunk. "Come on, Jackster. Today you eating with the men."

"I eat where I want," snapped Darnell.

"Why wouldn't you want to eat with us?" asked Lucus.

Darnell mumbled—then obeyed Lucus's gesture to lead the way.

A table emptied when Lucus and his cellmates sat at it.

Lunch was brown and brown and gray, with coffee.

Jackster kept sneaking looks to other tables, locking eyes with bros from his old neighborhood.

H.L.S. ran down "chumps I have known."

Like Dozer, a Valium freak who bypassed a pharmacy's alarm system, peeled its narco safe, then overindulged in booty and nodded off in the Pampers aisle. The cops woke him.

And Two Times Shorty, a midget who took it to the Stroll to bully an indy whore into being his bottom lady. She chased him through horn-honking curbside shoppers and lost tourists, pinned him on the hood of a Dodge, and pounded about a hundred dents in him with her red high-heeled shoe. Tossed him buck naked into a Dumpster. Climbing out, pizza parts stuck to his naked torso, Shorty grabbed the offered hand of a fine-looking woman. What the hell, he figured, second time's the charm, and he reeled off his be-mine pimp spiel. She slapped policewoman bracelets on him.

Then there was Paul the Spike, who tested heroin on street dogs. While he was slicing and dicing a batch of Mexican he had to keep stepping on and then retesting, Paul got the knock on the door. Because of the 'sclusionary rule, he beat the narco charges but drew ninety days for cruelty to animals.

"Hard luck can bite anybody's ass," said Sam, "but it always eats up chumps."

"I ain't no chump," said the Jackster.

Sergeant Wendell appeared at the mess hall door, scanned the mostly empty rows of tables.

"Who said you were a chump?" said Lucus, his eyes leaving the sergeant to settle on Darnell.

"No fool better!"

Sergeant Wendell started toward them.

"Trouble with young punks today," said Sam, "they got no *finesse*. Our day, needed to smoke a guy, you caught him in private, did your business and everything's cool. These days, you young punks let fly on street corners and wing out some poor girl comin' home from kindergarten. No respect for nothing, no style or—"

"Style?" snapped the Jackster. "That what that 'finesse' bullshit means? You got no idea, man, no *idea* what style is!"

Corner of his eye, Lucus saw Sergeant Wendell, coming closer. Lucus said: "Why don't you explain style to us, Darnell?"

"Ellicott!" yelled Sergeant Wendell.

"Yes Sir?" answered Lucus.

"What the hell are you doing?"

"I was just—"

"You know your damn schedule as well as I do! Your ass belongs in Administrator Higgins's office as of ten minutes ago!"

"On my way, Sir!" said Lucus, standing.

H.L.S. pulled Lucus's tray so Lucus wouldn't need to bus it.

"Why'd you make me have to come fetch you?" Wendell command marched Lucus to visit the Administrator in front of a dozen sets of eyes; in front of Darnell.

"Just guess I ain't so smart," said Lucus.

"Don't give me that shit," said Wendell, who was no fool and a good Jerk, though no con had ever been able to buy him. "Move!"

"Yes Sir."

Assistant Administrator Higgins kept his office *almost* regulation. Sunlight streaming through the steel mesh grille over his lone window fell on a government low-bid desk positioned in line with the file cabinets and the Official Calendar on the wall next to Facility Authority and Shift Assignment charts. But Higgins had taken out the regulation two visitors' steel chairs bolted to the floor in front of his desk and risked replacing them with more inviting, freestanding wooden fold-up chairs that a strong man could use to batter you to death.

Higgins was a bantamweight in chain-store suits and plain ties. He wore metal frame glasses that hooked around his ears. Glasses on or off, his dark eyes locked on who he was talking to. That afternoon, he slowly unhooked his glasses, set them on the typed report in the middle of his otherwise blank desk, and fixed those eyes on the man sitting in the visitor's chair.

"So you have no questions or comments about this report?" Higgins asked Lucus.

"Figure it's written, I can read now, so that ain't what I gots to talk to you about."

"That was on our schedule." Higgins leaned back in his chair.

"The Administration," started Lucus, "they got to like what I been doing. They been catching hell on the news, in the TV ads from those two citizens running for Senator. I heard the Warden—"

"Chief Administrator," corrected Higgins.

"Oh yeah, I forgot. Change the names and everything's OK. Long as there's no trouble."

"What do you mean, 'trouble'?"

"There's some that say the understaffing helps you guys, 'cause it'll inspire something to happen, and then you all can say, 'See? We need more budget. Jobs.'"

"I don't see it that way."

"Maybe some of the guards do."

"The Officers are paid to watch inmates, not make policy. I need to be told about any of them who act differently."

"I ain't the telling kind," said Lucus. "I just sensitive to your problems about image and keeping up the good show so the Warden don't get bad press and take heat from his buddy the Governor and every politician looking to get elected."

"What's this got to do with anything?"

"I just glad to help out—with things like that charity program on your desk."

"You've done good work, Lucus."

"What will it get me?"

Higgins frowned. "You knew that wasn't the way this program would be when you signed on."

Lucus shrugged. "Things change."

"Don't go con on me now, Resident."

"Sir, you was the one who showed me about attitude, about getting out from behind it and how nothing would change if I didn't. So I been workin' on my attitude, what's behind it, what I do. But where's it getting me? Still right here."

"You're down for Murder One, five counts. Plus. Where do you expect to be?"

"Oh I'm a criminal," said Lucus. "No question about that. I can do the time for what I did, but man, let my crime justify my punishment."

"Five murders," said Higgins. "Plus."

"I already done my plus in chains." Keep it calm, rational. "But I never did no murders."

"The law—"

"Sir, I know *the law*. We were sticking up gamblers. The law made them crooks, which made them marks. *The law* did that—not me. Figure, heist a crook, he can't holler for cops. Rodney, he had the gun, had them fools lined up against that wall, told me check out the basement. We agreed before we went in there: in and out with cash, nobody hurt, nobody can do shit about us. I'm in the basement, looking for whatnot, I hears those *pop-pop-pops*. . . . Man, Rodney done me just as much as he done them dudes!"

"Not quite," said Higgins.

"Yeah, well, what's done is done, but I didn't kill nobody. It's the law and Rodney that made me guilty."

"You chose to rob, you chose to go with a trigger-happy partner, you chose your juvie record, your prior theft and assault rec—"

"Yes Sir," said Lucus, interrupting with police formality: Got to hurry Higgins on. "I admit I'm guilty, but fitting my crimes with two twenty-year stretches, back to back, no parole—no right man can do that kind of justifying."

"It's a done deal, Lucus. I didn't think you were fighting that anymore."

"I got a lot of time to mess with it. Nineteen years more."

"Might just be enough to make yourself a new life."

"Yeah. Starting when I'm sixty-two."

"Starting every time you breathe." Higgins's dark eyes blinked. "You want something."

"This new attitude you helped me get," said Lucus. "Working with the programs—with my Program in my head. Not getting in any beefs since I got out of chains—"

"At least," said Higgins, "caught for none in your jacket."

"I been doing good time—"

"The law isn't about doing good time. That's what you're supposed to do as a minimum. No matter what you do in here, every day is on the payback clock, and you gotta get to zero before you can claim you're owed."

"Maybe yes, maybe no. Maybe not always."

Higgins shrugged. "What do you want?"

"A transfer," said Lucus.

"*What?*"

"Out of here. Right now. Not a parole, you couldn't pull that off. But you could take a paper out of that desk, sign it, and there it is, a transfer out of the walls to the Minimum Security unit downstate. Effective soon as the ink is dry. Call the Duty Sergeant and—"

"You're down for hard time, Lucus. You're a five-count killer with one escape and one shot-up officer—don't tell me where that gun was found—plus a jacket full of incidents—"

"All before I changed my attitude."

"Never happen. I never bullshitted you it would. You've got to deal with that in the most pos—"

"The transfer ain't for me. It's for my son."

Higgins blinked.

Blinked again, and in the Administrator's dark eyes, Lucus saw mental file cabinet drawers slide open.

"Kevin," said Higgins. "Kevin Ellicott, down for . . ."

"Last year, a nickel tour for what they could get him on instead of big dope. He's done angel time for thirteen months."

"Your boy runs with the Q Street Rockers," said Higgins. "They're not a church choir."

"I didn't say he was a genius. What he is, Sir, is a juicer. Just about to become a full-bore alcoholic, if he stays in here much longer. And what's that gonna solve? How's that gonna make life easier for the Warden? What justice is—"

"Doesn't add up," said Higgins. "He can get pruno as easy at the Farm as here."

"Maybe if he gets into the Farm's Step program—"

"It's *his* maybes," said Higgins. "Not yours. Why isn't he asking? Why are you doing this?"

"He's my son. I wasn't there to bring him up. Hell, if I

had been around before I got my Attitude Program, probably wouldn't have done him much good. Maybe he could have learned better street smarts, but . . . He stays in here, he dies in here."

"Of alcoholism?" said Higgins.

"Dead is dead," said Lucus.

They watched each other for a dozen heartbeats.

"And you think a transfer to the Farm will keep him alive."

"It'll give him a chance."

"What aren't you telling me?" said Higgins.

"I'm telling you everything I can," answered Lucus.

"That you *can?*" said Higgins. "You got to learn that we create most of our own *cans* and *can'ts.*"

"We do?" Lucus waited, then said: "Thought you always said that we pay for them, too."

"That's right."

"Yeah," said Lucus. "That's right. So if somebody's already paid, then he deserves a *can.*"

Softly, Higgins said: "Don't blow it, Lucus. Whatever's going down, don't you blow everything you've accomplished."

"What's that, huh—*Sir?* Any way I cut it, I still got nineteen years to go. What could I blow?"

"The way you get to look at yourself in the mirror."

"I see a man there now. I'll see a man there tomorrow."

"If you won't help me," said Higgins, "I can't help you."

"I been helping you—Sir. Look at the report on your desk. Let the Warden take credit for it, keep his image shiny. I ain't asking nothing for me. Who I am, what I've done—what I can do, one way or the other, all that should be worth something."

Higgins shook his head: "You can't bargain for your son."

"Then what the hell can I do?"

"Let him do his own life."

"You telling me, no transfer for him?"

"That's the way it has to be."

"Thought we defined our own possibilities," said Lucus. "Are you through with me—Sir?"

"We're through, Resident."

Lucus walked to the door, turned back. "Answer me one question, Sir?"

"Maybe."

"Why you do what you do? Every day, come in here, locked up just like us, with us. Bucking the Administration and the Rules and the Law and the Word and the Attitudes: Why you do it?"

"I got kids, too."

Lucus nodded, and as he opened the door, said: "Too bad."

Clock in the sunshine on the wall facing the sergeant's desk: 1:57. Hour and a half to go.

Close that door behind you, thought Lucus. He said: "Hey, Sergeant, got some book work to do now. Can you cut me a library pass? It ain't my regular day till tomorrow."

Sergeant Wendell wrote the pass without bothering his boss behind the closed door. Wendell knew all about Lucus and his Help the Homeless Project and the grants and the reports.

The library filled the second floor of the Recreation Complex. Lucus shivered as he hurried through the open-air fenced tunnel from the Admin Building to the Rec. His exhales floated through the chain-link fence. The blade pressed against his arm was slick with sweat.

Inside the Rec, Lucus glanced at the standing-room-only crowd of blue jumpsuits watching a soap on the prison's big-screen TV that the Feds had confiscated in a drug bust. Cons laughed and joked, but soaked up the story about a beautiful blonde in slinky dresses and jewels who didn't know yet that the bearded dude she'd been banging was setting her up, secretly paying back a beef his father had with her father. With his glance, Lucus couldn't spot the face in the crowd, but he knew he was there.

The guard at the library door blinked at Lucus's pass with eyes that coveted first-floor duty where he could watch TV, too.

The A-Designate con working as librarian stood by the checkout desk, stacking books on a delivery cart to be rolled along the tiers. Another A-Designate replaced books on a shelf. Three Residents sat at tables by themselves, surrounded by lawbooks and yellow legal pads.

Over in the corner, reading at his Thursday table, Sir James Clawson.

A blue tent loomed in front of Lucus's view: Manster, the only creature in the Institution bigger than Cooley. Manster stayed out of chains because whatever he wanted from another con, the other con gave up. Outside, Manster pistol-whipped a cop to death.

"I'm here to see the Man," Lucus told Manster.

"Maybe." Manster held out a shovel-sized hand, not touching Lucus, but pinning the dude to the floor while Manster coughed to get Sir James's attention. Manster kept his eyes on Lucus, who everybody knew was one treacherous mother.

The three other ironmen between Sir James's table and the world made a space for their ruler to check out the petitioner. Sir James read to the end of the paragraph, glanced through the blue jumpsuits and let Lucus fall into his eyes.

"How you doin', J.C.?" said Lucus.

Manster exhaled a blimp of foul air: only Sir James's friends got to call him J.C.

Unless the mood was right.

"Lucus the lone wolf," said Sir James. "Join me."

So Lucus walked through the gauntlet of hard cons, sat in the chair across the table from the Man.

Sir James picked up some chump's pink Commissary Pass, used it as a bookmark for the page he was reading, then closed the volume. He turned the book so Lucus could see the cover: a picture of a suit-and-tie dude with a cocked sword in one hand and a briefcase in the other. The book's title read: *CORPORATE SAMURAI—Classic Japanese Combat Principles for the Twenty-First Century's Global Business Economy.*

"Are you still reading, Lucus?"

"Some. When I got time."

"You know what the underlying fallacy of this book is?" asked
J.C., who was working on his MBA, correspondence and good-
faith-in-your-prison-jacket style.

"Ain't read it."

"You don't' need to. Look at the cover."

The suit with a briefcase and sword and going-places face.

"Give a twelve-year-old a dime and a nine," said J.C., "and
he'll punch a dozen red holes in Mr. Global Business Corporate
Samurai before that classic sword even gets close."

A national gang once sent a crew from Angel Town to "nego-
tiate" Sir James's Outfit into their fold. A freezer truck carted the
five gangbangers back to L.A., dumped their meat in their 'hood.

"Business ain't my thing," said Lucus.

"It's the wave of the future," counseled J.C., who was down
on a drug kingpin sentence until well into the twenty-first century.

"I've got something for you," said Lucus.

"Ah."

"But I need something, too," said Lucus.

"Of course you do. Or you wouldn't be here. Respect and
such, you've been smart about it. But it's always been Lone Wolf
Lucus."

"I've had bad luck at partnering."

"Perhaps prison has taught you something."

"Oh yeah.

"Deal is," continued Lucus, "there's trouble coming down.
You run most of what moves inside here."

Sir James shrugged.

"Trouble comes down," said Lucus, "all the politics buzzing
outside, the Admin will tighten the screws, and that'll crimp your
business, be bad for you."

"The innocent always suffer," said J.C. "What 'trouble' has
made you its prophet?"

"There's a hit on, likely for this afternoon. The guarantee is it won't be quick and clean, and you don't need any out-of-hand mess tightening the screws on your machine."

"What's the 'guarantee'?"

"I am." Risk it. Maybe he knows, maybe not. Maybe he gave the nod, maybe he just heard the Word and let it melt in his eyes.

"The hit's on my boy—Kevin. He got drunk, got in a stupid beef over a basketball game in the yard. Trash flew, couple pushes before the Man walked by and chilled it down. Dude named Jerome's claimed the beef with my boy, and Jerome and his Orchard Terrace Projects crew gonna make it a pack hit."

"This just a beef? Not turf or trade?"

"Nothing ever stays clean, J.C. You know that. The Orchard Terrace crew does my boy, it'll make them heavy—balance of power shifts don't do you no good."

"Unless the teeter-totter dips my way," said J.C.

"Far as I know, you ain't in this."

Gotta be that way! Or . . .

J.C. sent his eyes to one of his lieutenants.

"Lucus's punk runs with the Q Street Rockers," said the man whose job it was to know. "Wild boys. Orchard Terrace crew, they been proper, smart."

J.C. sat for a moment. Closed his eyes and enjoyed the sunshine streaming through the grilled window.

"You're in a hard place," he told Lucus.

"Life story."

"What do you want from me?" asked J.C.

"Quash the hit—you could do it, no cost."

"Everything costs. What's in that play for me?"

"Your profits stay cool," said Lucus.

"Your concern for my profits is touching."

"We got the same problem here."

"No," sighed J.C., "we don't."

"If I squash the hit," he said, "then I tilt the teeter-totter. Even if you're right and the hit will cause trouble, unintended adverse consequences of my indifference, there'll be trouble no matter what. Why should I become the cause of trouble instead of just one of its bystanders?

"Your boy picked his crew—"

"It's a neighborhood thing, he didn't pick—"

"He didn't grow up," said J.C. "Now, if he runs to me out of fear, wants to join up . . . I'd be signing on a weak link. I'd gain more if I fed him back to the Orchard Terrace boys—then they'd owe me. Better to be owed by lions than to own one jackrabbit."

"I figured that already."

"What else is in your column of calculations?"

Fast, everything rushing so fast, too fast.

"You quash the hit," said Lucus, drawing the bottom line, "I'll owe you one."

"Well," said J.C. "Well, well.

"What would you owe me?" asked the man with a wallet full of souls.

"Eye for eye. One for one."

"Eye for eye *plus* interest." J.C. smiled. His teeth were white and even. "You really aren't a businessman, Lucus."

"I am who I am."

"Yes. You were a gray legend when I walked in here. Lone wolf and wicked. You mind your step, never push but never walk away. Smart. Smarter than smart—schooled."

"I'm worth it."

"You ever kill anybody, Lucus?"

"I'm down for five counts of murder—plus."

"My question is," said the man whose eyes punished lies, "have your hands ever drained the blood themselves?"

"Nobody ever quite died," confessed Lucus.

"Quite is a lot." J.C.'s smile was soft. "I know you're stand-up. You'd keep your word, wear my collar. But the fit would be too tight. And down the line, who knows what problems that would mean?"

Lucus felt his stomach fall away. His face never changed.

"So . . . I can't help you. Your boy's beef is none of my business—either way, I promise you that. He makes it clean, I'm not in his shadow. But his future is his future."

Lucus nodded. Pushed his chair back from the table slowly and felt the meats close in by his sides, ready.

"Whatever happens," said Lucus, "remember I gave you heads-up, fair warning. Nothing headed your way from me. Or my boy."

"We'll see." J.C. shrugged. "If we're square on that, we're square."

On his way out the library door, Lucus checked the clock: 2:01. Less than ninety minutes until the turn-out in the Yard.

What was left was the hardest thing.

Lucus found them in the TV room, backs to the wall, street cool, running their mouths and eyeing beautiful people in the tube.

"Well, what's up here," said one of them as Lucus rolled up.

Brush past that fool like December wind.

Look at yesterday's mirror—a young man against a wall, thick hair with no gray, taller and flatter muscles, no scar cross the bridge of the nose, but *damn:* a mirror.

"We gotta talk," Lucus told the apparition.

"Say what?" said the young man. Lucus smelled pruno on the boy's breath. Fear in his sweat.

Use your fear, telepathed Lucus. If you can't kill it, use it and ride it smart! But he said: "Say, *now.*"

"Old man," said his son, "anything you got to say, you say it right here, right *now,* in front of my bros."

"I thought you grew up to be enough of a man you didn't need nobody to protect you from facing your lone old man."

Catcalls and laughs bounced off Lucus—bounced off him and hit his son. Lucus knew they were all measuring Kevin, seeing how he'd handle this. Wondering if maybe Lucus could wolf their bro down. And if the old man could do it . . .

Kevin knows all that, too, sensed Lucus, and he felt proud that his son wasn't all fool.

"Well, shit!" said Kevin. "You been worrying 'bout talking to me for nineteen years, you might as well get it off your back now."

Kevin swaggered out of his crew, headed toward an empty corner by the moth-eaten pool table whose cues and balls hadn't been replaced after the last riot. Pressed his back against the wall, made Lucus turn his eyes from the distant crowd.

Good move! thought Lucus; he said: "We haven't got much time."

"You never did have the time, did you?"

"I never had much choice. Your Grandma didn't want to be bringing you down to no lockup and get you thinking that was just another part of family life, and your mother—"

"She'd have sold me for a nickel bag."

"She did what she could by you, got you to her mother. Gave up the one thing she ever loved all-out."

"I should drop by the cemetery, scrawl a thank-you on her stone."

"Don't throw your shit on her grave."

The chill in Lucus's voice touched his son.

"Why'd you two go and have me anyway?"

"Wasn't what we were thinking of," answered his father.

"Yeah, I know. A little under-the-blanket action sitting in chairs in Minimum's visitor hall, 'fore you got popped big time."

"Least you know who your father is."

"Hell of a family that gives me." Kevin shook his head. "I don't know who the hell you are. You're the big Never There."

"Nothing kept you from catching a bus out here when you turned eighteen, signing the visitors' log and calling me out."

Kevin shrugged: "I figured I'd make it here soon enough."

There it is, thought Lucus.

"Just like I could bust out in the hospital bus to see you when you was learning to walk and nobody was there to hold your hands but junkies and badasses and your spaced-out mama."

"You should have been smarter," muttered Kevin.

"Yeah," said his father. "I should have."

Got to tend to business!

But Lucus said: "Outside . . . You got a woman?"

Kevin looked away, said: "They's all bitches or whores."

"Thinkin' and talkin' like that," said his father, "no wonder you're in prison. No woman who's worth it will stick around you when you got that attitude."

"Yeah, well . . . No ladies no how was beating down my crib door." Kevin looked at his father; looked away, said: "That woman Emma, works in the dry cleaners. She calls herself your wife."

"We ain't got no law on it." Lucus shrugged, prayed for the clock not to tick. "Her old man died in a bustout, I got to know her through that. Phone calls, letters. We understand each other."

"You don't even have Minimum Security visiting privileges, the glass stays up when she visits you. What's she see in it?"

Lucus shrugged: "Safe sex."

Made his son laugh!

"We got no time," said Lucus. "The hit's on you today. Probably in the yard. They miss, they'll pick it up first chance."

Kevin blinked: "Jerome said—"

"Words are weapons! Ain't you learned that!"

"You ain't been my teacher, you can't give me grades!"

"If I'd been learning you, you wouldn't have gotten drunk and gotten in a beef over chump Yard basketball! And if you *had* run up against it, you would have done it right!"

"Yeah? Like how?"

"Like you'd have kept it *personal!* Man to man. Walked into Jerome's crew and called him out—put him on the spot. Then you'd have had a chance!"

"What chance did I ever have for anything!" hissed Kevin. "You think I'm chump enough to ask him—"

"You don't 'ask' for anything from anybody!"

"Force a throw-down, strap our arms together, toss the blade on the floor and—"

"And you got an even chance! You let it buck up to you dissin' him and his whole crew, you got a war, not a battle."

"I got my own crew!"

"Yeah, right. There's more of the other dudes, and the guys on your side would never sell anybody out—or miss getting cut up on accidental purpose. They gonna *die* for you."

"That's the way it is."

"If that's the way it was, this wouldn't be plea-bargain city."

"So what do you want me to do, Mr. Smart Time Con?"

"You got one chance. Go to the Admin. Feed them a pruno still—Robinson, Building 2, Tier 2, in the bus the auto mechanics practice on. Trade that bust for a crash transfer to—"

"You want me to rat? You a fool? That's evil! And suicide!"

"No, that's smart. Robinson wants to kick the juice—like you need to. He knows lockdown cold turkey is his only way.

"I already dealt it out with him," said Lucus. "You just gotta make your move—and right now."

"You're one treacherous mother," said Kevin.

"Believe it."

"But I go to the Farm, the Orchard Terrace guys—"

"They got no crew there."

"They will."

"That's tomorrow. You're scheduled to die today. With the time you done, keep your jacket clean and when the courts make the Admin thin the herd, you're a prime candidate for early release. Could be outta here in a year. Besides, we'll fix tomorrow when—"

"The Farm boys would know I ratted—"

"Not if Robinson puts out the Word how you two tricked the Admin."

"My crew would cut me loose."

"No loss."

"They're all I got!"

"Not anymore."

Lucus heard the babble behind him; knew a hundred eyes was checking them out. Knew the clock was ticking.

"You just don't understand," said Kevin. "If I run from—"

"You're not running *from*, you're running *towards*. And don't tell me I don't understand."

"I gotta do what I gotta do. If what's gonna happen's got to happen, that's just the way it's gotta be."

"Kevin?"

"Yeah?"

"Don't hand me bullshit street jive. That's all hollow words you stack in front of your face to keep from seeing you're too lazy or too stupid or too scared to fight so you can walk your own way. 'What's gotta be, gotta be' *shit:* you sit like a lame where the *'be'*-shit is, you ain't being stand-up strong, you making yourself the most powerless chump in the world."

"You don't get it, do you, old man?"

"Yes, yes I do."

"Why you doing this?" asked Kevin.

"Just because I done a lot of wrongs doesn't mean I can't do one right."

"Why this? Why me?"

"You're what I got," whispered Lucus.

Kevin pushed off the wall. "See you."

"I can save your life!"

"No, you can't," said his son. Nineteen-year-old Kevin spread his arms out like Jesus: "Besides, what's it worth?"

And he walked away. Strutted toward his *bros*.

Nowhere to run, nowhere to hide. Lucus went back to his cell.

Jackster and H.L.S. were there, waiting out the last few minutes before Yard time.

Nobody said anything.

Soon as Kevin got sent to the Institution, Lucas put the few pictures the boy's grandmother had grudgingly sent him in a paperback book where, like now, he could flip through them without a ritualized search that might betray his heart. With those childhood snapshots were pictures that somehow Emma had scissored from high school yearbooks for both years Kevin had attended.

Lucus glanced at his cell walls. Pictures of wide outdoors. Pictures of Emma—she sent him a new one every three months. *Who says we can't grow old together?* she once told him through the phone and glass in the Maximum Designates' Visitation Room.

Couple minutes to go, Lucus leaned on the bars. Stared nowhere.

"What you doing?" asked the Jackster.

"Nothing," mumbled Lucus.

"What you gonna do?" asked Jackster.

Lucus stood wordless until the Klaxon blared the "all out" for those Residents with permission to choose whether they wanted the ninety-minute Exterior Exercise, General Population Period.

The blade rode fine inside his sleeve, even when Lucus slipped into his blue cloth prison jacket.

As his cellmates grabbed their jackets, Lucus said: "Nice day out there."

The Yard.

Inside the big wall, chop a couple football fields and box them in a square with three mammoth cellblocks, double chain-link fences topped with razor and barbed wire. Put guard towers on two adjoining sides for right-angled sniper crossfire. Lay down a running track that circles inside the fence, a couple steps from the Dead Zone trip wire. Pave a dozen basketball half-courts in one corner, stick some rusted barbells and concrete benches beside them, draw some lines on a cellblock and call them handball courts. Smack in the center, throw up a water tower, run a chain-link fence around it like a dog-protector around a hydrant. Build four chain-link fence funnels from the cellblocks and Admin Building.

Loose the animals down those funnels.

The D-Designates clink out there with their chains for thirty minutes after breakfast. General Population gets ninety minutes in the afternoon. A-Designates have unlimited lunch to dinner access.

Institution Procedures assign twelve pairs of Corrections Officers to Roaming Yard Patrol during General Population Period. The budget that day sent five pairs of Jerks out amongst *them* in the Yard.

Several hundred inmates funneled through the tunnels.

Go to the core, thought Lucus. Go to the center of the Yard, where you can watch and be ready to move any which way.

H.L.S., casually strolling along a step behind Lucus's right.

No matter how the Jackster shuffled, the old dudes hung behind him a half step and herded him where they wanted at the same time.

Sir James and a squad paraded toward the concrete chess tables in the best sun. J.C. showed his empty face to Lucus; Manster sent the lone wolf a sneer.

As inmates walked into the air, Lucus thought: They'll take their time, make sure the play is set.

Kevin and a handful of his crew hit the yard, laughing loud.

Count six, thought Lucus: Q Street Rockers supposed to be a dozen strong.

Barry strolled by with three attentive supplicants under his protection. Barry's eyes never pointed toward Lucus.

The blue sea of inmates parted for Cooley. The hulk's beady eyes jumped around the Yard, seeking a fish.

"Yo, Jackster!" called a voice. An inmate Darnell's age popped out of the crowd twenty feet away, a worn brown basketball spinning in his hands. "We shooting hoops or what?"

"Ah . . ." Darnell looked to his cellmates: "I got a game."

"Better win," said Lucus. And he smiled.

Darnell got an empty stare from Hard Luck Sam.

Jackster followed the man with the ball to a court.

The Twitch stood by the water tower fence, alone, an invisible wind roaring around him. His gloves were gone, strips of an old blue shirt were wrapped around his hands. Twitch's eyes bored through Lucus.

Lucus used both hands to rub his temples, like to rub the pain away.

Jerome and a posse of his Orchard Terrace crew, a dozen dudes, strolled into the yard, headed for turf opposite Kevin and his bros. Like nothing was on.

Looking once at Jerome, the world couldn't tell him apart from Kevin.

There, in the crowd on Kevin's flank, positioning by the Dead Zone wire: one—no, two, three Orchard Terrace boys, the O.T.'s fanning out and holding, waiting.

Making the box, thought Lucus. No need to check the other flank, O.T.'s would be there, too.

Inside his shirt, the blade burned Lucus's forearm.

Across the Yard, a b-ball game filled a court, the ball clinking through the hoops' chains, wonging off the backboards.

Jackster caught a pass, made a fast break to the hoop and laid up an air ball. A teammate tipped it in. Dude on the other team slapped the Jackster five and jogged down the court with him, mouths a-working. Time out, and the five-slapper waved a sub in for himself. Time in. Standing on the sidelines, a spectator got the word on the game from the five-slapper. Dunk shot. Ball in play. Spectator got bored, strolled away from the courts, through the crowd, cut left, cut right, materialized alongside the O.T. posse. Whispered in the main man's ear. Got a nod. The main man put his arm around Jerome, leaned to his ear.

Standing beside Lucus, H.L.S. said: "Catch that?"

"Oh yeah," said Lucus. "The Jackster."

Two tan uniformed Jerks picked their way through the blue-clothed crowd: Adkins and Tate, a too-short and too-lean combo who always got stuck with Yard duty and always walked the same beat. They headed for their shake-the-water-tower-fence-gate check, after which they would angle toward the barbells.

Lucus saw the O.T. posse adjust their cluster, the flankers anticipating the two guards' patrol, not hiding, but not letting any-body use the guards' presence to outmaneuver the game plan.

Adkins, the lean guard, swung keys retracto-chained to his belt. Shorty Tate kept his eyes on the ground, like he was looking for something. Everybody knew his eyes were in the dust so the cons wouldn't see the fear.

As if they needed to see it. Fear hung like smoke over the small guard who wished Yard Duty Officers were armed and he didn't have to rely on the Wall Snipers to protect him.

Adkins swung his keys and complained about the Union and the World Series, Tate locked his eyes in the dust, thinking about how after checking the gate to the water tower, they'd only need to—

The Twitch kicked smack between Tate's shoulder blades.

The small guard crashed into the dirt.

Adkins dropped his keys and the retracto-chain snapped them back to his belt.

But before Adkins could whirl around, Twitch was on his back, looping a thick strip of old shirt around the guard's neck. One end of the strip was tied to Twitch's wrist. He looped the strip around his hand, cinched it tight so the knife in his fist was locked point-digging into the guard's neck.

"Nobody move!" screamed Twitch. "Anybody moves, I cut this head off and let the mice run out! Nobody moves!"

The cons cared zero about Adkins, but Twitch's play stunned them into stillness.

On the ground, Tate gasped, but managed to push the button on his belt radio.

Twitch backed toward the water tower, the guard Adkins hugged in front of him, pinned by the knife at the base of his skull.

Two pairs of Yard guards ran through the blue crowd, yelling into their radios.

"Nobody come any closer! Nobody move!" Twitch yelled to the charging guards: "Don't you clear the Yard! You clear the

Yard, I cut off his head and let the mice run out! Swear to Jesus, you clear the Yard, you come at me, he's dead! Dead! Mice! Ain't gonna let you clear the Yard! No Attica! No clean shots!"

The guard captain, reaching the inner ring of spectators not far from Lucus, yelled: "Everybody hold your positions! Everybody! No prisoner moves! Officers stay back!

"It's OK, Sidney!" the captain yelled to the Twitch as he backed toward the water tower fence. The captain's words flew over Guard Tate, who stayed facedown in the dust and prayed that the snipers' aim was true. "You're—"

"Nobody move! You shoot me, you'll kill him or falling on my knife will!"

A ReAct Squad of guards charged out of the Admin Building. Shotguns, man, buckshot loads bouncing on SWAT belts. They formed a picket line around the cons to be sure nobody tried to cop a point in this psycho play.

On the Wall, snipers ran to position. Lucus saw sunlight glint off a scope.

Twitch backed against the water tower wall as the Captain told him *it's OK, don't do anything stupid*. Twitch kept yelling *nobody move;* he made Adkins unlock the water tower gate and stayed pressed against the guard.

The Klaxon blared.

Higgins, radio in hand, panting, moved next to the guard captain as Twitch maneuvered himself and his hostage up the spiral steel staircase along the outside of the water tower.

"What the hell is he doing?" asked Higgins.

"We can't get a clean shot," said the captain. "Not without probably killing Adkins, too."

"Nobody move down there!" yelled Twitch. "Nobody move or we'll all die!"

Higgins radioed a report to the Warden.

In his mind, Lucus saw the State Police cars in the town a mile beyond the Wall, cops choking down donuts and slurping coffee as they turn on the party lights and race to the Pen.

Somewhere, Lucus knew, a TV news camera crew was running toward its helicopter.

Standing on the edge of a metal ledge fifty feet above the Yard, knife tied against the guard's spine, Twitch yelled down, *Don't move! Kill 'im if you do! Mice!*

Radios crackled.

The dudes started to buzz, whisper, but stood still 'cause the Admin had turned out shotguns and snipers.

Higgins's radio squawked, the Warden: "What does he want?"

Cool and careful, Lucus stepped forward.

"Administrator Higgins!" yelled Lucus, going for the man truly in charge. "I can do it!"

"Freeze and stow it!" yelled the guard captain. One of his men behind him swung a shotgun bore toward Lucus.

"I can do it!" pleaded Lucus.

"Do what?" said Higgins.

"Get your man down from there alive. Twitch, he thinks I'm like, one of him. You know I'm the only guy in here he believes."

Captain said: "What the—"

"He's crazy, Sir," said Lucus. "But he ain't stupid."

"He's a dead man!" snapped the captain.

"Drop him, your guy falls, too," said Lucus, adding: "Sir. Hell to pay for that. Hell to pay even if you just kill Twitch.

"TV cameras coming. Ask the Warden what he wants on the six o'clock news."

"Resident," snapped the captain, "you're ass—"

"How will you do it?" said Higgins.

"Careful, Sir. Real careful. I can do it, promise you that.

"But," added Lucus, "I'm gonna need something from you."

"We don't—" started the captain.

"What?" interrupted Higgins, who knew the true priorities.

"I can't bargain Twitch down off of there with just be-nice bullshit. He flat out don't care, plus he's seeing things—"

"Man's crazy!" said the Captain.

"Dead on, Sir. And there's nothing you can threaten him with he don't do to himself in his cell.

"But," said Lucus, "you let me tell him he can get transferred to the state hospital—"

"The courts put him here as sane," said Higgins.

"Wasn't that a smart move." Lucus jerked his thumb toward the men on the tower. "You can administratively transfer him to the state hospital for a ninety-day evaluation. Hell, they get him in there, 'less you or his lawyer squawks, they'll keep him on an Indefinite Treatment Term. No doctor gonna risk his state job turning loose a man with a knife talking about mice!"

"Why would that work?" said Higgins.

"'Cause I'll sell Twitch the truth. Hospital is co-ed. Even violents see women. Better drugs, better beds, more sun, people who treat him like he is: he might be crazy, but he ain't no fool.

"Course," added Lucus, "there is one more problem."

"What?" said the captain and Higgins.

"Why risk my ass to do that? Long climb up that tower."

"You get my man back," ordered the captain, "or—"

"Or what—Sir? My lockup order don't make me a hostage negotiator. I get punished for being only a model, no-volunteer prisoner, some lawyer will make the Admin eat it big time."

"What do you want?" said Higgins.

"Nothing much," said Lucus. "A righteous deal—Admin breaks its word on this, it'll get brutal in here, and real soon, Admin will need credibility with us Residents to save something else."

"What do you want?" repeated Higgins.

"That little matter we talked about earlier today will do."

The captain said: "What?"

Higgins pushed his steel eyes against Lucus. Lucus didn't fold. Higgins bargained in the radio with the Warden.

"That a helicopter I hear chopping close?" said Lucus.

Higgins lowered his radio: "Go."

Hard Luck Sam, Kevin, and Darnell, Cooley and Sir James and

Manster, Jerome and the O.T. posse, Barry, Higgins and the Admin—everybody watched Lucus. Heard him yell to Twitch that he was coming up. Heard him talking about deals, making it cool. Watched him climb that spiral staircase as his words faded into the wind.

Watched three men on a platform. Watched them with cold eyes and sniper scopes.

Maybe ten, maybe nine minutes: nobody took their eyes off the three men just to read a watch.

A helicopter chopped the air above the Institution.

Movement on the ledge—a sliver of glistening steel tumbled through the sky to the Yard.

Guard Adkins scurried down the steps.

Higgins, into the radio: "No fire! Repeat, no fire!"

Half a dozen guards grabbed Twitch when he reached the bottom, handcuffed him and led him away. Everybody knew the guards would use the hoses on him inside, but even the mean Jerks knew the deal had to stand.

Lucus walked toward Higgins and H.L.S.

Higgins said something to the captain, who frowned, but nodded when the message was repeated as a command.

Guard captain and two of his shotgun boys marched through the crowd of prisoners. Marched up to Kevin.

"You!" yelled the Captain: "Let's go!"

"Me!" said Kevin as the shotguns swung his way. "Hey! What's this shit! I didn't do anything! I didn't do anything!"

And as the guards hustled him away to pack his personal gear, the whole Yard watched.

Higgins nodded to Lucus, went home to his family.

The Klaxon sounded the return to cells. Shotguns on the Yard watched everybody shuffling back inside.

Sir James was lost in the crowd.

For a heartbeat, Lucus saw Jerome and the O.T. posse.

Roll up on that boy next Yard time, thought Lucus. Brace him, but let him back down. His posse won't be so hot to dance with him, and he'll know it. The Word will advise him to keep his cool: the sucker he wanted ain't there no more, the beef is over, and a respected, evil dude like Lucus . . . Don't mess with Lucus.

Walking beside Lucus, like he was reading his mind, H.L.S. said: "What about our spy boy Darnell?"

"Oh, I'll think of something for the Jackster."

"Hard luck," said Sam.

As they strolled toward the tunnel, the other dudes kept a safe and puzzled respectful distance.

Sam said: "I gots to know—just exactly what did you tell Twitch to make him drop the blade and climb down from there?"

Lucus whispered: "Same thing I said to make him grab the guard in the first place."

∎ *Jonathan Lethem* ∎

THE ONE ABOUT
THE GREEN DETECTIVE

I'd better start with the joke. It explains a lot, though not enough, of course.

The mailman comes to a house on the day before Christmas. He's pushing mail through the slot when the door opens. A woman is standing there. She says, "Why don't you come in and have some coffee? It's cold out there."

"Well, sure, why not?" says the mailman. She's a very attractive woman. And it is cold.

The woman sits the mailman down at the table and serves him not only coffee, but a full breakfast: waffles, bacon, syrup, orange juice.

The mailman is baffled, but he doesn't object. The food is delicious. The woman sits across from him, nursing a cup of coffee, smiling encouragingly.

The mailman finishes the meal and looks at the door. "Well, thanks, that was wonderful," he says. "I'd better—"

"Do you want to come upstairs?" says the woman.

The mailman's eyes widen, but the woman just nods and raises her eyebrows to reinforce the question.

So the mailman follows her to the bedroom. There they make slow, languorous love. The woman is generous and affectionate, but afterwards, when the mailman is stroking her hair, and readying a thousand questions, she says pertly, "Time to go."

The mailman bites his tongue, not wanting to question a good thing. He dresses and heads downstairs.

At the door, the woman stops him. "One last thing, I almost forgot." She fishes in her purse and pulls out a dollar bill, and hands it to him.

This is the straw that breaks the camel's back. "Listen lady," says the mailman. "First you give me breakfast. It was wonderful, I'm not complaining. Then we make love. It was fantastic. I don't understand, but it was fantastic. Now you're giving me a dollar. What's the game? I need an explanation."

"Well, it's almost Christmas," says the woman.

"Yeah?"

"This morning I reminded my husband that we should do something for the mailman. My husband said, 'Fuck him, give him a dollar.' "

"What about breakfast?" says the mailman.

"Oh, breakfast was my idea," says the woman brightly.

In 1959, when I was twenty-two years old, I went to work for the Conmoy Agency in Cleveland, Ohio. This is how it happened, and it isn't a joke, even if it starts like one. I was in a bar and the guy next to me said, "When'd you get out, soldier boy?"

"How'd you know I was Army?"

"So many different ways I couldn't pick one. You stink of Army. What you having?"

"Uh, a Manhattan."

"Give him another one," the man told the bartender.

I quickly emptied the drink in front of me, while the bartender made me another. "What do you do?" I asked the man.

"I'm a Conmoy Man. You know what that is?"

"It's a private security agency, right?"

"Conmoy leases his operatives for security sometimes. We're a detective agency."

Now he had my interest. Detective to me was Lew Archer. The base library had just gotten *The Doomsters* in hardcover and I'd burned through it in a night.

Other guys liked Hammer, but to me Spillane was kid stuff. Ross Macdonald's Lew knew life. I wanted some of that.

"What's the case you're on now?"

"Me, I work in the office now. But the Agency's always working on dozens of cases, not just one."

This was disappointing. It sounded like bureaucracy, not investigation. "Were you ever on a case I'd have heard of?"

"Sure, lots."

"Name one."

"The Nigger in the Candyshop. Everybody knows that one."

I had heard of that, though I couldn't say where or when. "You solve it by yourself?"

"Nobody solves it by themselves, soldier, except in the movies. We're a big outfit, lots of ears, lots of guys out pounding pavement. That's how things get done."

I was impressed enough. "There's always enough clients to keep a team that big in work?" I asked. "Or is that why you do security stuff?"

"Let me introduce myself," said the man, sticking out his hand. "L. J. Dranes."

"Lieutenant Oscar Fife," I said, and took his hand.

"Well, Oscar, pleased to meet you. Security work is good steady money, sure, but it also gets us out and about. In circulation. Work comes out of that. See, Conmoy isn't exactly like the usual snoop agency. We don't sit around waiting for clients to turn up. We generate the work ourselves, from the ground up."

"Really?" I said, not sure what he meant.

"Let me tell you about it. . . ."

By the end of the night I had an appointment for an interview at Conmoy.

"What's good today?" I said, laying one of the Agency's fives on the counter of the fish shop. I hated fish. "Why can't you tell me where you heard the joke?"

"Everything you see on the ice is good and fresh today. About the joke, I could tell you, I just don't want to."

"That guy Leonard was sure you were the one who told it to him. I'll take two of those flounders."

"Flounder, you mean," said the counterman. "Two flounder."

"Whatever. Where'd you hear the joke?"

"Maybe if I had an idea what the big interest was," he said, wrapping the fish.

I scuffed my feet in the sawdust. I'd memorized a list of Agency lines to use when I ran into resistance. Dranes had gone over it with me, and underlined the ones that would work, given my age. "My old man ran out on us," I recited. "He sent a card postmarked Akron so I came up here to look. He used to tell that old chestnut every time he touched the stuff."

Old chestnut. The emphasis was always supposed to be on how old and familiar the joke was, the closer you got. The hotter the trail.

I was on my own out here in Akron, with a pocket full of the Conmoy expense account, tracing the Mailman on Christmas Case. The man at the fish counter was the twenty-seventh link in the chain, further than I'd been before. I'd only worked two other cases: The Texan and the Golden Tuba, which had taken three weeks of research to peter out to nothing, until Conmoy closed it down, and The Gas Station Attendant's Beautiful Wife, which I'd worked for a week and then had yanked away from me the minute it got interesting. They'd sent a bunch of top Conmoy men out to California right after, but nobody in the office would tell me a thing. I might have been part of solving that case, for all I knew.

For all I knew.

Dranes had talked about pounding pavement. Now I was one of a million guys the Agency had out tracing jokes back, teller by teller, but all us lower-echelon guys were supposed to tell the office any time things felt like they were heating up. The fishmonger's stalling probably qualified.

Now he sighed and looked around, like he was afraid someone else was listening. He'd somehow changed his mind about telling me. "Well, I didn't hear it from your pa," he said. "My cousin Dewey is a regular card. When he told that joke it was funny, had a bunch of guys on the floor. Not like when you told it."

"I heard it too many times," I said. "It's not funny to me. Where can I meet your cousin?" As I said it I put the stinking package under my arm and laid another five on top of the one on the counter.

"That's too much for the flounder," he said.

"It's a tip," I said, getting witty. "I'm looking for a tip in return."

"Dewey and Leon Staley," he said, sweeping up the bills. "Staley's Tow and Pull, on Racine Avenue. They're both my cousins, but Dewey's the one with the sense of yuks. Bet he don't know your pa, though." He glared at me.

"Maybe, maybe not," I said. "Dewey and Leon Staley. Thanks."

"Don't get 'em mixed up," he said. "Leon's got a temper on him."

"Right. Thanks." I tossed the package in the trash right outside the fish shop. Its fluid heaviness made me nauseous.

The company car, a Nash Rambler, was parked around the corner. I unfolded my map of Cleveland and found Racine.

Rudy Conmoy himself sat in on my job interview, but it was another man who asked the questions, which included some pretty personal stuff. Family history, schooling, experiences with women. I did my best to make it a shortcut to what I figured they wanted to know: that I could cope with life's seamy underside. I probably sounded like an ass.

Rudy Conmoy broke in and told me a quick joke. It was the one about the chicken who goes into the library. He told it good, and the three of us laughed, me a little nervously.

"That's funny," he said. "Right?" He lit a cigarette and looked at me and I suddenly felt a chill.

"Sure," I said.

"Want to tell me why?" he said.

I thought a minute, but didn't risk anything.

He went on, "It's got animals in it, that's why. Like Bugs Bunny. The things Bugs does, they wouldn't be too funny if they happened to you, right?"

The way he said it made me afraid for Bugs if he ever met up with Conmoy. "No, sir."

"Call me Rudy. Around here, Oscar, jokes with people in them aren't funny. Jokes about violence, jealousy—not funny. They're serious business. They're the business you'll be in if you come work for us."

I just listened.

"You ever read Freud?"

I shook my head.

"Well, you should. Freud tells us how behind every joke there's something wrong, some kind of guilt or pain. Behind some of them there's a crime, Oscar. Not all, but some. Mr. Dranes told you how we find our own work, right?"

"Yes."

"All right." He stubbed out his cigarette, suddenly distracted. "Peter here will get you signed up. Nice meeting you, Oscar."

I found the Tow and Pull. It was a couple of offices fronted by a big lot full of tinker jobs. I wondered how many would ever run again. I parked across the street instead of pulling into the lot, not wanting the company car to attract attention. They sold DeSotos too, and if Dewey Staley was a big talker maybe I could play customer, get him rolling without tipping my hand.

Nobody met me in the lot. I went into the front office and tapped the bell. A grease-covered mechanic poked his head in from the side where he was working. "Leon's on the phone. It's gonna be a minute."

"Where's Dewey?" I said.

He looked at me like how could I want Dewey instead of Leon? But all he said was, "He's back there too."

I saluted him, and he went into the garage. I decided to find the men's. I went back out and around the side, thinking of it like a gas station. I didn't see the john, but there was a screen window, and I heard a voice leaking out.

"—you've got to be kidding, Phil. Nobody's gonna dig that crap back up. I made sure of that."

I crouched down there alongside a pile of fenders and listened.

"A kid with a crewcut. I'll look out for him. Okay. Okay, Phil. I got it covered."

I heard the mouthpiece clatter down into the cradle.

"You and your fucking jokes, Dewey," the voice said angrily.

"I told you I was sorry already," answered a meeker voice.

"Sorry don't cut it. This is costing me."

"But, Leon—"

"What?"

"You sure this isn't just one of Phil's fish stories?" The meeker voice laughed like a hyena.

"You wait," said the other voice humorlessly. "I'm gonna make a call."

I felt a weird thrill go through me. I'd stumbled into something. I was closer than I was supposed to be. I'm not sure I'd completely believed in the Conmoy Method until that moment. Now I believed in a big way.

My instincts were good, too good. I should have turned the case over when I got the hairy eyeball from the fishmonger. But there wasn't a chance in the world I was letting it go now.

I couldn't confront either Staley, not after they'd been warned. I needed another approach. I slipped back out along the side of the office and through the lot, thanking my lucky stars I'd parked across the street.

I drove up Racine a few blocks to a diner, went in and ordered coffee. It was almost two-thirty. I got the waitress to give me the Cleveland White Pages. Leon Staley was in there, Mr. and Mrs., with an address on North Wood. I jotted it in my notepad. Then I flipped to the front and found the post office that serviced North Wood.

I drove to the post office feeling so full of being a private eye I could have inflated the Goodyear Blimp by mouth.

I got directed to the route manager, a fat guy who sat like an octopus plumped in the center of a circle of mail bins. He had yellow, rheumy eyes. A drinking man.

"That's Cohen's route. You got a complaint about the service over there?"

"I'm looking for a guy who was in the service with my brother. Good-looking guy. This would've been a few years ago."

"Oh, Christ."

"What?"

"It isn't Cohen you want. You're thinking of that guy who went missing, whatsisname—" He put two clubby fingers on the tip of his chin.

"Missing?" I felt a hot flush, an intimation of real evil.

"Yeah. Kid about your age, I mean, he was back then. One day he just didn't show up. Missing persons case. Cops were out here about it."

"How long—?"

"Almost five years ago. We've still got his last paycheck in a drawer somewhere. His folks never came by for it."

"Around Christmas?" I said, a little breathlessly.

He began to nod, then stopped and looked at me. "What do you know about it?"

"Never mind. Thanks." I got out of there.

She was the one. I felt it the minute she let me into the house. I'd been telling the joke all week and I felt like I'd entered this house a hundred times already. Of course, it wasn't the house that gave me the feeling. It was her.

Mrs. Staley opened the door and then backed up to let me in like I was bringing an entourage. I shut it behind me and took off my hat.

She was in her thirties, but just, and she had the air of a teenager fitted into the career of housewife before she knew what hit her, before she'd tasted anything of life. Which is to say I imagined I *had* tasted life, enough to judge. All I really knew was that she had the body of an overripe teenager, and it was fitted into her apron with difficulty.

Her face had kept its youthfulness, but it might as well not have bothered, because her eyes ruined the whole effect. They were eyes that had worn themselves out tracing the limits of a cage, like a lioness in a zoo. They weren't hoping to escape anymore, just survive. And they didn't want anyone else coming into the cage without an invitation.

"Tell me again who you work for," she said.

I'd presented myself at the door as working for the Conmoy Insurance Agency. I'd taken my cue from some fake business cards I'd seen in L. J. Dranes's desk. I didn't have the faintest idea how a Conmoy operative actually introduced himself at this juncture. Or whether he did.

"I'm an insurance agent, ma'am," I said. "May I sit down?"

"Here," she said, pulling out a chair at the table in the kitchen nook. "The living room's a mess." She backed away again, as though I were going to somersault into the chair. "Would you like some coffee?"

"Sure," I said, marveling. It was like we were acting it out.

She went into the kitchen, and said from there, "I didn't hear anything from Leon about insurance."

"He took out a policy on his business, but it covers the home too," I said. I craned my neck to see her, but she was out of view. "That's one of the best features."

"Uh huh," she said.

I craned the other way, for a look at the living room. Sofa, Barcalounger, no television, but a big old Victrola. The room wasn't a mess as far as I could see.

She came out with coffee, two cups, and sat with me at the table. She seemed to have calmed herself a little in the kitchen. Popped a couple of mother's little helpers, I wondered? Her mouth didn't look so tense. But her eyes still cried for help.

I was sure I was Lew Archer now, plunging into some stifled past to let the pain and heartbreak free itself, like a doctor opening a festering wound.

"What do you need to see?" she said.

"Talking to you is as important as seeing the place," I said, and gave her my best smile. "Are you around the house most of the time?" It wasn't polite to ask a woman if she worked, those days. Assuming either way could get you in trouble.

"Yes. Why?"

"Premiums are lower if the place isn't left alone."

"Well, I sure fit that description." The boring talk clearly reassured her. She smiled back and took a pack of cigarettes out of a purse that lay on the table. "Care for one?" she said. "They're menthol."

"Sure." I'd only smoked a menthol cigarette once before. I lit hers and then mine. "No kids around," I said. "Why don't you get out more?"

A cloud crossed her expression. "Leon likes me to keep close to home. He wants a meal waiting." She brightened suddenly. "That's okay. That's what I like too."

I smoked and looked her over. "You don't get lonely?"

"Sometimes." She said it to herself. Then she put her cigarette into the ashtray and unlaced her apron and pulled it off, and my breath stopped. Her blouse wasn't as buttoned up as it could have been.

"Your name is Oscar?" she said.

"Oscar Fife," I told her again.

"How old are you, Oscar?"

I added a year. "Twenty-three."

"Do I look old to you?"

"No."

She smiled and picked up her cigarette and stared at me. I had an erection like a frozen Mars Bar.

"You seem like a nice kid, Oscar. Why are you doing this?"

"What?"

"Leon sent you to check up on me. See what I would do."

My jaw fell open. "No."

"Of course he did."

"That's not it at all," I managed.

"Tell me then."

"Is Leon a violent man, Mrs. Staley?"

The look on her face made me feel I'd recaptured the edge in this exchange. I rewarded myself with a drag on the cigarette, which I'd been neglecting. I nearly choked.

"You all right?" she asked.

"Yes, just—" I didn't want to stand because of the boner. "Could you get me some water?"

She went to the kitchen tap and came back with a glass. I gulped half down in one go.

"Don't ignore my question," I said. "Is he violent?"

She didn't say anything.

"You don't have to live like this," I said, throwing caution aside. A goddamn knight in tinfoil, with a stiffy under the table. "You don't have to protect him. Nobody will hurt you if you come forward."

"You'd better say what you mean," she said. Her voice was even but she was gripping the table like she wanted to break off a piece to dunk in her coffee.

"I know about the mailman," I said.

If she'd had a throat full of smoke it would have been her turn to choke. But her cigarette and coffee were on the table between us, growing as chilly as the look in her eyes.

"Would you excuse me for a minute?" she said.

"Sure."

She went upstairs. I heard a door shut, then a murmur that might have been a lowered voice. I thought about sneaking up to listen in case she was making a call. Then I spied the downstairs phone on the wall of the kitchen and thought about picking it up. I didn't do anything, and in a minute she was back downstairs.

It finally occurred to me to wonder where the Agency would find a paying client in a case like this. If Mrs. Staley wanted to cover for her husband, what was the Agency's angle?

That's me in a nutshell: always a step or two behind. If not five or six steps.

I wished all of a sudden that I'd called the Agency after my visit to the fish seller. Or at least that I hadn't told her the name Conmoy, so if I got out of there now my mistake couldn't come back to haunt me.

She only gave me a minute to think about it. Then she put her arms up on my shoulders and played with my hair. "Cute kid," she said quietly. "You should let it grow a little." Then she put her mouth up to mine.

I'd only kissed girls up to that point. Mrs. Staley made a real impression. She smelled like something only Archer would know about.

I don't know how long we stayed like that, me following her

lead. It felt like a lifetime, in a way. I certainly didn't have a look at my watch. The only time I opened my eyes I saw hers were closed.

The Leon Staley came through the door with a gun in his hand.

I hadn't gotten a look at him back at the Tow and Pull. He was at least ten years older than his wife. He was big, too. He looked like a guy who bullied prospective buyers to close deals at the lot. He made the gun look small. Mrs. Staley let me go and moved behind him. I stood there like a dolt.

"You like the way my wife tastes? You're gonna pay for that kiss, kid."

I didn't speak.

"In there," he said, pointing me into the living room with the gun. "Put the needle on the record, then put your hands in the air."

I did what he said. It was a comedy record, Mort Sahl live at the Hungry I. Mort was making fun of John Wayne.

"Make it loud."

"Why?"

"So if I have to shoot you it doesn't bug the neighbors," he said.

I turned it up. "Is that how you did the mailman?"

"Shut up, cop."

"I'm not a cop. I'm a detective."

"Aren't you a little young to make plainclothes?"

"I'm a private detective."

"Give me a break. If you're a private eye who hired you?"

"Conmoy Agency. We find our own work."

"Did you say *Conmoy*?" He looked at me more puzzled than angry for the first time.

"He called it insurance," said Mrs. Staley from the doorway.

"Conmoy?" he said again to me, ignoring her.

"That's right," I said, baffled by this turn.

"Anna, go upstairs," he said, without turning away from me.
"Leon—"

"Go." She went.

"Turn that down," he said to me. I did it. He let the gun sag, and he took another step into the room. "What the fuck is this, some kind of joke?"

"What do you mean?"

"I'm square with Conmoy. I don't need this shit. You shouldn't be coming around here. A deal's a deal."

"What?"

He squinted at me, then pulled the gun up straight again. "No, you don't really work for Conmoy. You're a rookie cop who thinks he's onto something. You're just throwing names around, hoping you'll get lucky."

"If you want to call the Agency you'll see I work for them."

"I already called the damn Agency from the lot, the minute I heard from Phil you were nosing into things. They're on their way up here."

I didn't know what to say to that.

"So just sit and listen to the funny man. We'll see who you work for."

"Can I put my hands down?"

"Go ahead."

We listened to Sahl.

Rudy Conmoy himself walked in about fifteen minutes later, with L.J. Dranes and another guy. They must have started from Cleveland as soon as they got the call. I don't know if Staley knew it was Conmoy he was talking to but Conmoy sure made an impression on him fast. "You did the right thing calling," he said. "We're pretty sure it stops with this kid. Our man inside the Akron force is checking it out, but there doesn't seem to be anything brewing."

"Well, I don't like it," said Staley, making jabbing motions at me with the gun.

"I understand. We'd like to make it up to you, Staley. Consider yourself square with us for a year, how's that?"

"That's something. But what about this kid?"

"We'll take care of him. Dranes, get the kid out of this man's house already."

"Wait a minute," said Staley. "The kid says he's with you."

"Never seen him before," said Conmoy. "But don't you worry about that. We'll figure out who he's with. It's not your problem anymore. Shouldn't have been in the first place."

I'd been practicing keeping my mouth shut, but this was too much. "Mr. Conmoy, tell him—"

"Shut up," said Conmoy in a way that made me do it. "Dranes, I said get him out of here." He opened his wallet, and said to Staley, "You deserve a reward, actually. You shouldn't have to do our work for us—"

I caught how Staley's expression changed when he saw the denomination of the bill in Conmoy's hand, then Dranes pushed me out the door.

We were in the insurance business after all. That was the funny part. The Conmoy Agency was a protection racket, was another way to put it. Dranes lit both our cigarettes and explained it to me in Conmoy's Lincoln while we waited for Conmoy to come out.

"There isn't any margin in solving cases like ours, Oscar. The jokes cover guilt. We do the same thing."

"The office files—that's all stuff you're covering up. You only solve them to put the squeeze on people. Those are blackmail files."

"Blackmail's an unpleasant word, Oscar."

"But why was I on the Mailman case? You already had Staley in your pocket."

"He was one of those fellows who get cocky and don't want to pay. We like to keep the pressure up, make sure the joke stays fresh. Your job was to give him a little hotfoot by getting close, then report back. It's a standard operation."

"You never even put me on an unsolved case?"

"The Gas Station Attendant's Wife was new," he said. "You did a good job with that, Oscar. Conmoy was impressed." He chuckled. "I guess you did a pretty good job on Staley, too." He chuckled a bit more.

Conmoy and his other man came out. "Don't use the word blackmail if you want to keep this job," said Dranes before they got to the car. He pulled the coffin nail out of my mouth and stubbed it into the ashtray.

Conmoy tapped on my window. I rolled it down. "Give me your keys. Andy's going to drive your car back." I gave him the keys, and he passed them to Andy. "Get in the back," he told me.

Dranes took the wheel, and Conmoy got in the passenger seat. He didn't say anything until we got on the highway back to Cleveland. Neither did Dranes.

Finally he said, "You want to star in a joke, Oscar?"

"What?"

"I said do you want to star in a joke?"

"No," I said.

He turned around and leaned over the seat and grabbed me by the collar. "You sure? Because you're close. You're this close." He jammed me back against the seat and the door. "I could put you in a joke in a New York minute." He wasn't yelling, just talking calmly. But there was a little fleck of spit on his lower lip.

"No, Mr. Conmoy."

"You want this job, Oscar?"

"I'm not sure."

"Not sure. Your little prodigy's not sure. Stop the car, Dranes."

"Come on, Rudy," said Dranes.

"Stop the car. I mean it."

We pulled over. It was dark now. We were on a stretch of highway that was nowhere. There was a water tower in the distance, and a ditch at the side of the road.

"Out."

"I'm sorry, Mr. Conmoy."

"Out."

That was some time ago. They left me there on the side of the road and I had to hitch back to Cleveland. Once or twice after that I saw someone I knew was a Conmoy man working security at some public event, but I never saw Dranes or Conmoy himself again. I did another stint in the service before I ended up in the insurance biz for a while, the real insurance biz. Ironic, isn't it.

That's all. What do you want, a punch line?

▪ *George Pelecanos* ▪

WHEN YOU'RE HUNGRY

The woman in the aisle seat to the right of John Moreno tapped him on the shoulder. Moreno swallowed the last of his Skol pilsner to wash down the food in his mouth. He laid his fork across the segmented plastic plate in front of him on a fold-down tray.

"Yes?" he said, taking her in fully for the first time. She was attractive, though one had to look for it, past the thick black eyebrows and the too-wide mouth painted a pale peach color that did no favor to her complexion.

"I don't mean to be rude," she said, in heavily accented English. "But you've been making a lot of noise with your food. Is everything all right?"

Moreno grinned, more to himself than to her. "Yes, I'm fine.

You have to excuse me. I rushed out of the house this morning without breakfast, and then this flight was delayed. I suppose I didn't realize how hungry I was."

"No bother," she said, smiling now, waving the manicured fingers of her long brown hand. "I'm not complaining. I'm a doctor, and I thought that something might be wrong."

"Nothing that some food couldn't take care of." They looked each other over. Then he said, "You're a doctor in what city?"

"A pediatrician," she said. "In Bahia Salvador. Are you going to Bahia?"

Moreno shook his head. "Recife."

So they would not meet again. Just as well. Moreno preferred to pay for his companionship while under contract.

"Recife is lovely," the woman said, breathing out with a kind of relief, the suspense between them now broken. "Are you on a holiday?"

"Yes," he said. "A holiday."

"Illiana," she said, extending her hand across the armrest.

"John Moreno." He shook her hand, and took pleasure in the touch.

The stewardess came, a round woman with rigid red hair, and took their plates. Moreno locked the tray in place. He retrieved his guidebook from the knapsack under the seat, and read.

Brazil is a land of great natural beauty, and a country unparalleled in its ideal of racial democracy. . . .

Moreno flipped past the rhetoric of the guidebook, went directly to the meat: currency, food and drink, and body language. Not that Brazil would pose any sort of problem for him; in his fifteen-odd years in the business, there were very few places in the world where he had not quickly adapted. This adaptability made him one of the most marketable independents in his field. And it was why, one week earlier, on the first Tuesday of September, he had been called to the downtown Miami office of Mr. Carlos Garcia, Vice-president of Claims, United Casualty and Life.

Garcia was a trim man with closely cropped, tightly curled hair. He wore a wide-lapelled suit of charcoal gray, a somber color for Miami, and a gray and maroon tie with an orderly geometric design. A phone sat on his lacquered desk, along with a blank notepad, upon which rested a silver Cross pen.

Moreno sat in a leather chair with chrome arms across from Garcia's desk. Garcia's secretary served coffee, and after a few sips and the necessary exchange of pleasantries, Moreno asked Garcia to describe the business at hand.

Garcia told him about Guzman, a man in his fifties who had made and then lost some boom-years money in South Florida real estate. Guzman had taken his pleasure boat out of Key Largo one day in the summer of 1992. Two days later his wife reported him missing, and a week after that the remains of his boat were found, along with a body, two miles out to sea. Guzman and his vessel had been the victims of an unexplained explosion on board.

"Any crew?" asked Moreno.

"Just Guzman."

"A positive identification on the body?"

"Well. The body was badly burned. Horribly burned. And most of what was left went to the fish."

"How about his teeth?"

"Guzman wore dentures." Garcia smiled wanly. "Interesting, no?"

The death benefits of Guzman's term policy, a two-million-dollar payoff, went to the widow. United's attorneys fought it to a point, but the effort from the outset was perfunctory. The company absorbed the loss.

Then, a year later, a neighbor of the Guzmans was vacationing in Recife, a city and resort on the northeast coast of Brazil, and spotted who she thought was Guzman. She saw this man twice in one week, on the same beach. By the time she returned to the

States, she had convinced herself that she had in fact seen Guzman. She went to the widow with her suspicions, who seemed strangely unconcerned. Then she went to the police.

"And the police kicked it to you," Moreno said.

"They don't have the jurisdiction, or the time. We have a man on the force who keeps us informed in situations like this."

"So the widow wasn't too shook up by the news."

"No," Garcia said. "But that doesn't prove or even indicate any kind of complicity. We see many different kinds of emotions in this business upon the death of a spouse. The most common emotion that we see is relief."

Moreno folded one leg over the other, and tented his hands in his lap. "What have you done so far?"

"We sent a man down to Brazil, an investigator named Roberto Silva."

"And?"

"Silva became very drunk one night. He left his apartment in Recife to buy a pack of cigarettes, stepped into an open elevator shaft, and fell eight stories to his death. He was found the next morning with a broken neck."

"Accidents happen."

Garcia spread his hands. "Silva was a good operative. I sent him because he was fluent in Portuguese, and because he had a history of success. But I knew that he had a very bad problem with alcohol. I had seen him fall down myself, on more than one occasion. This time, he simply fell a very long way."

Moreno stared through the window at the Miami skyline. After a while he said, "This looks to be a fairly simple case. There is a man in a particular area of Recife who either is or is not Guzman. I will bring you this man's fingerprints. It should take no more than two weeks."

"What do you require?"

"I get four hundred a day, plus expenses."

"Your terms are reasonable," Garcia said.

"There's more," Moreno said, holding up his hand. "My expenses are unlimited, and not to be questioned. I fly first-class, and require an apartment with a live-in maid to cook and to clean my clothes. And, I get two and one half percent of the amount recovered."

"That's fifty thousand dollars."

"Correct," Moreno said, standing out of his seat. "I'll need a half-dozen wallet-size photographs of Guzman, taken as close to his death date as possible. You can send them along with my contract and travel arrangements to my home address."

John Moreno shook Garcia's hand, and walked away from the desk.

Garcia said to Moreno's back, "It used to be 'Juan,' didn't it? Funny how the simple change of a name can open so many doors in this country."

"I can leave for Brazil at any time," Moreno said. "You know where to reach me."

Moreno opened Mr. Garcia's door and walked from the office. The next morning, a package was messengered to John Moreno's home address.

And now Moreno's plane neared the Brasilia airport. He closed the guidebook he had been reading, and turned to Illiana.

"I have a question for you, Doctor," Moreno said. "A friend married a first-generation American of Brazilian descent. Their children, both of them, were born with blue-black spots above their buttocks."

Illiana smiled. "Brazil is a land whose people come from many colors," she said, sounding very much like the voice of the guidebook. "Black, white, brown, and many colors in between. Those spots that you saw"—and here Illiana winked—"it was simply the nigger in them."

So much for the ideal of Racial Democracy, Moreno thought, as the plane began its descent.

Moreno caught a ride from the airport with a man named Eduardo, who divided his time as an importer/exporter between

Brasilia and Miami. They had struck up a conversation as they waited in line to use the plane's lavoratory during the flight. They were met at the airport by someone named Val, who Eduardo introduced as his attorney, a title which Moreno doubted, as Val was a giggly and rather silly young man. Still, he accepted a lift in Val's VW Santana, and after a seventy-mile-per-hour ride through the flat treeless landscape that was Brasilia, Moreno was dropped at the Hotel Dos Nachos, a place Eduardo had described with enthusiasm as "two and one half stars."

The lobby of the Hotel Dos Nachos contained several potted plants and four high-backed chairs occupied by two taxicab drivers, an aging tout in a shiny gray suit, and a bearded man smoking a meerschaum pipe. A drunken businessman accompanied by a mulatto hooker in a red leather skirt entered the lobby and walked up the stairs while Moreno negotiated the room rate. The hotel bellman stood sleeping against the wall. Moreno carried his own bags through the elevator doors.

Moreno opened the windows of his small brown room and stuck his head out. Below, in an empty lot, a man sat beneath a Pepsi-Cola billboard with this face buried in his hands, a manged dog asleep at his feet. Moreno closed the window to a crack, stripped to his shorts, did four sets of fifty pushups, showered, and went to bed.

The next morning he caught an early flight to Recife. At the airport he hailed a taxi. Several foul-smelling children begged Moreno for change as he sat in the passenger seat of the cab, waiting for the driver to stow his bags. Moreno stared straight ahead as the children reached in his window, rubbing their thumbs and forefingers together in front of his face. Before the cab pulled away, one of the children, a dark boy with matted blond hair, cursed under his breath, and dropped one American penny in Moreno's lap.

Moreno had the cab driver pass through Boa Viagem, Recife's resort center, to get his bearings. When Moreno had a general idea of the layout the driver dropped him at his *apartamento* in the nine hundred block of Rua Setubal, one street back from the beach. A uniformed guard stood behind the glassed-in gatehouse at the ten-story condominium; Moreno tipped him straight off, and carried his own bags through the patio of hibiscus and standing palm to the small lift.

Moreno's *apartamento* was on the ninth floor, a serviceable arrangement of one large living and dining room, two bedrooms, two baths, a dimly lit kitchen, and a windowless sleeper porch on the west wall where clothes were hung to dry in the afternoon sun. The east wall consisted of sliding glass doors that opened to a concrete balcony finished in green tile. The balcony gave to an unobstructed view of the beach and the aquamarine and emerald swells of the south Atlantic, and to the north and south the palm-lined beach road, Avenida Boa Viagem. The sliding glass doors were kept open at all times: a tropical breeze blew constantly through the *apartamento,* and the breeze insured the absence of bugs.

For the first few days Moreno stayed close to his condominium, spending his mornings at the beach working on his local's tan, watching impromptu games of soccer, and practicing his Portuguese on the vendors selling oysters, nuts, and straw hats. At one o'clock his maid, a pleasant but silent woman named Sonya, prepared him huge lunches, black beans and rice, salad, mashed potatoes, and pork roasted and seasoned with *tiempero,* a popular spice. In the evenings Moreno would visit a no-name, roofless café, where a photograph of Madonna was taped over the bar. He would sit beneath a coconut palm and eat a wonderfully prepared filet of fish, washed down with a cold Brahma beer, sometimes with a shot of aguardente, the national rotgut that tasted of rail tequila but had a nice warm kick. After dinner he would stop at the Kiosk, a kind of bakery and convenience market, and buy a bottle of Brazilian cabernet, have a glass or two of that on the balcony of his *apartamento* before going off to bed. The crow of a nearby rooster woke him every morning through his open window at dawn.

Sometimes Moreno passed the time leaning on the tile rim of his balcony, looking down on the activity in the street below. There were high walls of brick and cinderblock around all the neighboring condominiums and estates, and it seemed as if these walls were in a constant state of repair or decay. Occasionally an old white mare, unaccompanied by cart or harness, would clomp down the street, stopping to graze on the patches of grass that sprouted along the edges of the sidewalk. And directly below his balcony, through the leaves of the black curaçao tree that grew in front of his building, Moreno saw children crawl into the gray canvas Dumpster that sat by the curb, and root through the garbage in search of something to eat.

Moreno watched these children with a curious but detached eye. He had known poverty himself, but he had no sympathy for those who chose to remain within its grasp. If one was hungry, one worked. To be sure, there were different degrees of dignity in what one did to get by. But there was always work.

As the son of migrant workers raised in various Tex/Mex border towns, Juan Moreno had vowed early on to escape the shackles of his own lowly, inherited status. He left his parents at sixteen to work for a man in Austin, so that he could attend the region's best high school. By sticking to his schedule of classes during the day and studying and working diligently at night, he was able with the help of government loans to gain entrance to a moderately prestigious university in New England, where he quickly learned the value of lineage and presentation. He changed his name to John.

Already fluent in Spanish, John Moreno became degreed in both French and criminology. After graduation he moved south, briefly joining the Dade County sheriff's office. Never one for violence and not particularly interested in carrying or using a firearm, Moreno took a job for a relatively prestigious firm specializing in international retrievals. Two years later, having made the necessary connections and something of a reputation for himself, he struck out on his own.

John Moreno liked his work. Most of all, whenever his plane left the runway and he settled into his first-class seat, he felt a kind of elusion, as if he were leaving the dust and squalor of his early years a thousand miles behind. Each new destination was another permanent move, one step farther away.

The Brazilians are a touching people. Often men will hug for minutes on end, and women will walk arm and arm in the street.

Moreno put down his guidebook on the morning of the fourth day, did his four sets of fifty pushups, showered, and changed into a swimsuit. He packed his knapsack with some American dollars, ten dollars worth of Brazilian cruzeiros, his long-lensed Canon AE-I, and the Guzman photographs, and left the *apartamento*.

Moreno was a lean man a shade under six feet, with wavy black hair and a thick black mustache. His vaguely Latin appearance passed for both South American and southern Mediterranean, and with his newly enriched tan he received scarcely a look as he moved along the Avenida Boa Viagem toward the center of the resort, the area where Guzman had been spotted. The beach crowd grew denser, women in thong bathing suits and men in their Speedos, vendors, hustlers, and shills.

Moreno claimed a striped folding chair near the beach wall, signaled a man behind a cooler, who brought him a tall Antarctica beer served in a Styrofoam thermos. He finished that one and had two more, drinking very slowly to pass away the afternoon. He was not watching for Guzman. Instead he watched the crowd, and the few men who sat alone and unmoving on its periphery. By the end of the day he had chosen two of those men: a brown Rasta with sun-bleached dreadlocks who sat by the vendors but did not appear to have goods to sell, and an old man with the leathery, angular face of an Indian who had not moved from his seat at the edge of the market across the street.

As the sun dropped behind the condominiums and the beach draped in shadow, Moreno walked over to the Rasta on the wall, and handed him a photograph of Guzman. The Rasta smiled a mouthful of stained teeth, and rubbed two fingers together. Moreno gave him ten American dollars, holding out another ten immediately and quickly replacing it in his own pocket. He touched the photograph, then pointed to the striped folding chair near the wall to let the Rasta know where he could find him. The Rasta nodded, then smiled again, making a "V" with his fingers and touching his lips, blowing out with an exaggerated exhale.

"Fumo?" the Rasta said.

"Não fumo," Moreno said, jabbing his finger at the photograph once more before he left.

Moreno crossed the road and found the old man at the edge of the market. He replayed the same proposition with the man. The man never looked at Moreno, though he accepted the ten and slid it and the photograph into the breast pocket of his eggplant-colored shirt. Moreno could not read a thing in the man's black pupils in the dying afternoon light.

As Moreno turned to cross the street, the old man said in Portuguese, "You will return?"

Moreno said, *"Amanha,"* and walked away.

On the way back to his place Moreno stopped at a food stand—little more than a screened-in shack on the beach road—and drank a cold Brahma beer. Afterward he walked back along the beach, now lit by streetlamps in the dusk. A girl of less than twenty with a lovely mouth smiled as she passed his way, her hair fanning out in the wind. Moreno felt a brief pulse in his breastbone, remembering just then that he had not been with a woman for a very long time.

It was this forgotten need for a woman, Moreno decided, as he watched his maid Sonya prepare breakfast the next morning in her surf shorts and T-shirt, that had thrown off his rhythms in Brazil. He would have to remedy that, while of course expending as little energy as possible in the hunt. First things first, which was to check on his informants in the center of Boa Viagem.

He was there within the hour, seated on his striped folding chair, on a day when the sun came through high, rapidly moving clouds. His men were there too, the Rasta on the wall and the old man at the edge of the market. Moreno had an active swim in the warm Atlantic early in the afternoon, going out beyond the reef, then returned to his seat and ordered a beer. By the time the vendor served it the old man with the Indian features was moving across the sand toward Moreno's chair.

"*Boa tarde,*" Moreno said, squinting up in the sun.

The old man pointed across the road, toward an outdoor café that led to an enclosed bar and restaurant. A middle-aged man and a young woman were walking across the patio toward the open glass doors of the bar.

"*Bom,*" Moreno said, handing the old man the promised ten from his knapsack. He left one hundred and twenty thousand cruzeiros beneath the full bottle of beer, gestured to the old man to sit and drink it, put his knapsack over his shoulder, and took the stone steps from the beach up to the street. The old man sat in the striped folding chair without a word.

Moreno crossed the street with caution, looking back to catch a glimpse of the brown Rasta sitting on the wall. The Rasta stared unsmiling at Moreno, knowing he had lost. Moreno was secretly glad it had been the old man, who had reminded him of his own father. Moreno had not thought of his long-dead father or even seen him in his dreams for some time.

Moreno entered the restaurant. There were few patrons, and all of them, including the middle-aged man and his woman, sat at a long mahogany bar. Moreno took a chair near an open window. He leaned his elbow on the ledge of the window and drummed his fingers against wood to the florid music coming from the restaurant. The bartender, a stocky man with a great belly that plunged over the belt of his trousers, came from behind the bar and walked towards Moreno's table.

"*Cervejas*," Moreno said, holding up three fingers pressed together to signify a tall one. The bartender stopped in his tracks, turned, and headed back behind the bar.

Moreno drank his beer slowly, studying the couple seated at the bar. He considered taking some photographs, seeing that this could be done easily, but he decided that it was not necessary, as he was certain now that he had found Guzman. The man had ordered his second drink, a Teacher's rocks, in English, drinking his first hurriedly and without apparent pleasure. He was tanned and seemed fit, with a full head of silvery hair and the natural girth of age. The woman was in her twenties, quite beautiful in a lush way, with the stone perfect but bloodless look of a photograph in a magazine. She wore a bathing suit top, two triangles of red cloth really, with a brightly dyed sarong wrapped around the bottoms. Occasionally the man would nod in response to something she had said; on those occasions, the two of them did not look in each other's eyes.

Eventually the other patrons finished their drinks and left, and for a while it was just the stocky bartender, the man and his woman, and Moreno. A very tall, lanky young man with long, curly hair walked into the bar and with wide strides went directly to the man and whispered in his ear. The man finished his drink in one gulp, tossed bills on the bar, and got off his stool. He, the woman, and the young man walked from the establishment without even a glance in Moreno's direction. Moreno knew he had been made but in a practical sense did not care. He opened his knapsack, rose from his seat, and headed for the bar.

Moreno stopped in the area where the party had been seated and ordered another beer. As the bartender turned his back to reach into a cooler, Moreno grabbed some bar napkins, wrapped them around the base of Guzman's empty glass, and began to place the glass in his knapsack.

A hand grabbed Moreno's wrist.

The hand gripped him firmly. Moreno smelled perspiration,

partly masked by a rather obvious men's cologne. He turned his head. It was the lanky young man, who had reentered the bar.

"You shouldn't do that," the young man said in accented English. "My friend João here might think you are trying to steal his glass."

Moreno placed the glass back on the bar. The young man spoke rapidly in Portuguese, and João the bartender took the glass and ran it over the brush in the soap sink. Then João served Moreno the beer that he had ordered, along with a clean glass. Moreno took a sip. The young man did not look more than twenty. His skin had the color of coffee bean, with hard bright eyes the color of the skin. Moreno put down his glass.

"You've been following my boss," the young man said.

"Really," Moreno said.

"Yes, really." The young man grinned. "Your Rastaman friend, the one you showed the pictures to. He don't like you so good no more."

Moreno looked out at the road through the open glass doors. "What now?"

"Maybe me and a couple of my friends," the young man said, "now we're going to kick your ass."

Moreno studied the young man's face, went past the theatrical menace, found light play in the dark brown eyes. "I don't think so. There's no buck in it for you, that way."

The young man laughed shortly, pointed at Moreno. "That's right!" His expression grew earnest again. "Listen, I tell you what. We've had plenty excitement today, plenty enough. How about you and me, we sleep on top of things, think it over, see what we're going to do. Okay?"

"Sure," Moreno said.

"I'll pick you up in the morning, we'll go for a ride, away from here, where we can talk. Sound good?"

Moreno wrote his address on a bar napkin. The young man took it, and extended his hand.

"Guilherme," he said. "Gil."

"Moreno."

They shook hands, and Gil began to walk away.

"You speak good American," Moreno said.

Gil stopped at the doors, grinned, and held up two fingers. "New York," he said. "Astoria. Two years." And then he was out the door.

Moreno finished his beer, left money on the bar. He walked back to his *apartamento* in the gathering darkness.

Moreno stood drinking coffee on his balcony the next morning, waiting for Gil to arrive. He realized that this involvement with the young man was going to cost him money, but it would speed things along. And he was not surprised that Guzman had been located with such ease. In his experience those who fled their old lives merely settled for an equally monotonous one in a different place, and rarely moved after that. The beachfront hut in Pago Pago becomes as stifling as the center hall colonial in Bridgeport.

Gil pulled over to the curb in his blue sedan. He got out and greeted the guard at the gate, a man Moreno had come to know as Sergio, who buzzed Gil through. Sergio left the glassed-in guardhouse then and approached Gil on the patio. Sergio broke suddenly into some sort of cartwheel, and Gil stepped away from his spinning feet, moved around Sergio fluidly and got him into a headlock. They were doing some sort of local martial art, which Moreno had seen practiced widely by young men on the beach. Sergio and Gil broke away laughing, Gil giving Sergio the thumbs-up before looking up toward Moreno's balcony and catching his eye. Moreno shouted that he'd be down in a minute, handing his coffee cup to Sonya. Moreno liked this kid Gil, though he was not sure why.

They drove out of Boa Viagem in Gil's Chevrolet Monsa, into downtown Recife, where the breeze stopped and the temperature rose an abrupt ten degrees. Then they were along a sewage canal near the docks, and across the canal a kind of shantytown of tar paper, fallen cinderblock, and chicken wire, where Moreno could make out a sampling of the residents: horribly poor families, morning drunks, two-dollar prostitutes, men with murderous eyes, criminals festering inside of children.

"It's pretty bad here now," Gil said, "though not so bad like in Rio. In Rio they cut your hand off just to get your watch. Not even think about it."

"The *Miami Herald* says your government kills street kids in Rio."

Gil chuckled. "You Americans are so righteous."

"Self-righteous," Moreno said.

"Yes, self-righteous. I lived in New York City, remember? I've seen the blacks and the Latins, the things that are kept from them. There are many ways for a government to kill the children it does not want, no?"

"I suppose so."

Gil studied Moreno at the stoplight as the stench of raw sewage rode in on the heat through their open windows. "Moreno, eh? You're some sort of Latino, aren't you?"

"I'm an American."

"Sure, American. Maybe you want to forget." Gil jerked his thumb across the canal, toward the shantytown. "Me, I don't forget. I come from a *favela* just like that, in the south. Still, I don't believe in being poor. There is always a way to get out, if one works. You know?"

Moreno knew now why he liked this kid Gil.

They drove over a bridge that spanned the inlet to the ocean, then took a gradual rise to the old city of Olinda, settled and burned by the Dutch in the fifteenth century. Gil parked on cobblestone near a row of shops and vendors, where Moreno bought a piece of local art carved from wood for his mother. Moreno would send the gift along to her in Nogales, a custom that made him feel generous, despite the fact that he rarely phoned her, and it had been three Christmases since he had seen her last. Afterward Moreno visited a bleached church, five hundred years old, and was greeted at the door by an old nun dressed completely in white. Moreno left cruzeiros near the simple altar, then absently did his cross. He was not a religious man, but he was a superstitious one, a remnant of his youth spent in Mexico, though he would deny all that.

Gil and Moreno took a table shaded by palms near a grille set on a patio across from the church. They ordered one tall beer and two plastic cups. A boy approached them selling spices, and Gil dismissed him, shouting something as an afterthought to his back. The boy returned with one cigarette, which he lit on the embers of the grille before handing it to Gil. Gil gave the boy some coins, and waved him away.

"So," Gil said, "what are we going to talk about today?"

"The name of your boss," Moreno said. "It's Guzman, isn't it?"

Gil dragged on his cigarette, exhaled slowly. "His name, it's not important. But if you want to call him Guzman, it's okay."

"What do you do for him?"

"I'm his driver, and his interpreter. This is what I do in Recife. I hang around Boa Viagem and I watch for the wealthy tourists having trouble with the money and the language. The Americans, they have the most trouble of all. Then, I make my pitch. Sometimes it works out for me pretty good."

"You learned English in New York?"

"Yeah. A friend brought me over, got me a job as a driver for this limo service he worked for. You know, the guys who stand at the airport, holding signs. I learned the language fast, and real good. The business, too. In one year I showed the man how to cut his costs by thirty percent. The man put me in charge. I even had to fire my friend, too. Anyway, the man finally offered me half the company to run it all the way. I turned him down, you know? His offer, it was too low. That's when I came back to Brazil."

Moreno watched the palm shadows wave dreamily across Gil's face. "What about Guzman's woman?"

"She's some kinda woman, no?"

"Yes," Moreno said. "When I was a child I spotted a coral snake and thought it was the most beautiful thing I had ever seen. I started to follow it into the brush, when my mother slapped me very hard across the face."

"So now you are careful around pretty things." Gil took some smoke from his cigarette. "It's a good story. But this woman is not a poisonous snake. She is just a woman." Gil shrugged. "Anyway, I don't know her. So she cannot help us."

Moreno said, "Can you get me Guzman's fingerprints?"

"Sure," Gil said. "It's not a problem. But what you are going to get me?"

"Go ahead and call it," Moreno said.

"I was thinking, fifty-fifty, what you get."

Moreno frowned. "For two weeks, you know, I'm only going to make a couple thousand dollars. But I'll tell you what—you get me Guzman's fingerprints, and I'll give you one thousand American."

Gil wrinkled his forehead. "It's not much, you know?"

"For this country, I think that it's a lot."

"And," Gil continued quickly, "you got to consider. You, or the people you work for, maybe they're going to come down and take my boss and his money away. And then Gil, he's going to be out of a job."

Moreno sat back and had a swig of beer and let Gil chew things over. After a while Gil leaned forward.

"Okay," Gil said. "So let me ask you something. Have you reported back to your people that you think you have spotted this man Guzman?"

"No," Moreno said. "It's not the way I work. Why?"

"I was thinking. Maybe my boss, it's worth a lot of money to him that you don't go home and tell anyone you saw him down here. So I'm going to talk to him, you know? And then I'm going to call you tomorrow morning. Okay?"

Moreno nodded slowly. "Okay."

Gil touched his plastic cup to Moreno's and drank. "I guess now," Gil said, "I work for you too."

"I guess you do."

"So anything I can get you, Boss?"

Moreno thought about it, and smiled. "Yes," he said. "There is one thing."

They drove back down from Olinda into Recife where the heat and Gil's cologne briefly nauseated Moreno, then on into Boa Viagem where things were cooler and brighter and the people looked healthy and there were not so many poor. Gil parked the Monsa a few miles north of the center, near a playground set directly on the beach.

"There is one," Gil said, pointing to a woman, young and lovely in denim shorts, pushing a child on a swing. "And there is another." This time he pointed to the beach, where a plainer woman, brown and finely figured in her thong bathing suit, shook her blanket out on the sand.

Moreno wiped some sweat from his brow and nodded his chin toward the woman in the bathing suit. "That's the one I want," he said, as the woman bent over to smooth out her towel. "And that's the way I want her."

Gil made the arrangements with the woman, then dropped Moreno at his *apartamento* on the Rue Setubal. After that he met some friends on the beach for a game of soccer, and when the game was done he bathed in the ocean. He let the sun dry him, then drove to Guzman's place, an exclusive condominium called Des Viennes on the Avenida Boa Viagem. Gil knew the guard on duty, who buzzed him through.

Ten minutes later he sat in Guzman's living room overlooking the Atlantic where today a group of sailboats tacked back and forth while a helicopter from a television station circled overhead.

Guzman and Gil sat facing each other in heavily cushioned arm-chairs, while Guzman's woman sat in an identical armchair but facing out toward the ocean. Guzman's maid served them three aguardentes with fresh lime and sugar over crushed ice. Guzman and Gil touched glasses and drank.

"It's too much sugar and not enough lime," Guzman said to no one in particular.

"No," Gil said. "I think it's okay."

Guzman set down his drink on a marble table whose center-piece was a marble obelisk. "How did it go this morning with the American?"

But Gil was now talking in Portuguese to Guzman's woman, who answered him contemptuously without turning her head. Gil laughed sharply and sipped from his drink.

"She's beautiful," Guzman said. "But I don't think you can af-ford her."

"She is not my woman," Gil said cheerfully. "And anyway, the beach is very wide." Gil's smile turned down and he said to Guz-man, "Dismiss her. Okay, Boss?"

Guzman put the words together in butchered Portuguese, and the woman got out of her seat and walked glacially from the room.

Guzman stood from his own seat and went to the end of the living room where the balcony began. He had the look of a man who is falling to sleep with the certain knowledge that his dreams will not be good.

"Tell me about the American," Guzman said.

"His name is Moreno," Gil said. "I think we need to talk."

Moreno went down to the condominium patio after dark and waited for the woman on the beach to arrive. A shirtless boy with kinky brown hair walked by pushing a wooden cart, stopped and put his hand through the iron bars. Moreno ignored him, prac-ticing his Portuguese instead with Sergio, who was on duty that night behind the glass guardhouse. The shirtless boy left without complaint and climbed into the canvas Dumpster that sat by the curb, where he found a few scraps of wet garbage that he could chew and swallow and perhaps keep down. The woman from the beach arrived in a taxi, and Moreno paid the driver and received a wink from Sergio before he led the woman up to his *apartamento*.

Moreno's maid Sonya served a meal of whole roasted chicken, black beans and rice, and salad, with a side of shrimp sauteed in coconut milk and spice. Moreno sent Sonya home with extra cruzeiros, and corked the wine, a Brazilian cabernet, himself. He poured the wine and before he drank asked the woman her name. She touched a finger to a button on her blouse and said, "Claudia."

Moreno knew the dinner was unnecessary but it pleased him to sit across the table from a woman and share a meal. Her rather flat, wide features did nothing to excite him, but the memory of her fullness on the beach kept his interest, and she laughed easily and seemed to enjoy the food, especially the chicken, which she cleaned to the bone.

After dinner Moreno reached across the table and undid the top two buttons of the woman's blouse, and as she took the cue and began to undress he pointed her to the open glass doors that led to the balcony. He extinguished the lights and stepped out of his trousers as she walked naked across the room to the edge of the doors and stood with her palms pressed against the glass. He came behind her and moistened her with his fingers, then entered her, and kissed her cheek near the edge of her mouth, faintly tasting the grease that lingered from the chicken. The breeze came off the ocean and whipped her hair across his face. He closed his eyes.

Moreno fell to sleep that night alone, hearing from someplace very far away a woman's voice, singing mournfully in Spanish.

Moreno met Gil the following morning at the screened-in food shack on the beach road. They sat at a cable-spool table, splitting a beer near a group of teenagers listening to accordion-drive *ferro* music from a transistor radio. The teenagers were drinking beer. Gil had come straight from the beach, his long curly hair still damp and touching his thin bare shoulders.

"So," Gil said, tapping his index finger once on the wood of the table. "I think I got it all arranged."

"You talked to Guzman?"

"Yes. I don't know if he's going to make a deal. But he has agreed to meet with you and talk."

Moreno looked through the screen at the clouds and around the clouds the brilliant blue of the sky. "When and where?"

"Tonight," Gil said. "Around nine o'clock. There's a place off your street, Setubal, where it meets the commercial district. There are many fruit stands there—"

"I know the place."

"Good. Behind the largest stand is an alley. The alley will take you to a bar that is not marked."

"An alley."

"Don't worry," Gil said, waving his hand. "Some friends of mine will be waiting for you to show you to the bar. I'll bring Guzman, and we will meet you there."

"Why that place?"

"I know the man, very well, who runs the bar. He will make sure that Guzman leaves his fingerprints for you. Just in case he doesn't want to play football."

"Play ball," Moreno said.

"Yes. So either way we don't lose."

Moreno drank off the rest of his beer, placed the plastic cup on the cable-spool table. "Okay," he said to Gil. "Your plan sounds pretty good."

In the evening Moreno did four sets of fifty push-ups, showered, and dressed in a black polo shirt tucked into jeans. He left his *apartamento* and took the lift down to the patio, where he waved to a guard he did not recognize before exiting the grounds of his condominium and hitting the street.

He walked north on Setubal at a brisk pace, avoiding the large holes in the sidewalk and sidestepping the stacks of brick and cinderblock used to repair the walls surrounding the estates. He passed his no-name café, where a rat crossed his path and dropped into the black slots of a sewer grate. He walked by people who did not meet his eyes and bums who held out their hands but did not speak.

After about a mile he could see through the darkness to the lights of the commercial district, and then he was near the fruit stands. In the shadows he could see men sitting, quietly talking and laughing. He walked behind the largest of the stands. In the mouth of an alley a boy stood leaning on a homemade crutch, one badly polioed leg twisted at the shin, the callused toes of that leg pointed down and brushing the concrete. The boy looked up at Moreno and rubbed his fingers together, and Moreno fumbled in his pockets for some change, nervously dropping some bills to the sidewalk. Moreno stooped to pick up the bills, handing them to the boy, then he entered the alley. He could hear *ferro* music playing up ahead.

He looked behind him, and saw that the crippled boy was following him into the alley. Moreno quickened his step, passing vendors' carts and brick walls whitewashed and covered with graffiti. He saw an arrow painted on a wall, and beneath the arrow the names of some boys, and an anarchy symbol, and to the right of that the words "Sonic Youth." He followed the direction of the arrow, the music growing louder with each step.

Then he was in a wide open area that was no longer an alley because it had ended with walls on three sides. There were four men waiting for him there.

One of the men was short and very dark and held a machete at his side. The crippled boy was leaning against one of the walls. Moreno said something with a stutter and tried to smile. He did not know if he had said it in Portuguese or in English, or if it mattered, as the *ferro* music playing from a boombox on the cobblestones was very loud.

Moreno felt a wetness on his thigh and knew that this wetness was his own urine. The thing to do was to simply turn and run. But for the first time he saw that one of the men was Sergio, the guard at his condominium, who he had not recognized out of his uniform.

Moreno laughed, and then all of the men laughed, including Sergio, who walked towards Moreno with open arms to greet him.

The Brazilians are a touching people. Often men will hug for minutes on end, and women will walk arm and arm in the street.

Moreno allowed Sergio to give him the hug. He felt the big muscled arms around him, and caught the stench of cheap wine on Sergio's breath. Sergio smiled an unfamiliar smile, and Moreno tried to step back, but Sergio did not release him. Then the other men were laughing again, the man with the machete and the crippled boy too. Their laughter rode on the sound of the crazy music blaring in the alley.

Sergio released Moreno.

A forearm from behind locked across Moreno's neck. There was a hand on the back of his head, pressure, and a violent movement, then a sudden, unbelievable pain, a white pain but without light. For a brief moment Moreno imagined that he was looking at his own chest from a very odd angle.

If John Moreno could have spoken later on, he would have told you that the arm that killed him smelled heavily of perspiration and cheap cologne.

Gil knocked on Guzman's door late that night. The maid offered him a drink. He asked for aguardente straight up. She returned with it and served it in the living room, where Gil sat facing Guzman, and then she walked back to the kitchen to wash the dishes before she went to bed.

Guzman had his own drink, a Teacher's over ice, on the marble table in front of him. He ran his fingers slowly through his lion's head of silver hair.

"Where is your woman?" Gil said.

"She took a walk," Guzman said. "Is it over?"

"Yes," Gil said. "It is done."

"All this killing," Guzman said softly.

"You killed a man yourself. The one who took your place on the boat."

"I had him killed. He was just a rummy from the boatyard."

"It's all the same," Gil said. "But maybe you have told yourself that it is not."

Guzman took his scotch and walked to the open glass doors near the balcony, where it was cooler and there was not the smell that was coming off Gil.

"You broke his neck, I take it. Like the other one."

"He has no neck," Gil said. "We cut his head off and threw it in the garbage. The rest of him we cut to pieces."

Guzman closed his eyes. "But they'll come now. Two of their people have disappeared."

"Yes," Gil said. "They'll come. You have maybe a week. Argentina would be good for you, I think. I could get you a new passport, make the arrangements—"

"For a price."

"Of course."

Guzman turned and stared at the lanky young man. Then he said, "I'll get your money."

When he returned, Gil was downing the last of his drink. Guzman handed him five banded stacks of American fifties. Gil slipped them into his trousers after a careless count.

"Twenty-five thousand," Guzman said. "Now you've taken fifty thousand of my money."

"You split the two million with your wife. And there have been many others to pay." Gil shrugged. "It costs a lot to become a new man, you know? Anyway, I'll see you later."

Gil headed for the door, and Guzman stopped him.

"I'm curious," Guzman said. "Why did this Moreno die, instead of me?"

"His bid was very low," Gil said. "Goodnight, Boss."

Gil walked from the room.

Down on the Avenida Boa Viagem, Gil walked to his Chevrolet Monsa and got behind the wheel. Guzman's woman, who was called Elena, was in the passenger seat, waiting for Gil to arrive. She leaned across the center console and kissed Gil on the lips, holding the kiss for a very long while. It was Gil who finally broke away.

"Did you get the money?" Elena said.

"Yes," Gil said. "I got it." He spoke without emotion. He looked up through the windshield to the yellow light spilling onto Guzman's balcony.

"We are rich," Elena said, forcing herself to smile and pinching Gil's arm.

"There's more up there," Gil said. "You know?"

Elena said, "You scare me a little bit, Gil."

She went into her purse, found a cigarette, and fired the cigarette off the lighter from the dash. After a couple of drags she passed the cigarette to Gil.

"What was it like?" Elena said.

"What's that?"

"When you killed this one," she said. "When you broke his neck. Did it make a sound?"

Gil dragged on the cigarette, squinted against the smoke that rose off the ash.

"You know how it is when you eat a chicken," he said. "You have to break many bones if you want to get the meat. But you don't hear the sound, you know?

"You don't hear it," Gil said, looking up at Guzman's balcony, "when you're hungry."

Mark Olshaker

DOORWAY TO THE FUTURE

STATEMENT OF JONATHAN M. NIMROD, M.D.

IN THE MATTER OF: Events surrounding breaking and entering at the residence of Malcolm J. Westfield, M.D., and Gail O'Connor Westfield, M.D. (his wife), on August 21.
HELD ON: August 22, Metropolitan Police Headquarters, Municipal Center, 3rd Floor.
PRESENT: Detective First Class Vincent T. Robinson, Detective Third Class Cassandra L. Mansfield.

DET. ROBINSON: I know how difficult this must be for you, Dr. Nimrod. So just start wherever you think you need to to give us the whole story from your perspective.

DR. NIMROD: Okay, let me see, now. This is . . . I just don't know.

DET. MANSFIELD: Take your time, doctor. Would you like some water?

DR. NIMROD: Thanks. All right. I'm not sure where this all begins. I guess when we first met. Ever since I knew him, Malcolm was a hypochondriac. So was Gail, which probably had something to do with why they gravitated toward each other right from the beginning. The three of us met early in our first year in med school, and we just seemed to hit it off naturally. Maybe because we each thought so many of the others in the class were jerks.

There's a phenomenon that's pretty common among first-year med students. It's called the "disease of the week." Every time you study a new condition, at least a quarter of the class is going to come down with symptoms. For example, when you do motor neuron diseases, every twitch or fasciculation becomes a symptom of amyotrophic lateral sclerosis, rather than just simple fatigue, which is what it really is ninety-some percent of the time. Every headache is caused by a brain tumor, every sweat or low-grade fever becomes African hemorrhagic virus, and every vague chest pain signals the onset of a heart attack.

No matter what the disease of the week happened to be, Malcolm would be sure he had it. It became a classwide joke. When we studied cervical cancer, I said to him, "Well, there's one you probably don't have." He agreed, almost begrudgingly, it seemed to me. But Gail's anxiety more than made up for it. She ran out that very afternoon and got a Pap test.

Now I decided I wanted to go into psychiatry pretty early on, so I guess I was always analyzing everyone around me, and no one's more obnoxious than a psych student with all the answers. But I was convinced then—and now from the perspective of my years of practice and experience still am—that this shared neurosis of theirs was at least in part what motivated them to want to become doctors.

I mean, think about it: here were two people who were "deathly afraid of death," both going into the one profession that takes on death on a daily basis and tries to defeat it . . . or at least, postpone it. It also might explain why they both went into such intense fields—Malcolm into thoracic surgery and Gail into OB-GYN. Maybe it also explains why we became such close friends in spite of the fact that I was always in his shadow—I had a need to analyze other people and Malcolm had a need to analyze himself; over and over again.

Don't get me wrong, though. They were both terrific people; weird, crazy senses of humor and a lot of fun to be around. Malcolm and I were anatomy lab partners freshman year, and Malcolm developed a macabre fascination with body parts we progressively removed from our cadaver: one day as she opened her purse for the keys to her apartment, Gail reached in and found her hand gripping its well-endowed penis.

They were both tremendously good-looking and athletic. Students of the opposite sex—including me—lamented that they were attached to each other so early freshman year, effectively freezing out the rest of us. One day a truck actually crashed into a mailbox on campus as its driver became fixated watching Gail cross the street in an extremely short skirt. From that day on, she was known as "the traffic-stopper." She looked absolutely adorable on the tennis court with her little white tennis dress highlighting her long dancer's legs and terrific figure; adorable, that is, until she started beating the crap out of you.

They got as good as they gave, though. One night when Malcolm was trying to catch a little sleep during a thirty-six-hour ER rotation, a couple of the other students used a red pen to paint petechiae over all the exposed parts of his body. When he woke up, one of them innocently asked him what was wrong with his skin, then watched him freak out as he looked at himself in the mirror. They both took the ribbing everyone gave them with good grace, because if they were insecure about some things, they were totally secure in their abilities. And at the end of the four years, absolutely no one was surprised when they finished numbers one and two in the class and announced their wedding date for the day after graduation. They weren't just desirable catches for each other. They were both considered such premium candidates that Yale–New Haven Hospital accepted them as a "package" so they could do their internships together.

We stayed good friends throughout internship and residency and on into practice. I can't deny I was not only in awe of them but also somewhat jealous. Still in his residency, Malcolm was handling coronary bypasses and heart transplants on his own! Everyone who saw him operate said he was as sure and decisive as any surgeon they'd seen. Again, I'm being a shrink here, but it was as if this was the one area where he could overcome his own fears of disease and mortality by bringing seriously ill patients back from the brink by the sheer virtuosity of his own skill.

Malcolm was definitely going places in medicine. I'm not exaggerating when I say that he was largely responsible for getting me my position at the hospital here after he'd come down from Yale. It was typical of the type of charming control he tried to exert over all his friends and associates. I'd told him on the phone one night I didn't think I was going anywhere in Cleveland and he had said, good, because he "wanted" me working near him, anyway.

It wasn't two weeks later that I received a letter of invitation from the hospital, mentioning that Dr. Westfield had assured them I'd be a valuable addition to the clinical staff. There was no doubt even at that early stage that he was a star. They were grooming Malcolm to take over the transplant program and whatever he wanted, he got. That was okay, though. I was used to playing second fiddle to the handsome, brilliant, charismatic Malcolm J. Westfield.

So I have to admit I was both surprised and flattered when Gail called me one day. This was about seven or eight months after I'd moved to town. I was still single in those days and I was spending a fair amount of time at their place.

At any rate, as soon as I got on the phone I could tell she was in an agitated state. She said there was something they needed to talk to me about and asked if I could come right over. What was it, I asked, but she wouldn't tell me over the phone. So I raced right over there.

"What is it?" I asked as soon as Malcolm opened the front door. He and Gail looked grave.

"We're thinking of trying to have a baby," Gail explained.

That was what they'd called me over for?

"You're in OB, Gail," I replied, still not quite getting it, "you must know how it's done."

Malcolm finally cracked a smile. "No, that's not the point, Jon."

"Then what is the point, Malcolm? Certainly you don't need my permission to stop practicing birth control."

"We really want a child," Gail confessed. "We have for a long time."

"Is there . . . uh . . . any physical problem?" I asked.

"No, no. Nothing like that," Malcolm said. "None that we know of, at least. We've gone through all the tests. We're pretty sure if we try, we'll be able to conceive."

Typical Westfield—everything totally analyzed beforehand. "Then I really don't know what we're talking about," I said.

"We've been through a lot of emotional turmoil and soul-searching," he went on. "We're sharing this with you, not just because you're the best shrink I know, but because you're my best friend, too. I mean, here's the thing, Jonny: Are we mature and stable enough to responsibly bring a baby into the world?"

"What!" I stammered, incredulous. "Mal, you face life-and-death decisions every day in the operating room. Gail, you bring other people's children into the world every day. How much more mature and stable is there than that? I've seen the way you deal with your mothers and babies. You love kids."

She chimed in, "What Mal's asking, Jonny, is whether you think—and you have to be painfully honest, that's why we're asking—if you think all of our anxiety and insecurity and hypochondria would rub off on the child and make him—or her—crazy? With our personalities and all that's going on in the world today, I'm worried I'd be so afraid I wouldn't let a kid of mine cross the street by herself until she was ready for college. And if—God forbid—she got sick . . . What am I talking about, of course she'll get sick; all kids do, I'm just afraid I'd go to pieces and this child would grow up a hopeless neurotic. With all our hangups, do we have the right to be parents?" A tear trickled down her cheek.

My heart went out to both of them. So much of a therapist's time is spent trying to get his patients to truly see and accept themselves—faults, flaws, hangups, and all—and then to go on from there. These two friends of mine, both magnificently accomplished in their professional fields and the envy of those around them, had zeroed in on their own hangups like a heat-seeking missile and were beating themselves up over them. In a way, they were like a single organism: what one thought, the other thought; what one felt, the other felt.

I tried to explain to them that none of us is perfect, something they obviously knew on an intellectual level (though it was well-known that Malcolm would accept nothing less than perfection from his surgical team) but had to hear someone else say. I tried to get them to accept the proposition that being aware of and understanding your problems is the critical step in being able to deal with them.

We talked for a long time that night. There's no need to go into all the detail here, but gradually, I think I got them both to believe me when I said they would both make terrific parents. To these two people who were so afraid of disease and death, I tried to get them to accept the idea that the only immortality people can have is through their kids. Children are the one true doorway to the future.

By the end of the evening, I think they were both feeling a lot better about things. I could see it in their body language and general affect. It was very gratifying to me to seem to have such a positive effect so quickly. I thought it was about the best short-term therapy I'd ever conducted, and it was nice that I could do it for two people I felt so close to.

In the following weeks, I could tell that their entire attitude had changed. They seemed happier, more serene, better able to "face the world." They'd made peace with themselves and their own fears. They were almost like two teenagers together, giggling at any suggestive reference and making inferences about what they would do when they were alone together.

I'd say it was about three or four months later—actually it must have been four because it was at the neurology department picnic—that Gail sidled up to me, took me aside, and in an excited, girlish voice, whispered, "We're pregnant!"

I guess it kind of caught me by surprise because I remember blurting out, "Are you sure?"

She laughed. "Of course I'm sure. I'm a very good doctor!"

"And you're okay about it all now?"

"More than okay," she said. "I can't remember ever being happier. It's like I finally feel completely alive. Not just me—Mal, too."

In the weeks and months that followed, all their attention seemed to be centered around the expected new arrival. Gail started showing, gradually getting bigger and bigger, and, to use the old cliché, looking more and more radiant. She joked that she finally had credibility with her own expectant mother patients.

As soon as they knew from the tests that it was a boy, they began calling him Michael and outfitted a bedroom as the nursery. They painted the walls baby blue, accented them with Frank Lloyd Wright motifs, decorated them with characters from *The Wizard of Oz*, and hung a miniature Alexander Calder mobile above the modernistic-looking, acrylic crib.

"Michael's going to be exposed to culture as soon as he opens his eyes," Gail said proudly.

Then, in proof that they hadn't completely gotten away from their old hangups, Malcolm explained the room's special air filtration system he'd had installed. There was also a dedicated outlet wired to both the house's electrical system and a backup generator, just in case the kid should ever need a heart monitor, a respirator, an oxygen tent or any other emergency apparatus. That was okay, though, as far as I was concerned. As long as they kept this all in balance, I didn't see any harm in it. In the final analysis, Michael would live his own life, not theirs.

Everyone who came to the house was given a tour of Michael's room by the proud parents-to-be. With two months to go before the due date, the nursery was so full of stuffed animals you could hardly move around.

The big surprise to everyone who knew them was that as the big day approached, Mal and Gail announced that they were going the natural childbirth route and were going to have the baby at home. "Just as women did for thousands of years before the invention of hospitals and the introduction of impersonality and bacteria and sepsis," Gail declared.

Normally, I might have thought this move was a touch radical and counterculture. But, after all, Gail was an obstetrician, Mal was a surgeon, and if this was their way of trying to liberate themselves emotionally from their fears of "letting nature take its course," then it was all to the good. They were looking forward to the natural childbirth as a great adventure.

May I have some more water, please? Thanks.

(SUBJECT PAUSES.)

After all this, I cannot adequately describe to you what I felt when I heard that the baby was born dead. It was like a sick cosmic joke. At the last moment, apparently, the cord wrapped around his neck tightly enough to strangle him. If they'd been in the hospital rather than at home, who knows? Maybe they could have saved him. I was sure that's what was going through Mal's and Gail's minds, too.

A lot of what happened then is a blur, but I do remember them carrying their dead little boy, wrapped completely in a baby blue blanket, back to the hospital for the post . . . the autopsy. They both looked a hundred years older. The light had gone out of their lives. The funeral was probably the saddest event I have ever experienced.

The other image that stuck in my mind was the first time I was over their house again after that. The door to Michael's room was closed, locked tight with a heavy deadbolt. No one ever saw that door opened again.

DET. ROBINSON: And this all happened how long ago, doctor?

DR. NIMROD: This was . . . let's see . . . this was like . . . eighteen years ago. Yeah. Eighteen years ago.

DET. MANSFIELD: And they didn't have any more children after that?

DR. NIMROD: No. I could have predicted they wouldn't after this experience. It was as if God had just confirmed all their worst fears for them; that He was giving them a message. They said they wouldn't adopt children, either. They realized they couldn't stand the pain if anything happened to another child of theirs.

After a while—I'm talking several years—it was as if none of this had ever happened. I mean they never spoke of it; never mentioned it. Their friends knew never to bring up the subject. The door to the nursery remained closed and locked, but it was as if Mal and Gail had never tried to have a child. We see this a lot in psychiatry in terms of coping with a severe loss. The only way to deal with the pain is to compartmentalize it, just not let it be part of your daily life.

But obviously, the experience did have its effects on both of them. And not all negative, as paradoxical as that sounds. Mal had always been a brilliant surgeon, very up on all the latest technology and how to use it in new and creative ways in medicine. But after this, he became an even more sensitive caregiver. That is, he was really able to hone in on his patients' own fears and anxieties and help them cope. Whenever a patient died—and a lot of them do in his particular field—he shared the grief with family members and loved ones. He never explained where it came from, but those people could always sense that unlike the stereotype of the cold, mechanistic, and egocentric surgeon, Dr. Westfield really understood from his own life what they were feeling. By this time he'd become head of the hospital's transplant program—internationally known. And I always speculated that not being able to save his own child all those years ago had been at least part of the impetus for his drive to give as many others a second chance at life.

DET. ROBINSON: Tell us what happened last night, beginning with the call.

DR. NIMROD: Okay . . . let's see. This was about, oh, maybe ten minutes to ten, it hadn't been dark long. . . . I was home alone. My wife and one of the neighbors had taken all the kids to the movies. I got a phone call. It was Gail. She sounded hysterical. She asked me to come over right away. It sounded like she said Mal had been shot. How badly, I asked. She couldn't tell me. I asked her if she'd called an ambulance or the police. She said no, so I said I'd call them.

She said, "No! Don't do that!" She was adamant, but begged me to get over there.

I didn't know whether I should call for help or not, but they only live five or six minutes away, so I just raced out the door.

When I got there, Gail was waiting for me at the front door. She looked like she was in shock. I asked her where Mal was. Without saying anything, she quickly led me through the front hall and up the stairs. I could see furniture knocked over in the living room and den.

Mal was lying at the top of the stairs, his shirt stained with blood. I bent down to examine him. He was breathing. He opened his eyes slightly when I felt for his pulse. The wound appeared to be on the lower left side of his abdomen. There was a lot of skin laceration and he'd lost some blood, but so far as I could tell, nothing major had been hit. His pulse was strong, which was a good sign.

"We've got to call for help," I said to Gail.

"Not yet," Mal gasped.

"Mal says we should take care of things here first," Gail said, suddenly strangely calm and coherent. I was totally confused.

"What happened?" I asked. At that she started to come unglued again.

But I finally got out of her that they'd heard the sound of breaking glass from the patio doors in the back. Then they'd heard footsteps. Someone had broken in. Mal went down to see what had happened. Then Gail heard shouting from downstairs.

She came to the top of the stairs. She said she could see the intruder was a white man who looked like he was in his late twenties and was holding a gun. He was shouting that he knew Malcolm was a doctor and knew he had drugs in the house. Mal tried to tell him he didn't, but the guy seemed desperate. He raced through the living room and den, overturning furniture, forcing open drawers and cabinets, ransacking everything in his way.

He didn't find what he was looking for on the first floor, so he went back toward the stairs. But Mal stepped in front to block his way. Gail said the burglar smashed him on the shoulder with the gun butt and pushed past him. He scrambled up the stairs. Mal staggered after him.

When the robber saw the closed door at the end of the upstairs hallway, he assumed he'd found what he was looking for. He demanded that Mal unlock the door. Mal refused. Furious, he turned to Gail and ordered her to get the key. She pleaded that there was nothing in there he wanted.

She said the man turned and aimed the gun at Mal. He said, "Open the goddamned door!" Mal didn't budge.

Screaming, the robber pulled the trigger. Mal was hit, thrown backward against the wall. Gail screamed and rushed over to him.

The robber turned back toward the closed door, aimed directly at the dead-bolt lock and fired at it, again and again.

The edges of the door splintered. Gail screamed, "No!" She tried to stop him from going in, but he pushed her roughly out of the way. He threw the door open and rushed in, leaving Gail sobbing over her husband.

Then . . . just after that, I guess, was when she called me.

DET. ROBINSON: Just a second, doctor. Where was the intruder at this point? Was he still in the house?

DR. NIMROD: No. Gail said about half a minute after he shot the lock and went into the room, he ran out screaming. I guess he ran away.

So after I'd examined Mal and Gail had told me all this, I asked her if I could call the police and rescue squad now. She shook her head emphatically and . . . and pointed toward the shattered door.

I was pretty freaked out by that point. I stood up and moved kind of hesitantly over to the door, not understanding what possibly could have made the robber with a gun run out screaming. He would have to be pretty weirdly sentimental to be that affected by a long-dead baby's preserved nursery.

But as soon as I got in there and quickly glanced around, my . . . oh God . . . my blood froze. I don't know how to . . .

DET. MANSFIELD: Just try to describe what you saw.

DR. NIMROD: It was like nothing I'd ever seen before. The crib and baby furniture, the *Wizard of Oz* decorations, the stuffed animals, were all gone. In their place was an array of gleaming metal equipment that looked like it had come from the most modern intensive-care unit. The room was eerily silent except for the intermittent and persistent sounds of technology. A heart-lung machine burbled. A bank of monitors clicked and whirred and blinked, and small screens showed multiple continuous EEG and

EKG tracings and readouts for respiration, rectal temperature, and basal metabolism.

And in the middle of all of this, on a contraption that looked like an operating table, attached to all kinds of wires and leads and completely covered by a clear plastic tent was this . . . this body. There was a naso-gastric tube and several IV lines.

It was naked, the size of a small adult male with several open, bloodless wounds. Upon closer examination, I pegged the age at about eighteen or twenty from the facial hair and skin texture. The body was lean but the musculature was weak and flaccid, as it would be from a total lack of exercise or use. But the thing that struck me was the face: a soft, delicate face, in some ways commensurate with the age of the body but totally innocent and curiously blank, without any of the stress or character lines of experience or personal history, of pleasure or pain. Because clearly, this individual had had none. And with a shudder that turned my insides to jelly, now I knew beyond all doubt: this was Michael.

He hadn't died at birth. The body Mal and Gail had brought back to the hospital was another stillbirth she had somehow secretly secured. The natural childbirth at home eighteen years before had all been part of a carefully thought-through plan. The equipment had been here in this room all that time, the backup electrical system they'd installed had been put in to service it. They'd kept their baby in this room since the moment of his birth—continually shot up with something like Haldol or Prolixin, never moving, never actually becoming a person or taking part in life in any remotely human definition of the term.

I staggered out of the room, consumed with horror. "What have you done?" I gasped at Gail. But I knew the answer to that, too. These two brilliant, technically adept, pathologically insecure medical neurotics had planned, conceived and nurtured a living being to be nothing more than a bank of young, healthy, and genetically compatible "spare parts" for both of them. As a world-renowned transplant specialist, Mal faced every day the difficulty of obtaining suitable donor organs, and even when they became available, he fought the battle of tissue rejection in every case. So he and Gail set up their own private stock, ready and available for either or both of them to harvest whenever the need arose. Heart, lungs, liver, kidney, pancreas, intestines, eyes, vessels, bone marrow, everything, even the brain if they ever found a way to transplant pieces of that—it was all right here on this table waiting for them.

The only immortality people can have is through their kids, I had told them. It had been me who said that. Somehow, I managed to speak. "How . . . how could you? In the name of God?"

"Jonny, you're the one person who should understand," she pleaded. "There's never been a breakthrough like this before." She grabbed my arm, tried to pull me to her.

"Understand?" I repeated incredulously. "Understand? I understand that this is the most monstrous, unnatural thing I've ever seen. All these years I thought you were confiding in me . . . I thought I was helping you two. I didn't know. You both were playing God."

I can't tell you exactly what happened next, but I must have pulled myself loose from her. As if in a trance, I staggered back toward the nursery door. As she called after me, I went back in the room.

"Jonny, no!" Gail called after me, but I was oblivious to her. I was crazed, oblivious to everything as I lurched over the master control unit.

DET. MANSFIELD: And that's when you "pulled the plug"?

DR. NIMROD: Yeah. That's when I pulled the plug.

▪ *John Weisman* ▪

THERE ARE MONSTERIM

Jerusalem, July 1977

Liz's fifth birthday was on Saturday, and so Terry, the perfect father, took her to Nahariya on Wednesday for a long weekend at the beach. Sainted mother Maggie let them go without her.

They'd first thought of celebrating the kid's premier half-decade in Haifa, in a big room at the Dan Carmel where, from the terrace, they could look down on the bustling port and eat dinner at the perpetually crowded Romanian restaurant on the edge of the farmer's market. But while Terry had already telexed his "Summer Travel in the Holy Land" piece to the *New York Times* Tuesday, Maggie was still tied up polishing a profile of Foreign Minister Moshe Dayan that was due at *Woman's Day*. She wouldn't shake free until Friday night.

Besides, they decided, the Dan was expensive and he'd have to pay for a double room all five nights. Besides, they rationalized, Liz wasn't a big fan of Haifa anyway, preferring the construction of sand castles, wallowing in the surf, and the scarfing of fast food to romantic harbor views and Romanian steaks slathered with—in Liz's words—"Eecch, garlic."

So, after a brief parental discussion about four-year-olds' eating habits, family finances, and the fact that he'd be carless in Haifa until Maggie arrived, they chose to go farther north and stay at a modest pension they knew in Nahariya, chockablock close to a dozen falafel and shashlik stands, fifty yards from the water and, as it happened, one-fifth the price of the Dan.

Terry packed a duffel for himself and Liz, carefully stowed Liz's teddy bear Shmulik right on top of the bags, and then they all piled into the beat-up Renault 4 and Maggie dropped them at the taxi stand on Luntz Street, where they caught one of the Israeli communal jitney cabs known as a sherut, to Haifa. The big gray Mercedes diesel car was just about to pull out. Maggie gave them quick pecks on the cheek and shooed them on their way. They shared the two-hour ride with a Hasid who smoked incessantly, a middle-aged yenta who fell asleep just after the turnoff to Abu Gosh and snored contentedly for the rest of the trip, and two Israeli Army girls on leave.

Liz, too, slept most of the way to Haifa, waking only briefly when the sherut stopped at the Herzlyia interchange to take on a passenger, then dropping back into full snooze, her knees curled fetally, head on Terry's lap.

He, the conscientious parent, developed lock-joint in his knees by the time they pulled into Haifa, his long legs having been frozen uncomfortably in one position for forty-four kilometers.

In Haifa they switched to an aged Egged bus that chugged and wheezed, Lizzie insisted, like the Little Engine That Could, gears grating and the red-faced driver, a cigarette clenched between tight lips, cursing the autos that had the audacity to pass on the narrow, two-lane highway north of Akko. Terry watched Liz as she kneeled, nose pressed to filthy window glass, remarking on every olive grove, every banana tree, hitching soldier, donkey, and tractor in the fields as the bus lurched inexorably northward.

Four-year-olds, the father thought, were incredible. He never stopped marveling at the creature he and Maggie had created: he took pleasure at watching Liz sleep; doted on her when she was awake; snapped endless pictures of her antics, her poses, her wide-eyed grins.

He sometimes wondered whether this perpetual enchantment with his daughter was the result of his becoming a father so late in life, or whether it was based on his own middle-aged fears of mortality and the deep-rooted, primordial need to procreate in order to see one's self reflected in another human being. Those were two possible answers, of course. But more basically, he simply loved his daughter with a love so total, absolute, and all-consuming that, from time to time, the enormity of that love frightened the hell out of him.

He reached over and caressed Liz's cheek tenderly with the back of his hand. She'd gotten herself all dolled up for the trip north, declining Maggie's practical suggestions of jeans or shorts with a maverick shake of golden hair and insisting instead on wearing a bright pink and white plaid "Mommy dress," as she called it, accompanied by a quartet of plastic, sparkle bangle bracelets, a necklace of fluorescent green beads, and a rhinestone barrette carefully placed askew atop her head.

"Etonnant!" Maggie'd exclaimed as she coolly perused the defiant combination of colors, then giggled and swept the child into her arms to rearrange the barrette. "You are your mother's daughter."

Even after her sherut nap, Terry realized, the kid was tired by the time they reached Nahariya in midafternoon, and so instead of going down to the beach immediately they shared a pair of greasy falafels spiked with piquant tomato sauce and a couple of grapefruit sodas swigged from the bottle at a kiosk near the bus stop. Then Terry swung the duffel bag over his left shoulder, swept up Liz with his free arm, lugged the two bundles three blocks, and checked into a first-floor room at the Pension Har Zion that had a three-by-six-foot balcony overlooking an alley and lots of other three-by-six-foot balconies, and the two of them lay down for an hour on squeaky camp cots.

They woke at six-thirty, sweaty and grungy. Terry turned on the shower (it wasn't much of a shower but it was wet) and put Liz into it first, then dried her off and while she dressed herself he rinsed off the travel grime, shampooing his red hair twice and lathering quickly with the hard hotel soap as the water temperature dropped precariously fast. Wrapped in a towel he stepped back in the room to find his daughter singing to Shmulik, whom she held cradled in small arms.

He started to speak but she put a finger to her lips.

"Quiet, Daddy. Shmulik's tired from the long trip and he's afraid because it's a different bed and I'm singing him to sleep." So he followed orders and watched silent as Liz, who'd put her T-shirt on inside out, rocked the steady teddy, three days younger than she was, and sang an incredible melange of English and Hebrew nonsense syllables as the creature stared up at her lovingly with button eyes.

She was a bright child. Precocious, Terry though proudly; always the coquette. Her habit (just like her mother) was to stand, legs slightly apart, feet planted firmly, hands on her hips, and, well, command. She'd spoken words at nine months, sentences at sixteen, and after having lived in Israel more than half her life she could make do in Hebrew almost as well as either of her parents, learning the language by osmosis from Orli, the Yemenite maid who came daily to clean and watch her while Terry and Maggie pursued their writing chores. Bright, hell, she was a pistol. Take Shmulik the bear. Originally his name had been Bar-Bar, which was short for bear-bear. But seven or eight months after they'd arrived in Israel Liz announced that the teddy had been rechristened.

"Shmulik," she said, oozing the syllables. "Shmu-u-u-ulik." And Shmulik he'd been ever since.

They'd come to Israel three years before, moving from Rome in the fall of 1974. The nomadic, vaguely newlywed American Family Robinson on a Great New Adventure. Maggie was the one with the job: an associate producer for a U.S. television network whose news panjandrums decided to expand Middle East coverage by opening a minibureau in Jerusalem.

Terry, who made his living freelance writing and occasionally editing English-language texts, had lived overseas for two decades, a confirmed bachelor well into his late thirties, until he'd met the beautiful, auburn-haired Maggie Ross on a blind date in Rome, wooed her for sixteen months with flowers, white Italian truffles, and weekends in Tuscany, and finally—finally—convinced her, twelve years his junior and ambitious as hell, that marriage to a struggling journalist entering early middle age was the fate to which she'd been doomed.

Eleven months after they set up housekeeping in a small but comfortable house with a huge garden in Jerusalem's German Colony, Maggie's network got a new vice president for news and a new set of budget priorities, which did not include a Jerusalem minibureau. So, twenty-six weeks' severance pay in their pockets, the network American Express card cut in two and express-mailed to New York, they were suddenly on their own in the Promised Land, evicted from the expense-account Eden of network news. They thought about going back to Rome, but they'd rented out the five-room flat Terry owned in Parioli—a four-year lease to an American diplomatic couple. Besides, they rationalized, Rome was expensive, while the house in Jerusalem cost a mere $350 a month and Israel's living costs were lower than anywhere in Western Europe except Portugal. The country was beautiful, the people were friendly. Moving would be a hassle. They decided to stay on, as long as they could make ends meet.

Maggie, a natural scrambler, got work as a free-lance producer whenever Barbara Walters or Walter Cronkite or some other network luminary came to town and needed extra hands. She also pitched article ideas about many of the Israeli political contacts she'd made to every American magazine she could think of—and a few paid off. The *Woman's Day* profile of Dayan was her first big-time assignment and she fretted over each comma and semicolon.

If the magazine bought and published it, it would be a breakthrough—not to mention the $3,500 fee, enough to keep them going for four months if they were cautious about how they spent it.

There was other money, of course. The net income from Terry's apartment was a thousand a month. His freelance articles brought in four to six thousand a year. A one-day-a-week editing stint at the *Jerusalem Post*'s International Edition was good for another fifteen hundred per annum. And if things got really rough there was the account in Switzerland, a numbered account containing just under five hundred and fifty thousand U.S. dollars in Swiss francs, Terry Robinson's accumulated pay as an NOC—Non-Official-Cover—contract agent for the Central Intelligence Agency, for which he'd worked on and off since graduating from Brown University twenty-three years before.

He wasn't one of those gun-toting cowboys of suspense fiction. Not his style, although he'd qualified with a handgun during a training session back in the States a decade earlier. Nor was he an expert on ciphers and satellite transmissions.

Terence Robinson was an information gatherer, an evaluater, a shrewd judge of others. He was adept at recruiting and setting up networks of agents, running them, and protecting his people. His cover was perfect: as a freelance journalist, a writer of ephemeral articles on travel (and, very occasionally, Euro-politics), he got to see a lot of things and meet a lot of people.

Much of the information he gleaned he passed on to Langley through a series of case officers. In Italy he spent his time writing about tourism, even publishing a paperback on Tuscany. He wrote occasionally about the labor movement for the *Wall Street Journal* and a somewhat overdramatic, he thought at the time, piece on the rise of domestic Italian terror for *Playboy*. But for the most part, Terry Robinson stayed clear of controversial themes. They were dangerous because they pegged you one way or another, and his entire existence depended on his not being pegged as anything but a nondescript freelancer, a generic American expatriate.

Maggie knew what he did of course.

Johnny T, Terry's case officer when he'd gotten married, had encouraged him to tell Maggie the truth.

"There are secrets and there are secrets," Johnny had said, long fingers drumming idly on a Formica table at a nondescript trattoria just off the crowded Piazza Farnese. "If Maggie doesn't know, it could be worse for you in the long run." Besides, Johnny'd explained, the Agency was leery of agents who couldn't share one of the most basic facets of their existence with their wives.

So, shortly after their marriage he'd taken Maggie to San Gimignano for the weekend on the pretext of researching a piece on some of the small wineries in the area. They stayed at a simple hotel in Pancole, a few kilometers outside the town, and over wine, crusty peasant bruschetta, salad made of wild greens, and thick grilled veal chops he quietly explained to his bride just what he did for a living.

"You're kidding," she said, her hand clapped to her mouth. When he didn't smile, she dropped her hand and said, genuinely shocked, "You're not."

And then, perceptive reporter that she was, she cut to the heart of the matter: "Why, Terry?"

He played with his wine glass. "Because there are bad guys out here, and the only way to keep them from winning is to do everything you can to be one of the good guys."

She frowned. "Everything you can?"

"All I can—the best I can."

She shook her head. "But history—"

"Nobody really understands history. Not really. Not all the way."

She nodded in agreement. "Okay—let's leave history out of it. What makes me so afraid right now, is the 'everything you can' thing. If you do *everything* you can to stop the world's bad guys, don't you end up committing the same kind of crimes you most want to prevent?"

"Sometimes. If you let yourself," Terry said evenly. He looked at her, his face dead serious. "But I'll never let myself."

Her eyes told him she wasn't sure about that.

"Believe me, Maggie," he said, "I could never become the same thing I'm fighting against." He took a sip of wine and returned her stare. "Because if you do that, you stop being political—you simply become a criminal. I know—I've seen it happen. And I don't like it."

He saw she had tears in her eyes. "What's the problem?"

"I love you so much," she said.

And so they agreed to a truce. He was never totally explicit with her about the details of his covert existence. There were clandestine meetings that he went to, and trips he took suddenly. But the specifics were never discussed between them. She had insisted on that, and he honored her request. Unlike Terry, who used his writing as a cover and considered himself a dilettante, Maggie's appointed role in life was professional journalist, and sometimes she felt torn between the ideals she had learned as a student at Northwestern University's Medill Graduate School of Journalism.

She had been twenty-six when she'd met Terry; less than three years out of grad school, the Midwest patina of her childhood in Lakewood, Ohio, barely scrubbed away. She had known from the age of twelve she would be a journalist, and she had worked hard to achieve that goal, waitressing her way through Ohio State University, winning a scholarship to Medill, and, following her graduation, moving to New York and a greenhorn's slot on the assignment desk of NBC News. She was vibrant and energetic and

filled with the righteous indignation common to young prac-
titioners of the journalist's craft. Her job, she argued (often
passionately), was to comfort the afflicted and afflict the comfortable.

It took her some months to reconcile what she did with what
Terry did. She was a child of the sixties blessed (or cursed) with
the antagonism toward government common to most of her generation. And yet she respected, albeit somewhat grudgingly, what
Terry did. He supported the system and was willing to put himself on the line for his beliefs. And so, despite Maggie's negative
feelings about such things as the war in Vietnam, Nixon's presi-
dency, and the way Henry Kissinger ran U.S. foreign policy, she
understood Terry's commitment (perhaps it was her conservative
Lakewood upbringing) to his agency and to their Nation.

Not that she didn't experience emotional conflicts. She ap-
proved of what her husband did. But she also realized the disas-
ters that could befall them if her friends and colleagues from
Rome's American journalistic community ever found out about
Terry's covert activities. Like it or not, Maggie was drawn inside
the double-edged existence shared by all spies' families: the cover
stories and outright lies that have to be told in order to survive.
Lying to her friends and colleagues did not sit easily with her. And
yet she did what she had to do, because her husband's safety depended on her constancy and consistency.

She'd experienced more of those conflicts in Italy than she did
in Israel. Italy in the mid-seventies was fertile turf for Terry's clandestine operations. The Red Brigades were active. The Libyans,
rich with petrodollars and vehemently anti-American, bought
their way into foundering Italian corporations. The Communist
Party controlled newspapers, labor unions, and thousands of local politicians. In Italy there was a lot for Terry to do—and he
worked continually on Agency business while Maggie produced
infrequent two-minute news stories about the Pope, earthquakes,
and the anarchy of Neapolitan society, all the time fretting quietly
about her husband's safety.

In Israel things were different. Liz made the biggest change in their lives, of course. The kid had been unplanned, the result of a trip to Venice. Terry had asked her to come along with him at the last minute, she'd forgotten to pack her diaphragm, and the rest was history. Maggie had always sworn to herself she wouldn't have a child until she had won her first Emmy. The day Liz was born she'd realized what a real award she'd been given. Not that she was any less ambitious, it was simply that her ambitions now had two objectives: a terrific daughter and great news stories. After her layoff, she found herself less and less inclined toward the eighteen-hour days she'd willingly put in as a network producer, preferring to spend time with Liz and putter in the garden between writing assignments.

Their move from Italy, she noticed, had affected Terry as well. Israel was an ally, a friendly oasis in a hostile environment. If Terry were operating in Jerusalem, he showed no sign of it, working on freelance journalism and his part-time job at the *Post*'s grimy Romema headquarters and most every day coming home for lunch, a nap, and a couple of hours' playtime with Liz. He'd told her that Israel would be a virtual vacation for him, and that seemed to be the case.

"Friends don't spy on each other," he'd insisted. "I'm an expert on Communist labor unions, not the Histadrut."

And the PLO?

"Geez, Mag, the Israelis have those guys cold. I couldn't find out one thousandth of what the Shin Bet's got on Arab terrorists even if I were fluent in Arabic and had Yasser Arafat his bloody self on my payroll."

Still, he'd developed professional contacts—Maggie was sure of it—among the left-wing members of Israel's parliament, the Knesset. And he went out of his way to cultivate a few of the more moderate West Bank Palestinian Arabs.

Israel was not Italy. There were no late-night assignations, no dead drops, or one-time cipher books. There were no calls to Maggie from pay phones that went, "I gotta see a man about a horse, darlin'," his way of letting her know he might not be home for a few hours or a few days. There was none of the perpetual, gnawing, unspoken dread Terry Robinson had come to know in his gut, the brickbat pain that hit him like an ulcer when he worked the streets alone and unprotected. He'd felt those twinges for twenty years, in Rome, Paris, Amsterdam, and London.

No, Israel was different. Strange for him, a Christian in a Jewish homeland, that he felt so comfortable in this rough country of olives and orange groves and scrub-brush wadis, this raw, unsophisticated place with its boy soldiers and bearded Hasids and breakneck drivers. He loved Israel's vitality, took pleasure in its adolescent chauvinism, its matter-of-fact fatalism, its almost professional irreverence. He'd come to feel safe walking Israel's crowded streets and visiting its historic sites.

He watched as Liz laid the bear on her cot, fussing, tucking it under the covers tightly, its nappy head right in the middle of the pillow.

She turned to him, bright-eyed, her index finger touching pursed lips, the bracelets up around her elbow. "Okay, Daddy, we can go. But we have to leave the light on because Shmulik is scared by the monsterim."

"Monsterim?" He was amazed. She'd fixed a Hebrew plural suffix onto an English word.

Hands on her hips, she glared up at him, her face serious, and stage-whispered, "You know—monsters."

He nodded sagely. "Any special kind of monsters?"

"Big ones. With teeth—" She spread her hands two feet apart.

"I've seen those big monsters before," he said. "I know all about them. But Shmulik doesn't have to worry."

"Why not?"

"Because." He scanned the room quickly. It was Spartan: paneled walls, a single bare-bulb lamp with clip-on shade for light, an armoire where they'd hung their clothes, and, hidden by the panels' vertical joints, a spring-closed storage closet where the extra bedding and a third cot were kept. Terry went to the section of panel where the faint outline of the storage closet could just be seen and pressed the hidden door. It sprung open. He gestured. "See? All Shmulik has to do is run in there and close the door and he'll be safe."

Liz scampered over and looked inside, wrinkling her face disapprovingly. "Eecch, Daddy, it's smelly. I'd rather leave the lights on."

He laughed. "Okay, okay. Shmulik gets the lights."

They walked hand in hand through the crowded streets, marveling at the electric lanterns that were strung above their heads. On the beachfront Terry headed toward a restaurant he remembered from their last trip, and after obtaining Liz's approval they commandeered a table facing the water, and the attention of an overworked waiter. Terry ordered a Gold Star beer; Liz decided on Coke. Solemnly, they poured the drinks into streaked glasses and touched rims.

"Cheers, my birthday girl."

"Daddy—it's not till Saturday."

"Well, it's soon enough to say cheers."

She shook her head. "No it isn't. You can only say 'cheers, my birthday girl' when it's my birthday."

She was so literal. Just like her father, he thought. "Okay," he improvised, "cheers, my non-birthday girl."

"You're silly, Daddy."

"Of course I'm silly. I'm a daddy. You know what you are?"

She shook her head.

"You," he paused, waiting for the desired effect, "are an imp."

Reaction achieved. "Am not. There's no such real word like *imp*."

"Oh yes there is. I can show it to you in the dictionary when we get home. Or we can call your mother and ask her to look it up."

Inquisitive: "What does imp mean?"

"It means Liz Robinson."

Defiant: "No it doesn't."

"It means Liz-who-wears-dresses-on-the-bus-and-tucks-in-her-teddy-Robinson."

Petulant: "No it doesn't."

"It means Liz-who-likes-Coca-Cola-because-it-makes-her-nose-wrinkle-Robinson."

"It means what you're doing, Daddy. Being mischiev . . . mis-chievoonieous."

Where the hell did she come up with the damn words? He laughed. He agreed. "When I was your age I was an imp."

Triumphant: "You are an imp, too, Daddy." She took her glass in two hands and slurped contentedly on Coke. "We are *impim!*"

They dined royally, so far as Liz was concerned, on kebab sand-wiches and french fries drowned in ketchup. Terry had two more Gold Stars, Liz another Coke.

After he paid the bill they walked down the beach and Liz took off her sandals and scampered down to the water. Terry rolled his trouser legs, shed his Top-Siders and followed. Then they went for ice cream, *glida* in Hebrew; coconut ice cream in a sugar cone that had, to Terry's dismay, a bad leak. He wiped at Liz's chin and the top of her T-shirt with an inefficient, wax-coated napkin then gave up and swabbed wholeheartedly with his pocket handker-chief.

By nine-thirty, Liz was feeling tired again so they abandoned the streets for their hotel room. He peeled Liz out of her clothes, sent her to the bathroom and waited as she brushed her teeth, them dumped her playfully into her bed, Shmulik resting com-fortably in the crook of her arm.

"Daddy?"

He kissed her forehead. "What, Liz?"

"Would you stay here with me?"

"Sure, honey. Why?"

"This bed is lumpy and I'm not sure I can get right to sleep but I'm tired and I want to sleep and I—"

He cut her off. "Not to worry, imp. Daddy's here." He slipped onto the narrow bed and cradled his daughter. He kissed her cheeks and her forehead and held the child to him. "Not to worry. Daddy's here."

He was still on Liz's bed, lying fully clothed and dreaming when the shots awoke him. He didn't know what time it was and his head was foggy with sleep but the shots were unmistakable: automatic weapons fire coming from close by.

Instinctively he rolled out of the bed. Liz, too, was awake and she started, startled, to go with him but he pushed her head gently back onto the pillow and looked her straight in the face. "Stay here, baby, stay here."

He moved quickly to the door of the balcony, cracked it open and peered outside, wincing as the firing grew closer, bullets whining ricochets off nearby stone. There were shouts, cries, and then an explosion from somewhere down below. He looked back at the bed where Liz lay frightened. He called to her: "Lizzie, hit the deck. Get down on the floor and stay there."

"Daddy—"

"Liz—do exactly what I say. Now!"

He couldn't tell where the firing was coming from, or from whom, or—

More shots. Closer. Now from inside the hotel. Down the stairs. Down the hall. Were they coming—they—terrorists? Soldiers? He crawled toward the door and pressed his ear against it. *Shouting*.

But not Hebrew shouting. Arabic shouting.

Terrorists. Oh, goddamn to hell terrorists. Liz. Terrorists. His heart raced. They were trapped. A twenty-foot drop to hard pavement outside and maybe the goddam terrorists were waiting for them there, too. He tried to ease his racing pulse. Okay. Think. You are a goddamn professional. You are supposed to know what to do.

He went onto automatic pilot. Light? No light. Dark room.

Dark equals safety. He rolled to the desk and reached up ("Oh, damn, Lizzie," as he heard the adjacent door splinter) and smashed the bulb.

Now—shelter. His mind worked in milliseconds debating the possibilities. Under the bed. No protection. Bathroom. No protection. Closet.

Closet: dark room; closet hidden. Grab Liz. Stay quiet. Wait. Roll to the left. Take Liz.

Her eyes were frightened, panicked saucers. She began to cry out and he realized that she was reflecting his own state. He forced himself to calm down. Whispered shushing noises in her ear as he held her and crawled to the paneled wall, found the hidden door, pulled the two of them inside and then, fingers searching desperately for an exposed piece of wood, clicked the door closed. Exhausted, he lay panting in the small black space, his body wrapped around the child.

He found her ear and kissed it. "Lizzie—there are bad men outside. Very bad. We have to lie here very, very still until we hear them go away."

The child began to sob uncontrollably. He covered her mouth and whispered in her ear again. "Can't do that, Lizzie. Can't cry, or talk or anything because if they find us they'll hurt us." His mind raced. All his training; all his experience—nothing to show for it. Lying in a dark place waiting to be killed. Waiting for the child to be killed. Take me—leave Liz. Hostages. Gunshot wounds. Grenades. Knives in Liz's throat. Liz's head severed.

Liz cried. He held her mouth tighter. "No, no, no, baby. No crying. Can't cry."

"Shmulik," she gargled. "Shmulik—" and she clawed at the wood door, trying to push it open in the suffocating blackness.

Terry held her down, wrestling his body atop hers, his eyes wide in the stifling, airless hidey-hole.

"No-no-no-no," he wheezed, his hands tightening on the child's mouth and nose. Hurting her, he knew, but he had to, to protect her. "Shmulik's okay, Liz. He's okay right where he is. He's a big bear. He can take care of himself."

The outside door splintered. Terry could hear the wood give way and he cringed as automatic weapons raked the place. Loud voices. Arabic. Screams. Liz echoed them, or tried to—Terry held her down as she struggled. More shots. More screams. From . . . somewhere, a drum beat loudly, incessantly, against his ear. He realized it was the pulse in his wrist. He tried to still it. Took the knuckle of his index finger and put it in his mouth. Bit down hard. The pain would kill the noise. Under him, Liz calmed down, her sobbing stopped. Now the loudest noise in the black was his own heartbeat.

Other voices. Gunshots. Distant voices. How long had they lain there? Minutes? Hours? His eyes closed in the darkness, Terry waited, waited, waited.

Other voices closer now. Hebrew or Arabic? He bit on his finger until tears came to his eyes. Quiet, Lizzie, or they'll hear us. The monsterim. Big teeth. Sharp knives.

Lights outside their hiding place. Oh, God, we're found out . . . be killed. Voices. Shots. Hebrew. English. English English English: "Mr. Robinson—Mr. Robinson, this is the Army."

Pounding. Sudden brilliant light. His eyes couldn't take it.

Wincing, he saw a lethal silhouette, a helmeted face, a hand holding an Uzi submachine gun.

Arms dragged him and Liz into the room.

Hands lifted him. Quick frisk then onto the bed. God it was cold. A body was sprawled on the floor, red-and-white keffiyeh splotched with blood covering the head. Nearby, two grenades and an AK-47 rifle with long, curved ammo clips taped back-to-back. The corpse was reaching for the weapons with stone-dead hand.

He tried to find his daughter. "Liz? Liz? You okay, kiddo? We made it, Lizzie. The army's here. The bad men are all gone (They are gone, aren't they? You killed the sons of bitches, didn't you?) Don't worry, Liz, the bad men all gone."

Where the hell's the bear? Where's Shmulik? Lizzie wants Shmulik. She'd cried for Shmulik. Where's the goddam bear?

"Sit up Mr. Robinson," said a voice. "Please sit up."

He obeyed, his eyes still unaccustomed to the brightness of the room. "Liz—where's Liz?"

The commando had her. The hooded commando in black SWAT clothing, dripping state-of-the-art ordnance, looking like a character out of a Ninja fantasy had Liz in his arms and he was KISSING HER? KISSING HER ON THE LIPS? Terry launched himself across the room but strong arms held him back.

The commando's eyes raised toward Terry but his mouth never left Liz's lips. He lowered the child onto the floor, pushing on her chest, muttering a cadence in Hebrew, "Echad, shtyim, shilosh, arba, shesh . . ." then blowing in her mouth.

The commando's eyes locked with his own. Dead gray eyes, Terry would recall much, much later. Dead gray eyes peering through holes in the black balaclava hood.

There was a lot of muted conversation carried on in Hebrew as he sat on the edge of the bed, the hands of soldiers, strong young men in khaki and black who blocked his view, resting on his shoulders while his own hands supported his head. He didn't understand a word of it. But something was terribly wrong.

Finally, a captain knelt by his side. Terry stared at the man uncomprehending, noting—absurdly, he thought for an instant—the crow's-feet around the officer's eyes and the deep scar along the man's neck and wondering where he'd gotten them. The Israeli put his arm around Terry's shoulder and squeezed.

"She is gone, Mr. Robinson. I'm sorry."

Sorry? Gone? Who's gone? Gone where? Gone how?

Then, he saw. Then he realized what he'd done.

The commando was laying Liz on a stretcher, oxygen mask obscuring most of her small face, still pushing down on her chest and counting the goddamn Hebrew syllables, "Echad, shtyim, shilosh, arba," and Liz, Liz, Liz's eyes were closed and—"Ooh, God—NOOOO!"

He screamed and lurched toward the stretcher where they were tying down the corpse of his daughter his love his child oh, God, no. "Please—God, take me now. Take me, take me, take me. Not her. Not Liz. Oh, please, God—Maggie—God, my baby, my baby. Dear God, no!"

Things went black and white. The soldiers held him down, he fighting against them, nauseated by the sweaty jumble of arms and bodies smelling of fear and death. From somewhere a hand with a syringe appeared and it went into his upper arm right through the shirt and then the room started to spin crazily, bright lights blinking neon like Piccadilly in the rain and he felt himself disappearing into a crystal vortex and the last words he heard himself scream were, "Don't you idiots understand? Take her teddy, take her teddy—there are monsterim."

. *Jan Adkins* .

BARRATRY

A Small Tale of Maritime Misadventure

Even a man who is pure of heart, and says his prayers each night, may become a wolf when the wolfbane blooms, and the moon is full and bright.

I have this on good authority: the gypsy woman in *The Wolf Man,* a very high-minded and selfless old dear who looked after Lon Chaney, Jr., around his time of the month. I can't say that I have ever needed a shave as much as Lon Chaney, but I know there is a wolf in me, and in you.

Neither of us will be padding around in the park ripping the throats out of deer and coeds but we all share a delight in our dark sides and, given the right circumstances or phase of the moon, we will fall on the side of larceny. Old hippies (like me) or ice yuppies, we all love to thumb our noses at the Majesty of the Law. Larceny is the sex of ethics, a titillation to be enjoyed in private. We have a special place in our hearts for moonshiners, desperados, flimflam men, D. B. Cooper, Dirty Harry, the Great Impostor, Willie Sutton . . . and pirates. Pirates did for me—Howard Pyle's thick-fingered, sash-and-bandanna buccaneers lured me toward my own dark side.

And Bill. I will call him Bill Barrister, for he is a lawyer and still carrying on in a high-handed way that argues against using his real name. Bill's delight in capering close to the edge of things is probably one of the reasons I like him so much.

He is an untidy, loud, perennially adolescent, and annoying guy with the social graces of a golden retriever kept in the house too long. He makes all wives shudder and you would not introduce him to your sister. Even at this late date he thinks James Bond was cool with women. He would be a social pariah but he is outrageous enough to be in demand at dinner parties for driving a certain kind of politically pious woman to the brink of spluttering hysteria.

You've had a roommate or a friend like Bill, someone who can make you cringe, embarrass you, take your breath away with a howling gaffe at your expense, but he will be there when you want to shoot yourself in the head because you miss your ex-girlfriend, and he will be there when you beg her to come back, and he will be there when you hate everyone, including Bill.

A good thing about unreconstructed men of my generation is that we still believe in friendship. We were friends. With the wry, disguised, insulting, locker-room loyalty that marks our generation, we stood up for one another.

Bill and I were not alike. Our professions, our backgrounds, our families, our taste in food and women and books were different but we had two common connections that bridged enough of the gap: we both remembered most of *Casablanca* verbatim, and we both loved to sail.

Bill, the love of sailing, and that delicious surrender to larceny were the reasons I was a barrator, "a member of a ship's company whose actions cause harm to the ship's owner." This is a serious maritime crime, a hanging offense in the old, pre–Exxon *Valdez* days, but there I stood at the wheel of a boat I didn't own, stealing out of Saltworks Creek on a moonless night under sails as dim as used winding-sheets. I was a thief, wincing at every ratchet of the winch pawls as I played the jib and the main to wheedle steerageway out of fitful night airs.

It was Bill's boat, stolen in friendship, and a sweet boat it was. *Sorrento* was a Weldon 42, a handsome cruising sloop built at the Weldon Works on the Eastern Shore. In a naval sense she was Bill's prize, the spoils of a financial raid he and his former partners had made on Weldon Boatbuilding when it was caught against a lee shore of debt. In the takeover—not entirely hostile but not really amiable—Bill and one of his partners had appointed themselves panjandrums of the corporation and, in lieu of salaries, had awarded themselves the twin 42's that were being finished that spring. Whether or not the sale of the finished boats would have hauled the boatworks out of the financial shallows is moot, since Weldon died a few months after launching them for the new owners.

You're right, Bill can be a sonofabitch. He gouged the boat-yard and the boats out of old Skip Weldon without a regret. But then he sat with him in the hospital for two weeks when he was dying. Maybe practicing law does that to you: lets you separate what's on paper from what's lived too damned easily.

Sorrento, like most of the Weldons, was laid out generously and finished to a polish, a comfortable boat for cruising the Chesapeake. But Skip Weldon must have made a mistake with the 42's because he settled for once on a sweet set of hull lines and a powerful rig. Unlike all the other "wholesome cruisers" in his overbuilt gold-plater fleet, the 42 had a nice turn of speed and answered her helm with the enthusiasm of a sailing dinghy. Bill and I took her all over the Upper Bay for years, lurching from one piece of muddy bottom to another, learning the hydrology by

Braille. I had sold my own boat and I exercised my nautical ad-
diction as the titular first mate. She was docked at the Weldon
Works, then, and we cruised the Bay almost every weekend. We
entertained our "drowning parties" of friends less than half as
much as we entertained ourselves by running aground everywhere—the Upper Chesapeake is a big farm pond, anyway, mud
bottomed and forgiving, so we held onto tacks too long or
pushed too far into tiny gunkholes. Both of us danced on the
edge with *Sorrento,* maneuvering that big 42 into miniature town
docks and finding out-of-the-way anchorages at cocktail time
where the grain smell of the Eastern Shore farm fields came down
to the green scent of shore and the pleasant musk of the water.

Bill loved that boat; he named it after his father's birthplace in
Italy. For both of us *Sorrento* was a playground and a refuge. We
sat a hundred nights in *Sorrento*'s cockpit looking at the stars,
talking about books and law, politics and history and, of course,
women.

Women as well as pirates put me at *Sorrento*'s wheel in this cut-
ting-out expedition, skulking out of my own creek.

No moon, there were only stars that night, and damn few of
those between patchy clouds, so it was as dark as a coal miner's
nightmare. The creek writhes a bit and then almost chokes off before it opens into the Severn River. *Sorrento* takes six feet of water
and this was a very bad time to run aground. Yes, there's a delicious thrill in sneaking away in the middle of the night, but knowing that you are stealing about a hundred thousand dollars from
some very heavy folks who are due to show up any minute gives
you an uncomfortable pucker. My eyes flicked back and forth, trying not to miss anything in the night-vision hole at the center of
my vision, assembling the dim scene in my head more than my
eyes. Easing out of one reach I jibed, bringing the boom across as
quietly as I could under Willie Mealy's window, close to the creek
where it turned. Sleep soundly, Willie. Running the narrow channel at the creek's mouth, where it bars up, would be critical. I
reached out for Deb's arm and she started.

"What?" she hissed, obviously unaccustomed to theft in the night.

"Behind the companionway steps is a flashlight with a red filter."

"Good. Great. What do you want me to do about it?"

"Don't get fussy, Deb. Use it to turn on the navigation instruments. I need the depth sounder. You'll find the switch . . ."

"Where the hell do I turn it on?" She whispered like an overheated radiator.

"The flashlight or the navigation instruments?"

"The navigation thing, you jerk."

"I'm trying to tell you."

"Then tell me, dammit."

"It's on the starboard breaker panel over the navigation station."

"Just tell me where the hell it is!" A steamed radiator in heavy traffic.

"To your right as you go down the stairs, over the desk, the big row of switches. It's toward the bottom. 'Navigation Instruments,' that's what the label says."

I was not only a barrator but I was making my new wife an accomplice.

I felt about my friendship with Bill the way die-hard New Yorkers feel about Manhattan: it was an acquired taste I didn't expect or even want everyone else to share, my best horror stories revolved around the inconvenience of it, it was expensive and annoying, but I insisted that the subject of my perseverance was worth it.

He was, I will admit, a rat with women. I had known a long string of his girlfriends. Some of them were well-bred, expensively dressed Washington power brokers, and they didn't care for our bohemian boat life. Some were politicians and lobbyists, women who had lost their ability to carry the truth in a bucket from making too many deals. Some were other Washington lawyers, and it's never pretty to watch sharks mate; the water is cloudy with lust, anger, and blood. He was a rat to all of them. Then there was Malice Alice.

Bright white light lanced out of the companionway hatch, burning away my night vision, announcing us to any wakeful soul on the creek.

"Kill that light, Deb!" I stomped the sole of the cockpit with a boom and the light went off.

"Sorry," her voice came out of the cabin, "Wrong light. I can't see anything."

"I can't, either, Deb. We're probably about to plow into the *Andrea Doria*."

"I said I was sorry."

"Okay, okay. Just get the red-filtered flashlight. It's small and black."

I could just make out the shifting red glow from the cabin as she found the chart-reading flashlight and then the breaker panel. For a second the spreader lights went on, illuminating the whole deck in the middle of the Creek, defibrillating my heart, challenging my bladder control, screwing my night vision again. They went off with a huffy curse from below and in a few moments the navigation panel lit up. I had eleven feet of water under us. I couldn't see a damned thing but we were still in deep water. Deb came back up the companionway ladder. "Did I just turn the wrong thing on for a second?"

"I never liked you. I married you out of pity."

"You never had it so good."

She was right but she needn't have been so smug about it.

Bill had watched our explosive courtship over several years, had commiserated with me after half a dozen breakups, and had been one of a dozen guests at our small wedding on the dock, *Sorrento*'s big mast nodding over us.

Malice Alice was the reason *Sorrento* had been moved to my dock, and she was also the reason Deb and I were cutting her out in the night. Alice Nailor and her husband, Harold, had been Bill's partners in the Weldon takeover. They had taken the other

Weldon 42, the exact twin of *Sorrento*. They named it *Aphrodite,* even though the goddess of love had little effect on their marriage, an arrangement as practical and flavorless as the legal announcements section of the *Washington Post*. Harold and Alice continued their daily business dealings but, file by file and blouse by blouse, Alice moved her base of operations to the Weldon Works, a separation that did not appear in conversation or on the legal notice page of the *Post*. She took over the old sail loft as her office, *Aphrodite* as her bedroom, and—without much resistance from a truly unprincipled sex dog—Bill as her bunkmate.

Business raiders find romance on high seas, sail into sunset. If this were a tale of romance instead of an account of a felony I could bring up the music, ask for a G major chord, and roll the credits. But life isn't tidy.

For one thing, Bill's life was imploding, collapsing in on itself like a dying star. One afternoon in the early eighties, Ronald Reagan had deregulated the petroleum industry and Bill's profession as an oil lawyer ceased to exist, along with his high roller's six- and sometimes seven-figure salary. On that afternoon every cent of Bill's grown-up Monopoly money was in play, except for the taxicab money in his Brooks Brothers pockets. Without a flow of cash to support his investments they came crashing in on him. Of course he had his real estate. But owning property in Washington in the late eighties was like owning a balloon stand in a hurricane. For several years Bill understandably felt that he needed his resources more than the government (look what they did to his job, after all). Pressed by tax requests that were less and less polite, he orchestrated a desperate yard sale of rental and residential properties to avoid a new job of making license plates for the District. His file at the IRS was no longer labeled "Shoot On Sight" but had an unhealthy radioactive glow and didn't bear close inspection. That was when Bill's life collapsed entirely. He dropped out of public sight and became a black hole.

It was also when he discovered that Alice was genuinely crazy. How many times, sitting in *Sorrento*'s cockpit, had we shaken our heads at the quirks of someone's girlfriend (usually mine) and re- cited the Three Great Rules of Life? Never eat at a place called "Mom's." Never play cards with a man called "Doc." And never *ever* get mixed up with a woman who is more screwed up than you are. Even the smartest men are wise only in the abstract.

I liked Alice at first. We sailed together a few times and she was always nice to me. It seemed that she wanted to help him in every way. She was a wealthy woman and offered him cars, loans, trips. She insisted that he wasn't living up to his potential as the brilliant lawyer and business mind he really was and she wanted him to shine. I thought it was about time he had a lady that lasted more than three dates and an overnight.

He was flattered at first. No one had paid him so much atten- tion in a long time. But her attention became increasingly minute. He began to find Post-it notes on the papers in his briefcase, opening with suggestions of better deals he could make, adjuring him to stand up for himself and be tough, ending with detailed and specific sexual scenarios she wanted to play out that evening. The invasion of his briefcase rankled him but the sex flogged him on, even when a Polaroid—a gynecological self-portrait by Al- ice—fell out of his notes and onto a document being stamped by the small claims court commissioner. The invasion of his sock drawer was next. Returning to his supposedly secret borrowed apartment one evening he noticed that all his spices had been al- phabetized and his sock drawer had been completely regimented in groups: crew socks by color and over-the-calf socks by pattern. Later that week his bathroom became spotless and contained a new green clothes hamper. A Post-it note on the mirror sug- gested that he use the hamper for towels, only (underlined), and use the new mesh bags in his closet for colored, white and dry- cleaning. Also, he must never again put gym clothes on the car- pet, please. The sock drawer did it. Sex was a good thing, surveillance was a bad thing.

Bill stopped by my place on the way to the Weldon Yard dur- ing the third week of his domestic improvement. He had a beer on the dock and allowed that "This thing with Alice is becoming mondo weirdo. That bimbo is following me, calling to see if I'm in the apartment. She doesn't even have the decency to breathe hard, just hangs up and shows up, like by accident, five minutes later. With a can of whipped cream or a coil of sash cord or some sex-toy routine. I'm not getting any sleep."

"Poor you."

"Come on, you've seen *Fatal Attraction*."

"We all liked the first reel."

"Alice is nuts. Nuts. Whacked. I never noticed how dead her eyes are. Ever notice that? She could . . . do something."

"Have you got a pet rabbit?"

"Laugh, go ahead. You just wait until someone's following you. This is crazy. I'm going down to call it off. That's it. Put this back on a business footing where it belongs. No wonder Harold was so nice to me. You want to sail this weekend?"

When I drove down to sail that weekend *Sorrento*'s deck was tight with Bill's goods from the Weldon Works. The other sailors who kept their boats at the yard and occasionally stayed aboard were bidding him goodbye. Alice was in New York but her boat was sitting beside Bill's, identical except that all her woodwork was buffed, all her brasswork shined, and geraniums smiled from cute little boxes screwed to the pilings on her side of the dock. It was like a page out of *Little Toot*.

"What's up?" I asked.

"I'm getting out of here. Hey. Do you mind if I take *Sorrento* up to your dock for a few days? Look at this layout. This is just too cozy. And she didn't exactly go for being dumped. I don't want to leave the boat here, okay?"

That is how *Sorrento* became a resident at my dock for three years. And for two of them Bill was a resident, too. He quit his apartment in the District—he said too many people knew where it was—and lived on the boat. I didn't mind. Truth to tell, I liked it. It was like a boy's club for a long while, and that was when Deb and I had called it off and expressed our mutual mistrust and loathing. I was lonely.

No more Ms. Nice Guy, Alice became Malice Alice, then. She would case the dock and see if Bill was gone and somehow—we never found out quite how she did it—get past the locks and hatch-dogs into *Sorrento* while I was asleep and make up Bill's rumpled bed as if she were going to use it with him, leaving a Hallmark card full of bittersweet endearments on his pillow. Endearments. They were really veiled reproaches, "Thinking about you with longing and wishing you could see how dangerous anger and bitterness are to your soul." She never left a mint but we wouldn't have eaten it, anyway. During that time she began to meet him, as if by casual coincidence, in a client's lobby or at a restaurant, where she would accelerate from a cool hello to tears and shouting like an exotic fuel dragster. On an April afternoon she waited until Bill left his office for lunch and strode confidently into the fourth floor tank he shared with a school of similarly ruined sharks. She said something that led the bored part-time secretary to believe that she was Bill's squeeze and did not take out her screwdriver until she was in Bill's office. She did not clean up and she did not warn him against leaving gym clothes on court papers. With the efficiency of a really bright, really crazy woman who is accustomed to working on boats she removed the hard drive from his computer and left with it three minutes later.

This ritual emasculation drove Bill deeper underground and into a deeper depression. Lawyers opposing Bill in lawsuits suddenly knew more than they could have discovered legitimately. His box score at the courthouse suffered. A woman lawyer representing a former client of Bill's found reasons at this time to sue him for malpractice and threatened him with disbarment; the menacing lawyer was, incidentally, a friend of Alice's. Someone with specific knowledge of Bill's finances rekindled the Internal Revenue Service's interest in Bill's case; there was new information about a small hoard of cash he kept and about a sweetheart loan from his hometown bank with which he had bought a car. You may have no guilty secrets but would you really want your life systematically laid out for the IRS? Poor Bill. He had bags full of guilty secrets.

The car was sold, the IRS temporarily held at bay with the proceeds, and in a six-hundred-dollar Buick station wagon Bill disappeared for months, something he'd never done before. He maxed out another credit card on a cross-country drive, stopping to camp and fish and sample topless bars near the Interstate. From the few postcards that struggled back from his national odyssey it sounded like a refusing-to-come-of-age road novel.

As grisly as all this sounds, it was not without its features. Bill was part of my own past, a crucible bubbling with unfinished stuff fuming and sparking with inappropriate remarks, bitter pronouncements, and enough yuks to cover up his loneliness. The rawness in Bill was something I recognized and loved, as you can love your younger, less-controlled self without wanting to return—except, perhaps, on Friday nights. Now, for the first time I could see another Bill emerging, a softer, stronger man. Football coaches can posture about winning being the only thing, but defeat is more powerful than victory. Defeat builds. You never learned a damn thing from doing it right. From a lot of defeat and a lot of pain, Bill was becoming a real person. A mensch. I was not altogether sure I wanted it to happen. Bill was such a prodigy as an asshole, so enthusiastic and unashamed, that seeing him change was like losing a living national treasure. But I knew it was the best thing for my friend.

You can change all you want, mend your ways, manage all twelve steps, put on saffron robes and do holy works, but crazy ex-girlfriends like Malice Alice will still be coming to get you as if you were your nasty old self. And Bill wasn't that far from it yet. She was on her way.

Bill returned to the city without rippling the surface, stepping out of his car in a cascade of empty soda cans onto my driveway one afternoon. He was full of tales from the golden West, bristling with new schemes, and full of resolve to make something comfortable and sensible out of his life. In the next few months he avoided offending any prominent figures and actually carried through several projects. He made a new start at a modest civil practice and looked into some real estate work, going to ground at night in a borrowed basement room. He protected his friends from legal inquiry by keeping his burrow's location a secret. *Sorrento*, all but ignored, grew weed on her bottom while Bill applied himself to the long climb out of his hole.

It's possible Bill's resolve had inspired me, but I was running again, trying to build up wind for tennis. I was braving the heat wave on a summer afternoon, puffing alarmingly, sweating wonderfully (I don't know if sweating is good for you but every man I know equates it with virtue) and had reasonable hopes of surviving another fight-or-flight session without an infarction. I had made the turn at Point No-Point Road and was on my way to the barn, running left-side, against traffic, when a car pulled in ahead of me and its tinted window rolled down.

Malice Alice. A little tip for a long life: in the presence of madness, evil, or absolute power, smile. "Hello, Alice. I haven't seen you since Hector was a pup, girl. You're looking great!" She looked puffy and pale and I remember hoping she had something terminal. But not fast.

"Hi there, stranger," she said sweetly, "I was just in Annapolis and thought I'd stop by to see you. How is everything?"

The cool air spilling out of her window smelled of stale cigarettes and too much perfume. "So far, so good, Alice . . ."

"And how is our Bill?" She cut in a half a second too quickly; she was an accomplished but not a graceful liar. "Is he still living on his boat? Is he back in Washington?"

"Beats the hell out of me, Lieutenant. Haven't seen him for a while, either. He must be busy somewhere."

"Well, I'll run into him one way or another, I guess." There was a gladness embedded in her tone that sent a little shiver along my back.

"If I see him, shall I tell him you're looking?"

"Oh, that's all right. I'll surprise him."

I'll bet you will.

We shook out some banalities for most of a minute and she drove away, a little too fast. I stretched out a minute and then continued my run, wanting to forget the entire incident. But I couldn't.

She had passed me coming toward my house but hadn't stopped. She stopped on her way out. I'm probably as recognizable running out as I am running in. She wanted to see if *Sorrento* was still at my dock, and if Bill was on it. She had also known that Bill had been out of town. I suddenly felt that someone's-behind-the-door feeling, when the soundtrack changes to scratchy violin music in a minor key. Bright day, nice run, creepy violin music in my head.

I shook out my shoulder as I ran into my own yard. I walked around puffing and trying not to wheeze, thinking about the sudden appearance of Malice Alice. Still breathing hard, I walked around to the back of the house, toward the water. You can't see my dock from the road. I stood at the head of the steep stairs down to the dock and looked at *Sorrento,* safe but weedy, resting at the end of the dock. By the toe of my Nikes there was a cigarette butt. I don't smoke. Now here's the cool part: I picked it up and smelled it, rolled it between my fingers. It smelled awful. But fresh. Cool, I felt like Sam Spade, I wanted to call my hard-boiled secretary, Alma, but I didn't have one. I called Bill instead.

"Hey, Buddy." He sounded busy and happy.

I told him that I'd just met Alice on the way back from my run, that she'd passed me going in without stopping, and that she'd walked around the house and had a cigarette at the head of the dock stairs. "It probably doesn't mean anything, right? But something just jangled. Something strange about the whole thing. Bill? You there?"

"This is not good."

"How's that?"

"I was going to call you. A tax lien on the boat came yesterday afternoon. She shows up today at the dock. This isn't coincidence. She wants her pound of flesh and she wants ten percent, to boot."

"Ten percent?"

"If she rats me out, tells the feds where my boat or any other resources are, she gets ten percent of the value. She wants to get paid for having her revenge on me. They're going to get *Sorrento*. There's someone gearing up to come and get it right now. Oh shit."

Thick-fingered, sash-and-bandanna pirates answered Bill. I didn't. "What if the boat isn't there when they come?"

A pause developed and Bill's voice gathered more confidence. "You're speaking entirely theoretically, of course."

"Of course."

"Because I wouldn't want to know about any disappearance of my boat. If someone should ask me where it is I would want to be able to say, with all candor, that it was at the dock when I saw it last, that other people sometimes use it, and that it must be off on a cruise somewhere. That's what I'd want to say."

"Who knows where it would go?"

"I don't," Bill said, "and I don't want to know."

"Well, I've got to go shower and look at some charts."

"Okay, whatever. Whatever, buddy. And you know?"

"What?"

"I should never have played cards with that guy called Doc."

"Or eaten at Mom's."

And here we were, pirating out of our own creek with a boat that belonged to the IRS, at least ninety percent of it, trying to get away clean and not run aground. I was at the helm about to run the gut at the mouth of the creek. My night vision was returning and Deb was beginning to get into the titillating unfamiliarity of sneaking around at night. She had her arms around me, biting the back of my neck.

"Right. Now you're turned on. You can't get turned on at

some more convenient time? Like when we're not committing a felony? How sick are you?"

She was beginning to describe, in a fairly interesting way, just how sick she was when I caught a light out on the river. "What's that?"

"I said that we could get in the back of the car at the far end of the Metro parking lot . . ."

"Not that, Deb. Out there on the river."

I throttled down and took the diesel out of gear. We drifted toward the creek's mouth. A red running light with a white light over it. A motorboat across the river in the channel, coming up-river along the beacons. It could be a fisherman coming back from a long day, or a cruiser coming home. The red light stayed but was joined by a green light. Trouble: the boat had just turned toward us and was showing her green starboard and red port running lights. I dropped *Sorrento*'s diesel into reverse and the way came off her. I throttled up and we began to move astern.

It's not like backing a car into your driveway. The rudder at the stern doesn't work worth a damn backwards. The cove behind us was dark and overhung with trees. A little Herreshoff twelve and a half swung at a mooring in front of one of the cove's docks. I began to play the rudder and back toward the other. The practice I'd had in backing *Sorrento* out of my cove and all those little gunkholes on the Eastern Shore paid off. I spun the wheel one way and then the other, balancing the push of the rudder under me with the gentle sternway and what wind there was. We retreated behind the headland and couldn't see the motorboat, now.

"Deb, I'm going to come up to that dock behind us, with our stern toward the land. When we get close to the pilings, grab on and stay low. We've got a boat coming and it may be the repo man. We'll try to look like we belong at the dock. Don't let them see any movement or any light."

"Is this like *Islands in the Stream* or *To Have and Have Not?*"

"Yeah, like both." I was distracted, looking backward, working the wheel and rudder and throttle. I took her out of gear and we pivoted into the cove. We had thirty seconds at the outside. I put her in forward and spun the wheel. She touched bottom in the mud behind her for a brief, knee-weakening moment, and pulled out, turning into the dock. Deb was forward on the port side, leaning out with the boat hook, smart girl. In neutral, now, drifting along the pilings, I slipped *Sorrento* into reverse, goosed the throttle, and she came to a dead stop beside the dock. Out of gear, throttle down, I jumped across the cockpit for the jib sheet and looped it over a piling. "Got it?" I called to Deb, as softly as I dared.

"Got it," she replied, holding the far piling as she lay behind the coach house on the deck. The diesel was idling quietly but the occasional sprays of water from her exhaust sounded like Sousa's Marine Band to me. I crouched in the cockpit as the lights of the motorboat appeared beyond the trees. I could hear it throttle down, headed straight into the creek. It made the turn at the little entrance buoy and headed for the Naval Academy hurricane moorings. Whoever it was knew the creek. It passed fifty yards away, working slowly into the creek. I could just make out the block lettering on the topsides and the big towing bitt aft, a SeaQue Towing boat. It was one of the scavengers who camp out on the distress frequencies and appear beside disabled cruisers wallowing in the middle of the Bay. Not exactly angels of mercy, they offer a quick exit from discomfort and embarrassment, but comfort comes at a high price when you really want it. They were not here to rescue a disabled boat.

To give them credit, they organized this raid quickly, between three in the afternoon and three in the morning. Not bad. They would take their time going in, four minutes to my cove. *Sorrento* was a big piece of hardware. They would see she wasn't there right away, but they would poke around back in the creek wondering if they really had the right dock for what, another ten minutes? Not that much. Then they'd be back, probably searching the banks with spotlights. How much time did we have, then?

Conservatively, twelve minutes in all. At six knots I could cover almost a mile and a quarter. But would *Sorrento* do six knots waving all this weed under her? Could we get out of here and hide somewhere else? Not if we waited too long. We'd count on their concentration forward and push off when they were a little farther into the creek, while they were still in view.

"Let go and give a push out," I called to Deb.

"They'll see us!"

"They're looking for us up there, not back here. We've got to get out of here before they come back."

Risks. I spun the big boat past the moored Herreshoff and took the entrance buoy on the wrong side, knowing that the tide was high. I headed out to clear the bar that reaches into the Severn. If I went downriver they'd pick me up for sure. I headed upriver, cutting the marker at the end of the bar and grinding away tooth enamel as I waited to fetch up on the mud. The depth sounder read out depths as the bottom rose toward our keel . . . 17.5 . . . 12.2 . . . 08.3. . . . At 6.7 feet the shallow water alarm began to weep a little repetitive tune and then stopped as we crossed the bar . . . 13.6 . . . 20.8 . . . 26.8. I gave it all the throttle I had, knowing that they couldn't hear me unless they turned off their big power plant. If I could make the headland upriver and stop her against the trees they wouldn't see a moving boat, they might search downriver, the logical place for me to go.

Even if we did elude them tonight, they would scour the river and the rivers all around Annapolis tomorrow. I had a big stolen boat; that's not like smuggling diamonds or even drugs. I couldn't hide it in or about my person. I couldn't get away from anyone, even if her bottom wasn't a seaweed garden. I should have had her hauled and scraped and painted this spring. . . .

A very piratical idea spoke to me, a middle-of-the-night, almost bloodthirsty ruse. Captain Edward Teach would have liked it. I liked it.

We made it to the headland and slipped into the background confusion of the trees and docks before we saw lights in my creek.

Red and white running lights and spotlights, playing the shore. I nosed *Sorrento* between two docks. The SeaQue boat hesitated at the mouth of the creek, turning, playing their spotlights behind and then out onto the Severn River. The spots swept past us, flaring in our eyes. I could hear Deb gasp but I put my arm around her, "They can't see much at this range, just a tangle of boats. We're almost a mile away. Let's hope they do the logical thing."

They did. The spotlights went out and the boat spun. I could see her green starboard light, then green and red together, then just red, and she headed downriver, the faint line of a big wake behind her. A few seconds later the angry growl of her big engine reached us. She would patrol the harbor and the near Bay for *Sorrento,* but I had no intention of obliging Malice Alice or the IRS.

We headed upriver. "Take the helm, babe," I said. "Keep that green flasher well on your left and keep the red quick flashing light just on your right." Deb took the wheel and I went below to retrieve my false colors.

It had taken me five minutes with a tape measure and twenty-two dollars to have Signs-For-U make a new transom. I unrolled the white printed vinyl and leaned over the stern. I stripped off the waxed-paper backing and laid the pressure sensitive film over the nicely lettered name *Sorrento.* With an Exacto knife I trimmed the excess that fluttered beyond the transom's edge. *Sorrento* was now *Jean Valjean* out of Hugo Cove, Maryland. An hour later we anchored behind St. Helena Island among other cruising boats and went below to sleep for a few sweet hours, drunk on our larceny.

Gavin's Marina is tiny and rough, a contrast to the swank yachting marinas in Annapolis and Eastport. It's hard to find by water and takes something of an expedition to arrive by land, but it has a big travel-lift and eight feet at the dock. At eight-thirty the new-christened *Jean Valjean* was tied up at the gas dock, waiting. A man who looked comfortable enough to be the owner came down with a cup of coffee in his hand to unlock the gas pumps.

"Hey there," he called, "What can I do you for?"

"Morning," I said, "I've got a foul bottom. Need antifouling paint, new zincs. And I need to do a little caulking on my topsides. Can you haul me and put me over under the trees?"

"Hell yes I can haul you. Haul you this morning, you're first in line. But you sure you want to be under the trees? Get sap and bird shit on your deck, suchlike." He sipped his coffee and seemed to enjoy it.

"We'll probably be coming back and forth, staying on the boat sometime. I'd like the shade, to keep her cool."

"If that'll make you happy, you got it. You want a power wash, of course, and disk-sanded?"

"Look her over and give me a price. Take your time. If you've got someone to sand her and paint her, let's do it."

I played her into the slip and killed the engine. Deb and I stepped off and watched as the travel-lift crew slung the bands under her and lifted her right up, her keel dark with weed and spotted with barnacles, water sheeting, then streaming, then dripping off her centerline and propeller and rudder as she lost her connection to the Bay. We sat against the pilings watching the rainbows of backsplash as they blasted her hull with the power washer, then followed her diminishing trail of water in a kind of procession across the lot to the far side, under the trees, out of sight from the water. They propped her upright on screw-poppets and lent us a ladder. I bought two blue plastic tarps and a coil of Samson Braid at the marina store and snugged them down across the deck house and the forward hatch. If I could have bought her a false nose, I would have done that, too.

We called a taxi, then, and went home. The dock looked bare without her.

"Bill?" I called him late in the afternoon, "I've got some bad news for you."

"What's that?" he asked agreeably.

"Damndest thing. Your boat's gone. Wasn't there this morning. A lot of folks are looking for that boat, too. The SeaQue launch was up here about three in the morning shining their spot-lights on the dock. But she was gone by then. They must have been disappointed."

"Oh, they were," Bill said, "they've already called me about it, wondering where that fine boat of mine is. I told them she was probably out cruising with friends and would be back any day, now. But I could be wrong."

"You could be. You in the mood for a hamburger tonight?"

"Sure."

"We ought to get one around seven."

He knew where to meet us. The local Fuddrucker's is loud and bright but the burgers are prime. I looked for Alice's car as we drove in but couldn't find it. I suspected it was nearby. She does not give up easily. After all, her injured persistence was the only reason we were skulking around like this.

We settled into attacking our half-pounders, medium rare, and slowed down for the french fries and onion rings. I paused for a drink and asked him, "What's your position at the Weldon Works?"

"Very humble. I don't own anything, anymore."

"But are you on the board or an officer of the corporation or anything like that?"

"Well, they haven't reorganized that I know of. I guess I'm still an officer of sorts."

"Could you get into the yard if you really needed?"

"But I don't have anything there."

"But if you needed to get into the fiberglass shed, could you do it? And would it be legal?"

"Let's say that it would be defensible."

"Most of Skip Weldon's tools are still there, all the plugs and molds for making boats?"

"Haven't gone anywhere. Haven't made any boats, either."

"We don't want to make a boat. We want to remake one."

"What?"

I love fiberglass. I can say this with authority because I've owned five wooden boats. They all sank. Some slow, some fast. Wood is sweet, beautiful stuff but it's full of holes. If you build a boat out of wood, it sinks. They all do. Fiberglass is a polymer resin, impermeable and almost infinitely formable. It's ideal stuff for boats. Fiberglass boats don't sink without a reason. Even if they do sink, you can repair anything, a holed hull or a stove bow, and it's as good as new. For five millennia boats were cobbled up out of wood because no one had any good polymer resin ready. If God had wanted us to have wooden boats, he would have made boat-shaped trees.

Alice was not in residence at the Weldon Works that night; her boat and her sail-loft office were dark. The fiberglass shed smelled of paint and solvent and raw resin. The shapes of the plugs and molds for the Weldon boats were stacked high at one end. A few yard dinghies leaned against one another inside the big sliding door. Our flashlights made broken shadows from the smooth hull shapes of the plugs and we were less directed than we should have been. It's hard when you love boats to be surrounded by their swelling, feminine forms and still pay attention to good larceny. What we were hunting was small and simple. We didn't know exactly what it looked like but at length we found it, touchingly worn and old-fashioned. Skip Weldon had used it a lot over twenty years, a homely little device for molding numbers into fiberglass. We picked up a few other items—a disk sander, an extension cord, some pots and scrapers and tins and paper tubs—and left. I was sad to leave, I admit, sad that Bill's raid on this old boatworks had come to so little and sad not to have known crusty Skip Weldon as well as Bill had known him. We talked about him all the way back to Annapolis.

We were sitting on my dock the next evening, drinking beer and conspiring. We watched a blue heron work the shallows for a few minutes. "We've got one logistic problem," I said. "We've got to keep Alice away from the boatyard for one whole night."

"How are we going to do that?"

"Ask her out to dinner in Washington and sleep with her."

"Shoot me. Give the IRS my boat and shoot me. Drop me into a cement mixer. It'd be less painful."

"We also need something to cover up noise."

"This isn't going to work."

"Sure it will. It's elegant. We just haven't figured out the details."

We still hadn't figured out the details when Deb found us on the dock at sundown. "What's the matter?" she asked.

"Here's the problem," I began. "We've got to chase Malice Alice out of her boat for a whole night. We've also got the problem of covering of some noise so anyone staying on a boat at the docks won't know what we're doing."

She picked a piling of her own. She's an engineer and twice as nasty as either of us. We waited.

"Ha," she said. "Do you remember when we sailed into that marina up on the Chester River to pick up some soda and beer?"

"Last year, in August, when that guy . . ."

"Talk about pollution," Bill began, then that Mack-the-Knife smile spread over his gremlin face. "Deb, I take back some of those rotten things I said about you. This is even more rotten."

It's a little disturbing when you realize that your new wife is capable of diabolic plotting. A wonderful talent directed toward Malice Alice, but what surprises can I expect if . . . make that *when* . . . she's angry with me?

We did some careful work on the *Jean Valjean* that week, put all our wicked ducks in a row, made a critical call for routine maintenance at the Weldon Marina, and on the following Tuesday afternoon we waited near the Weldon Works under an oak, watching the yard through binoculars. At four-thirty the Honey Bee System truck groaned into the yard followed by a cloud of dust and a swarm of flies. Arthur Janeway, proprietor and service man, climbed down from the cab and surveyed the location of the Weldon sanitary tank. This EPA-mandated device was built to store the waste from boat holding tanks. The holding tanks were connected to the boats' toilets. The Weldon sanitary tank had not been pumped since the collapse of the yard's financial structure last year. We had seen this man work several times before, once with Deb on the Chester River. Janeway was and probably still is the clumsiest, least efficient, most accident prone, sloppiest honey dipper on the Eastern Shore, an area not known for its crisp professional standards. He was a man with a sweet face who was totally unaware of any discomfort his hydraulic mismanagements might cause citizens nearby. We watched and were not disappointed as he began by misconnecting the draw lines and the pressure lines to the holding tank. A few moments after he started his pump and pulled the pressure lever, gouts of black fluid spurted from the tank vents, traveling yards across the lot and wetting down a curious spaniel. The spaniel spun round and round and headed for its owner's boat. While Janeway shook his head in accustomed confusion and shut down the pump, the spaniel bounded along a dock, onto a boat, and down a companionway hatch. There was a moment when it seemed that the boat had accepted the soiled spaniel in Christian forgiveness, but the offending dog reemerged in midair from the hatch, sailed across the cockpit, and rebounded from the lifelines like a WWF wrestler from the ring ropes. The pet fancier erupted from the hatch himself, holding his arms away from his body and spitting. Even at that distance his howl carried and rose above the spaniel's. He looked around in confusion, then seized the suitably groveling dog by its matted pelt and hurled it into the water. The spaniel surfaced, barking. In a shaking, hopeless frenzy its master jumped in after it.

Heads popped out hatches. Shouts and curses drifted across the water. Janeway held up his hands: Sorry, I've got this job to do. But we could see that by pausing to reassure his customers, he had dropped a conduit which was rapidly draining his pumper truck's accumulated night soil into the parking lot behind him.

Alice appeared at the sail-loft door, stopped for a horrified moment and launched herself at Arthur Janeway like an Exocet missile. The strike was aborted by olfactory countermeasures but she
danced back and forth in the gravel, keeping her distance from
the unclean Janeway, stumping up puffs of white dust as she ges-
ticulated and shouted. At that distance she sounded like a squeaky
fan. Janeway made placatory gestures: Things happen, everything
would work out, it would come out right in the end. Alice danced
and looked around for something long and heavy. The honey
truck drained into the gravel. The man was spectacularly incom-
petent.

Half an hour later the last car's dust was settling in the parking
lot, Janeway was attempting to recoil his balky black hoses, and
the Weldon Works—cleared and protected by a reeking miasma of
lower human processes—was ours.

Mirth and shit are old partners in half the jokes you ever heard.
We coughed and choked a little at first but, to us, it was part of a
joke and it wasn't that bad. We laid our extension cords as soon as
the Honey Bee System sanitary representative departed and we
went to work on an eight-inch section of *Aphrodite*'s transom.
I've told you, fiberglass is wonderful stuff. You can replace and repair it, and—with a little care, some gel-coat, and three grits of
wet sanding, a good wax and some buffing—you'd never know
the repair had been done. One, two, three, we were out of there
in three hours and headed across the Bay Bridge. We entered the
house triumphant, but Deb shooed us out ignominiously, insisting that we take all our clothes off on the porch. Apparently a
remnant of the Janeway miasma had traveled with us.

After that we were all virtue, believe me. You see, my con-
science got the better of me, my government had a legal right to
its property, and ethically I could no longer be a barrator. So I
turned in Bill to the IRS.

We had a picnic for the occasion, Bill and Deb and I. We took
some sandwiches and a cooler of beer and went to the Weldon

Works. The smell had gone down some. We were dragging one of the yard dinghies to the water when Alice took notice from her office window.

"Bill," she called from her door, ignoring Deb and me, "how are you?"

He only smiled in return. We didn't say anything to her as we inserted the drain plug in the dinghy's transom and slid it into the water.

"Bill," she called again, "where are you going? Have you had lunch? How about a cold beer, Bill?"

He pointed across the creek to the far bank against a field of ripe corn. We put our blanket and bags and cooler into the dinghy and shoved off.

She couldn't take it. We had not even unwrapped the sandwiches before she launched another dinghy and was pulling across the long reach of creek toward us. She arrived winded but trying hard to be girlish and appealing. Deb actually walked down to help her out of her boat, something that surprised me. "So. This looks nice," she said, inviting herself, "a picnic under the trees. Very civilized. What kind of sandwiches do you have? What have you been doing with yourself, Bill? I haven't seen you in much too long. We have a lot to catch up on."

"Well, Alice, I've been busy, you know. I've been reflecting on my wasted youth and I've decided to go straight."

"That's hopeful, Bill. You sound like things could turn around in your life. I'd love to help in any way I can, of course."

"I know you would, Alice. And you will."

Deb was watching all this with her least angelic expression, tossing something from hand to hand. I could hear a boat coming up Weldon Creek, a throaty big-engined growl.

"Anything at all, Bill. You know I've always been your greatest advocate. I could help you in a lot of ways."

"Alice, you have. I know about some of the ways you've helped me."

"What do you mean? You don't think I'd ever do anything to

hurt you, do you? Why, I'd sooner hurt myself than you, Bill. You know how I feel."

"Not really," Bill said, watching the boat past Alice's hopeful smile. "I've never really understood how you could be so damned helpful and so damned destructive at the same time."

"Bill, you just don't understand what's best for you. I've only done what's in your best interests, even when you couldn't see what they were."

"Mm." Bill commented, watching an impressive display of small craft handling at the Weldon Works yard.

"If you would give me the time to explain how your life could be better, with a little help from me, you'd understand."

"Don't think so, Alice." He was distracted by the efficiency of the three men from the big yellow boat in the yard, the boat with the green lettering on the side, SeaQue Towing.

Alice looked around, following his gaze. "What are they doing to my boat?"

"They're not doing anything to your boat."

"That's my boat they're pulling out of the slip."

"No, Alice, that's hull number WW42304. The number is cast right into the transom. Did you see them check it? They have to check the hull number when they impound a boat."

"They're going to tow it away!"

"Like I said, I'm going straight. WW42304 is *my* hull number, Alice. They've just checked it. That boat will square me with the IRS once and for all. I'm glad to make everything legal with them at long last."

"That's my boat!" She leaped up.

"Don't think so, Alice. You can check the number yourself. It's in the files up in the office. WW42304, Bill Barrister. WW42305 belongs to Alice and Harold Nailor. What ever happened to your boat, Alice? You didn't sell that and not report the income, did you?"

"You slimy little son of a bitch. I'll get you for this!" She was pushing off her dinghy. "Stop!" she screamed at the SeaQue crew, but I'll bet people have yelled things like that at them before, and they didn't stop.

She threw herself onto the oars and started across the creek at a furious pace.

"Beer?" Deb asked, and we replied, "Yes, thank you. How civilized."

The SeaQue boat backed the *Aphrodite,* hull number WW42304, out of her slip. The VHF antenna caught one of the geranium pots and dumped it on the dock. The antenna snapped upright and waved wildly. "Hey, you guys!" I called, "Be careful with that boat! Ten percent of it is mine!"

Alice's rowing was not going well. She was rowing just as fast but not getting as far. The dinghy rode lower and lower in the water and then sank entirely. Deb held up the plug she had been tossing around. "Abrupt woman," she commented. "Left without this little plug thing that keeps the water out. What do you call this if you're talking sailor talk."

"Little plug thing, Deb."

"Makes sense. Should we help her?"

Alice was shaking her fist at the retreating SeaQue boat, *Aphrodite,* and us while trying to tread water.

"No," Bill said after a few sentences of distant invective. "She can swim. I think."

Alice had kept up hull number WW42304 very professionally and she was assessed well. Ten percent of her price paid for the yard bill at Gavin's very nicely, with enough left over for a *bon voyage* dinner at Cantler's in the spring when they launched the *Jean Valjean,* hull number WW42306. Bill was taking her south. He'd always wanted to cruise the Caribbean and maybe start a pasta place on the beach, do a little light legal work, and use his natural talents as a troublemaker in the islands. And we had to face the facts: his life wasn't worth a nickel around Washington, especially after the IRS was through with Malice Alice. It seems that someone intimately acquainted with Alice's business dealings had informed the tax hounds about a series of under-the-table deposits made over two years. She insisted that the deposits were rent checks from a property she owned that had, mistakenly, been forgotten in her tax records. But there was a clear record of a boat she and her husband owned at about that time, a valuable boat that disappeared without an insurance claim. Did she sell it and pocket the money? Did she owe our government for capital gains? Once she explained that situation away or paid the taxes due on it she would be less distracted and would probably turn all of her attentions toward our Bill. Best he went south.

You can't trust anyone. Someone ratted Malice Alice out to the IRS. And even I ratted Bill, my good friend, out to the same people. There's a moral there. There's another moral to this story of barratry, a lesson in life, true in every detail even though I must apologize for it in advance: People who live in glass boats shouldn't throw stones.

John Lutz

SHOCK

It was odd the way people in shock had a protective, calming armor against emotion, almost like a powerful, deadening drug. And this was a shocking scene. Every lamp in the beach cottage blazed, illuminating detail and making it all the more vivid, the deeper to be etched into memory.

Gloria lay with her throat slit, obviously dead, though blood still flowed in a sluggish current from the gaping wound. The pool of blood that framed her thin body on the floor was still spreading.

Next to her, seated on the floor with his back against the sofa and his legs splayed, was a man with a brilliant red rim of blood around his white collar, a bib of blood covering his chest and tie.

By the sofa stood a tall man with blond hair and stunned blue eyes. He was wearing faded jeans and black leather sandals, a loose-fitting white T-shirt with a leaping swordfish emblazoned on its chest above the letters OCEAN YACHT CLUB.

The man who had just entered the beach cottage said, "Who are you?"

"Peterson's my name," the blond man said in an unnaturally calm voice, apparently in shock. "I live here. Are you the police?"

"No." The pounding of the surf carried in on the warm sea breeze, a throbbing sound like a slow heartbeat. "Are you sure your name's Peterson?"

"Of course I'm sure."

"Hmm . . . What in God's name happened here?"

"It's obvious," the blond man said. "Jorgen killed her, then he slit his own throat."

"Jorgen?"

"Gloria's brother. He's had serious mental problems. Just released from an institution, you know."

"I didn't know."

"Oh, yes. Devious character. And he can improvise like the devil himself."

Outside in the night, a seagull screamed. "Did you say the dead woman's name is Gloria?" the man who'd just entered the cottage asked.

"Yes. She's— She was my wife."

"If you'll forgive me for saying so, you don't seem terribly upset."

"I suppose I'm in shock." It was possible, Peterson thought. Gloria *had* been his wife, after all. And he might indeed be in shock, even though he was glad she was dead. She'd been a hideous woman inside a beautiful shell.

Within months after their wedding she'd emerged from that shell and blatantly proclaimed that she'd married him only for his money; she not only didn't love him, she hated him. Hideous woman.

Peterson had heard about her mad brother Jorgen but hadn't met him until now. It was pointless to say hello.

The man just inside the cottage door said, "I'm Nat Crancer. This is all so . . . tragic and lurid, I suppose I'm in shock myself. My God, anyone would be! I own the beach cottage half a mile south of this one. I was walking past and happened to glance in through those wide glass doors. The drapes are open and the lights are all on, so I couldn't miss seeing . . . all of this. I thought I might be of help."

"That was terribly considerate of you," Peterson said in his strangely flat voice. "There are further problems you might help me with." He brought his right hand around from where it had been concealed behind his back. In it was a long knife with a sharp point and a serrated blade, the sort that might be used for scaling fish. There was blood on the blade. "The murder weapon," he explained. "I picked it up off the floor, just as he planned."

" 'He' being . . . ?"

"Jorgen. Gloria's crazy brother. I hired a private detective and obtained proof of Gloria's infidelity. My attorneys would have seen to it that our divorce netted her small profit. She'd intended to financially rape me and share a much larger settlement with Jorgen. When she told him I had proof of her extramarital activities and their plan wouldn't work, Jorgen apparently became distressed, slit her throat, then his own. But not without planting clues suggesting I was the killer." He pointed to the floor near Gloria. Her bloody finger still lay near the last letter where she'd scrawled DAVI in her final moments. "My first name is David, you see."

"And you *are* holding the murder weapon."

"That was the idea. Jorgen knew that in my shock at finding the body, I'd reflexively pick up the knife. He used Gloria's finger to write the first four letters of my name before killing himself. Tried to make it look like a dying message. That, along with the common knowledge that Gloria and I hadn't been getting along, would in his twisted mind be enough to convict me. He might be right, I'm afraid."

"Why wouldn't he assume you'd smear the blood and make the letters unintelligible?"

"Now, how would that look? The scene tampered with, my fingerprints on the murder knife, my unfaithful wife dead in my beach cottage?"

"It would look glum for you, all right."

"Probably Jorgen wanted me to panic and act exactly in the manner you described."

The ocean continued pounding the beach a few hundred feet away in relentless, rhythmic surges, the pulse of the planet. "What bothers me somewhat, Peterson, is that, while proof of infidelity might have weakened Gloria's legal position in divorce proceedings, you're obviously a very rich man. She still would have come away from a divorce with something."

"No, no. She'd never have contested the terms my attorneys laid down. Her only condition would have been that her extramarital affair remain secret."

"That seems a bit optimistic of you, considering what you've told me about her."

"Not actually. You see, this clandestine affair she was having was with Jorgen—her own brother."

"Ah, I do see. That throws a different light on things. An incestuous relationship explains Jorgen's violent reaction, his rage and desire to get even with you. In fact, it almost seems justified."

"Well, I don't think so." Peterson set the knife down on the back of the sofa and walked over to a wet bar in the corner. He ran tap water and held his hands beneath it, rinsing them diligently for several minutes.

When he turned around and reached for a towel, he saw this neighbor, this man who said his name was Nat Crancer who had seemed so detached and in shock, staring longingly and regretfully at Gloria.

"Why are you looking at her that way?" Peterson asked.

Crancer said, "I'm wondering if you're really Peterson, or if Peterson is the man on the floor with his throat slit."

"Absurd. If the dead man is Peterson, who would I be?"

"Jorgen."

"That's wild. I saw the way you were staring at Gloria. Might not *you* be Jorgen?"

"Might. I might even be the real Peterson. But I'm not. I walked in when you were already here, and these two were already dead."

"That means absolutely nothing. You could have left, then seen me here and returned to deal with the situation."

The man who said he was Nat Crancer walked around the sofa and advanced on the man who said he was Peterson.

Peterson backpedaled in a wide circle, returning to the sofa, and picked up the knife again.

"That stuff about you thinking I'm Jorgen is just talk," Crancer said. "Nothing but bluff." He moved closer to Peterson. "Why don't you hand me the knife, then sit down and try to remain calm while I phone the police."

"You seem afraid," Peterson said.

"*You* seem afraid." Crancer slowly reached for the knife, thinking Peterson, who in truth seemed eerily detached rather than afraid, would hand it to him. He knew what he'd do with it once he had it.

The struggle was brief.

The man who'd said his name was Nat Crancer dropped heavily to the floor, stabbed cleanly through the heart.

"There!" Peterson proclaimed, like a ten-year-old who'd bested an opponent in a schoolyard scuffle. He was vaguely aware that this shock he was in continued to insulate him from all emotion, which was a blessing.

But he was still capable of surprise when the dead man who'd been sprawled braced and bloody against the sofa suddenly stood up.

Peterson realized his throat hadn't been slit at all. He must have heard Peterson approaching and used Gloria's blood to make it appear he'd killed himself as well as her, then feigned death. Peterson and Crancer, in their shocked states, had simply assumed he was dead because of all the blood. He was standing straight upright now, very tall, smiling above his bib of Gloria's blood, not dead in the slightest!

He was holding a second knife.

Peterson was truly shocked.

"Please!" he managed to say, before the broad blade slashed savagely across his throat.

Jorgen placed the serrated knife in Peterson's hand. The broad-bladed knife that had killed Gloria and Peterson he placed in Crancer's hand. He yanked the phone from an end table and placed the receiver in Gloria's hand. Then he walked the half-mile to Crancer's cottage, where he showered, leaving traces of Gloria's blood, and placed one of Gloria's bras beneath Crancer's bed. Several strands of Gloria's pubic hair that he'd plucked, he placed *in* the bed.

Then he returned to Peterson's cottage. He cradled Gloria's head in the crook of his right arm, then let it fall back. Her throat hadn't been cut deeply; it had taken her awhile to die. She might actually have been alive though fading when Crancer appeared.

Jorgen called the 911 emergency number, made a few inarticulate choking sounds, then hung up. A few minutes later he phoned again, from the phone in the kitchen, and pleaded desperately for the police.

It would be obvious what had happened: Gloria had been having an affair with Crancer, they quarreled, and Crancer thought he'd killed her. Then he'd gone to his cottage and cleaned up.

He returned to make it appear that Peterson was the killer, scrawling the first four letters of Peterson's name on the floor with Gloria's blood. Maybe he realized then that Gloria was still alive, or maybe he never noticed. Because that's when Peterson interrupted him, they'd struggled, and Crancer had slit Peterson's throat as Peterson was stabbing him through the heart. Jorgen would say he'd arrived just in time to see that happen, though he'd been unable to prevent it. Gloria, barely alive, had managed to reach the phone to call 911 for help, but was unable to speak. She'd died in Jorgen's arms, and he'd finished the call for her.

If the police believed his story, it meant officially that Peterson had died first.

Which meant that Gloria had inherited Peterson's money before she'd died.

Which meant that Jorgen would now inherit Gloria's money. And the police would believe him. He was a plausible sort. He could improvise like the devil himself.

▪ *Art Monterastelli* ▪

STRAIGHT SHOOTER

In a town characterized by every kind of excess and self-aggrandizement, Hank Snapp was an unusually humble man. Like many people he came to Los Angeles because of a desire to be in the movie business. He went to UCLA Film School, but didn't quite fit in with the fast-track crowd. After graduation he got a job editing and then producing public service announcements. He married a beautiful red-haired woman he met at a church fundraiser and became a reserve policeman to supplement their income. Fourteen years went by. The public service announcements proved to be a dead end to the real Hollywood. His beautiful red-haired wife turned out to have a fondness for cocaine and the occasional one-night stand. Hank handled her betrayals well. He told his

weekend patrol partner, Curtis Thornberry, that during the in-
evitable breakup of the marriage he had been tempted by violence
only once, when they were dividing up community property.

"She wanted to keep my one-sheet from *King's Row.*"

"What the hell's a one-sheet?"

Having grown up in South Central, and being an extremely
agile two-hundred-and-sixty-pounder, Curtis had always been
more interested in football than movies.

Hank explained what it was. Curtis scrunched his nose, more
puzzled than ever.

"Let me get this straight. The bitch was screwin' around on
you and you got upset about a *poster?*"

Hank blushed, the way he always did when Curtis used such
language. He explained that the poster was autographed by Ronald
Reagan, the Gipper himself. In Hank's estimation *King's Row* was
the best movie Reagan ever made.

"Hank," Curtis responded, "don't take this the wrong way,
but you need to rethink your pri*orities.*"

A few weeks after his divorce Hank received a call from Ray Washburn, an old film school professor who was now a postproduction
honcho at Warner Bros.

"Hank, Blackguard Studios is looking for someone to cut their
trailers and promos. There's room for advancement and, off my
recommendation, the job is basically yours."

"Who do I have to sleep with?" Hank jokingly asked.

"You don't have to sleep with anybody, but you'll be working
for Pig Bledsoe." Ray paused. "I'm not gonna lie to you. Bledsoe's the meanest, most abusive sonofabitch on the planet. You'll
learn a world of skills from him if he likes you. If he doesn't, you
won't last two days."

"All I can ask for is an opportunity."

"I want you to think about this."

"C'mon, Ray, when do I meet him?"

"Day after tomorrow."

"I'll put some little extra starch in my collar."

Blackguard Studios produced action/adventure television shows for first-run syndication. The shows weren't particularly good but there were a lot of them, which resulted in a nearly nonstop workload for the postproduction people. The studio was in east Hollywood, in an area frequented by junkies and homeless teens. The parking lot was surrounded by a ten-foot cyclone fence, topped off with a double coil of razor wire. Hank's first day on the job he heard a muffled groan from one of the giant Dumpsters in the lot. Two vagrants had found a tear in the fence and set up house inside the Dumpster. They looked like a single two-headed beast as they "went at it," race and gender barely distinguishable in a roil of matted hair, tattered clothes, and putrid garbage. Ever the gentleman, Hank got their attention by clearing his throat.

The wild-eyed male looked up at him.

Hank smiled politely and said, "You know, there are laws against doing this kind of thing in public."

"This ain't fucking public! This is our *home,* you fucking pervert!"

Hank's smile never wavered.

"It's private property and I happen to be a reserve police officer. If you don't move out of here quietly, I'm gonna have to arrest you."

It wasn't until Hank showed them his gun that they finally believed him. After that it was a fairly peaceful exit. Hank felt good about letting them go. They obviously had not had the benefit of a good Christian upbringing, even lacked the basics of modern hygiene, but they were God's creatures nonetheless. Besides, it was his first day of work and he didn't want to cause trouble for anyone.

Pig Bledsoe, however, failed to see the value of such fellowship. Word got back to him about Hank's encounter with the vagrants and after lunch he summoned Hank into his office. Pig sat behind his desk sucking on the gnawed end of an aqua-filter cigarette holder. Two hundred and thirty-two pounds of muscle and bloated

gas crammed into a five-foot, eight-inch frame. The wall behind
him was plastered with photographs of fighter jets and special effects explosions.

"Ray Washburn told me you were a reserve cop."

"I am."

"He said you pack a gun. Nine-millimeter, to be precise."

"Well, not everywhere I go but—"

"Did you have it with you this morning?"

Hank hesitated for a moment.

"Yes I did."

"Then why the hell didn't you shoot those two vagrants you
found fornicating in my Dumpster?"

Hank smiled faintly; he couldn't tell whether the man was serious or not.

Pig Bledsoe was dead serious. He raged on for twenty minutes
about property rights, airborne viruses, contaminated water supplies, and the general decline of the republic. As he sat silently
through this harangue two thoughts occurred to Hank: one, that
Pig might have had too much caffeine that morning; two, that he
might not be entirely sane. Sane or not, Hank liked the man. He
had values.

"Those two trailers I showed you this morning? I want you to
recut them."

"I thought they were locked?"

Pig clenched the gnawed aqua-filter between his teeth.

"I thought," Hank continued, "they had to be delivered to the
distributor first thing tomorrow morning?"

"They do, you're gonna have to stay up all night. I'll meet you
here 5:30 A.M., we'll check the reels together."

Hank didn't know what to say.

"I'm looking for a good man, Snapp. Washburn tells me you
could be that man. He says you're a straight shooter."

Hank nodded his head, almost imperceptibly.

"All the bullshit you've heard about me, there's one thing
that's true. I appreciate loyalty."

Pig lowered his voice, narrowed his eyes.

"You understand what I'm saying?"

Hank recut both trailers and completely restructured a twenty-second promotional reel. Pig rewarded him by working him night and day for the next two weeks. Two weeks turned into two years. Word spread around town. Pig Bledsoe had finally found his number-two man.

For his part Hank couldn't have been happier. Pig was teaching him the business. ADR, special effects, foley, he was becoming one of the true wizards of postproduction. He was learning so much that the dream of directing his own movie, having laid dormant for so many years, gradually reasserted itself. Around this same time something happened outside of Blackguard that brought that dream even more forcibly to the surface.

During one of Hank's growingly infrequent stints as a reserve policeman, he and his partner Curtis answered a domestic violence call in an upper-middle-class neighborhood of Van Nuys. It was a ranch-style house with a circular drive and a couple of fruit trees in the yard. The front door was open when they arrived, the interior of the house dark. Hank and Curtis announced themselves. When they received no reply they entered, Curtis a couple of steps ahead of Hank. The foyer led into a large living room at the back of the house, two sets of sliding glass doors looking out on a swimming pool. The light from inside the pool was the only source of illumination and was reflected in aqueous blue strips across the glass doors.

"Something spooky about this place," Curtis said.

One of the doors was cracked open and the sound of someone crying drifted in from outside. As Hank moved around Curtis's right side he saw there was a woman standing by the pool. Her hair was cut short and a flimsy camisole covered her shivering figure, nothing more than a pair of panties beneath that. Hank was momentarily struck by the image of this woman by the blue pool, its almost cinematic quality, when he heard the explosion from the other side of the room. Two barrels from a Remington over-and-under shotgun. If Curtis hadn't been such a big man the blast would have taken Hank out as well. As it was the impact knocked Curtis, all six foot three, two hundred and sixty pounds of him, off his feet and right into Hank, dropping both of them to the floor. For a heart-numbing moment Hank was trapped beneath his dying partner. He was able to get to his radio before his gun.

"This is one-adam-twenty, officer needs assistance." Even to Hank, standard procedure seemed absurd. He could hear the life sucking right out of Curtis's body, an eternity between each lumbering breath, blood seeping warm and sticky down the back of his own neck. He screamed into the radio: "It's my partner, god-dammit! My partner's been shot!"

The man with the shotgun, suddenly aware that he'd shot a policeman, disappeared into a back hallway. The woman outside still stood beside the pool, a faint look of surprise on her face, her delicate beauty frozen in time. Hank struggled to get out from under Curtis's tremendous weight.

"It's gonna be all right, partner. I promise you, it's gonna be all right."

There was no reply from Curtis, only a strange sucking sound; not unlike a balloon with a hole ripped through it, trying to refill itself with air.

And then, from somewhere in the back of the house, there was a second explosion of shotgun barrels. And for Hank, time got scrambled all over again.

After the death of his partner, Hank went off active reserve duty. He put in the same long hours at Blackguard, but his heart was no longer in the work. One day, in the middle of a dubbing session, Pig Bledsoe walked into the control room and offered to take Hank out for a drink. It was three o'clock in the afternoon.

Pig decided on the bar of a cheap Italian restaurant a block off Sunset. Autographed pictures of Vic Damone, Mario Lanza, and Frank Sinatra gathered dust above a facade of plastic wine casks.

The cracks in the red leather booth they occupied were patched over with duct tape.

"The woman stood out by the pool the whole time."

"Who was in the bedroom again?"

Pig was more focused on his scotch than he was on the story he had asked Hank to tell.

"Her husband."

"Who had just blown his brains out."

Hank nodded.

"She knew it was her husband? In the bedroom."

"I don't know what she knew. Her face just sort of went blank. The whole thing was strange. Being inside of it, I mean. From the moment we walked in the door it was like there was something else going on, beyond what we could see. And that something just *sucked us in*. And then it clobbered the hell out of us."

Hank looked down at his own scotch. He pushed an ice cube to the bottom of the glass with his finger. He held it there for a moment, before letting it bob back to the surface.

"It's like there was the surface of the thing," he tried to explain, as much for his own benefit as Pig's. "And then there was the thing itself."

Pig stared back at him with a blank gaze. Then he thrust his hand in the air and waved for the bartender.

"Two more of these!"

He smiled at Hank. "And the whole thing started because he caught her cheatin' on him."

"I guess."

"Yeah," Pig nodded. "That explains it."

It didn't explain anything for Hank. Whatever the initial motive had been, he was still struck by the aura or texture of the event; however elusive, it seemed to hold more truth than the facts. When the bartender set two more scotches down in front of them, Hank took a big gulp of his.

"I'm thirty-eight years old, Pig." There was a slight tremor in Hank's voice. "I need to change my life."

"You need to quit that cop shit is what you need."

"I need to get out of Blackguard, too. It's starting to swallow me up."

An odd look shadowed Pig's face.

"You're absolutely right, Hank. You need to look at this as your wake-up call; a chance to look into your own heart. And you know what you're gonna find there?" His voice grew thick with conspiracy. "The need to direct your own movie."

"A movie?"

"Not exactly a *movie* movie but a film, an honest to God film. Paniflex camera, cranes, lights, the whole shebang!"

Pig leaned closer over the table, barely containing his hushed excitement.

"I've seen you in the editing room, I've seen your inserts; you're a natural, Hank. The only reason it hasn't happened before is because you've been too much of a mensch. Spielberg, Stone, Coppola, they'd pimp their own mothers for the right shot; but you, you've got *integrity*. That's why you're the perfect guy for the job."

Hank started to feel a little light-headed.

"What exactly *is* the job?"

A couple of nights later Hank received a call from Ray Washburn.

"I hear Pig's roped you into one of his nefarious little schemes."

"He's giving me a chance to direct, Ray."

"You're talking about a commercial."

"If I do a good job on the commercial they're gonna give me a small feature."

"They being Pig and Justin Duchette."

"That's right, Pig and Justin have a deal together."

"I know all about their 'deal.'" Ray said, a certain edge creeping into his voice. "Pig was supposed to produce three commercials for fifty grand apiece. He spent the money for the first one on some other harebrained scheme, or maybe he just lost it at the racetrack, I don't really give a rat's ass. The point is I don't want to see you get sucked in with this guy Duchette. He's as sleazy as they come and right now he's got Pig by the short ones."

Hank had never heard his old professor talk this way.

"Ray, you know I'm indebted to you for setting me up with Pig in the first place, but I'd appreciate it if you didn't talk him down so much. He's treated me fair and I owe him plenty."

"Hank, I shouldn't be telling you, but Pig's in trouble. On top of his gambling debts and all the ex-wives he owes money to, he's about to get nailed with a sexual harassment suit. It's happened before but this time, when it becomes public, Blackguard's gonna dump him." Ray's voice softened. "Play your cards right they're gonna tap you to replace him."

Hank thought about the prospect of being named head of postproduction.

"I don't think I can play those cards, Ray. It's not in me to take advantage of situations like that."

"Situations like that are what careers are made of."

Hank thought about it again.

"I've already made up my mind, Ray. I don't want to disappoint you, but I'm gonna direct this thing for Pig."

"Yeah, well, don't say I didn't warn you."

The first creative meeting between Hank, Pig, and Justin Duchette didn't go as well as Hank had hoped. Duchette was a baby-faced thirty-three-year-old sporting a beautifully tailored Armani jacket over a plain white shirt and a pair of jeans with the knees ripped out. He sat in Pig's chair, feet up on the desk, scrutinizing Hank's shot list.

"You don't look too happy," Hank ventured.

Duchette stared vacantly at the sheets of paper in his hand. Then he crumpled them into a single ball and tossed it into the wastebasket across the room.

"We're selling Spa Scent, Hank. That's the product. Nobody cares how the house is lighted, the fancy way you move your camera, or the color of the sky." He held up his hand and counted off a finger for each item he listed. "You've got your trained seals, which is a nice opening gimmick. You've got your middle-aged bald guy, who should be funny. And you've got your blonde with big tits. These are your three essential components."

He got up from behind Pig's desk and walked to the door.

"Just the essentials, Hank. Everything else is a come shot."

There was an uncomfortable silence after Duchette left the room. Pig, who had been quiet throughout the meeting, did his best to avoid Hank's eyes.

"I'm not sure he understands what I'm trying to do," Hank finally said.

"Forget him, Hank. He's totally a money man."

Pig fished the shot list out of the trash and handed it back to Hank.

"Your shot list is fine."

He straightened one of the fighter jet photographs on the wall as he moved around his desk.

"One thing, though. That blonde, Nicole?"

"The one who couldn't remember the dialogue."

"Yeah. I think it would be a good idea if you cast her anyway. Duchette's kind of sweet on her."

In the weeks that followed Hank threw himself into the chaotic labor of preproduction. He looked at nearly fifty hours of film before deciding on the right cameraman who was ready to be bumped up to director of photography. He hired a location scout and subsequently made a deal with a woman in Van Nuys named Marla Milkie to use her backyard pool and spa for the shoot. Along with Rusty Bender, the animal trainer who would be wrangling the seals, he choreographed that part of the commercial that would take place in the pool. Through it all the only time he saw Pig was when he needed his signature on a check.

"You sure this is the best deal you can make on film stock?"

"It's half priced. The guy at Kodak is doing us a tremendous favor."

"What about short ends?"

"You never know when short ends are gonna run out. It's a bad choice for a project like this; especially if we want to shoot the whole thing in two days."

Pig signed the check, begrudgingly, and then went back to figuring out his picks for the ninth at Santa Anita.

"Nobody told me the slimy things were actually gonna be inside the pool!"

It was the night of the tech rehearsal and Marla Milkie suddenly had a problem with the seals. As Hank crossed over from the other side of the pool Rusty Bender ambled up alongside him, his ponytail swaying in the breeze.

"She's lying, Hank," Randy said quietly. "I took her through the whole thing. Shot by shot."

"Let me handle it," Hank replied, putting on his best reserve-cop smile as he approached Marla.

"There's a misunderstanding about the seals?"

"I had no idea they were actually going in the water." The shocked look was etched on her face as carefully as the mascara and ruby red lipstick, and Hank realized she had spent at least as much time perfecting it.

"I'll have to drain the entire pool. It's not healthy for humans to swim in the same water as marine animals. And on top of that," she adroitly shifted gears, not even bothering to conceal the coyness in her eyes, "aren't you supposed to get some kind of special permit from the city?"

Hank wrote the check, an extra five hundred dollars for "seal clean-up," from his own account.

"Rusty, how we doing?"

Rusty's seals were swimming loops inside the perimeter of the pool. It was the first night of shooting and they were already two hours behind schedule.

"I need a couple more practice runs, Hank. They're still over-excited from the drive over."

Hank scratched his head. The seals looked fine to him, but then Rusty was the expert. He walked away from the camera to the spa area. Wally, the balding middle-aged man they'd hired to play the balding middle-aged man, sat on the edge of the jacuzzi. He had a robe over his bathing suit, his feet dangling down in the hot water.

"Those seals are terrific. Did you see that trick they did with the beach ball?"

"We're going to try and get it on film, Wally."

"That would be terrific. Really terrific."

"Where's Nicole?"

"She went in the house with Marla. I guess she's not too crazy about getting in the water with the seals."

By the time Hank got to the kitchen, Nicole was finishing off her second vodka and tonic. Her bathrobe hung open and the bikini she wore under it barely concealed the most private of her private parts. Marla was at the kitchen counter, dumping ice, fresh fruit, and vodka into a blender.

Hank crouched down in front of Nicole and gently took the glass of vodka out of her hand. "It's not a good idea to have alcohol in your system before you—"

"I'm not getting in no hot tub with no goddamn mountain lion!"

"Sea lion, honey. Those are what you call sea lions," Marla volunteered.

Hank took Nicole's hand and held it the way he would a small child's.

"They're not sea lions, they're seals, and they're never going to be in the jacuzzi with you. One of them is going to slide across the spa ledge and kiss Wally. That's it."

Nicole bit down on her bottom lip, still not entirely convinced. "Do they have names?"

Hank had to think about this for a moment. To the best of his knowledge, they didn't. But Nicole, a Valley Girl from Reseda who'd probably never read anything more challenging than the *Hollywood Reporter*, needed reassuring.

"The lead seal's name is Timmy," he said. And without a thought, he added, "The other one's name is Lassie."

Nicole's mouth was agape. A spark of hesitation burned dully in her eyes.

"Which one does Wally have to kiss?"

Hank went with his first instinct.

"Timmy."

Nicole giggled.

"Does he have to give him any tongue?"

Behind them, Marla hit the switch on her blender without putting the top on. The mangled concoction of ice, fruit, and booze erupted all over her cherry-wood cabinets and Formica countertop. Marla herself slipped on a puddle of it and landed on her ass in the middle of the floor, the blender still churning away at full bore above her, her own laughter the only thing competing with the high-speed metallic squeal. Hank took a quick look to make sure she was physically okay. Then he led Nicole out of the kitchen.

Two hours before dawn they were shooting only their second master of the night: two seals racing across the length of the pool, passing a beach ball between them, Wally and Nicole sitting in the jacuzzi in the background. Pig had showed up sometime after one A.M., taken a cursory look around the set, and then disappeared into the kitchen with Marla. Hank was too busy to worry about either one of them. Right after Pig arrived Duchette dropped by to see how Nicole was doing. It wasn't long after this that he was permanently encamped behind the camera, looking over Hank's shoulder on every shot.

"That last one seemed pretty good to me."

"We were too far ahead of the lead seal when the ball went into the air," Hank replied.

Duchette glanced at his watch. "Hank, we're making a commercial, not a fucking Stanley Kubrick film."

Pig came out of the kitchen, swaggered across the patio, a fresh vodka and juice concoction in his hand.

"Leave my director alone, Duchette."

"Excuse me?"

"You're supposed to leave the creative end to me and my people. That's the deal we made."

"All I'm suggesting is that we move on to the next shot. The way your 'director' is shooting we're never going to finish the whole thing tonight."

Hank's jaw went slack. When Pig didn't say anything Hank turned to Duchette himself.

"Excuse me, but it was my understanding that we're budgeted for two production days."

"That's right," Pig blurted out. "Two production days!"

Duchette never raised an eyebrow.

"You're talking about an extra ten to fifteen thousand dollars that I don't see in the budget, Pig."

The entire crew, Hank included, held their breath.

"Why you yuppie-scum-sonofabitch—"

Pig made a fist with the hand that wasn't holding the cocktail glass. As he started towards Duchette, dipping instinctively into his fighter's crouch, he lost his balance on the edge of the pool and started to teeter over. Hank reached out and pulled Pig back by his belt strap, before returning his attention to Duchette.

"Mr. Duchette, I have to be honest with you. There's no way we can get the rest of the coverage we need. It's going to be daylight pretty soon."

"So what?"

"The shots won't match. It'll be night when we first see the seals in the pool and then it'll be daytime when we move in on Wally and Nicole in the jacuzzi."

Duchette took a moment to think about this.

"If the people at Spa Scent don't accept the commercial because of technical incompetence, you and Pig eat the cost. That's the deal we made."

This part of the deal had never been explained to Hank. He looked away from Duchette for a moment. Pig had collapsed into a lawn chair and was petting one of the seals. Most of the crew members, who had been hauling ass all night, were also looking for places to sit down, their spirits noticeably sagging. Wally and Nicole were out of the jacuzzi, bundled in robes and sound blankets to keep warm, eager to find out what all the excitement was about.

Duchette sidled up beside Hank and whispered in his ear, "Bledsoe's taken me to the cleaners on this. Tonight's his last shot. After this, we *all* end up in court."

The wretched sound of Pig vomiting turned everybody's head. Duchette kept his mouth near Hank's ear, creating a strange intimacy. "He's a real beauty, isn't he? I should shoot myself for getting into business with him in the first place." He shook his head disgustedly and moved away. "You really can't expect me to throw good money after bad, Hank."

Hank stared at the uninspiring image of Pig, now passed out in the lawn chair, a tendril of vomit hanging off one sleeve. The dream that had brought Hank down from Fresno all those years ago, for the first time truly within his grasp, was starting to slip away. From his years as a reserve policeman he knew one thing for certain: a command decision was needed.

"I'll put up the money myself."

Duchette stopped walking.

"Say that again."

"I'll put up my own money for the second night. We'll amend the contract so I get it back after the commercial goes on the air."

A hushed silence fell over the entire backyard; even the seals were quiet. One side of Duchette's mouth curled into a faint smile. He stuck out his hand.

"Hank, you've got yourself a deal."

Hank was at the bank that morning before the doors opened. When they finally did he had a cashier's check drawn up for ten thousand dollars, his entire life savings. He dropped the check off at Duchette's offices on San Vicente, explaining the necessity of it being deposited that day to the most responsible looking of the three young and very attractive secretaries. He went back to his own house in North Hollywood with the intention of getting some sleep. But there was too much on his mind. He went back over his shot list for the second night, realizing there was still one more shot he needed to get with the seals alone, isolating the beach ball. And realizing also that Duchette had been right, he had spent far too much time on his "beauty" shots; his own perfectionism had cost him the ten thousand dollars. The upside was, if he could trust what he was seeing on the video feedback, the film itself looked good. Still too wound up to sleep, Hank popped a cassette of John Ford's *The Searchers* into the VCR and settled back on the sofa with the remote, freeze-framing the transitions from masters to individual coverage, concentrating on the way Ford had composed each frame. An hour and a half into this, maybe fifteen minutes into the film itself, he finally fell asleep.

On his way to the set that night Hank drove by the house where Curtis had been killed. He said a silent prayer for Curtis's soul and then another one for his family's well-being. The house itself was as dark as it had been that fateful night, a "For Sale" sign posted in the middle of the front yard. Hank replayed the events in his head. He saw the slender short-haired woman caught in the swimming pool's blue light. He heard the blast from the over-and-under shotgun and remembered the impact of Curtis's body pitching into his. Once again he tried to make some sense out of what had happened, but it went against instincts that had been honed by more than fifteen years on the job. When you're a cop, even a reserve cop, bad shit happens. Sometimes it happens to people you don't know, sometimes it happens to your partner, and sometimes it happens to you. If they had walked into that house at even slightly different angles, he would have been the one to catch the shotgun blast and Curtis would be the one sitting there trying to make sense of it—a simple calculus of chance and circumstance. Hank's real quandary was figuring out how God fit into it. A lifetime of prayer, however, had taught him to be patient with questions like that. Besides, it was getting late and he had a movie to direct.

With a more realistic shot list than he had had the previous night Hank was able to get the final master in forty-five minutes. He picked up a nice medium shot of Timmy jumping straight up out of the water, a beach ball perched on the tip of his snout; with a sudden flick of the seal's head the ball sailed across the pool in the general direction of the spa. The composition of the shot as the ball left the frame lended itself perfectly to an eventual tighter cut of the ball landing in the spa.

"Do they have to stay in the jacuzzi between shots? Nicole's nipples are getting cold."

It was the first time Duchette had opened his mouth that night. Hank and Reed Marlowe, the DP, were already picking up the camera and tripod, hurrying around the side of the pool to the next setup. Duchette grabbed the apple crate Reed had been standing on top of and hurried along with them, leaving the heavier aluminum camera cases to the gaffer.

"I was thinking we could pitch a tent in the backyard. I happened to have a rather nice one in the trunk of my Jag."

Hank exchanged a quizzical look with Reed.

"I uhm don't think we're going to have time for that. Nicole's in every shot from here on in."

"Just as long as Nicole's happy."

Since the camera was focused on the spa now, Rusty donned a wet suit and climbed into the pool to work more closely with the seals. Pig and Marla were nowhere in sight and nobody seemed to miss them. Once the lights were set and the camera was ready to roll, Hank crouched down in front of the spa to talk to his actors.

"Okay, Wally, when you bring the bottle around from behind your back—"

"Second position."

"Right, second position. When the bottle's in second position, make sure we can see the words 'Spa Scent.'"

Wally held the bottle stomach high.

"Perfect, now when you drop the bottle—"

"Third position."

"That's right, Wally, third position. Just make sure we see the logo when the bottle hits the water."

The camera was tight on Nicole as she stood at the other end of the spa, facing away from Wally. She was perfectly in character, her lips pouty and bored, her breasts accentuating the bottom of the camera's frame. Hank recited the lines that would eventually be supplied by the off-screen narrator: "Tired of the same old bathwater experience?"

"I'm tired of everything," Nicole purred. "I wish we'd invested in a Lamborghini instead of this dreary old thing."

"Yew-hew, Nicole!" Wally piped in at the appropriate moment, his pale potbelly outside the frame. "Wally has a surprise for you!"

Hank, standing behind the camera, whispered into his headset microphone: "Start the seals."

Rusty received the order at the other end of the pool and hung an anchovy in front of Timmy's eyes. Timmy swallowed the fish and promptly took off across the pool. At the same time the camera was pivoting wide to include Wally in the shot with Nicole, shooting over Nicole's left shoulder as she turned towards him.

"Oh, Wally!" Nicole cried, responding to the luxuriant froth of bubbles emanating from the spa's filter-head.

"It's Spa Scent!" Wally exclaimed.

Nicole closed her eyes, tilted her head back, and slithered down into the bubbling hot water.

"Mmmmm, I feel a thousand little fingertips caressing every inch of my body." Consciously or not her own fingers began caressing her skin as she slithered back up out of the sudsy water.

"Does Wally get a little spa kiss?"

"Wally gets a *big* spa kiss."

The camera moved in for a close-up as Wally closed his eyes and puckered his lips. And right on cue, with everybody behind the camera breathless with anticipation, Timmy the seal slid across the jacuzzi ledge and met Wally's lips with a big juicy kiss.

"Cut!"

Hank scrambled around the camera. He squeezed Nicole's shoulder. "That was great, don't change a thing."

"Thanks, Hank."

Wearing a heavy sweater, short pants, and tennis shoes, Hank stepped right into the jacuzzi and put his arm around a nervous-looking Wally.

"How about me?"

"You're doing fine, Wally." He took a dramatic pause, holding his index finger to his lips. "One thing, though. The moment before the seal slithers up to you?"

"Yeah?"

"You're anticipating the kiss."

Wally looked crestfallen.

"It's okay, we're talking nanoseconds here. We're going to do it one more time so—"

Wally started to say something. Hank cut him off with a wink of his eye.

"Trust the moment."

And so the night progressed. Hank was in the zone, his perfectionism matched only by his adroit management of the clock. It took him four more takes but he finally got the shot he wanted of Timmy kissing Wally. He did a pick-up of the Spa Scent bottle hitting the water in front of Nicole's crotch, logo facing up. He cleared the actors out of the jacuzzi and got a shot with Timmy floating by himself in the frothy foam for the coda. And when it was time to shoot from the other side, it took Reed and the gaffer less than thirty minutes to adjust the lights.

"Hank!" Rusty bellowed from across the pool. "I'm running out of anchovies!"

"As soon as we get this shot you can wrap the seals."

It was the kiss, with the camera looking over Wally's shoulder instead of Nicole's. They shot it three times and each time Timmy's timing was off. Hank started feeling a little anxious, there was less than two hours left before daybreak. He decided to move the shot in tighter, thereby giving the seal more latitude for his arrival.

"Wally, you're gonna have to cheat your shoulder back an inch or two."

The frame was readjusted. They were about to start rolling film when they heard Marla scream.

Hank raced toward the house, half the crew on his heels. By the time they got inside Pig was ripping a sliding closet door off its track in the main foyer, trying to get at Marla. They were both drunk, a deck of playing cards and a pile of clothing strewn across the living room carpet. Having stripped down to her bra and panties, by all evidence voluntarily, during the course of their game, Marla was now screaming her lungs out and pulling every piece of clothing in the closet down between her and the rampaging buck-naked Pig. Hank managed to get a hand on Pig's shoulder as Pig tore in half a purple velour smoking jacket that separated him from his prey.

"Pig!"

Pig swung an elbow back, catching Hank in the eye. Marla used the distraction to kick Pig square in the scrotum, which only incensed him more as he emitted a primal wail and launched his

body like a torpedo right on top of her. As Hank struggled to re-
gain his bearings in the cramped closet, his one eye swelling shut,
various limbs flayed out at him. Rusty and two other crew members knocked the second sliding door off its track and finally managed to pull Pig off Marla.

"I want that maniac out of my house!"

It was Duchette who came to Marla's assistance, having ground
up several Valium and camouflaged them in the straight vodka
both Marla and Pig were drinking. One sip of this potent libation
and Marla lost the desire both to scream and to keep her eyes
open. The recalcitrant Pig, on the other hand, drank nearly twice
as much of the same brew, threw the glass across the room, and
stormed out of the house, scratching his injured scrotum with
one hand while holding his pants and shoes with the other. Without bothering to put the pants on, and before anyone could stop
him, he climbed into his '72 El Dorado convertible and sped away
into what little night remained.

"Keep that piece of meat on it, Hank."

Hank sat on a chair in the kitchen, a raw piece of steak pressed
over his forehead and right eye. Rusty was rummaging through
the kitchen drawers, looking for a screwdriver to repair the closet
door.

"How's Marla?"

"She's passed out in the bedroom. Duchette's in there with
her, making sure her heart doesn't stop."

"How're your seals doing?"

"They're getting real hungry, Hank."

Hank lifted the piece of meat off his head.

"We better get to it."

With one eye swollen shut Hank's field of vision was considerably
altered. He wasted nearly forty minutes trying to decide on the
frame and angle that would match everything else he had shot.
On top of that one of the big klieg lights they were using started

shorting out. They replaced the bulbs but the light continued to flicker. Somebody finally traced the power cable back to the generator, which was parked in the front yard, and found that the cable itself had been frayed.

"Looks like somebody ran over it with a lawn mower."

Hank was huddled with Rusty, Reed, and one of the grips. The grip had wrapped the lacerated section of cable with electrical tape and was suggesting that they flip ends in order to keep an eye on this section while they were shooting. There was some debate about time or, rather, the absence of it.

"Let's just grab this shot and get out of here, Hank," Reed said, starting to show some strain.

In spite of everything that had happened, in spite of the throbbing pain in his right eye, Hank felt a strange sense of calm. He wasn't happy with this last shot. And he would not allow himself to be rushed.

"It's a bullshit shot, Reed," Hank replied. "I didn't come this far not to get the shot I want."

Reed nodded his head. "We've got about forty minutes of real night left. What's the shot you want?"

Hank took a couple of steps back and surveyed the area. For some reason, maybe the sudden change in his own vision, he latched onto the idea of forced perspective—changing the audience's perspective with a sudden unexpected camera angle. He remembered a Scorsese film where Robert De Niro kidnapped Jerry Lewis and tied him to a chair with several rolls of surgical tape. Scorsese cut from a series of eye-level shots of De Niro talking about what he was going to do to a jolting overhead shot as he actually started wrapping him with the tape. Hank thrust his arm into the sky and pointed two fingers down, the fingers symbolizing the camera.

"I want to shoot down for the kiss. I want to be able to cut from Wally puckering his lips to a high shot of the seal sliding up to meet him."

Reed scratched his head.

"It's the shot I want."

Using a corroded swing set from a forgotten corner of the yard, they were able to jury-rig a camera platform above the jacuzzi. It took them thirty-five minutes and the sun was threatening to come out at any time. But spirits were high, everybody, including Duchette, chipping in with the work. Hank was crouched on the edge of the jacuzzi, reassuring his actors that their performances were to remain the same. Reed was directly above him on the top bar of the swingset, adjusting the camera.

"Hank, we've got shadows on both sides of Wally."

"How bad?"

"Bad enough. We either have to move the swing set around or move one of the lights."

The camera platform on top of the swing set was held together with clamps and duct tape. Hank realized that if he moved it he risked having the whole thing fall apart.

"Let's move the lights."

A streak of magenta started to reveal itself under the eastern sky. Hank and Reed noticed it at the same time.

"Rusty, get your seals ready! We're going to roll film while we're moving the lights. Places, everybody!"

They had all worked on enough sets to know what this meant, time was no longer precious, it was virtually extinct. Duchette saw two of the grips struggling with the main klieg light and instinctively picked up the cable behind them. Marla wandered into the backyard in her underwear, a pale ghostly figure trying to fight off the cobwebs of her narcotic slumber, wondering what two seals and all these crazy people were doing in her backyard.

"Action!"

The seals took off as the two grips were lugging the klieg light around the far side of the pool. There was something sublime in the first loop they made around the pool and, even though the camera wasn't on them, everybody noticed. It was like watching a great actor deliver an off-camera performance with the intention only of helping a lesser actor with his close-up. Even Duchette was moved. As Timmy and Lassie segued into their final loop Duchette marveled at their beauty, gliding so effortlessly through the water. It was at this moment that he felt something hot and sticky in his hands. He glanced down at the length of cable he still held and realized it was the electrical tape covering the lawn-mower lacerations. A short inside the cable was melting the tape. There was a hard tug on the cable as the two grips ahead of Duchette tried to signal to him that they needed more cable to set the lights.

"No, wait—"

It was too late. The tape itself started unraveling in Duchette's hands. Sparks shot out of the exposed wire. The grips saw the sparks, so did practically everybody else on the set, but they couldn't stop the motion they'd already started. Their last tug jerked the cable completely out of Duchette's hands and, just as Timmy and Lassie were submerging for the beach ball finale, *into the swimming pool.*

An electrical current shot across the water. Rusty scrambled up the ladder at the shallow end of the pool. Even though there was a barrier between pool and spa Hank yanked Nicole and Wally out of the jacuzzi with single arm jerks. Duchette, aware that he was standing in a puddle of pool water, jitterbugged backwards until he reached the grass, where he careened into a spaced-out Marla, knocking both of them to the ground.

And in what seemed like an eternity every person on the set turned their attention at the same time to that spot in the middle of the pool where Timmy was supposed to come rocketing out of the water. But there was nothing but a deathly silence. Broken, finally, by the anticlimactic "plop" of the beach ball breaking the surface.

Neither Timmy nor Lassie followed.

A week later Pig sat in his office finishing off a quart of Glenlivet he'd been saving for the millennium. All the fighter jet and special effect photographs were off his wall, stacked neatly in a cardboard box next to a single-drawer filing cabinet that contained his personal papers. An autographed Dodger baseball bat stood by the door. A hole the size of Pig's fist marred the exposed plaster of the opposite wall. A little before noon Hank walked in wearing a baggy windbreaker over a shirt and tie. The windbreaker concealed his belt-holstered 9mm; in anticipation of his legal bills, he had begun working extra shifts for the U.S. Marshal's office.

"I hear you're taking off for Mexico."

"No sense stickin' 'round here. I got Animal Rights in my front yard, three lawsuits, a tax audit, and no job."

"I can't believe Blackguard's letting you go, Pig. It's a pretty shitty thing to do, even for a studio."

"It's a pretty shitty world, Hank."

Hank sank down in his chair. Pig filled a Styrofoam cup with twelve-year-old scotch and passed it over. Hank drained half the cup without so much as blinking his eyes.

"If Duchette would just let me take a whack at that footage, I could save us all."

"This isn't about being a good Christian, Hank."

"The footage is good, Pig. It's all there. If the Spa Scent people could just see the finished product—"

"Duchette doesn't want them to see it. If the film is deemed undeliverable because of technical defects, you and I are liable. That's the deal I made. Duchette not only doesn't have to pay us, he can sue us for what he's out of pocket *and* there's a good chance the settlement will give him clear ownership of the film, which he can then deliver to Spa Scent at a later date." He swallowed some scotch. "He doesn't give a shit about us or the fucking seals."

"It doesn't seem right."

"It's not right, Hank. We're getting fucked every which way from Sunday. That's why I'm heading to Mexico."

Hank fell into a rare funk as they silently finished the bottle of scotch between them. He knew Pig was serious about going to Mexico. His own options were hamstrung by his respect for the law and a burning desire to see the film he had directed cut together. He said as much to Pig.

"I told you, that's not the point."

"I *know* it's not the point, Pig. But I can't sleep at night. I want to see it for my own sanity. I want to know what I did was good."

"It's under lock and key, Hank."

"I don't care about that either."

Pig stared at him for a long time.

"Shit," he said finally, finishing his scotch. "Why don't we go take a look at it together."

Duchette was storing the negative at Caudex Film Labs, a cement and reinforced-steel compound in the heart of Hollywood. Rumor had it that during the riots of '92 there was a traffic jam of Mercedes and Land Rovers outside the gates of Caudex, pusillanimous studio executives figuring it was safer to hide there than risk the drive home. Pig and Hank drove over in Pig's El Dorado, the top down, empty beer cans clattering together in the backseat, what little hair they had between them blowing in the wind. Pig called in a favor on his cellular phone from an editor who worked inside the compound. The editor disconnected a trip alarm and let them in a side door off Yucca Street.

"Your film's downstairs by the processing labs. But I can't take you down there, Pig." The editor looked genuinely scared. "I'm hanging onto this job by a pubic hair."

"Anybody I know in the lab?"

"Shelly Walker."

Pig smiled.

"He ain't a soft touch no more. He's clean and sober five years now."

"It don't matter. Old Shelly's a film lover."

They found Shelly checking proofs for a cable movie. Pig explained the situation to him, emphasizing the fact that he and

Hank only wanted to take a look at the printed footage, to gain some sense of completion for all the work they had put into it. Shelly agreed to let them see it. It turned out the footage was not only already assembled but one of the second-shift editors, having heard about the seals, decided to make a first cut. The word in the halls of Caudex was that the film looked good. Pig and Hank were about to see for themselves.

"The intercom's not working so if you want me to stop it or roll it again just wave your hand."

Shelly said this on his way to the projection booth.

Pig and Hank sat in the front row of the small screening room as the lights came down, each of them lost in a welter of expectation. Wondrous light flooded the room and for the next minute and a half they were bombarded with big-screen images like none they had ever seen before: a plaintive Timmy trailing Wally around the side of the pool, Wally booting the beach ball across the water to lose the pesky little seal; Nicole looking bored and voluptuous in the bubbling hot water, Wally's perfect timing as he revealed the bottle of Spa Scent for the first time; Nicole's grace and beauty as she slithered up and down through the cloying froth. There was even more. Timmy and Lassie's perfect synchrony as they swam loop after loop around the inside perimeter of the blue pool; the climactic kiss between Timmy and Wally, even with Hank's intrusive cut to an overhead angle, more poignant than anyone could have imagined; and Timmy's final frolic in the jacuzzi, a pair of Ray Bans on his snout, a bottle of Spa Scent floating beside him. It was all there.

Seeing the film nearly frame by frame, Hank was overcome by too many emotions to think clearly. There were things, the forced perspective among them, that he obviously wanted to change. But he was overcome by the feeling that the piece as a whole was greater, far greater, than its individual parts. Cut together it had a vibrancy, an originality, that went beyond even Hank's wildest dreams.

Pig, equally dumbstruck, had tears in his eyes.

Then the lights came up.

When they turned to look behind them Justin Duchette's hand was on the switch, two armed security guards standing behind him blocking the door.

"You're trespassing, Pig," Duchette said, without a trace of humor or goodwill.

"You're also violating a court order."

Pig advanced toward him silently, tears streaming down his flushed and angry face.

Even with two armed guards standing behind him Duchette's first reaction was to backpedal.

"You're already in a world of trouble, Pig. I wouldn't make it worse."

Pig kept coming.

The two guards collapsed alongside Duchette in an awkward retreat to the hallway, their hands moving nervously to the handles of their .38's. Hank was a half step behind Pig, aware that the moment was taking on a life all its own.

Shelly Walker wheeled a metal cart out of the projection booth directly behind Duchette and the two security guards. A single reel of 35mm film sat on top of the cart. Pig's eyes latched onto it immediately.

"That's my film!"

Pig lurched toward the cart.

"Don't let him out of here with that film!" Duchette ordered, retreating to a position of even greater safety as everyone else rushed past him.

Shelly Walker, old pro that he was, abandoned cart and film and slipped back inside the projection booth.

The first guard had his hand on the back of Pig's neck. "That's private property," he exclaimed.

Pig responded with his trademark elbow to the face. As the half-conscious guard dropped to the floor he made a feeble attempt to tackle Pig with his arms. Pig kicked him in the head and bolted for the emergency door. The second guard, at Duchette's urging, had his gun out and was drawing a tremulous bead on Pig's own head.

"Hold it right there, Mr. Bledsoe!"

Pig kept going. It was at this point that Hank reached inside his windbreaker for his 9mm. He aimed it at the second guard as the guard was squeezing off a warning shot at Pig. The guard's shot was wide to the left, but the bullet ricocheted off a fire extinguisher and hit Pig under his shoulder blade.

"Drop your gun!" Hank shouted at the second guard. "I'm a reserve policeman!"

In the confusion the second guard turned toward Hank, seeing the gun in his hand without registering the words "reserve policeman." He started to aim his gun a second time, but before he could get it steady Hank squeezed off two shots of his own. Both bullets ripped through the guard's right shoulder, flailing him back against the side wall. He slowly slid down the wall to the floor, a spasm of blood marking the spot where the bullets had rended muscle and bone. At the end of the hall Pig, still clutching the reel of film, managed to bang his head down on the handle of the emergency door and fall halfway through the opening. The mind-numbing blare of the alarm overwhelmed everything, including the echo of the gunshots.

The first guard was on the floor a few feet away from Hank. He made a feeble attempt to reach for his own gun. Hank didn't even bother to point the 9mm at him. Instead, in a weary voice he simply repeated, "I'm a reserve policeman."

The alarm continued to blare. Ever the professional, Hank pocketed both guards' guns before walking down to the emergency exit. He gently dislodged Pig's head from between door and doorjamb. He checked the pulse in Pig's carotid artery to verify what he already sensed in his heart: Pig was dead. He sat on the floor and cradled Pig's head in his lap, the slender reel of 35mm film beside them.

Toward evening of the next day Ray Washburn paid Hank a visit at the Hollywood Division police station. They were keeping Hank in a holding cell while the D.A.'s office tried to figure what, if anything, they were going to charge him with. Although they had talked several times on the telephone in the past few years, it was the first time Hank had actually laid eyes on his old professor in more than a decade. They sat across from each other in the small interview room usually reserved for lawyer/client meetings.

"You look good, Ray. Must be all that clean living."

Ray returned Hank's smile, but only for a moment. He had a Palm Springs suntan, a five-thousand-dollar gold Rolex on one wrist, and the burden of unwanted responsibility in his eyes. It was the watch that gave Hank pause, remembering the old film school adage *everything in the frame is important*.

"I'm gonna cut to the chase, Hank. This is a messy situation all around."

"You should see it from my end."

"The thing of it is, the D.A.'s office is willing to work with us. They've got an honest eye towards protecting the community here."

Hank's eyebrows furrowed.

"If you're willing to admit you and Pig broke into Caudex with the intention of stealing that film, they'll let you cop a plea. One count felony burglary. Reduced sentence. Hell, you'll probably get off with probation."

Ray had the expression of someone who was trying to do someone else a tremendous favor. It was an expression Hank found inappropriate.

"I've got a release form here, says Duchette's company is sole owner of the film. It's just a formality given the fact he put up all the money."

"That's, um, not entirely true, Ray."

Ray shifted his eyes ever so slightly.

"I put ten thousand dollars of my own money into this project," Hank said. "In fact, there was a lawyer in here earlier who says I have just as much right to that film as Duchette. He's going over the contracts tonight, but you can see how that messes up the burglary angle."

Ray's face was pinched with discomfort.

"Hank, you put two bullets through the shoulder of a Caudex security guard. I don't know much about the law but that seems pretty serious to me."

Hank smiled, aware that Ray was more concerned with "Caudex" than with the fate of some security guard.

"I'm an officer of the court myself," Hank said. "And even if it turns out the film belongs to somebody else, that guard was in error when he shot Pig. You can't use deadly force to protect private property."

Ray was silent for only a moment.

"You were in error yourself, slim. And you've got three witnesses who'll testify you fired your own weapon without due cause. We're talking some *major* prison time."

Although Hank still harbored some affection for his old teacher, Ray had turned their conversation into a poker game. And at that moment Hank had the irrepressible feeling that he was holding the winning hand.

With just the right touch of regret, he said, "I guess I'll have to take my chances in court."

There was nothing left to be said. No matter whom he was representing, Ray was the company man and Hank was simply a problem to be solved. Ray stared him straight in the eye for a moment, to make sure they perfectly understood each other. They did. Ray nodded his head and left without a word, his gold Rolex reflecting the overhead light. A guard came in and led Hank back to his cell. Hank sat down on the metal cot and closed his eyes, the sound of the cell door clanging shut not bothering him in the least. Whatever the outcome, he knew he had done right; he had Pig's reputation to protect as much as his own. Besides, it wasn't even about them anymore, it was about the work they had done together. The quality of that work was manifested in a little over a minute and forty seconds' worth of film. And evidenced by the other side's desire to keep it—the film was good.

James Lee Burke

THE CONVICT

My father was a popular man in New Iberia, even though his
ideas were different from most people's and his attitudes were un-
compromising. On Friday afternoon he and my mother and I
would drive down the long, yellow dirt road through the sugar-
cane fields until it became a blacktop and followed the Bayou
Teche into town, where my father would drop my mother off at
Musemeche's Produce Market and take me with him to the bar at
the Frederic Hotel. The Frederic was a wonderful old place with
slot machines and potted palms and marble columns in the lobby
and a gleaming mahogany-and-brass barroom that was cooled by
long-bladed wooden fans. I always sat at a table with a Dr. Nut
and a glass of ice and watched with fascination the drinking ritu-

als of my father and his friends: the warm handshakes, the pats on the shoulder, the laughter that was genuine but never uncontrolled. In the summer, which seemed like the only season in south Louisiana, the men wore seersucker suits and straw hats, and the amber light in their glasses of whiskey and ice and their Havana cigars and Picayune cigarettes held between their ringed fingers made them seem everything gentlemen and my father's friends should be.

But sometimes I would suddenly realize that there was not only a fundamental difference between my father and other men but that his presence would eventually expose that difference, and a flaw, a deep one that existed in him or them, would surface like an aching wisdom tooth.

"Do you fellows really believe we should close the schools because of a few little Negro children?" my father said.

"My Lord, Will. We've lived one way here all our lives," one man said. He owned a restaurant in town and a farm with oil on it near St. Martinville.

My father took the cigar out of his teeth, smiled, sipped out of his whiskey, and looked with his bright, green eyes at the restaurant owner. My father was a real farmer, not an absentee landlord, and his skin was brown and his body straight and hard. He could pick up a washtub full of bricks and throw it over a fence.

"That's the point," he said. "We've lived among Negroes all our lives. They work in our homes, take care of our children, drive our wives on errands. Where are you going to send our own children if you close the school? Did you think of that?"

The bartender looked at the Negro porter who ran the shoeshine stand in the bar. He was bald and wore an apron and was quietly brushing a pair of shoes left him by a hotel guest.

"Alcide, go down to the corner and pick up the newspapers," the bartender said.

"Yes suh."

"It's not ever going to come to that," another man said. "Our darkies don't want it."

"It's coming, all right," my father said. His face was composed now, his eyes looking through the opened wood shutters at the oak tree in the courtyard outside. "Harry Truman is integrating the army, and those Negro soldiers aren't going to come home and walk around to the back door anymore."

"Charlie, give Mr. Broussard another manhattan," the restaurant owner said. "In fact, give everybody one. This conversation puts me in mind of the town council."

Everyone laughed, including my father, who put his cigar in his teeth and smiled good-naturedly with his hands folded on the bar. But I knew that he wasn't laughing inside, that he would finish his drink quietly and then wink at me and we'd wave goodbye to everyone and leave their Friday-afternoon good humor intact.

On the way home he didn't talk and instead pretended that he was interested in mother's conversation about the New Iberia ladies' book club. The sun was red on the bayou, and the cypress and oaks along the bank were a dark green in the gathering dusk. Families of Negroes were cane fishing in the shallows for goggle-eye perch and bullheads.

"Why do you drink with them, Daddy? Y'all always have a argument," I said.

His eyes flicked sideways at my mother.

"That's not an argument, just a gentleman's disagreement," he said.

"I agree with him," my mother said. "Why provoke them?"

"They're good fellows. They just don't see things clearly sometimes."

My mother looked at me in the backseat, her eyes smiling so he could see them. She was beautiful when she looked like that.

"You should be aware that your father is the foremost authority in Louisiana on the subject of colored people."

"It isn't a joke, Margaret. We've kept them poor and uneducated and we're going to have to settle accounts for it one day."

"Well, you haven't underpaid them," she said. "I don't believe there's a darkie in town you haven't lent money to."

I wished I hadn't said anything. I knew he was feeling the same pain now that he had felt in the bar. Nobody understood him—not my mother, not me, none of the men he drank with.

The air suddenly became cool, the twilight turned a yellowish green, and it started to rain. Up the blacktop we saw a blockade and men in raincoats with flashlights in their hands. They wore flat campaign hats and water was dancing on the brims. My father stopped at the blockade and rolled down the window. A state policeman leaned his head down and moved his eyes around the inside of the car.

"We got a nigger and a white convict out on the ground. Don't pick up no hitchhikers," he said.

"Where were they last seen?" my father said.

"They got loose from a prison truck just east of the four-corners," he said.

We drove on in the rain. My father turned on the headlights, and I saw the anxiety in my mother's face in the glow from the dashboard.

"Will, that's only a mile from us," she said.

"They're probably gone by now or hid out under a bridge somewhere," he said.

"They must be dangerous or they wouldn't have so many police officers out," she said.

"If they were really dangerous, they'd be in Angola, not riding around in a truck. Besides, I bet when we get home and turn on the radio we'll find out they're back in jail."

"I don't like it. It's like when all those Germans were here."

During the war there was a POW camp outside New Iberia. We used to see them chopping in the sugar cane with a big white P on their backs. Mother kept the doors locked until they were sent back to Germany. My father always said they were harmless and they wouldn't escape from their camp if they were pushed out the front door at gunpoint.

The wind was blowing hard when we got home, and leaves from the pecan orchard were scattered across the lawn. My pirogue, which was tied to a small dock on the bayou behind the house, was knocking loudly against a piling. Mother waited for my father to open the front door, even though she had her own key, then she turned on all the lights in the house and closed the curtains. She began to peel crawfish in the sink for our supper, then turned on the radio in the window as though she were bored for something to listen to. Outside, the door on the tractor shed began to bang violently in the wind. My father went to the closet for his hat and raincoat.

"Let it go, Will. It's raining too hard," she said.

"Turn on the outside light. You'll be able to see me from the window," he said.

He ran through the rain, stopped at the barn for a hammer and a wood stob, then bent over in front of the tractor shed and drove the stob securely against the door.

He walked back into the kitchen, hitting his hat against his pants leg.

"I've got to get a new latch for that door. But at least the wind won't be banging it for a while," he said.

"There was a news story on the radio about the convicts," my mother said. "They had been taken from Angola to Franklin for a trial. One of them is a murderer."

"Angola?" For the first time my father's face looked concerned.

"The truck wrecked, and they got out the back and then made a man cut their handcuffs."

He picked up a shelled crawfish, bit it in half, and looked out the window at the rain slanting in the light. His face was empty now.

"Well, if I was in Angola I'd try to get out, too," he said. "Do we have some beer? I can't eat crawfish without beer."

"Call the sheriff's department and ask where they think they are."

"I can't do that, Margaret. Now, let's put a stop to all this." He walked out of the kitchen, and I saw my mother's jawbone flex under the skin.

It was about three in the morning when I heard the shed door begin slamming in the wind again. A moment later I saw my father walk past my bedroom door buttoning his denim coat over his undershirt. I followed him halfway down the stairs and watched him take a flashlight from the kitchen drawer and lift the twelve-gauge pump out of the rack on the dining-room wall. He saw me, then paused for a moment as though he were caught between two thoughts.

Then he said, "Come on down a minute, Son. I guess I didn't get that stob hammered in as well as I thought. But bolt the door behind me, will you?"

"Did you see something, Daddy?"

"No, no. I'm just taking this to satisfy your mother. Those men are probably all the way to New Orleans by now."

He turned on the outside light and went out the back door. Through the kitchen window I watched him cross the lawn. He had the flashlight pointed in front of him, and as he approached the tractor shed, he raised the shotgun and held it with one hand against his waist. He pushed the swinging door all the way back against the wall with his foot, shined the light over the tractor and the rolls of chicken wire, then stepped inside the darkness.

I could hear my own breathing as I watched the flashlight beam bounce through the cracks in the shed. Then I saw the light steady in the far corner where we hung the tools and tack. I waited for something awful to happen—the shotgun to streak fire through the boards, a pick in murderous hands to rake downward in a tangle of harness. Instead, my father appeared in the doorway a moment later, waved the flashlight at me, then replaced the stob and pressed it into the wet earth with his boot. I unbolted the back door and went up to bed, relieved that the convicts were far away and that my father was my father, a truly brave man who kept my mother's and my world a secure place.

But he didn't go back to bed. I heard him first in the upstairs hall cabinet, then in the icebox, and finally on the back porch. I went to my window and looked down into the moonlit yard and saw him walking with the shotgun under one arm and a lunch pail and folded towels in the other.

Just at false dawn, when the mist from the marsh hung thick on the lawn and the gray light began to define the black trees along the bayou, I heard my parents arguing in the next room. Then my father snapped: "Damn it, Margaret. The man's hurt."

Mother didn't come out of her room that morning. My father banged out the back door, was gone a half hour, then returned and cooked a breakfast of *couche-couche* and sausages for us.

"You want to go to a picture show today?" he said.

"I was going fishing with Tee Batiste." He was a little Negro boy whose father worked for us sometimes.

"It won't be any good after all that rain. Your mother doesn't want you tracking mud in from the bank, either."

"Is something going on, Daddy?"

"Oh, Mother and I have our little discussions sometimes. It's nothing." He smiled at me over his coffee cup.

I almost always obeyed my father, but that morning I found ways to put myself among the trees on the bank of the bayou. First, I went down on the dock to empty the rainwater out of my pirogue, then I threw dirt clods at the heads of water moccasins on the far side, then I made a game of jumping from cypress root to cypress root along the water's edge without actually touching the bank, and finally I was near what I knew my father wanted me away from that day: the old houseboat that had been washed up and left stranded among the oak trees in the great flood of 1927. Wild morning glories grew over the rotting deck, kids had riddled the cabin walls with .22 holes, and a slender oak had rooted in the collapsed floor and grown up through one window. Two sets of sharply etched footprints, side by side, led down from the levee, on the other side of which was the tractor shed, to a sawed-off cypress stump that someone had used to climb up on the deck.

The air among the trees was still and humid and dappled with broken shards of sunlight. I wished I had brought my .22, and then I wondered at my own foolishness in involving myself in something my father had been willing to lie about in order to protect me from. But I had to know what he was hiding, what or who it was that would make him choose the welfare of another over my mother's anxiety and fear.

I stepped up on the cypress stump and leaned forward until I could see into the doorless cabin. There were an empty dynamite box and a half-dozen beer bottles moted with dust in one corner, and I remembered the seismograph company that had used the houseboat as a storage shack for their explosives two years ago. I stepped up on the deck more bravely now, sure that I would find nothing else in the cabin other than possibly a possum's nest or a squirrel's cache of acorns. Then I saw the booted pants leg in the gloom just as I smelled his odor. It was like a slap in the face, a mixture of dried sweat and blood and the sour stench of swamp mud. He was sleeping on his side, his knees drawn up before him, his green-and-white, pin-striped uniform streaked black, his bald, brown head tucked under one arm. On each wrist was a silver manacle and a short length of broken chain. Someone had slipped a narrow piece of cable through one manacle and had nailed both looped ends to an oak floor beam with a twelve-inch iron spike. In that heart-pounding moment the length of cable and the long spike leaped at my eye even more than the convict did, because both of them came from the back of my father's pickup truck.

I wanted to run but I was transfixed. There was a bloody tear across the front of his shirt, as though he had run through barbed wire, and even in sleep his round, hard body seemed to radiate a primitive energy and power. He breathed hoarsely through his open mouth, and I could see the stumps of his teeth and the snuff stains on his soft, pink gums. A deerfly hummed in the heat and settled on his forehead, and when his face twitched like a snapping rubber band, I jumped backward involuntarily. Then I felt my father's strong hands grab me like vise grips on each arm.

My father was seldom angry with me, but this time his eyes were hot and his mouth was a tight line as we walked back through the trees toward the house. Finally I heard him blow out his breath and slow his step next to me. I looked up at him and his face had gone soft again.

"You ought to listen to me, Son. I had a reason not to want you back there," he said.

"What are you going to do with him?"

"I haven't decided. I need to talk with your mother a little bit."

"What did he do to go to prison?"

"He says he robbed a laundromat. For that they gave him fifty-six years."

A few minutes later he was talking to mother again in their room. This time the door was open and neither one of them cared what I heard.

"You should see his back. There are whip scars on it as thick as my finger," my father said.

"You don't have an obligation to every person in the world. He's an escaped convict. He could come in here and cut our throats for all you know."

"He's a human being who happens to be a convict. They do things up in that penitentiary that ought to make every civilized man in this state ashamed."

"I won't have this, Will."

"He's going tonight. I promise. And he's no danger to us."

"You're breaking the law. Don't you know that?"

"You have to make choices in this world, and right now I choose not to be responsible for any more suffering in this man's life."

They avoided speaking to each other the rest of the day. My mother fixed lunch for us, then pretended she wasn't hungry and washed the dishes while my father and I ate at the kitchen table. I saw him looking at her back, his eyelids blinking for a moment, and just when I thought he was going to speak, she dropped a pan loudly in the dish rack and walked out of the room. I hated to see them like that. But I particularly hated to see the loneliness that was in his eyes. He tried to hide it but I knew how miserable he was.

"They all respect you. Even though they argue with you, all those men look up to you," I said.

"What's that, Son?" he said, and turned his gaze away from the window. He was smiling, but his mind was still out there on the bayou and the houseboat.

"I heard some men from Lafayette talking about you in the bank. One of them said, 'Will Broussard's word is better than any damned signature on a contract.' "

"Oh, well, that's good of you to say, Son. You're a good boy."

"Daddy, it'll be over soon. He'll be gone and everything will be just the same as before."

"That's right. So how about you and I take our poles and see if we can't catch us a few goggle-eye?"

We fished until almost dinnertime, then cleaned and scraped our stringer of bluegill, goggle-eye perch, and sacalait in the sluice of water from the windmill. Mother had left plates of cold fried chicken and potato salad covered with wax paper for us on the kitchen table. She listened to the radio in the living room while we ate, then picked up our dishes and washed them without ever speaking to my father. The western sky was aflame with the sunset, fireflies spun circles of light in the darkening oaks on the lawn, and at eight o'clock, when I usually listened to "Gangbusters," I heard my father get up out of his straw chair on the porch and walk around the side of the house toward the bayou.

I watched him pick up a gunnysack weighted heavily at the bottom from inside the barn door and walk through the trees and up the levee. I felt guilty when I followed him, but he hadn't taken the shotgun, and he would be alone and unarmed when he freed the convict, whose odor still reached up and struck at my face. I was probably only fifty feet behind him, my face prepared to smile instantly if he turned around, but the weighted gunnysack rattled dully against his leg and he never heard me. He stepped up on the cypress stump and stooped inside the door of the houseboat cabin, then I heard the convict's voice: "What game you playing, white man?"

"I'm going to give you a choice. I'll drive you to the sheriff's office in New Iberia or I'll cut you loose. It's up to you."

"What you doing this for?"

"Make up your mind."

"I done that when I went out the back of that truck. What you doing this for?"

I was standing behind a tree on a small rise, and I saw my father take a flashlight and a hand ax out of the gunny sack. He squatted on one knee, raised the ax over his head, and whipped it down into the floor of the cabin.

"You're on your own now. There's some canned goods and an opener in the sack, and you can have the flashlight. If you follow the levee you'll come out on a dirt road that'll lead you to a railway track. That's the Southern Pacific and it'll take you to Texas."

"Gimmie the ax."

"Nope. You already have everything you're going to get."

"You got a reason you don't want the law here, ain't you? Maybe a still in that barn."

"You're a lucky man today. Don't undo it."

"What you does is your business, white man."

The convict wrapped the gunnysack around his waist and dropped off the deck onto the ground. He looked backward with his cannonball head, then walked away through the darkening oaks that grew beside the levee. I wondered if he would make that freight train or if he would be run to ground by dogs and state police and maybe blown apart with shotguns in a cane field before he ever got out of the parish. But mostly I wondered at the incredible behavior of my father, who had turned Mother against him and broken the law himself for a man who didn't even care enough to say thank you.

It was hot and still all day Sunday, then a thundershower blew in from the Gulf and cooled everything off just before suppertime. The sky was violet and pink, and the cranes flying over the

cypress in the marsh were touched with fire from the red sun on
the horizon. I could smell the sweetness of the fields in the cool-
ing wind and the wild four-o'clocks that grew in a gold-and-
crimson spray by the swamp. My father said it was a perfect
evening to drive down to Cypremort Point for boiled crabs.
Mother didn't answer, but a moment later she said she had
promised her sister to go to a movie in Lafayette. My father lit a
cigar and looked at her directly through the flame.

"It's all right, Margaret. I don't blame you," he said.

Her face colored, and she had trouble finding her hat and her
car keys before she left.

The moon was bright over the marsh that night, and I decided
to walk down the road to Tee Batiste's cabin and go frog gigging
with him. I was on the back porch sharpening the point of my gig
with a file when I saw the flashlight wink out of the trees behind
the house. I ran into the living room, my heart racing, the file still
in my hand, my face evidently so alarmed that my father's mouth
opened when he saw me.

"He's back. He's flashing your light in the trees," I said.

"It's probably somebody running a trotline."

"It's him, Daddy."

He pressed his lips together, then folded his newspaper and set
it on the table next to him.

"Lock up the house while I'm outside," he said. "If I don't
come back in ten minutes, call the sheriff's office."

He walked through the dining room toward the kitchen, peel-
ing the wrapper off a fresh cigar.

"I want to go, too. I don't want to stay here by myself," I said.

"It's better that you do."

"He won't do anything if two of us are there."

He smiled and winked at me. "Maybe you're right," he said,
then took the shotgun out of the wall rack.

We saw the flashlight again as soon as we stepped off of
the back porch. We walked past the tractor shed and the barn
and into the trees. The light flashed once more from the top of

the levee. Then it went off, and I saw him outlined against the moon's reflection off the bayou. Then I heard his breathing— heated, constricted, like a cornered animal's.

"There's a roadblock just before that railway track. You didn't tell me about that," he said.

"I didn't know about it. You shouldn't have come back here," my father said.

"They run me four hours through a woods. I could hear them yelling to each other, like they was driving a deer."

His prison uniform was gone. He wore a brown, short-sleeved shirt and a pair of slacks that wouldn't button at the top. A butcher knife stuck through one of the belt loops.

"Where did you get that?" my father said.

"I taken it. What do you care? You got a bird gun there, ain't you?"

"Who did you take the clothes from?"

"I didn't bother no white people. Listen, I need to stay here two or three days. I'll work for you. There ain't no kind of work I can't do. I can make whiskey, too."

"Throw the knife in the bayou."

"What 'chu talking about?"

"I said to throw it away."

"The old man I taken it from put an inch of it in my side. I don't throw it in no bayou. I ain't no threat to you, nohow. I can't go nowheres else. Why I'm going to hurt you or the boy?"

"You're the murderer, aren't you? The other convict is the robber. That's right, isn't it?"

The convict's eyes narrowed. I could see his tongue on his teeth.

"In Angola that means I won't steal from you," he said.

I saw my father's jaw work. His right hand was tight on the stock of the shotgun.

"Did you kill somebody after you left here?" he said.

"I done told you, it was me they was trying to kill. All them people out there, they'd like me drug behind a car. But that don't make no nevermind, do it? You worried about some no-good nigger that put a dirk in my neck and cost me eight years."

"You get out of here," my father said.

"I ain't going nowhere. You done already broke the law. You got to help me."

"Go back to the house, Son."

I was frightened by the sound in my father's voice.

"What you doing?" the convict said.

"Do what I say. I'll be along in a minute," my father said.

"Listen, I ain't did you no harm," the convict said.

"Avery!" my father said.

I backed away through the trees, my eyes fixed on the shotgun that my father now leveled at the convict's chest. In the moonlight I could see the sweat running down the Negro's face.

"I'm throwing away the knife," he said.

"Avery, you run to the house and stay there. You hear me?"

I turned and ran through the dark, the tree limbs slapping against my face, the morning-glory vines on the ground tangling around my ankles like snakes. Then I heard the twelve-gauge explode, and by the time I ran through the back screen into the house I was crying uncontrollably.

A moment later I heard my father's boot on the back step. Then he stopped, pumped the spent casing out of the breech, and walked inside with the shotgun over his shoulder and the red shells visible in the magazine. He was breathing hard and his face was darker than I had ever seen it. I knew then that neither he, my mother, nor I would ever know happiness again.

He took his bottle of Four Roses out of the cabinet and poured a jelly glass half full. He drank from it, then took a cigar stub out of his shirt pocket, put it between his teeth, and leaned on his arms against the drainboard. The muscles in his back stood out as though a nail were driven between his shoulder blades. Then he seemed to realize for the first time that I was in the room.

"Hey there, little fellow. What are you carrying on about?" he said.

"You killed a man, Daddy."

"Oh no, no. I just scared him and made him run back in the marsh. But I have to call the sheriff now, and I'm not happy about what I have to tell him."

I didn't think I had ever heard more joyous words. I felt as though my breast, my head, were filled with light, that a wind had blown through my soul. I could smell the bayou on the night air, the watermelons and strawberries growing beside the barn, the endlessly youthful scent of summer itself.

Two hours later my father and mother stood on the front lawn with the sheriff and watched four mud-streaked deputies lead the convict in manacles to a squad car. The convict's arms were pulled behind him, and he smoked a cigarette with his head tilted to one side. A deputy took it out of his mouth and flipped it away just before they locked him in the back of the car behind the wire screen.

"Now, tell me this again, Will. You say he was here yesterday and you gave him some canned goods?" the sheriff said. He was a thick-bodied man who wore blue suits, a pearl-gray Stetson, and a fat watch in his vest pocket.

"That's right. I cleaned up the cut on his chest and I gave him a flashlight, too," my father said. Mother put her arm in his.

"What was that fellow wearing when you did all this?"

"A green-and-white work uniform of some kind."

"Well, it must have been somebody else because I think this man stole that shirt and pants soon as he got out of the prison van. You probably run into one of them niggers that's been setting traps out of season."

"I appreciate what you're trying to do, but I helped the fellow in that car to get away."

"The same man who turned him in also helped him escape? Who's going to believe a story like that, Will?" The sheriff tipped his hat to my mother. "Good night, Mrs. Broussard. You drop by and say hello to my wife when you have a chance. Good night, Will. And you, too, Avery."

We walked back up on the porch as they drove down the dirt

road through the sugar-cane fields. Heat lightning flickered across the blue-black sky.

"I'm afraid you're fated to be disbelieved," Mother said, and kissed my father on the cheek.

"It's the battered innocence in us," he said.

I didn't understand what he meant, but I didn't care, either. Mother fixed strawberries and plums and hand-cranked ice cream, and I fell asleep under the big fan in the living room with the spoon still in my hand. I heard the heat thunder roll once more, like a hard apple rattling in the bottom of a barrel, and then die somewhere out over the Gulf. In my dream I prayed for my mother and father, the men in the bar at the Frederic Hotel, the sheriff and his deputies, and finally for myself and the Negro convict. Many years would pass before I would learn that it is our collective helplessness, the frailty and imperfection of our vision that ennobles us and saves us from ourselves; but that night, when I awoke while my father was carrying me up to bed, I knew from the heat of his heart that he and I had taken pause in our contention with the world.

Jeremiah Healy

EYES THAT NEVER MEET

One

Marla Van Dorn owned a condo in one of those bay-windowed brownstones on Commonwealth Avenue. The living room had a third-floor view of the Dutch-elmed mall as it runs eastward through Back Bay to Boston's Public Garden. The view westward tends toward the bars and pizza joints of Kenmore Square and derelicts on public benches, so most people with bay windows look eastward for their views. As I was.

Behind me, Van Dorn said, "When the leaves are off the trees, you can see straight across Commonwealth to the buildings on the other side. Even into the rooms, at night with the lights on."

I nodded. Ordinarily, I meet clients in my office downtown, the one with JOHN FRANCIS CUDDY, CONFIDENTIAL INVESTI-

GATIONS stenciled in black on a pebbled-glass door. But I live in Van Dorn's neighborhood, so stopping on the way home from work at her place, at her request, wasn't exactly a sacrifice.

She said, "It might be helpful if we sat and talked for a while first, then I can show you some things."

I turned and looked at her. Early thirties, *Cosmo* cover girl gone straight into a high-rise investment house. Her head was canted to the right. The hair was strawberry blond and drawn back in a bun that accented the cords in her long neck. The eyes were green and slightly almond-shaped, giving her an exotic, almost oriental look. The lipstick she wore picked up a minor color in the print blouse that I guessed was appropriate business attire in the dog days of July. Her skirt was pleated and looked to be the mate to a jacket that I didn't see tossed or folded on the burlappy, sectional furniture in the living room. The skirt ended two inches above the knee while she was standing and six inches farther north as she took a seat across a glass and brass coffee table from me. Van Dorn made a ballet of it.

The head canted to the left. "Shall I call you 'John' or 'Mr. Cuddy?'"

"Your dime, your choice."

The tip of her tongue came out between the lips, then back in, like it was testing the wind for something. "John, then. Tell me, John, do you find me attractive?"

"Ms. Van—"

"Please, just answer the question."

I gave it a beat. "I think you're attractive."

"Meaning, you find me attractive?"

"Meaning based on your face and your body, you'd get admiring glances and more from most of the men in this town."

"But not from you."

"Not for long."

"Why?"

"You're too aware of yourself. The way you move your head

and the rest of you. I'd get tired of that and probably tired of trying to keep up with it."

Her lips thinned out. "You're a blunt son of a bitch, aren't you?"

"If you don't like my answers, maybe you shouldn't ask me questions."

A more appraising look this time. "No. No, on the contrary. I think you're just what I need."

"For what?"

"I'm being . . . I guess the vogue-ish expression is 'stalked.' "

"There's a law against that now. If you go to—"

"I can't go to the police on this."

"Why not?"

"Because a policeman may be the one stalking me."

Uh-oh. "Ms. Van Dorn—"

"Perhaps it would be easier if I simply summarized what's happened."

She didn't phrase it as a question.

I sat back, taking out a pad and pen, show her I was serious before probably turning her down. "Go ahead."

She settled her shoulders and resettled her hands in her lap. "I was burglarized two months ago, the middle of May. I came home from work to find my back window here, the one on the alley, broken. I've since had security bars installed, so that can't happen again. Whoever it was didn't take much, but I reported it to the police, and they sent a pair of detectives out to take my statement. One of them . . . He called me on a pretext, about checking a fact in my statement, and he . . . asked me to go out with him."

Van Dorn stopped.

I said, "Did you?"

"Did I what?"

"Go out with him?"

"No. He was . . . unsuitable."

"Did you hear from him again?"

"Yes. I'm afraid I wasn't quite clear enough the first time I turned him down. Some of them just don't get it. The second time, I assure you he did."

"What'd you tell him?"

"I told him I don't date black men."

I looked at her, then said, "His name?"

"Evers, Roland Evers. But he told me I could call him 'Rollie.' "

"Then what happened?"

"Nothing for a week. I travel a good deal in my job, perhaps ten days a month. When I'd get back from a trip, there would be . . . items waiting for me, downstairs."

When I came into her building, there had been a double set of locked doors with a small foyer between them and a larger lobby beyond the inner door. "What do you mean by 'downstairs'?"

"In the space between the doors, as though somebody had gotten buzzed in and just dropped off a package."

"Buzzed in by one of your neighbors, you mean?"

"Yes. The buzzer can get you past the outer door to the street but not the second one."

"What kind of package?"

"Simple plain-brown-wrappers, no box or anything with a name on it."

"What was in the packages?"

"Items of women's . . . The first one was a bra, the second one panties, the third . . ." Van Dorn's right hand went from her lap to her hair, and she looked away from me. "The bra was a peek-a-boo, the panties crotchless, the third item was a . . . battery-operated device."

I used my imagination. "Escalation."

"That's what I'm afraid. . . . That's the way it appears to me as well."

"You said the burglar didn't take much."

Van Dorn came back to me. "Excuse me?"

"Before, when you told me about the break-in, you said not much was taken."

"Oh. Oh, yes. That's right."

"Exactly what did you lose?"

"A CD player, a Walkman. Camera. They left the TV and VCR, thank God. More trouble hooking them up than replacing them."

"No items of . . . women's clothing, though."

"Oh, I see what . . ." A blush. "No, none of my . . . things. At first I assumed the burglary wasn't related to all this, beyond bringing this Evers man into my life. But now, well, I'm not so sure anymore."

"Meaning he might have pulled the burglary hoping he'd get assigned to the case and then have an excuse for meeting with you?"

Van Dorn didn't like the skepticism. "Farfetched, I grant you, but let me tell you something, John. You've no doubt heard burglary compared to violation. Violation of privacy, of one's sense of security."

"Yes."

"Well, let me tell you. Living in this part of the city, being such a target for the scum that live off drugs and need the money to buy them and get that money by stealing, I've come to expect burglary. It's something you build in, account for in the aggravations of life, like somebody vandalizing your Beemer for the Blaupunkt."

Beemer. "I see what you mean."

"I hope you do. Because this man, whoever it is, who's leaving these . . . items, is grating on me a lot more than a burglary would. Than my own burglary *did*. It's ruining my peace of mind, my sense of control over my own life."

"You just said, 'whoever it is.' "

"I did."

"Does that mean it might not be Evers?"

"There's someone else who's been . . . disappointed in his advances toward me."

"And who is that?"

"Lawrence Fadiman."

"Can you spell it?"

"F-A-D-I-M-A-N. 'Lawrence' with a 'W,' not a 'U.'" Van Dorn opened a folder on the coffee table and took out a photo. A nail the color of her lipstick tapped on a face among three others, one of them hers. "That's Larry."

Thirtyish, tortoiseshell glasses, that hairstyle that sweeps back from the forehead in clots like the guys in Ralph Lauren clothes ads. The other two people in the shot were older men, everybody in business suits. "How did you come to meet him?"

"We work together at Tower Investments."

"For how long?"

"I started there three years ago, Larry about six months later."

"What happened?"

"We were on a business trip together. To Cleveland of all places, though a lot of people don't know what that city is famous for in an investment sense."

"It has the highest number of *Fortune* 500 headquarters outside New York?"

Van Dorn gave me the appraising look again. "Very good, John."

"Not exactly a secret. What happened in Cleveland?"

"A few too many drinks and 'accidental' brushings against me. I told him I wasn't interested."

"Did that stop him?"

"From the unwanted physical contact, yes. But he's made some other . . . suggestions from time to time."

"And that makes him a candidate."

"For the items, yes."

"You talk with Fadiman or his superior about sexual harassment?"

"No."

"Why not?"

Van Dorn got steely. "First, Larry and I are peers. I'm not

his subordinate, not in the hierarchy and not in talent, either. However, if I can't be seen to handle his . . . suggestions without running to a father figure in the firm, there would be some question about my capability to handle other things—client matters."

"Your judgment. Evers and Fadiman. That it?"

"No."

"Who else?"

"A bum."

"A bum?"

"A homeless man. A beggar. What do you call them?"

I just looked at her again. " 'Homeless' will do."

Van Dorn said, "He's always around the neighborhood. He stinks and he leers and he whistles at me when I walk by, even across the street when I'm coming from the Copley station."

The subway stop around the corner. "Anything else?"

"He says things like 'Hey, lovely lady, you sure look nice to-day,' or 'Hey, honey, your legs look great in those heels.' "

She'd lowered her voice and scrunched up her face imitating him. In many ways, Van Dorn was one of those women who got less attractive the more you talked with them.

I said, "Any obscenities?"

"No."

"Unwanted physical contact?"

Van Dorn looked at me, trying to gauge whether I was making fun of the expression she'd used. She decided I wasn't. "Not yet."

"You have a name for this guy?"

"You can't be serious?"

"How about a description?"

"Easier to show you."

She stood, again making a production of it, and swayed past me to the bay window. "Over here."

I got up, moved next to her.

Van Dorn pointed to a bench on the mall with two men on it. "Him."

One wore a baseball cap, the other was bareheaded. "Which one?"

"The one closer to us."

"With the cap on."

"Yes."

"Does he always wear that cap?"

"No."

"You're sure that he's the one?"

"What do you mean?"

"Well, it's kind of hard to see his face under the cap."

Van Dorn looked at me as though I were remarkably dense. "I couldn't describe his face if I tried. I mean, you don't really *look* at them, do you? It's like . . . it's like the eyes that never meet."

"I don't get you."

"It was an exhibit, a wonderful one from Greece at the Met in New York the last time I was there. There were a dozen or so funeral stones from the classical period, 'stelae' I think is the plural for it. In any case, they'll show a husband and wife in bas relief, her sitting, giving some symbolic wave, him standing in front of her, sort of sadly? The idea is that she's died and is waving goodbye, but since she's dead, the eyes—the husband's and the wife's—never meet."

I thought of a hillside in South Boston, a gravestone that had my wife's maiden and married names carved into it. "And?"

"And it's like that with the homeless, don't you find? You're aware of them, you know roughly what they look like—and certainly this one's voice—but you never look into their faces. Your eyes never meet theirs."

It bothered me that Van Dorn was right. "So, you think the guy in the cap might be leaving these items for you?"

"He's around all the time, seeing me get into cabs with a garment bag. God knows these bums don't do anything, they have all the time in the world to sit on their benches, planning things."

"The items . . . the pieces of underwear in the packages, were they new?"

"Well, I didn't examine them carefully, of course. I threw them away."

"But were they new or old?"

"They seemed new."

"And the device."

The blush again. "The same."

"Where would a homeless man get the money to buy those things new?"

"Where? Begging for it, stealing for it. For all I know, he's the one who broke into this place. Fence the CD and such for whatever money he needed."

I looked down at the guy in the cap. He didn't look like he was going anywhere for a while. "Anybody else?"

"Who could be leaving the packages, you mean?"

"Yes."

"No."

"How about a neighbor?"

"No."

"Jilted boyfriend?"

"John, I haven't had a *boy*friend in a long time."

She looked at me, catlike. "I do have some very good *men*friends from time to time, but one has to be so much more careful these days."

I nodded and changed the subject. "What exactly is it that you want me to do, Ms. Van Dorn?"

She swayed back to the couch, rolling her shoulders a little, as though they were stiff. "What I want you to do is pay all these men a visit, rattle their cages a little. Let them know that I've hired you and therefore that I treat this as a very serious issue."

I waited for her to sit again. "It's not very likely one of them's going to break down and confess to me."

"I don't care about that. Frankly, I don't even care who it is who's been doing these things. I just want it to stop because I made it stop through hiring you."

Through her getting back in control. "I can talk to them. I can't guarantee results."

A smile, even more like a cat now. "I realize that. But somehow I think you achieve results, of all different kinds, once you put your mind to it."

I folded up my pad.

Van Dorn let me see the tip of the tongue again. "You may regret not finding me attractive, John."

"Our mutual loss."

The tongue disappeared, rather quickly.

Two

I left Marla Van Dorn's building through the front doors, holding open the outer one for a nicely dressed man carrying two Star Market bags and fumbling to find his keys. He thanked me profusely, and I watched to be sure he had a key to open the inner door, which he did. Most natural thing in the world, holding a door open for someone, especially so they could just drop off a package safely for someone in the building.

Before crossing to the mall, I walked around the corner to the mouth of the alley behind Van Dorn's block, the side street probably being the one she'd use walking from the subway station. The alley itself was narrow and typical, cars squeezed into every square inch of pavement behind the buildings in a city where parking was your worst nightmare. I moved down the alley, a hot breeze on my face, counting back doors until I got to the one I thought would be Van Dorn's. There were bars across a back window on the third floor, but a fire escape that accessed it. Before the bars, nobody would have needed anything special to get up and in there, just hop on a parked car and catch the first rung of the escape like a stationary trapeze.

I walked the length of the alley and came out on the next side street, turning right and taking that back to Commonwealth. I crossed over to the mall and started walking down the macadam path that stretched like a center seam on the eighty-foot-wide strip of grass and trees. And benches.

The way I was approaching them, the guy in the baseball cap was farther from me than the other man, who looked brittly old and seemed asleep. The guy in the cap was sitting with his legs straight out, ankles crossed, arms lazing over the back of the bench. He wore blue jeans so dirty they were nearly black, with old running shoes that could have been any color and a chamois shirt with tears through the elbow. He was unshaven but not yet bearded, and the eyes under the bill of the cap picked me up before I gave any indication I was interested in talking to him.

The guy in the cap said, "Now who might you be?"

"John Cuddy." I showed him my ID folder.

"Private eye. Didn't think you looked quite 'cop.' "

"You've had some experience with them."

"Some. Mostly Uncle Sugar's, though."

The eyes. I'd seen eyes like that when I strayed out of Saigon or they came into it. "What's your name?"

"Take your pick, John Cuddy, seeing as how I don't have no fancy identification to prove it to you."

I said, "What outfit, then?"

The shoulders lifted a little. "Eighty-second. You?"

"Uncle Sugar's cops."

The cap tilted back. "MP?"

"For a while."

"In-country?"

"Part of the while."

He gestured with the hand closest to me. "Plenty of bench. Set a spell."

"I won't be here that long."

The hand went back to where it had been. "Why you here at all?"

"A woman's asked me to speak to you about something that's bothering her."

"And what would that be?"

"You."

A smile, two teeth missing on the right side of the upper jaw, the others yellowed and crooked. "Miss Best of Breed?"

"Probably."

"Saw you going into her front door over there."

"You keep pretty good tabs on the building?"

"Passes the time."

"You seen anybody leaving things in the foyer?"

"The foyer? You mean inside the door there?"

"That's what I mean."

"Sure. United Parcel, Federal Express."

"Anybody not in a uniform and more than once?"

"This about what's bothering her?"

"Partly."

"What does 'partly' mean?"

"It means she isn't nuts about you grizzling her every time she walks by."

The cap tilted down. "I don't grizzle her."

"She doesn't like it."

"All's I do, I tell her how good she looks, how she makes my day better."

"She doesn't appreciate it."

The guy tensed. "Fine. She won't hear it no more, then."

"That a promise?"

The guy took off the cap. He had a deep indentation scar on his forehead, one you didn't notice in the shadow of the bill. "Got this here from one of Charlie's rifle butts. The slope that done it thought he'd killed me, but he learned he was mistaken, to his everlasting regret. When I was in, I found I liked hand-to-hand, picked up on it enough so's the colonel had me be an instructor."

"What's your point?"

"My point, John Cuddy, is this. You come over here to deliver a message, and you done it. Fine, good day's work. But you come back to roust me some more, and you might find you're mistaken and regret it, just like that slope I told you about."

"No more comments, no more whistles, no more packages."

"I don't know nothing about no packages. What the hell's in them, anyways?"

"Things that bother her."

"What, you mean like . . . scaring her?"

"You could say that."

The head drooped, the arms coming off the back of the bench, hands between his knees, kneading the flesh around his thumbs. "That ain't right, John Cuddy. Nossir. That ain't right at all."

Three

The Area D station that covers my neighborhood is on Warren Street, outside Back Bay proper. The building it's in would remind you of every fifties black-and-white movie about police departments. Inside the main entrance, I was directed to the Detective Unit. Of eight plainclothes officers in the room, there was one Asian male, one black female, and one black male.

The black male looked to be about my size and a good stunt double for the actor Danny Glover. He was sitting behind a desk while a shorter, older white detective perched his rump on the edge of it. The black guy wore a tie and a short-sleeved dress shirt, the white guy a golf shirt and khaki pants. They were passing documents from a file back and forth, laughing about something.

I walked up to the desk, and the black detective said, "Help you?"

"Roland Evers?"

"Yeah?"

"I wonder if I could talk to you."

"Go ahead."

"In private?"

The white guy swiveled his head to me. Brown hair, clipped

short, even features, the kind of priestlike face you'd tell your troubles to just before he sent you away for five-to-ten. "Who's asking?"

I showed them my ID holder.

The white guy said, "Jesus, Rollie, a private eye. I'm all a-quiver."

Evers said, "Can't hardly stand it myself, Gus. Alright, Cuddy, what do you want?"

"Without your partner here might be better."

Gus looked at Evers, but Evers just watched me. "Partner stays."

Gus said, "You need to use a name, mine's Minnigan."

I decided to play it on the surface for a while. "You two respond to a B & E couple months back, condo belonging to Marla Van Dorn?"

Evers blinked. "We did."

"The lady's been getting some unwelcome mail. She'd like it to stop."

Minnigan said, "We never made a collar on that, did we, Rollie?"

Evers said, very evenly, "Never did."

Minnigan looked at me. "Seems we can't help you, Cuddy. We don't even know who did it."

"You spend much time trying?"

"What, to find the guy?"

"Yes."

Minnigan shook his head. "She lost, what, a couple of tape things, am I right?"

I said, "Walkman, CD player, camera."

"Yeah, like that. She never even wrote down the serial numbers. That always amazes me, you know? These rich people, can afford to live like kings and never keep track of that stuff."

"Meaning no way to trace the goods."

Evers said, "And no way to tie them to any of our likelies."

"That's alright. I'm not sure one of your likelies is the problem, anyway."

Minnigan said, "I don't get you."

"Van Dorn's not sure it's the burglar who's become her admirer."

Evers said, "Who does she think it is?"

"She's not sure." I looked from Evers to Minnigan, then back to Evers and stayed with him. "That's why I'm talking to you."

Minnigan said, "We already told you, we can't help you any."

Evers said, "That's not what Cuddy means, Gus. Is it?"

I stayed with Evers. "All she cares about is that it stops, not who's doing it or why. Just that it stops."

Minnigan glared at me.

Evers said, "You don't push cops, Cuddy."

"Is that what I'm doing?"

"You push a man, you find out he can hurt you, lots of different ways."

"I'm licensed, Evers."

"Licenses get revoked."

"Not without some kind of cause, and when you stop to think about it, everybody's licensed, one way or the other."

Minnigan came down off the glare. "Hey, hey. What are we talking about here?"

Evers glanced at him, then back to me. "Okay, let me give you the drill. I ask the woman out one time, she says 'no' like she maybe means 'maybe.' Fine. I ask her a second time, she gives me a real direct lecture on why she thinks the races shouldn't mix. I got the hint, you hear what I'm saying?"

I looked at both of them, Minnigan trying to look reasonable, Evers just watching me with his eyes as even as his voice.

I nodded. "Thanks for your time."

Outside the building, I took a deep breath. Halfway down the block, I heard Gus Minnigan's voice say, "Hey, Cuddy, wait up a minute."

I stopped and turned.

Minnigan reached me and lowered his voice. "Let me tell you something, okay?"

"Okay."

"Rollie's going through a divorce. I know I been there, maybe you have, too."

"Widowed."

"Wid—Jeez, I'm sorry. Really. But look, he's just out on his own a month, maybe two, when we answer the call on that Van Dorn woman. And you've seen her, who wouldn't try his luck, am I right? But that don't mean Rollie'd do anything more than that."

"So?"

"So, cut him a little slack, okay?"

"As much as he needs."

Minnigan nodded, like I meant what he meant, and turned back toward the Area D door.

Four

When I got off the elevator on the forty-first floor, I let my ears pop, then turned toward the sign that said TOWER INVESTMENTS, INC. The receptionist was sitting at the center of a mahogany horseshoe and whispered into a minimike that curved from her ear toward her mouth like a dentist's mirror. She gave me the impression she'd hung up however you have to in that kind of rig, then smiled and asked if she could help me.

"Lawrence Fadiman, please."

As she looked down in front of her, a man came through the internal doorway behind her. He wore no jacket, but suspenders held up pin-striped suit pants and a bow tie held up at least two chins. He looked an awful lot like one of the two older men in the photo Marla Van Dorn had shown me.

The receptionist pushed a button I could see and stared at a screen that I couldn't. "I'm afraid Mr. Fadiman's out of the office for at least another hour. Can someone else help you?"

"No, thanks. I'll catch him another time."

As I left, I heard the older man say, "Fadiman's not back yet?" and the receptionist say, "No, Mr. Tice."

The lobby of the building had a nice café with marble table-tops over wrought-iron bases that Arnold Schwarzenegger would have had a time rearranging. I chose a table that gave me a good view of the elevator bank servicing floors 25 through 50. I'd enjoyed most of a mint-flavored iced tea before the man in the tortoiseshell glasses and clotted hair came through the revolving door from outside. He wore a khaki suit against the heat, the armpits stained from sweat as he checked his watch and shook his head.

I said, "Larry!"

He stopped and looked around. Seeing no one he knew, Fadiman started for the elevator again.

"Larry! Over here."

This time he turned completely around. "Do I know you?"

"Only by telephone. John Cuddy."

"Cuddy . . . Cuddy . . ."

"Mr. Tice upstairs said I might catch you if I waited here."

The magic word in the sentence was "Tice," which made Fadiman move toward me like he was on a tractor beam.

He said, "Well, of course I'd be happy to help. What's this about?"

As we shook hands and he sank into the chair opposite me, I said, "It's about those nasty little packages Marla's been getting."

Fadiman looked blank. "Marla Van Dorn?"

"How many 'Marlas' you know, Larry?"

"Well, just—"

"The packages have to stop."

"What packages?"

"*The* packages."

"I don't know what—"

"Larry. No more of them, understand?"

He looked blanker. If it was an act, he was very, very good. "I'm sorry, but I don't have a clue as to what—"

"Just remember, Larry. I want them to stop, Marla wants them to stop, and most important of all, Mr. Tice would want them to stop if I were to tell him about them."

Blank was replaced by indignant. "Is this some sort of . . . veiled threat?"

I stood to leave. "No, I wouldn't call it 'veiled,' Larry."

Five

When I got back to the office, I called her at Tower Investments.

"Marla Van Dorn."

"John Cuddy, Ms. Van—"

"What the hell did you say to Larry?"

"Not much. If he isn't the one who's been sending the packages, he wouldn't have guessed what was in them."

"Yes, well, that's great, but you should have seen him fifteen minutes ago."

"What did he do?"

"He grabbed me by the arm, pulled me into a cubbyhole and hissed at me."

"Hissed at you?"

"Yes. At least, that's what it sounded like. He told me he didn't appreciate my 'goon' accosting him across a crowded lobby."

I liked "accosted." "The lobby wasn't that crowded."

A pause. "What I mean is, I think you've rattled his cage enough."

"He say anything else?"

"Just that if I stood in the way of any opportunities he had here, he'd know what to do about it."

I didn't like that. "Maybe I rattled a little too hard."

"Don't worry about it, I can't say I feel sorry for him. Did you see the others?"

I told her about Evers and the guy in the cap.

"Well, then, I guess we just . . . wait and see if the packages stop?"

"I guess."

"Unless you have something else in mind, John?"

"No."

"Well then." Brusquely. "I have things to do if I'm going to be out of here by six."

She hung up. I pushed some papers around my desk for a while, trying to work on other cases, but I kept coming back to Marla Van Dorn. I turned over what I'd learned. Lawrence Fadiman may have confronted her at work, but he wasn't likely to do anything violent there. Her condo was a better bet, and with the back window barred, that left the front entrance as maybe the best bet of all.

The paperwork on my desk could wait. I locked the office and headed home to change.

The guy in the baseball cap was already on the bench with the best view of Marla Van Dorn's likely route from the subway station down the side street toward Commonwealth. Even with me wearing sunglasses and a Kansas City Royals cap of my own above and a Hawaiian shirt, Bermuda shorts, and black kneesocks below, I thought he might recognize me. So I sat with my Boston guidebook and unfolded map on the next bench up the mall, keeping my eye on the side street as best I could, which really meant just from the alley mouth to Commonwealth. I checked my watch. Five-forty.

While I waited, taxis stopped, dropping off some fares and picking up others. United Parcel and Federal Express trucks plied the double-parked lane, moving down a few doors at a time. Owners walked dogs and summer-school students played Frisbee and nobody thought to ask the obvious tourist if he needed any help.

Out of the corner of my eye, I noticed the guy in the cap straighten. Looking over to the side street, I saw Marla Van Dorn walking, left hand holding a bag of some kind, hurrying a little as she approached the mouth of the alley, accentuating her figure under the cream-colored dress she wore.

Then one of the UPS trucks entered the intersection, its opaque, beetle-brown mass blocking my eyes for a frame. Before it passed, the guy in the ball cap was up and running hard, crossing Commonwealth toward the side street. As I got up, the UPS truck went by, and I could see the mouth of the alley again. But not my client.

I started running, too.

The guy in the cap disappeared into the alley, and I heard two cracks and a man's yell and a woman's scream. I drew a Smith & Wesson Chief's Special from under the Hawaiian shirt and flattened myself against the brick wall at the mouth of the alley, using my free hand as a stop sign to the people starting to stream down the side street. The two cracks had sounded to me like pistol shots, and both the man and the woman in the alley were still making noise, him more than her.

That's when I looked around the wall.

Marla Van Dorn was on her hands and knees, the front of the dress torn enough to see she was wearing a white bra and white panties. On his back on the ground in front of her was the guy in the cap, but he was bareheaded now, the cap still boloing near him from the hot breeze in the alley. The yelling was coming from Detective Gus Minnigan, whose right arm was pointing at an angle from his shoulder that God never intended, a four-inch revolver about twenty feet away from him.

I came into the alley fast, Minnigan clenching his teeth and yelling to me now. "The goddamn bum broke my arm, he broke my goddamn arm!"

Hoarsely, Van Dorn said, "This bastard . . . was waiting for me . . . grabbed me and pulled me into the alley."

Minnigan said, "She don't know what she's saying!"

Van Dorn looked up at me. "He put his gun in my . . . between my legs and said, 'What, you don't care about who's sending you the undies and the toy, I don't mean that much to you?' "

I remembered Minnigan in the Area D station, glaring at me when I told him and Evers that.

310

Minnigan said, "She's lying, I tell you!"

I said, "Shut up or I'll break your other arm."

Rocking back onto her ankles, Van Dorn pointed at the guy lying in front of her. "Then he came out of . . . nowhere. He ran right at us, against the gun. . . . The shots . . . He broke this bastard's arm and kicked the gun away, then fell. He came right through the bullets."

I looked down at the guy in the cap. His eyes were open, but unfocused, and I knew he was gone. Two blossoms of red, one where a lung would be, the other at his heart, grew toward each other as they soaked the chamois shirt.

"Why?" said Van Dorn staring at the man's face from communion height above his body. "Why did you do that?"

I thought, eyes that never meet, but kept it to myself.

▪ *Andrew Vachss* ▪

HOMELESS

When I was a little kid, I saw this demonstration in the park near my house. A lot of people, screaming and yelling. Most of the men had long hair. The man who lived with my mother would have said they were fags. There was a big sign. BRING THE WAR HOME it said.

I thought if those fags could be in my home, they would know it already was.

I hated them.

That was easy. Things like that come easy to me.

When I was a kid, I liked fighting. I was real good at it. I don't feel pain much. My mother's boyfriend taught me that.

Crying only made him happy. Hurting me made him happy.

I always made him happy until the day I stabbed him. I thought that would make me happy, but it didn't, not really. He died so quick, and then there wasn't nothing more to do to him.

They put me in a place they called a Juvenile Home. It wasn't so bad. They let the kids fight a lot. The bosses liked that. On Fridays, they let us fight with gloves on. Sometimes they even had people from the outside come in to watch.

I was pretty good at that, even with bigger kids.

One day, a man came in to watch. He said he would take me out of that place. I could go and live with him. He was going to train me to be a fighter.

I was almost sixteen then, so I said okay. The man fixed it with the bosses, and they let me go.

Where this man lived, it was like a farm. "This is your home now," he said.

All my life, I was in homes.

He trained me all the time. I wore the mouthpiece all day long, so I would always breathe through my nose. I did situps with a heavy thing around my forehead, so my neck would get strong. He showed me how to use my hips when I punched. How to punch through things, instead of just at them.

That didn't make sense to me except when I could spar. I liked to punch through people.

He put me in amateur fights. Big pillow gloves and headgear. It was hard to really hurt somebody—if you got them hurt, the referee would step in and stop the fight.

I hated it when they did that.

The man wanted me to win medals, fighting amateur. But I would get too excited when I hurt someone. I got disqualified in a lot of fights. After a while, they wouldn't let me in the tournaments.

The man said that was okay—I could turn pro when I was eighteen.

I did that. I won a lot of fights quick. One time I was fighting this black guy. He was real slick. I couldn't hurt him no matter what I did. I lost the fight, but that didn't make me mad. I was mad I couldn't hurt him.

I kept fighting, but I hated it. The rules, that's what I hated. So I went away. I just got on a bus and went away.

I had some money. Not much. I didn't need much. I found a room. I got a job in a car wash, but I got fired.

A whore asked me what I did, so I told her I was a fighter. She told me about these fights. In a basement. No gloves, just fighting. The people watching bet on the fights.

I liked that better. Nobody stopped the fights.

I could see the people watching got excited too. That made me mad. Hurting people was just for me.

I started doing that.

It always made me excited. The more I did it, the more I liked it.

At the first trial, they said I killed a lot of people. I got sentenced to life. The judge made a speech. He said the prison was going to be my home forever. He wouldn't look me in the face. He was too scared.

They didn't have the death penalty there, so another state asked for me. They took me out in chains, and I had another trial.

They said the same thing, but this time the judge said I had to die.

I've been here a long time. In this one room. People write me letters. Women want to marry me. They write disgusting things to me.

It used to make me frustrated, being here. It was hard to get to anyone. I got one guy, on the way to the showers. They don't let me out when there's other people around anymore.

A doctor came to talk to me once. He asked me why I did it. I told him I liked it. He asked me why I never killed women. Like he was disappointed. I tried to get him to come into my cell, but he wouldn't.

A priest came too. He told me there was things I could do. Before they killed me. Things that would make it all right later. If I didn't do the things, I would go to hell.

They're going to do it tomorrow night. Lethal injection, that's what they use in this state.

The warden came to the bars. He asked me, did I want anything before they did it. He called me "son." I wanted to hurt him so bad that I felt it deep inside my body.

Some organization sent me a copy of a telegram they sent to the governor. They're against the death penalty.

There are people outside—I can see it on the TV they have in the corridor. A demonstration. People carrying signs saying they shouldn't kill me.

I hate them all.

I'm not afraid.

I'm not glad either.

It doesn't matter—I'm going home.

▪ *Julie Smith* ▪

STRANGERS ON A PLANE

Wendell

A hundred times, lying on my bunk with my hands behind my
head, I've thought back to that time, those few minutes before
she spoke, and wondered how I missed her, why I failed to notice
her. A mist of Opium, red-painted nails and silky legs—generic
glamour. Southern women were like that. Who cared?

I didn't. I wanted a drink, and then another drink. I wanted to
revel in the situation of moving, feel the figurative wind in my
face, get it clear that miles were opening up between Atlanta
and me.

She asked if I lived in New Orleans and I must have looked at
her as if she were speaking Tagalog. What did New Orleans have
to do with anything?

"Excuse me," she said. "You must have been in another world."

She was quite beautiful, in that Southern way, that way they are. Long legs, green eyes, creamy skin, blond curly hair—doesn't any Southern woman have straight hair?

My wife does; Janet. She spends hundreds of dollars getting it to look like this woman's—at least she did; I wouldn't know anymore.

This woman looked like Janet a little, but she was younger, a little—tartier, perhaps.

A lot sexier.

She was exactly the sort of woman I'd have noticed if I'd been up to noticing anything.

I murmured some kind of answer; some apology, I guess—New Orleans was our common destination.

I had already made an ass of myself, but by now I wanted to talk to her. More to the point, I wanted her to talk to me. The sensation of speed was okay for a while, for a few minutes, but those minutes were past. I hadn't had a drink yet and I was already beginning to feel sweat on my upper lip—but not because I was an alcoholic.

Because of the fear.

I could keep it at bay with alcohol, and with distraction, and perhaps, I thought, with this woman.

I told her I was going to New Orleans on business and she said that she was too, which gave me an opening. I think she sensed in some way that I didn't want to talk about myself—at least not then, though there was a part of me that was crying, deep inside, to pour it all out.

"What sort of business?" I asked.

She said, "I don't think I can tell you yet."

I liked the "yet." It meant she planned to keep talking. "Why not?" I said.

"I have to work up to it."

I looked at my watch. "We have time. Why don't we start with your life story?"

"You tell me one interesting fact about you and I'll tell you one about me."

She was flirting.

There we were sitting next to each other on a short hop to New Orleans, we'd exchanged barely three sentences, and she was flirting. I looked at her eyes to be sure.

They had that light in them, that playful arrogance women get. "I'm from Atlanta," I said.

"I'm not."

"I'm—" I'm what?

Married?

Hip-deep in shit?

A fool. An idiot.

Crazy.

"An art dealer," I said. I wasn't.

"Ohhh, how interesting." The right reaction; a little intimidated.

"Now say what you do."

She said two words that sounded like a sneeze.

"Say that again?"

"Feng shui," she said. "Fung shway." That was how she pronounced it.

"What might that be?"

"I can't tell you yet."

"Why?"

"You might think I'm flaky."

Flaky. This woman had possibilities. "What's your name?"

"Lele."

"I'm Wendell." I let a beat pass. "Now why would I think you're flaky?" I said, and waited for her to giggle.

She obliged charmingly, and for the first time in weeks, I began to relax. I actually felt good.

Of course by then I had had a drink, so that helped. I ordered another.

She said, "You look like—I don't know—some kind of corpo-

318

rate executive. You'd think feng shui's weird." Her earrings were quartz crystals. In another minute she was going to start babbling about pyramid energy. "Anyway, it's your turn. Are you married?"

"No. Are you?"

"No. Why are you so unhappy?"

"I'm not." *Does it show that much?* "What do you mean? I'm the happiest guy in the world. Are you busy tonight?" *She's going to blush,* I thought, the second before she did.

"I don't know. I mean, I . . ."

"Come on. Let's have dinner."

She was a lot younger than I was, fifteen years, probably. I loved her for that—for her youth, her naïveté, her country-girl-in-the-big-city sort of appeal. It was what I needed that night—and what I miss now. What I miss more than anything on the outside, even my daughter.

How many nights have I lain here in my cell, listening to the assholes yell and mutter and fart and fuck each other and kill each other, and thought about Lele? How many more will I do it?

Thousands probably. I'm going to die here.

It all came out—her perfectly uneventful, utterly enviable, delightfully flaky life. She had grown up in Thomasville, Georgia, where her father was a cop. She had what she described as an "ordinary, boring childhood," but she was a nonconformist by the standards of Thomasville, at least as Lele told it: she believed in angels. That is, she had actually seen an angel one day in church, which she was pretty sure you weren't supposed to do in Thomasville.

So she had moved to Atlanta and studied massage. She lived with three other roommates and spent hardly a dime, saving and taking courses, some of them in whatever New Age subject caught her fancy, but some in business, and one in jewelry making. Eventually, she was able to start her own business, making and selling crystal jewelry like the earrings she wore.

That was all we had time for on the plane, but I did succeed in snagging her for dinner.

She wore a white dress and looked about seventeen. She told me about feng shui that night. Fortunately, it was complicated: I liked watching her mouth move.

She got into it because her jewelry business wasn't "fulfilling," she said, which probably meant it wasn't doing well. So naturally, she took a course.

"It's this ancient Chinese system," she explained, "that makes your environment work for you."

I have to laugh with I think about that now. This is an environment she could hardly have foreseen.

She drew a picture for me, which she called a "baghwa," an octagon with each side representing some desirable life aspect, like money, fame, marriage, or helpful people. "I could sure use some of those," I said, when she got to that one. *That's about the only thing that could get me out of this goddamn mess I'm in.*

She raised an eyebrow. "Oh?"

"Couldn't we all," I said.

"Well, I think I can help you. Every room in your house can be divided into eight parts. 'Helpful people' is just to the right of the entrance. You need to put a plant or a lamp there."

"A lamp?"

"Sure. Or some kind of machine—a computer or something."

"How about a television? That's where my television is, in my bedroom."

"Perfect." She smiled. "Benefactors are on the way, probably as we speak."

"Wait a minute. Hold it. How the hell is a television supposed to do anything?"

"Feng shui works metaphorically. Electricity is energy; you understand?"

I didn't, but apparently there were those who did. Whereas the crystal jewelry business probably hadn't come to much, she was now making about $1,000 a day plus expenses, flying around the world improving people's environments. She was staying at the Windsor Court (the same place I was), her luggage was Vuitton, and her clothes Donna Karan. (I know this last because, in her room later that night, I saw her labels.)

Lele was one hell of an interesting person—a combination of charming dingbat and clever businesswoman; half small-town girl, half sophisticate; nearly all seriousness. She didn't smile much, didn't laugh much, but then neither did I in that period of my life.

I ordered a bottle of wine, thinking we'd both get a little loose and giggly, but I couldn't help noticing, when about half the bottle was gone, that she hadn't touched hers. She drank water instead and she didn't order meat or dessert.

As a result, I drank more than I should have. And talked a great deal more than I should have.

We held hands afterwards and strolled on the Moonwalk. "Wendell, what is it?" she whispered. "Tell me what's bothering you."

"What makes you think anything's wrong?"

"You should wear a warning sign: 'contents under pressure.' You're going to have a stroke if you don't talk about it."

Perhaps it was the alcohol or the half-light, but I could have sworn there were tears in her soft blue eyes. She was a person who felt for others, who absorbed their pain; I knew it, I could see it. And I needed a sponge right then, so I told her.

"I'm not an art dealer," I said. "You were on the money when you said I looked like a corporate executive. I am one. A partner in a smallish firm."

"You're married too, of course. What firm?" For a moment, I stared at her in surprise. Once she'd set herself the task of extracting information, it was stunning how quickly she got down to business.

I told her its name. "What we do is . . ." I realized I didn't care enough anymore even to explain it. "It doesn't matter. What matters is what happened. Have you ever dug yourself into a hole so deep you can't imagine ever getting out again?"

"Oh, yes." Her tone was oddly bitter, and she turned away

quickly, but I saw something before she did. That time her eyes not only filled but overflowed.

For the first time, I realized there was more to this girl than I'd thought. Something was wrong in her life as well. One of my many regrets, here with all this time to kill, these infinite endless nights, is that I didn't offer her what she offered me, that I never gave her a chance to talk to a stranger: to pour it all out to a sympathetic soul she'd never see again.

"My wife is quite a bit younger than I am."

"Like me."

"No! Not like you. My wife is . . ."

"Yes?"

"An acquisitive bitch."

"And you think I'm not?"

It was strange, her saying that. I didn't know if she was or wasn't. I didn't know nearly enough about her to form an opinion—and yet I had. Somehow, in my drunken, half-crazy state, I'd started to think of her as something like that angel she saw, back in Thomasville.

"Are you?" I said.

She smiled and shook her head. "No. I have faults, but that's not one of them."

"What are your faults?"

"Oh, I get too involved with other people's problems. That's probably why you're telling me—you sense a sympathetic ear." She grinned with just the slightest tinge of irony.

She probably reads books on codependency, I thought. *She's probably trying to kick the habit and not getting anywhere.*

I knew about this because my first wife, the one before Janet, had made me read one once. Someone into feng shui was probably into pop psych as well.

But I did sense a sympathetic ear. I knew Lele would listen, and she wouldn't judge, and she'd probably want to make it better; and the way she'd make it better would involve taking her clothes off. I was pretty sure of that, but it didn't matter: I wanted to tell her anyhow.

"I don't know how it happened; I swear to God I don't know how it happened. But she wanted things—Janet, my wife, did. And next thing you know I convinced myself I wanted them too. We had a house and a swimming pool, and a new car every few weeks, it seemed like, and she had designer clothes; and we always went somewhere on weekends.

"That wasn't too bad, but then you never knew when something was going to break. You know—a car, a boat, an air-conditioning system. Two or three things did at once, one time, and my daughter's tuition was due. So I saw a way out."

"Yes?" Her blue eyes were huge and luminous; eyes you could tell anything to.

"We had this client account, you see. Well, it's complicated, but . . ."

"No. It sounds perfectly simple. The money wasn't yours and you borrowed it."

"I wasn't on salary. I got money when it came in, and I knew a big chunk was due. I just had a slight cash-flow problem, so I borrowed the money to cover it. Just for a few days.

"But then Janet got in an accident and we had to have the car fixed, so I took a little more. And by the time I got the chunk, I didn't really have enough to cover what I'd taken. But guess what? I had access to this other account that was just sitting there, so I took a little from there too. Well, no problem. In about a week, I had everything straightened out again.

"But then, Janet wanted to go to Europe with some friends, and I thought while she was gone I could assess things, get my life back in order. I was starting to realize just how unhappy I was, and I wanted to think about it. But I didn't have any money to send her off, so I borrowed some more and then . . . I don't know . . . the house needed painting or something—"

"And pretty soon you were in way over your head."

"Yes." I stared out at the Mississippi, feeling a freshening breeze on my cheek, thinking how far out of sync that was with the rest of my stale, spent life.

"How long ago was this?"

"At its height, I guess . . . three weeks ago. It went on for six months, and they were the worst of my life. I mean, they *are,* there's no were about it. William, my partner, found out last week, and he's in the process right this minute of deciding just how bad to fuck me." I knew how pathetic I sounded, but I couldn't stop myself.

"Know what I did this afternoon? Left the office, bought some clothes and a bag—I mean charged them—I can't pay for anything else, why should they be any different? Drove to the airport, and got a ticket to the first place that sounded appealing."

She looked alarmed. "You've run away from home?"

I sighed and didn't speak for about a minute. I picked up a chunk of rock and threw it in the river. "I wish. I really do wish that were an option. But I'm not made that way—I'm just not. I'll probably call Janet tomorrow and say it's a business trip and go home Sunday afternoon."

At her puzzled look, I said, "I've done this before. When the alcohol doesn't work anymore, when I think I'm going to jump out of my skin, I just . . . evaporate."

Evaporate. That was what I *wanted* to do. Hopping a plane wasn't good enough.

She smiled and took my hand. "Are you glad you met me?"

At that moment I would have proposed if the idea hadn't been utterly preposterous.

She stayed with me that night, or most of it. I don't know when she left, or how she managed without my knowing, but in the morning she was gone.

Somehow that was an eventuality that hadn't occurred to me. I'd assumed we'd spend the morning making love, then drinking coffee at the French Market, getting powdered sugar from the beignets all over our T-shirts; laughing.

I didn't even stay through till Sunday. I was bereft by her absence and flew home as soon as I could pack, not even stopping for breakfast.

Janet wasn't home when I got there, probably hadn't even noticed my absence. I left her a note and got in the car. I still felt like being away, like doing anything except going home, being anyone except me. I drove north and then south, and then east and then in circles, perhaps, not caring; just moving.

I got home about six and they arrested me that night.

I deserved to go to jail, I'm not saying I didn't. But I've always thought it was kind of ironic they got me on something I didn't do.

Sure, Wendell, tell it to the judge.

That's what they said, and what I did, and I guess, when all's said and done, that I wouldn't have believed me either. I had a damn good motive and no alibi, and he was killed with my gun, with my prints on it. No matter that I'd given it to him after he got mugged—two members of the jury actually laughed out loud when my lawyer mentioned that one.

Lele

Wendell reminded me of myself, I guess, or maybe of my little sister, Pammie. I've taken care of Pammie all my life, but she thinks deep down I'm as helpless and lost as she is. Right now maybe I am.

There was a time when I thought things would be all right and maybe Pammie and I could live like normal people, but I've given up on that, I guess. She has no idea of the danger she's in, and will always be in, and nowadays, that her children are in.

I would have wished a better life for her than marrying some alcoholic gas-pumping bozo from a town no bigger than Thomasville, but at least he doesn't smack her around like the other one and at least, thank God, she's alive. I wish to hell I'd meet one of those helpful people I arrange for my clients, but it just never seems to happen. Maybe some people are destined to be helped and others are the helpers.

Things could be a lot worse. I'm glad my life is what it is. At least it's a life. At least I *can* help people.

Of course it's run by pond scum, but as long as I don't say no to them, they leave me alone and pay me well, which means I have plenty of money to spend on Pammie and little Noah and Jeananne. A good thing because Hugh certainly doesn't. The husband.

It's amazing how much he reminds me of our dad, Pammie's and mine. And more the more I know him. Something about his personality, I don't know what. And of course the drinking. But at least he isn't violent, like Daddy was, and he doesn't carry a gun.

Daddy being a cop, the gun was legal and everything, but that didn't mean he got to pull it out and point it at us and threaten to kill us whenever we did anything he didn't like. Or more likely, didn't do something, like clean up our room.

He took me out in the backyard one day when I was six and shot Snowflake, our angelic long-haired cat, just to show me what that heavy, shiny thing could do.

The noise! Oh my God, the noise! And then my poor little white cat, suddenly just a red, sopping fur sock full of something small and light, something that wasn't Snowflake. How could that be? How could you turn something into nothing like that?

After that, I used to pee on the floor whenever I saw the gun, or at least whenever he drew it, and then he took me out in the woods and taught me to shoot it so I wouldn't be afraid.

He thought it worked, because I did quit terror-peeing, but actually it was Dominick that got me through it.

Dominick was my angel, who I met because Mama made me go to church every time the doors opened.

The way Mama handled life with Daddy was, she was a Bible-thumper who spent most of her time at home on her knees praying for deliverance. I'd say, "Mama, are you askin' God to take us away from here?" and she'd say, " 'Course not, Leila Jane, I'm not prayin' for deliverance from your father—I'm prayin' for deliverance *for* him."

"You want God to take Daddy away?"

She hit me when I said that. "Watch your mouth, girl! I'm prayin' God will make him a Christian, that's all."

"Why, Mama?"

"Because a Christian man wouldn't act like he does. Wouldn't hit his own wife and daughters."

The earlier part of the conversation had made me too savvy to question that part. Anyway, I didn't mind the hitting so much as I minded him shooting Snowflake.

Mama took Pammie and me to church with her because she said Christian strength would get us through this life. Pammie wasn't but six or eight at the time and how she was supposed to understand anything that was going on, I really don't know. I remember when I was her age, how I would squirm and fidget, and how Mama would take me home and tell Daddy and he'd make me take down my pants and bend over the bed while he hit me with his belt.

Pammie was a born lady, though. She could sit still for hours at a time, no expression at all on her little rosebud face. I used to wonder what she thought about to get her mind off things.

I thought about what angels looked like. I was pretty sure they didn't look like babies with wings, but on the other hand I did think they had wings. I listened to every mention the preacher ever made of them: "the angel Gabriel," "the Angel of the Lord," "the cherubim and seraphim," and I'd try to imagine them— great tall things, all in white feathers. They weren't birds, of course, but they must be related, I thought, because of the wings.

Then one Sunday, while I was sitting in church, the light from this big old candelabra they had on one side of the altar began to swirl around above it, and then it split off and started to spin around the room, until it finally stopped at front-row center, and got bigger and bigger and whiter and whiter and less and less vague in its shape, and finally just—I don't know how to say it, exactly—it just filled out and it was an angel. I don't exactly mean it became an angel, because I knew, even then, that it had always been one. It revealed itself, I guess you could say.

Or himself. This was most definitely a male angel, very large and protective. He had a great mane of white hair, giant shoulders, and for some reason, a staff. He didn't have feathers after all, but a robe of soft, white, shiny stuff—some kind of celestial silk, I thought.

"Leila Jane," he said, "no one else can see me."

I heard him in my head. I could talk to him that way. So I said (in my head), "Are you my guardian angel?"

He said, "If you like." And then he dissolved.

I thought that was pretty casual for a guardian angel—I mean, either he was or he wasn't, right? But the thing about him was, he never talked much. At least in the usual sense.

Next I thought, *I wonder what his name is.* And I knew it was Dominick. That was the way he communicated.

What I mostly knew about him was, whenever I needed him, I'd just think, *Dominick, get me through this alive,* and he would. He wouldn't stop Daddy from doing anything, he wouldn't vaporize him or anything, but he'd get me through it okay, and I stopped peeing my pants.

Naturally, I tried to teach Pammie about him. I told her what he looked like, and how he came to me, and how you just had to think his name when Daddy came around with his belt or his gun or anything, and you could get through okay. Pammie asked me to spell his name, and I wrote it down for her and everything so she'd be sure to get it right, but I didn't know that all the time we were talking, Mama was in the den folding laundry and heard every word.

Well, she just listened till I told Pammie the whole thing and didn't even say a word to either of us. Then she got in the car and went to see the minister about it, and he told her Dominick was the devil in disguise. He said you could tell because of his first initial, "D" like devil, and because of the last part of his name, "Nick," like "Old Nick."

The other thing that upset him was that I told Pammie what I knew that time Dominick appeared to me—that he was very definitely a male angel. I think I said it just that way, because that was the way I always thought about it. Pammie didn't ask me why I thought that, but the preacher sure did. Mama brought him back to the house with her and that was the first thing he wanted to know.

"I just know," I said, which was the truth.

"Did you see his penis?" the preacher asked.

"What's a penis?" I asked.

"A male organ."

Since I thought an organ was something like a great big piano, it took a little while to get that straightened out, but I never could say whether I saw his penis or not, since I wasn't exactly sure what it would have looked like if I had.

So the preacher decided I had, and that was another sign that Dominick was the devil and the fact that I was trying to convert my little sister to Satanism was still another sign of it. Well, Daddy was home by this time, and he'd had a few drinks, which had made him mean.

He never went to church or anything, but when Mama and the preacher explained about me and Satan, he just went batshit. But he didn't do it till the preacher left.

He got real quiet at first and told the preacher that he'd see that I was properly disciplined and the minute the preacher was out of there, he grabbed me by the hair and marched me to Pammie's and my room, where Pammie was sitting on the floor, dressing eight or ten of her Barbies.

He pulled me right in the doorway and my head hurt so bad I thought I was going to pass out, but when my knees buckled, he just pulled up on my hair, so that I stood up again, and shook me by it. He said, "You see that sweet child over there? You know what you've done to her? You've rurned her, that's what!"

I remember him saying "rurned" for "ruined," the way they did in Thomasville, just like it was yesterday.

"That's what you've done, Leila Jane, you've rurned that sweet child."

I tried to explain to him that it wasn't true, that Dominick was an angel and not the devil at all, but he said no one could believe a word I said because now I was a handmaiden of the devil and one of his servants, and so was Pammie.

He said Pammie was rurned and there was nothing to do but shoot her.

I said, no, to shoot me instead, and he said, oh, he was going to, but first he was going to whip me within an inch of my life and then he was going to make me watch him shoot Pammie.

And he did whip me within an inch of my life, without a stitch of clothes on. I had red marks all over me, which was lucky, as it turned out.

But no way was I going to watch him shoot Pammie. I just waited till he went into the bathroom. I knew he'd do that because he always did after he whipped me. When he did, I got his gun.

Then I shot Mama.

I hated to do it, because I wouldn't have hurt her for the world, but I knew I had to to keep Pammie alive. Besides, I didn't kill her; I was real careful to shoot her in the shoulder. The minute the gun went off, Daddy came out of the bathroom like a hurricane out of Florida.

I very calmly shot him dead as a doornail.

And then I grabbed Pammie and I raced outside screamin'. I said Daddy'd whipped me and said he was gon' shoot both me and Pammie, but Mama tried to stop him, so he shot her, but I got the gun away and shot him.

Mama never told anyone the truth and never mentioned it again except once. In the hospital, she said, "Leila Jane, your daddy wouldn't have shot you and Pammie. I don't know why you'd think a thing like that."

Since I was naked and had red welts all over me, and since the whole town knew what Daddy was like, everybody just kind of let the whole thing slide. We never even heard a word out of that preacher again.

And everything changed for me that night.

I've never been scared a day in my life since then. I've felt—as they say nowadays—*empowered*.

I won't exactly say I enjoyed killing Daddy—in fact, I can hardly remember doing it, it was just a part of the whole complicated plan I was carrying out. I mean, no sooner did I do it than I had to run outside and start screaming—I really had no time to sit around deciding how I felt about it.

But, now, I did enjoy it when I killed Denny. Because by then I was a completely different person—not scared; able to know how I felt. *And* able to make it on my own. I was still a massage therapist at the time, but I was already working with crystals, on my way to being a successful businesswoman.

It was a time when I was feeling good about myself. That massage therapy—making people feel better, feeling their pain disappear under my hands—was one of the things I always did best. I truly enjoy helping people. That's why the jewelry business didn't quite do it for me and why I'm so good at feng shui. Whenever I get a new client, I always think they're already doing great in their "helpful people" department because they've got me. Feng shui can change people's lives, and I like being the angel of that change, the way Dominick was of mine.

After I saved Pammie's life, I knew what God put me on Earth to do, and I knew it involved what I just said—helping people; protecting them like Dominick protected me. (Although after the Denny incident, things did take an unexpected turn.)

To make a long story short, Denny was Pammie's boyfriend, and he beat her every chance he got. Pammie'd kill *me* if she knew what I did, but I'm sorry, I wasn't about to stand by and watch that keep happening. We had enough violence in our lives when we were kids.

What I didn't know about Denny—though I probably would have blown him away even if I had—was that he was some kind of small-time mobster. Somehow or other, one of his business associates saw me shoot him—my guess is, it was somebody planning to shoot him himself, otherwise why would he have been watching him?

But naturally, the gentlemen of the mob didn't play it that way. They came and got me and said I'd killed their colleague and there was only one thing I could do to keep them from killing me *and* Pammie.

You got it—I did such a nice job on Denny, they had another close colleague they wanted erased. Naturally, I did it. What choice did I have? I hadn't killed two men to keep my sister alive just to let these creeps get her. I did it and I did it real well.

So now I work for the wise guys on what you might call a contract basis. When I was a kid and my dad was about to punish me, he'd say, "You made your bed; now lie in it." I guess this is my bed and I'm trying to lie in it without falling out.

Sometimes I try to look on the bright side. For instance, a nice thing is that it leaves me plenty of time for feng shui, which is my real love right now. And conversely, feng shui is a perfect cover for the other thing.

So was Wendell.

I always find someone like him. It's part of the job—establishing an alibi.

The night I met him, I did my gig while he was changing to go out for dinner— just a few minutes' work, since the target was in another French Quarter Hotel; and perfectly safe, since I was a dykey brunette at the time. (The wig and clothes went in the river with the gun.)

The way it all worked was, the feng shui job was in Atlanta on Saturday. So I just flew there on Friday, from the little Southwest town where I live with a cat and a fax machine, checked into a hotel, and flew to New Orleans under another name. That way if anybody tried to trace where I went, the trail would lead to Atlanta. But if they figured out I'd left, I had Wendell as a back-up alibi—not foolproof, but logically pretty sound, because hardly anybody would think you could really pull off a hit in twenty minutes, which is about all the time I was out of his sight.

All that may seem elaborate, but I am nothing if not a consummate professional. However . . . that doesn't stop me being soft-hearted.

I liked Wendell, and I felt sorry for him. I knew everything about getting in over your head—about feeling powerless because your life is in someone else's hands, about knowing that no matter how hard you try, you can never dig yourself out of the hole you're in.

And I was touched by the way he felt so guilty about his itty-bitty crime—I mean, itty-bitty by my standards. I've probably whacked fifteen men and gone scot-free, and here was this poor dude who was about to go to the Big House for stealing from some asshole who probably deserved it.

I wanted to do one tiny thing for him, to be his guardian angel, you might say.

So, look, it wasn't even a day's work for me to go kill his partner. I knew the name of the firm and I knew the target's first name. I cased his office, and when I found a gun in William's desk, that settled it. I could shoot him with it and make it look like suicide. All I had to do was call up, say I had some information about his crooked partner, and get him to meet me at his office.

Then kill him with his own gun and disappear.

I was fine because I had no motive, Wendell was fine because he was in New Orleans. No fuss, no muss. Just a simple favor for a friend.

I truly love doing stuff like that—random acts of kindness, you might say, one good deed that costs you nothing, but can change another person's life. And the best part is, you're an anonymous donor—they'll never know you're the person who did it.

That's the way I've lived my life. It's the thing that makes it possible to go on. No matter what I have to do or who I have to answer to to survive, I know I'm still a good person.

I think about Wendell sometimes. I'll never forget the way he kind of did a double take on that plane, how he finally saw who he was sitting next to, and he got this goofy look on his face, as if he couldn't believe his good fortune.

I'll always remember him that way, knowing it's the look he got about ten minutes after they told him William was dead, when things shook down and he caught onto what it meant.

ABOUT THE AUTHORS

Jan Adkins
Jan Adkins has written several crime and adventure novels, notably *Cookie* and *Deadline For Final Art*. He has been nominated for the National Book Award and the Newbery and is also an award-winning children's book author and illustrator.

Jessica Auerbach
Jessica Auerbach is the author of four novels: *Winter Wife; Painting on Glass; Sleep, Baby, Sleep;* and *Catch Your Breath*. She lives in Ridgefield, Connecticut.

James Lee Burke
James Lee Burke is the author of eleven published novels and one collection of stories. He has been the recipient of a Guggenheim and a Bread Loaf fellowship, an NEA grant, and an Edgar Award.

David Corn
David Corn, Washington editor of *The Nation* magazine, is author of *Blond Ghost: Ted Shackley and the CIA's Crusades*. He has written for *Harpers, The New Republic, The Washington Monthly, The Washington Post, The New York Times,* and many other publications.

James Grady
James Grady is the author of eleven novels, including *Six Days of the Condor*, and winner of national prizes for short stories. He has written extensively for Hollywood.

Jeremiah Healy
Jeremiah Healy is a professor at the New England School of Law and the current president of the Private Eye Writers of America. He has been nominated for a Shamus Award three times, winning it for the John Francis Cuddy mystery *The Staked Goat*. His latest books include *Four-*

some, Blunt Darts, So Like Sheep, Swan Dive, Yesterday's News, Right to Die, and *Shallow Graves.*

Jonathan Lethem

Jonathan Lethem is the author of the novels *Occasional Music* and *Amnesia Moon.* Born and raised in New York City, he now lives in Berkeley, California. His collection of short stories, *The Wall of the Sky, the Wall of the Eye,* will be released in the spring of 1996 by Harcourt Brace.

John Lutz

John Lutz is the author of *SWF Seeks Same* from which the hit movie *Single White Female* was made. He has twice won the Private Eye Writers of America Shamus Award, most recently for *Kiss* (1989), as well as the Mystery Writers of America Edgar Award. He lives near St. Louis, Missouri.

Art Monterastelli

Art Monterastelli lives in Los Angeles with his wife and two children. He has worked as a writer and writer/producer on such television dramas as *Nowhere Man, Sirens,* and *NYPD Blue.* His fiction has also appeared in the *Pacific Review.*

Joyce Carol Oates

Joyce Carol Oates is the author of several novels, including *Foxfire* and *American Appetites,* as well as *The Time Traveler,* a poetry collection. She received a National Book Award for her novel *Them* and has won several O. Henry Prizes and Pushcart Prizes. In addition, she is an editor of *Ontario Review.*

Mark Olshaker

Mark Olshaker is both an Emmy Award–winning filmmaker and a critically acclaimed author. His novels include *Einstein's Brain, Unnatural Causes, Blood Race,* and *The Edge.* He has also written the history-biography *The Instant Image: Edwin Land and the Polaroid Experience* and co-authored the nonfiction book *Mindhunter.*

George Pelecanos

George Pelecanos is the author of five novels: *Down by the River, The Big Blowdown, Shoedog, A Firing Offense,* and *Nick's Trip.* He is also involved with Circle Films, the independent film company best known for producing *Blood Simple* and *The Killer*. He lives in Silver Spring, Maryland, with his wife and two sons.

Benjamin M. Schutz
Benjamin M. Schutz is a multiple Shamus and Edgar Award winner.

Julie Smith
Julie Smith's *New Orleans Mourning* won the 1991 Edgar Award for novels, making her the first woman to win the award in that category since 1956. Ms. Smith is the author of several detective/mystery novels including *Other People's Skeletons* and *Huckleberry Fiend*. She lives in Oakland, California.

Jim Thompson
James Myers Thompson (1906–1977) was the author of twenty-nine novels and two screenplays (for the Stanley Kubrick films *The Killing* and *Paths of Glory*). Films based on his novels include *Coup de Torchon (Pop. 1280), Serie Noir (A Hell of a Woman), The Getaway, The Killer Inside Me, The Grifters,* and *After Dark, My Sweet. Savage Art,* a biography of Jim Thompson, was published by Knopf in 1995.

Andrew Vachss
Andrew Vachss has been a federal investigator in sexually transmitted diseases, a social caseworker, and a labor organizer, and has directed a maximum security prison for youthful offenders. He is now a lawyer in private practice. Mr. Vachss is the author of several novels in the "Burke" series, and his nonfiction work has appeared in *The New York Times, Parade, Antaeus,* and numerous other forums.

John Weisman
John Weisman is the author of six novels: *Evidence, Watchdogs, Blood Cries, Rogue Warrior, Rogue Warrior: Red Cell,* and *Rogue Warrior: Green Team,* and one nonfiction book, *Guerrilla Theater,* which was nominated for a National Book Award. He is currently writing the fourth novel in the *Rogue Warrior* series, *Designation Gold.* He and his wife divide their time between homes in Chevy Case, Maryland, and the Blue Ridge mountains of Virginia.

VINTAGE CRIME / **BLACK LIZARD**

___ **No Beast So Fierce** by Edward Bunker	$10.00	0-679-74155-0
___ **Double Indemnity** by James M. Cain	$8.00	0-679-72322-6
___ **The Postman Always Rings Twice** by James M. Cain	$8.00	0-679-72325-0
___ **Fast One** by Paul Cain	$9.00	0-679-75184-X
___ **The Big Sleep** by Raymond Chandler	$10.00	0-394-75828-5
___ **Farewell, My Lovely** by Raymond Chandler	$10.00	0-394-75827-7
___ **The High Window** by Raymond Chandler	$11.00	0-394-75826-9
___ **The Lady In the Lake** by Raymond Chandler	$10.00	0-394-75825-0
___ **The Long Goodbye** by Raymond Chandler	$11.00	0-394-75768-8
___ **Trouble Is My Business** by Raymond Chandler	$9.00	0-394-75764-5
___ **Dead Lagoon** by Michael Dibdin	$12.00	0-679-75311-7
___ **The Dying of the Light** by Michael Dibdin	$9.00	0-679-75310-9
___ **The Last Sherlock Holmes Story**	$10.00	0-679-76658-8
___ **I Wake Up Screaming** by Steve Fisher	$8.00	0-679-73677-8
___ **Black Friday** by David Goodis	$7.95	0-679-73255-1
___ **The Burglar** by David Goodis	$8.00	0-679-73472-4
___ **Cassidy's Girl** by David Goodis	$8.00	0-679-73851-7
___ **Night Squad** by David Goodis	$8.00	0-679-73698-0
___ **Nightfall** by David Goodis	$8.00	0-679-73474-0
___ **Shoot the Piano Player** by David Goodis	$7.95	0-679-73254-3
___ **Street of No Return** by David Goodis	$8.00	0-679-73473-2
___ **The Big Knockover** by Dashiell Hammett	$13.00	0-679-72259-9
___ **The Continental OP** by Dashiell Hammett	$12.00	0-679-72258-0
___ **The Maltese Falcon** by Dashiell Hammett	$9.00	0-679-72264-5
___ **Red Harvest** by Dashiell Hammett	$10.00	0-679-72261-0
___ **The Thin Man** by Dashiell Hammett	$9.00	0-679-72263-7
___ **Ripley's Game** by Patricia Highsmith	$11.00	0-679-74568-8
___ **Ripley Under Ground** by Patricia Highsmith	$11.00	0-679-74230-1
___ **Ripley Under Water** by Patricia Highsmith	$11.00	0-679-74809-1
___ **The Boy Who Followed Ripley** by Patricia Highsmith	$11.00	0-679-74567-X
___ **The Talented Mr. Ripley** by Patricia Highsmith	$11.00	0-679-74229-8
___ **A Rage In Harlem** by Chester Himes	$8.00	0-679-72040-5
___ **The Laughing Policeman** by Maj. Sjöwall and Per Wahlöö	$9.00	0-679-74223-9
___ **The Locked Room** by Maj. Sjöwall and Per Wahlöö	$11.00	0-679-74222-0
___ **The Man on the Balcony** by Maj. Sjöwall and Per Wahlöö	$9.00	0-679-74596-3

VINTAGE CRIME / **BLACK LIZARD**

___	**The Man Who Went Up In Smoke** by Maj. Sjöwall and Per Wahlöö	$9.00	0-679-74597-1
___	**Roseanna** by Maj. Sjöwall and Per Wahlöö	$9.00	0-679-74598-X
___	**After Dark, My Sweet** by Jim Thompson	$7.95	0-679-73247-0
___	**The Alcoholics** by Jim Thompson	$9.00	0-679-73313-2
___	**The Criminal** by Jim Thompson	$8.00	0-679-73314-0
___	**Cropper's Cabin** by Jim Thompson	$9.00	0-679-73315-9
___	**The Getaway** by Jim Thompson	$10.00	0-679-73250-0
___	**The Grifters** by Jim Thompson	$8.95	0-679-73248-9
___	**Heed the Thunder** by Jim Thompson	$10.00	0-679-74014-7
___	**A Hell of a Woman** by Jim Thompson	$10.00	0-679-73251-9
___	**The Killer Inside Me** by Jim Thompson	$9.00	0-679-73397-3
___	**Nothing More Than Murder** by Jim Thompson	$9.00	0-679-73309-4
___	**Now and On Earth** by Jim Thompson	$9.00	0-679-74013-9
___	**Pop. 1280** by Jim Thompson	$9.00	0-679-73249-7
___	**Recoil** by Jim Thompson	$10.00	0-679-73308-6
___	**Savage Night** by Jim Thompson	$8.00	0-679-73310-8
___	**South of Heaven** by Jim Thompson	$9.00	0-679-74017-1
___	**A Swell-Looking Babe** by Jim Thompson	$9.00	0-679-73311-6
___	**Texas by the Tail** by Jim Thompson	$9.00	0-679-74011-2
___	**The Transgressors** by Jim Thompson	$8.00	0-679-74016-3
___	**Wild Town** by Jim Thompson	$9.00	0-679-73312-4
___	**Blue Belle** by Andrew Vachss	$11.00	0-679-76168-3
___	**Born Bad** by Andrew Vachss	$11.00	0-679-75336-2
___	**Down In the Zero** by Andrew Vachss	$11.00	0-679-76066-0
___	**Hard Candy** by Andrew Vachss	$11.00	0-679-76169-1
___	**Sacrifice** by Andrew Vachss	$11.00	0-679-76410-0
___	**Shella** by Andrew Vachss	$11.00	0-679-75681-7
___	**Strega** by Andrew Vachss	$11.00	0-679-76409-7
___	**The Burnt Orange Heresy** by Charles Willeford	$7.95	0-679-73252-7
___	**Pick-Up** by Charles Willeford	$9.00	0-679-73253-5

Available at your bookstore or call toll-free to order: 1-800-793-2665.
Credit cards only. Prices subject to change.